THE
SHADOW
PATROL

THE SHADOW PATROL

ALEX BERENSON

headline

First published in 2012 by Putnam, an imprint of Penguin Group (USA).
This edition published in arrangement with Putnam.

First published in Great Britain in 2012 by
HEADLINE PUBLISHING GROUP

1

Cataloguing in Publication Data is available from the British Library

Hardback ISBN 978 0 7553 8138 8
Trade paperback ISBN 978 0 7553 8139 5

Typeset in Times by Avon DataSet Ltd, Bidford-on-Avon, Warwickshire

Printed and bound in Great Britain by Clays Ltd, St Ives plc

Headline's policy is to use papers that are natural, renewable and
recyclable products and made from wood grown in sustainable forests.
The logging and manufacturing processes are expected to conform
to the environmental regulations of the country of origin.

HEADLINE PUBLISHING GROUP
An Hachette UK Company
338 Euston Road, London NW1 3BH

www.headline.co.uk
www.hachette.co.uk

To all the men and women still fighting

Disappointment must be dealt with. You must wander in paradise just once more before you decide not to take the stuff again. A trifle more.

– A Coffin for Dimitrios, *Eric Ambler*

Certainly there is no hunting like the hunting of man and those who have hunted armed men long enough and liked it, never really care for anything else thereafter.

– 'On the Blue Water: A Gulf Stream Letter,' Ernest Hemingway, Esquire, *April 1936*

PROLOGUE

Amman, Jordan
June 2009

Marburg.

The trigger for everything.

What really happened.

The cab, a battered blue Nissan, pulled over a hundred meters from the front gate of the headquarters of Jordan's General Intelligence Directorate – the *mukhabarat*. The passenger handed over twenty Jordanian dinars and stepped out without waiting for change. He brushed imaginary dust from his tailored blue suit as the Nissan pulled away. The cars and trucks speeding by didn't bother him. He was a light-skinned Arab, dapper and slim. He wore a thick gold bracelet on his right wrist, a steel Rolex on his left.

The gate guards were more puzzled than alarmed at his approach. His suit fit too well to hide a suicide vest. He didn't look dangerous. But most Jordanians were wise enough to give the *muk* a wide berth. Especially ones dressed like him. Before he reached the gatehouse, two guards emerged, AKs at the ready. They put him on his knees and pulled a hood over his head and dragged him inside to explain himself.

His name was Dr Ahmad Rashid. He was a cardiologist at a hospital in eastern Amman. And – as he told the *muk* and then the CIA – he wanted to go to Pakistan's North-West Frontier, infiltrate al-Qaeda, and destroy it. He blamed al-Qaeda for the death of his brother, Farhad, who had killed himself a year earlier in a suicide bombing in Baghdad.

'This very day, one year ago. Twenty-two years old, but he could hardly read or write. If he went a few streets from our house, he was lost. A child. They filled his head with angels and virgins.'

Rashid's potential was obvious. For nearly a decade, the CIA had sought reliable sources inside al-Qaeda, men who might narrow the search for Osama bin Laden and his deputy, Ayman al-Zawahiri. Eventually, of course, the agency and NSA would track bin Laden to a compound less than fifty miles from the Pakistani capital of Islamabad. SEAL Team Six would do the rest. But in 2009, bin Laden was still a ghost. The agency had no hard information on him. Rashid could fill the gap.

Assuming he was genuine, of course. Brad Stanley, the station chief at Amman, feared that Rashid might be a con man, or – worse – a double agent sent by al-Qaeda. But his story held up under scrutiny from Amman station and the *muk*. The Jordanians reported that Rashid belonged to a moderate mosque and wasn't on their watch lists. Amman school records showed that his brother had dropped out in sixth grade. Army files confirmed a suicide bombing in Baghdad by a Jordanian, first name Farhad, last name unknown, on June 16, 2008.

With those preliminaries out of the way, Stanley decided that Rashid was worthy of surveillance. He put a four-man team on Rashid, led by Todd Laitz, his best watcher, maybe the best in the Middle East. For two weeks, Laitz and his men tracked Rashid. He jogged every morning at a gym in downtown

Amman. He stayed late at the hospital most nights. He visited his mosque only for the Friday midday prayer, which was more or less obligatory. Laitz summed him up to Stanley in four politically incorrect words: 'Even whiter than you.'

'Doubtful.' Stanley had played lacrosse at the University of Maryland, which made him practically albino. 'What do you think?'

'I think there's plenty of upside and we can limit the downside. I'd do it.'

Stanley agreed. So did the bosses in the Counterterrorist Center back at Langley. On July 16, the DO – as everyone still called the unit now officially known as the National Clandestine Service approved Rashid's recruitment. The CIA gave him the code name Marburg, after an African virus that caused its victims to bleed to death. The agency hoped that Rashid would do the same to al-Qaeda.

Running Rashid from Amman didn't make sense. He was handed off to Marci Holm, a senior case officer in Kabul. Making Rashid report to a female operative offered another test for him. The agency believed that a genuine jihadi wouldn't want to take orders from a woman. Plus Holm was a rising star, a tall, angular woman who had managed a half dozen successful ops in Afghanistan.

Rashid didn't complain when he was told Holm would be his controller. Their first meeting came in late August, in Dubai. They walked the giant Mall of the Emirates as Holm gave Rashid a three-hour crash course on tradecraft. No dead drops or chalk marks, just e-mail addresses and keywords. *Cricket* to schedule a meeting, *pulse* if he believed he'd been discovered.

'You shouldn't have trouble getting in and out,' she said. They were speaking English. Holm's Arabic was good. Rashid's English was better. 'They won't want to keep you in the mountains. They don't have many men who can travel as freely as you.'

'Maybe they'll want me to take care of them.'

'Even then they'll let you leave to get the drugs you need to treat them. As long as they trust you, it won't be a problem. And your brother martyred himself for them.'

'Animals.'

'They're not stupid. You need to be cautious. No unnecessary risks. I don't have to tell you what happens if they question your loyalty.'

'I understand.'

'But yes, we think they'll accept you. We think it's possible that within a few months you could meet their top men.'

'Bin Laden.' Rashid whispered the name.

'As far as we can tell, only a few people ever see him. Al-Zawahiri's more likely. You understand, he sets the strategy. He's the one who decides to use boys like Farhad as martyrs.'

'I know you don't trust me,' Rashid said, apropos of nothing.

'If I didn't trust you, I wouldn't be here.'

'It's all right. I'll prove myself to you.'

They'd walked the mall twice, end to end, Rashid's loafers clacking on the polished floors. Along the way they'd stopped at a Polo store, where he tried on a salmon-colored long-sleeved shirt. 'Do you like it?'

'It's very nice.' *He's not a terrorist*, Holm thought. *Can't be. Terrorists don't wear pink Polo shirts*.

Now they had looped back to the mall's signature attraction, its indoor ski hill, an almost criminal waste of energy, considering that the temperature outside was 101 degrees. But Dubai – like Las Vegas, its American twin – pretended to exist outside the laws of nature. Dubai created wants, and then satisfied them at a tidy profit. Put skiing in the desert, and people who'd never seen snow would buy twelve-hundred-dollar Prada jackets to skid down a two-hundred-foot hill. Yet Holm had to admit she enjoyed visiting the place, its glass-and-steel towers so unlike Kabul's shattered blocks. She'd take endless consumerism over endless war.

Rashid watched the skiers. 'Shall we try it?' As if they were on a date. His manners matched his clothes. He was old-fashioned, almost courtly.

'Not me.' She'd grown up in Oregon, snowboarding at Mount Hood. She wasn't renting a parka for this foolishness. 'But you should. Have you ever skied before?'

'No. But I shouldn't make you wait—'

'Go. I'll watch.' A bar overlooked the hill. Inevitably, it was styled as an après-ski lodge and called the St. Moritz Café. Holm sat by the natural-gas fireplace and sipped hot cocoa and watched Rashid ski. He moved cautiously, like most first-time adult skiers. But she saw that with a little training, he'd learn fast. He never let the skis run away from him. He saw her watching, waved. She waved back, and as she did—

Realized—

He's too smooth. Has been all along. If he can pick this up this quick, then he can fool you a dozen different ways. Get rid of him. Burn him. Now.

She kept waving. The feeling faded as fast as a sunset. She had no reason to distrust this man. She felt as though she'd embarrassed herself, flinched in public. Though she hadn't said a word aloud.

An hour later, he appeared, his hair mussed, grinning.

'Fun?'

'In point of fact, I enjoyed it enormously.'

'That means yes, right?'

'You missed out, Miss Simmons.' Her cover name.

'Next time.'

They walked to the mall's giant parking garage and found the Toyota minivan she'd rented. There they went through the usual end-of-meeting housekeeping. She pushed five thousand dollars on him over his objections and gave him a Motorola that looked like a stock smartphone but was satellite-capable. 'You get in trouble, you send the distress signal, we'll come get you. Anywhere in the world.'

'Thank you, Miss Simmons. But I don't intend to get in trouble.'

'Nobody ever does.'

'Until I see you next, be well.'

'You, too.'

He walked away without looking back.

Back in Kabul, she decided to tell Manny Cota, station chief, about her premonition. 'Maybe we should slow it down with Marburg. Check him again.'

'What now?'

She explained. Cota was less than supportive. Much less. 'I'm hearing this right, you want to lose this guy because you didn't like the way he skied. Because he skied too well?'

'I'm telling you I've never had a feeling like this before.'

'And that's good. I never pegged you as paranoid, Marci. You think those boys found this guy in Amman, convinced him to infiltrate us. And don't forget the Jordies are on board, they think he's a hundred percent copacetic.'

'I'm just saying—'

'And I'm saying we're going to see what he gives us. You don't want to be involved, okay. But this is happening. And if it happens without you, it won't be good for you. Or Pete either.'

Pete was Peter S. Lautner, her husband, another case officer. They'd met five years before in Kabul, been together ever since. Like her, he was a rising star, just promoted to become the agency's top liaison with the Afghan *muk*.

'You can't put this on Pete.'

'It is what it is. Your career, his career, all tied up.'

Giving her something else to worry about. 'Can I tell you something? You are a grade-A prick.' She tried to make her tone lighter than the words. She failed.

'Sticks and stones, Marci. I take it I have your cooperation.'

'As always.'

She talked the situation over with her husband that night, as they ate at the rough-hewn wooden table in their kitchen. Junior CIA officers lived in the Ariana Hotel. Even with wifi and a twenty-four-hour cafeteria, the hotel was depressing, its rooms low and dark, shadowed by tinted blastproof windows. More senior officers were assigned to homes in the walled zone around the hotel. Holm and Lautner had a two-bedroom brick house a block from the Ariana. Holm thought she might even miss it when they left.

She swirled a glass of the red wine she'd bought the day before in the Dubai airport, a thousand light-years away. 'What do you think?'

He hesitated. 'The guy's been vetted pretty close.'

'You think I overreacted.'

'I wasn't there, Marci.'

'I love you, husband, but that's the wrong answer.'

But she knew she was beaten. The next morning, she filed her report on Rashid to Langley, hinting at her concerns in passive language only a bureaucrat could love. *Marburg appears trustworthy, but it is important to note that his reliability has not been tested. Until he provides actionable intelligence, reasonable precautions as to his handling are dictated.*

In September, Rashid arrived in Peshawar, the Pakistani city that had been a jihadi hub for thirty years. As the CIA had expected, he connected easily with al-Qaeda. His medical degree made him useful. His brother's death made him trustworthy. A few days before Halloween, he reported that three midlevel Talib commanders would meet in a village northwest of Peshawar. The agency confirmed the report with another source, and a Predator drone sent the Talibs into the next world with a Hellfire missile.

In mid-November, Rashid informed Holm that he'd seen a weapons cache hidden in a village near the Afghan border. Satellite overheads showed two pallets of artillery shells and a case of AKs. The CIA's lawyers refused to allow a missile strike because of the risk of civilian casualties if the shells blew. Even so, the agency counted the tip as Rashid's second success.

A few days later, he reported meeting two German Turks at a safe house in Peshawar. The men had come to receive training for an attack in Berlin. They hadn't given up specifics, but Rashid had learned their names. The agency confirmed with its German counterpart, the BND, that the men were members of a Hamburg mosque known for its radicalism. They had left Germany three weeks before. CIA and BND agreed that they would merit a very close look when they returned. Rashid's stock rose further.

Then he sent an urgent message requesting a face-to-face with Holm. They agreed to meet in the giant Pakistani port city of Karachi. The agency had two safe houses there, but the Pakistani Inter-Services Intelligence agency knew of both, so Holm preferred not to use them. Instead she picked a two-star hotel at random. Two-star hotels worked best for these meetings. They were crummy enough that the clerks didn't ask questions, not so terrible that someone like her would attract attention.

She arrived at four p.m., two hours early. Two security officers and a tech operative were posted across the hall. The hotel was shabbier than she'd expected, linoleum floors and peeling yellow paint. It smelled of curry from the restaurant next door. Holm's room, 308, was a ten-by-eight cell with a sagging twin bed and a broken television.

Holm locked the door, closed the curtains, and waved her handheld RF detector over the walls. Finding no bugs, she tucked the detector away and pulled a black lipstick tube from her cosmetics case. The tube was actually a fish eye camera and microphone, with a transmitter that fed a recorder in the room across the hall. The images weren't great, but the sound quality was excellent. She looked for a place to hide the camera, but couldn't find one. Instead, she left it out on the nightstand. Men never noticed cosmetics. 'Testing, one, two, three,' she said.

A minute later, she heard two knocks on her door, the tech across the hall letting her know the camera and mike were live. After that, she just had to wait. People outside the business never understood that spying was mainly waiting. Waiting for HQ to approve a mission. For a source to show up. For the excuse he'd give if he didn't. For the nugget of information he'd been hoarding, lead disguised as gold. Waiting in dirty rooms, mall atriums, subway cars, armored Jeeps. Waiting and watching and hoping that the other side was just as bored.

At 6:05, she heard three quick taps on the door. Then two more. She opened up, and Rashid stepped in. Though if she hadn't expected him, she might not have known who he was. The dapper doctor in the thousand-dollar suit had become a white-robed villager with a scraggly black beard and sunken cheeks. He closed the door, sat on the bed, smoothed his robe. '*Salaam aleikum*, Miss Simmons.'

'*Aleikum salaam.*'

'How are you?'

'Fine. More important, how are you? You look different.'

'You think so? I don't see it.' He smiled, and for the first time she recognized him. His smile, simple, almost shy, hadn't changed.

'Are you hungry?' She'd put out bags of chips and bottles of soda. Case officers were supposed to have snacks at these meetings. Usually they went uneaten. Not today.

Rashid gulped down half a bottle of Coke. 'I suppose I'm hungry. They took me to a camp. In the mountains. Then a missile hit another camp a few kilometers away. So none of us could go anywhere.'

'They blamed you for the attack?'

'No, no. Just when one camp is hit they keep the others quiet for a few days. They know that the drones watch for movement after an attack. So we were stuck. And this camp was low on food. We had to be careful we didn't run out.'

'It sounds difficult.'

'I wasn't used to it, that's all.'

I was wrong, she thought. *I should never have suspected you.* Yet some corner of her mind still wasn't convinced. The brave smile, the patchy beard. Was he acting? He couldn't be. If he could pull this off, he belonged in Hollywood. If she wasn't going to disappear into the counter-counterespionage funhouse, she had to believe in her agents. Anyway, Rashid had no reason to make up this story. He was a spy, not a charity case. He knew the agency would judge him on the intel he produced. Rashid – no, *Marburg* – had given them three solid reports in two months. Reason enough to trust him.

'But you got out.'

'On Wednesday, Abu Khalid – that's the man who runs the camp, at least what he calls himself – said I could leave. *Hamdulillah.*' Thanks be to God.

'Abu Khalid.' Holm didn't recognize the name, but al-Qaeda commanders regularly changed their pseudonyms. 'If I showed you pictures, could you recognize him?'

'Yes.'

'And where the camp is?'

'No. They made me leave my phone, all my things, before they picked me up in Peshawar. Then they blindfolded me and drove for a long time.'

'Today's Sunday. That means you left the camp four days ago.'

'Yes.'

'When was the bombing?'

'The bombing happened, I want to say, five days before that. Yes. Nine days ago. Friday night.'

'You have such a good memory, Rashid. So specific and detailed.'

'I do my best.'

Specificity and detail were good, in theory. She could check the time line he'd provided against records of drone attacks. But if he was a double agent, he'd expect her to check. He wouldn't make up an attack, slip on something so obvious. So all his specificity and detail proved nothing, in the end.

''Round and 'round we go,' she said. 'Where we stop, nobody knows.'

'I don't understand.' He opened another Coke, drank deep. His thirst, at least, was genuine.

'You've grown a beard, too.'

'All the men up there have them. I expect the next time you see me, it will be even bigger.'

'Unless they want you to shave it so you can travel more easily.'

'I think they want me to stay up there. That's why I asked for this meeting, Miss Simmons.'

'Call me Marci. Please.'

'Yes. Marci. They've told me a top man is sick. Some kind of heart trouble. They say they want me to see him.'

'Do you know who?'

'They haven't told me, no. From the way they've talked about it, I think it must be someone very senior. But Abu Khalid told me that if they even suspect I might betray this man, they'll kill all my family. He showed me a picture of my house in Amman to prove he was serious.' Rashid's black eyes were hard and desperate. 'You must promise you won't let that happen.'

'I guarantee, you get us al-Zawahiri or bin Laden, we'll move your whole family to America. And don't forget the reward.' The twenty-five-million-dollar reward the United States had offered for the capture of al-Qaeda's top leaders.

'You promise that?'

'You'll be a hero. You'll meet the president. Now, please, tell me about the meeting with Abu Khalid.'

'After he showed me the picture of my house, he went through the man's symptoms. That he feels tired all the time and has sharp pains in his chest that make him lie down. He asked what was wrong with the man. I told him the truth, my best guess. This man may have had a heart attack. Now his heart is giving out. Congestive heart failure, we call it. And the altitude and the cold make it worse. But I can't be sure without seeing him. This kind of thing, you have to hear the heartbeat, touch the skin, talk to the patient.'

'What did Abu Khalid say?'

'He asked me, "If you see him, can you treat him?" I told him it depends how sick he is. And the medicines he needs, some are only in Karachi or even Dubai. Abu Khalid told me to get everything that I might need. He said he would let me know in a few days whether they would bring me to the patient.'

Holm thought through the options. 'Don't push. Don't reach out to Abu Khalid. Pressing will only scare them.'

'And if they tell me to see this man? Do you want me to bring some sort of transmitter?'

'No. If this is al-Zawahiri, they'll strip you naked before they take you to him. Check every pill bottle you have. They may even make you take the medicine you're giving him. One for you, one for him. They'll be paranoid. They find anything suspicious, they'll shoot you, be done with it.'

'So what do I do?'

'You treat him, Doctor. As best you can. Make him feel better. That's the best way to make him trust you.'

Rashid nodded.

'Just don't cure him or he won't need to see you again.'

'Don't worry, Miss Simmons – Marci. There's no cure for heart failure.'

'Good, then. So you'll help him. And the next time they take you to him, they'll relax. A little bit. That's all we need. But before then, we'll need to meet –'

'We –'

'A few of us will want to debrief you.' *You'll be pure gold, and half the agency will want the credit for this*, Holm didn't say. For the next hour, she refreshed him on codes and contact information. He told her his plan. It was simple enough. He would buy the medicines he needed. Finding them would take a day or two. Then he'd go back to Peshawar and wait for instructions.

'Are you ready for this?' she said.

'I don't want to make any grand speeches, Miss Simmons. But I'm sure in my heart that these men must be punished.'

'Good luck, Doctor. Go with God.'

'The same God for us all. I wish we could remember that.' He extended his hand and shook hers briefly. Then he disappeared. She listened as his steps shuffled down the hallway and the stairs and into the Karachi night. Trying to track him would be pointless, and anyway she knew where he was going. Back into the mountains. To trap Ayman al-Zawahiri.

Unless the trap was meant for her.

Back in Kabul, Cota was thrilled. The agency put a Special Operations squad on what was called 'black watch.' The term meant the unit, a twelve-man team, couldn't be used for any other mission, no matter how important. Basically, the squad was under house arrest at Bagram Air Base, waiting for a shot at al-Zawahiri.

Holm was in a similar position. Cota pulled her off her other jobs. A week after she returned, he stepped into her office at the Ariana and gave her a salute. 'I shouldn't tell you. But Duto' – Vinny Duto, the CIA director – 'briefed the White House about the op.'

'We're way ahead of ourselves. Marburg may not even get the call.'

'He doesn't, no one's going to put it on you. You handled him great. I watched the video from Karachi. He likes you, he trusts you.'

'I hope so.'

He sat down across from her. He tried to look sympathetic, but his tone was irritated. 'So what's wrong? You nervous that he'll blow his cover, get strung up? He's a big boy, he went in with his eyes open.'

'It's not that.'

'Not the *skiing*, again. He's not a double, Marci.'

'I like him, you know. He's got better manners than anyone I've ever met.'

'Better than me?'

'I've seen you pick your nose, Manny. You aren't even in the same time zone.'

'Congratulations to him.'

'What if he's too good to be true?'

'Marci. You keep forgetting, we're not dealing with the KGB. These guys, their idea of tricky is Semtex instead of ANFO. No way they could run a double as sophisticated as this.'

'Maybe they got lucky with Marburg. We think we got lucky with him, right?'

'Give me something specific. Anything.'

'He's not nervous.'

'What do you mean?'

'Even before I met him. The way he approached the *muk* in Amman. Walked right up to the gate. Who does that? He's never nervous.'

'Maybe he doesn't have a nervous disposition. Anyway, I saw the tape of you and him. He was nervous when he talked about his family.'

'Only for a few seconds, before he dropped it.'

'Because you reassured him. You did your job.'

'Or because he wanted to bring it up for sympathy, then let it go. He's so afraid for his family, how come he didn't ask for specifics of how we're going to get them out of Amman? A written guarantee.'

'Written guarantee? You think he wants a contract that says,

"If I deliver al-Zawahiri, my family gets free passage to the United States." What's he going to do, keep it in his underwear?'

'I could hold it—'

'Then it's really useful to him. Come on. You're overthinking this. The guy's a moderate Muslim, they do exist. He's pissed that his brother killed himself, that's a totally reasonable motive. Now he's helping us. You've got evidence to the contrary, speak now or forever hold your peace.'

She had nothing to say. He rapped his knuckles on her desk.

'Good girl.'

Four weeks passed, no word. Despite – or because of – her fears about Rashid's reliability, Marci was desperate to hear from him. For the first time, she understood what other case officers had meant when they said an assignment had eaten them alive. She felt almost literally as if she were being consumed. She hardly ate. She'd always been skinny, but now she could count her ribs. She pressed her husband for sex two and three times a day. Finally he rebelled.

'What you're doing, it's obvious.'

'I thought you'd like it.'

'Being used like a fence post so you can distract yourself. No. I don't like it. I keep waiting for you to call me Marburg. "Oh, yeah, Marburg. That's so good. Gimme some of that."'

She had to smile. 'I really have been unbearable, haven't I? Thank you.'

'For what?'

'For putting up with me, you ninny.'

'Didn't know I had a choice.'

She rested her arm on his chest. CIA guys came in three sizes: muscled-up ex-military types, trim guys who'd run in college, and chubby desk jockeys. Pete was a runner, with narrow shoulders and tightly knitted abs. 'Have I ever told you you have a great body?'

'Never.'

'Well, you do.'

'I love you, Marci.'

'Love you, too.'

Outside, the wind howled from the north, promising fierce weather. She closed her eyes and slept without dreams for the first time in a month.

The note arrived in her in-box the next morning. Rashid was supposed to use e-mail only to set up meetings. Instead he'd sent a full report – his first tradecraft mistake:

I have met our mutual friend. He is quite sick. In America, he would receive a pacemaker immediately. Unfortunately, I do not know where he is or how you can find him. They did as you suggested they would. I told them that to be searched in such a way was humiliating and unnecessary, but they insisted. This was in Peshawar. They even poured out my medicines and looked them over. They allowed me to keep the pills and bottles, but nothing else. They gave me new clothes, a robe and sandals. They put me in a van and blindfolded me and drove for hours. Then moved me to another vehicle.

When the second car stopped, I was led into a building. My blindfold was removed. I found myself inside a concrete room, no windows. I heard cars passing. After a minute my guards escorted me into another room with a long wooden table. They searched me again. This time they allowed me to keep on my clothes. We waited together – I don't know how long. Finally, a car stopped outside. A minute later, our friend walked in, with four guards. He looked me over and said, 'He has been checked?' and my guard said, 'Completely.' He dismissed the guards, and

I examined him. With the results I have already reported, I cannot do much for him here. Again as you suggested, his guards picked two pills at random from the bottles of medicine I'd given him and forced me to take them. I did not argue.

This meeting took place ten days ago. Until yesterday, I was confined at the house. They told me that they wanted to be sure the medicine 'worked.' I told them that I was loyal and didn't like being treated this way. Also that I wanted to consult with a specialist in heart failure to see if I could improve his treatment. Finally, they let me go. But I am sure they will bring me back to see him again.

I know I have gone on too long and that this is not the proper channel for this communication and I apologize. I am fearful now, but I believe that we have been given a great opportunity for justice. Whether they are watching me, I don't know, but I am certain that I can find a way to disappear for a few hours if necessary. I look forward to seeing you soon.

The note was . . . perfect. Like everything else Rashid had given them. She forwarded it to Cota without comment. Three minutes later, he walked into her office.

'We've got to get a tracker on him. One they won't find even if they strip him down again.'

'The pills could be the best way. They won't check those twice.'

'Or he can tell them that he needs to bring some medical equipment this time. Point is, we want options for him when we meet him, and that's going to take a couple days. Let's aim for next week. At Holux.' Holux was a small CIA base near the Pakistani border. Two dozen CIA officers and contractors lived there, mostly directing drone strikes.

'You want to meet him on our base?'

'At least ten people are gonna be at this thing, Marci—'

'Too many.'

'Let him drive over the border, leave his car in Jalalabad, and we'll pick him up and sneak him in.'

'Are you sure about this, Manny?'

'You don't like it, you hand it off. I'm through debating. I reread the whole package, the walk-in, the surveillance in Amman, everything. And not just me. Both the Teds and Big Mike' three of the top officers in the DO – 'have looked it over. We agree. Marburg is clean. Marburg is gold.'

'I'm aware of the consensus.'

'You're so worried about him, why'd you meet him one-on-one?'

'I had security across the hall.'

'We have a chance here to catch a guy we've been chasing a long time. End of story.'

Three e-mails later, she had set the meeting for Holux. As Cota had suggested, Rashid would cross into Afghanistan alone and meet a CIA pickup at Batawul, a village east of the camp.

Back at Langley, the geeks in the Division of Science and Technology worked on trackers. A transmitter hidden inside a pill would have to be a low-powered radio unit that could be monitored only at close range. The DST preferred to hide a satellite transponder inside a heart monitor. When Rashid delivered the monitor to al-Zawahiri, satellites would autolock on him.

The night before the meeting, Holm couldn't sleep. Around three a.m., she gave up, turned on a lamp. Her husband sat up, stretched his arms as if he'd been asleep, though she knew he hadn't. 'What if we're wrong?'

'He's already given us a bunch of guys. He's proven himself.'

'I know I'm being irrational. Maybe it doesn't make sense unless you're a woman. But we've all had one of them. In college if you're lucky, high school if you're not. He's older, picks you up at a bar. Doesn't try to take you home that night. Gets your number, takes you to dinner, and he's got a nice car. He's so polite. Charming. Not like the stupid boys you know. You're happy you dressed up for him. Then after dinner he takes you back to his place for a drink, and before you know it your skirt is off, and whether you want it or not, it's happening. And when it's done, he never calls again—'

'Did this happen to you?'

'I told you we've all had one of them. The point is, that's the feeling Marburg gives me. He's too good. Do anything to get in our pants.'

'Make sure they pat him down tomorrow. Before he gets inside.'

'I asked Manny and he says no. We haven't searched him before, we can't start now. Especially since he told us how much he hated those guys stripping him down.'

They were silent. Finally she said, 'You know I can't walk away now. It's too late. Anyway, Manny has me believing I'm crazy to worry about this. Tell me I'm crazy.'

'The craziest woman I've ever met. Why I love you.'

She leaned over, kissed him. 'Good night, sweetie.'

In the morning, she felt fine, chipper, even. She saw the truth. Marburg was not a double. He was her agent. He was about to give them Ayman al-Zawahiri. She showered and dressed and drank two big mugs of coffee and headed out.

The day was clear and crisp. A breeze splashed in from the mountains. They saddled up and flew to Camp Holux on two Black Hawks. The team totaled ten officers in all, including Cota and his deputy, the two top officers in Afghanistan. The most junior guy in the group was Tom Lautner, her husband's brother, on his first tour in Kabul. He had been assigned to help provide security. She liked having him there.

The base was spartan, brick outbuildings that the CIA had rented from a local farmer, ringed with sandbags and barbed wire and low concrete blast walls. A South African contractor managed security, hiring Nepalese Gurkhas for the guard tower and locals to patrol outside the wire. In the one-room brick building that served as the communications center, Holm hailed Ted Khan, the officer overseeing Rashid's pickup, on an encrypted radio.

'Stinson One, this is Holux, do you copy?'

'Copy. Awaiting subject. Over.' Even on encrypted frequencies, Khan wasn't chatty. Holm was glad he was handling the pickup. He was half Afghan, and though he'd grown up near Los Angeles, he spoke perfect Pashtun.

Cota's sat phone buzzed. 'Yes, sir . . . Soon as we hear, sir.' He clicked off. 'Erie wishes us luck,' he said to Holm. Erie was the code name for the deputy director of operations, the agency's second-highest officer.

'It's not even five a.m. back there.'

'He's calling from home. Putting that encrypted line to good use.'

The radio crackled again a few minutes later. Holm reached for the handset but Cota grabbed it. 'Firecracker here.' The code name for the chief of station.

'This is Stinson One. I have eyes on the subject. Umm, he's wearing a jacket.'

'What kind of jacket?'

'A windbreaker type, not too puffy, but maybe loose enough to hide a vest. Request permission for a physical search.'

Do it, Holm mouthed at Cota. He raised a finger to his lips.

'Does he seem nervous? Head down, shuffling his feet?'

'Negative. He's looking around for me, checking his watch.'

'No search. Subject is friendly and we're gonna treat him that way. If you think he's wearing a vest, you're authorized to take action. But don't be wrong.'

'Roger that. We'll bring him in, then.'

The radio clicked off.

'Don't say it,' Cota said.

'A windbreaker's not his style. He's never worn one before.'

'Come on. It's thirty degrees. And I told Khan he was authorized to take action.'

'You also told him not to be wrong.'

'I think after today Marburg's getting another case officer.'

They were all locked in, Holm saw. Cota was counting the promotions he'd get for running this op. The security guys would do what Cota said. She wanted to object, but it was too late.

Ten minutes later, Tom Lautner appeared. 'They're at the gate.'

The officers formed an impromptu welcoming party outside the communications center. The gate rolled open and Ted Khan piloted his rusty old Toyota pickup through the chicane of concrete barriers just inside. Holm waved, and from inside the Toyota, Rashid waved back.

The pickup stopped a hundred feet from the CIA officers. Khan stepped out as Holm walked toward the SUV's passenger side. Lautner and other security officers followed, their pistols holstered. Cota had told them no rifles. Too intimidating.

The front passenger door opened. Rashid stepped out, careful to make sure his gown didn't touch the pickup's muddy side panels. 'Doctor—'

He stepped toward her. 'Miss Simmons, *salaam aleikum*—'

Before he finished the greeting, she knew. His face was even thinner than it had been in Karachi. But under his windbreaker, his body was thicker. Squarer. Whoever had built the vest had done a good job. It wasn't obvious. If it had been obvious, Khan would have been sure, instead of just worried.

But it was there.

Rashid took another step toward her. His eyes opened wide. He smiled. She saw he wanted her to know. He wasn't nervous either. He was ready. He was *looking forward* to this.

'Bomb!' Holm yelled. 'Bomb!' No time to say anything else. She pushed Cota aside and down—

Behind her the security officers reached for their pistols—

They were all too late.

Ahmad Rashid, code name Marburg, reached under his sweater and pushed the detonator on his suicide vest. The seven pounds of Semtex strapped to his body blew. The blast wave tore Marci Holm into pieces so small that her remains could be identified only by her wedding ring. It ripped off the back of Manny Cota's head. It killed seven other CIA officers, including Tom Lautner. Marci's body partly protected him from the blast. He might have survived, but the overpressure wave caught him awkwardly and snapped his neck. Six other officers were seriously wounded, Ted Khan worst of all. The explosion blasted the 4Runner's windshield into shards that cut up his eyes before he could blink. In a way he was lucky. He couldn't see what had happened to his face.

Even before the wounded were loaded onto medevac choppers for transport to Bagram and then Germany, the Critic-coded transmissions began.

EXPLOSION HOLUX ... MULTIPLE KIA ... MULTIPLE WIA ... EMERGENCY TRANSPORT EN ROUTE ... REPEAT

EXPLOSION INSIDE WIRE HOLUX. PERIMETER SECURE NO FURTHER ATTACK. SUICIDE BOMB SUSPECTED. MARBURG ASSUMED RESPONSIBLE.

REPEAT MARBURG ASSUMED RESPONSIBLE.

In the days to come, the dimensions of the catastrophe would become evident. A less important station would have been temporarily shut. Not Kabul. Not for a month or a week or even a day. Not with the Taliban spreading and the Afghan government too corrupt to function. Not with al-Qaeda regrouping over the border in Pakistan. Even before Manny Cota was buried in Georgia, Duto and his deputies on the seventh floor at Langley were deciding who would replace him. Duto himself flew to Kabul to rally his officers.

'We've lost a battle,' he said. 'A terrible battle. The war goes on.'

PART ONE

ONE

Forward Operating Base Jackson,
Zabul Province, Afghanistan
Present day

Growing up in the scrubland of west Texas, Ricky Fowler had done some stupid things. The usual nonsense, nothing the cops cared much about. Mailbox baseball. Spraying a 1 beside the 75 on speed-limit signs. A couple times, drunk, he shot firecrackers at bulls. Roman candles and such. He wasn't proud of that little trick, but he never hit anything. The longhorns didn't even notice.

But these Afghans, they took the cake on stupid. Yeah, they were tough fighters, tricky little bastards who could get by forever on tea and stale bread. But tough and smart were two different things. Guys in his platoon had a name for the nonsense they saw outside the wire every day: *SATs*. Stupid Afghan Tricks.

Like last month, on patrol, this dude sitting on a donkey so short the dude's feet touched the ground. Plus the donkey's sides were so loaded with sticks that it looked like it had a Christmas tree growing out of its butt. Even so the rider was grinning like he'd won the lottery, like, *That's right, suckers. I got a donkey, so I do not have to walk. How you like me now?* Smiling with those big white choppers all the Afghans had, even though they'd never seen toothpaste in their lives. Maybe because they couldn't afford to drink soda. Fowler didn't know. Mystery number 101 about this country.

Fowler was an E-3, a private first class, in 1st Squad, 3rd Platoon, Bravo Company, 1st Battalion, 7th Stryker Brigade. The unit's name didn't make much sense. The Army didn't have but four Stryker brigades. But Fowler had given up trying to figure out the military's logic on names, or anything else.

For six months, 3rd Platoon had been more or less orphaned from the rest of its company, peeled off to provide extra support for the supply convoys that ran on Highway 1 from Kandahar to Kabul. The convoys ran only once or twice a week, so the rest of the time, they got thrown onto random jobs that other units in the brigade didn't want. They set up roadblocks to register motorcycles. They guarded detained Afghans who were scheduled to be moved to the big jail at Kandahar. They didn't have a defined area of responsibility, and they rarely saw their company captain, much less their battalion commanders. As far as Fowler could see, the battalion had more or less forgotten they existed.

At least they lived on the same base as the rest of Bravo, Forward Operating Base Jackson. Jackson was a pile of trailers and blast walls in Zabul province. Like its neighbor to the west, Kandahar province, Zabul was the ass end of Afghanistan. No mountains here. Western Zabul and Kandahar were a mix of low brown hills and desert. Its soil supported two crops: poppies and the Taliban. More opium grew in Kandahar and the next-door province of Helmand than in the rest of the *world* put together. Not that you'd know it. Southern Afghanistan was dirt-poor. Literally. The locals lived in mud-walled compounds, no electricity or plumbing, just a bunch of dusty kids and goats and sheep.

But here they were, 3rd Platoon, the Lost Boys of Bravo Company. Now they were going down to Hamza Ali, a speck of a village fifteen miles from their base, for a 'strongman show.' Sounded to Fowler like they'd be seeing more Stupid Afghan Tricks.

The show itself was a perfect example of the kind of jobs the platoon always got. It was part of COIN, which stood for counterinsurgency warfare. COIN meant, get into the villages and show the locals how much you want to help them. Pretend to care while they yell at one another about who stole whose goat. Give them a few bucks to rebuild the walls that the Strykers knocked over. Help them build a real country. Back in Vietnam, it had been called 'hearts and minds'.

Fowler bet that COIN looked good on the presentations the generals gave the president. In reality, far as he could see, the Afghans were as close to building a real country as the hamsters he'd had in first grade. They were happy enough to take the free food and blankets and radios that the Army gave them. Then they kept their mouths shut when the Talibs came by planting bombs. They knew that sooner or later Fowler and his buddies would pack up and go home, and the Talibs would settle every score.

The Afghans might be stupid, but they weren't *dumb*.

Meanwhile, when the elders of Hamza Ali invited Colonel Sean Brown, the commander at FOB Jackson, to see a show at their school, he followed the COIN doctrine. He said yes quick as if they'd offered him fifty-yard-line Cowboys–Giants tickets. Not that Brown had any intention of going. He kicked the visit to his executive staff, who sent it all the way down to 3rd Platoon.

*

On this mission – using the word *mission* loosely – the drive was the most dangerous part. A lottery, more or less. The Strykers were armored personnel carriers that carried eleven guys, two driving and nine in the hole. They were twenty-ton beasts, with tall wheels and inch-thick armor. They looked indestructible.

But they weren't. The Taliban's most lethal weapon was what the Army called IEDs, or improvised explosive devices, giant homemade land mines. A big enough IED, say one built out of an old artillery shell, could turn a Stryker's passenger compartment into a nine-man oven. A Stryker from Jackson had gotten popped about three months back. The bomb was huge, two 155-millimeter shells, a thousand pounds of explosive. Six guys had died. The others had been taken to the Army's burn center at Fort Bliss in San Antonio. Word was they didn't have faces anymore.

The good news was that bombs that big were rare. The bad news was that riding in the Strykers still stank. They had no windows or side doors, just hatches on top and a ramp in back. Fowler understood the logic. Doors and windows were weak points. The Stryker was meant to be a vault on wheels. But the inside felt like a vault, too, a cramped hold stinking of fear-sweat, cut off from the world except for a little screen that ran black-and-white video from the camera on the hull. Once the back ramp closed, the guys inside couldn't do anything but wait. Not for nothing did soldiers call the Strykers Kevlar coffins.

Some guys slept during rides. Not Fowler. Inevitably, he caught himself thinking of the idiotic cartoon Smurfs. In almost every episode, the Smurfs, those miserable blue nitwits, wound up on the run from the evil wizard and his cat. Along the way, they whined constantly to Papa Smurf: 'How much farther, Papa

Smurf?' 'Not far now.' A few seconds later: 'How about now? Much farther now, Papa Smurf?' 'No, not too much.' And then: 'What about now? Is it much—' Until finally Papa Smurf, that old coot, lost his temper and yelled, 'Yes, it is!' It was, too. Much farther. But in the end the Smurfs got where they were going. No cartoon IEDs ever blew their cartoon asses to cartoon heaven. Fowler figured that was why he found them comforting.

Today at least they were on a hard-packed road, only a few big rocks to bounce them around. Even so, the convoy never got out of second gear. Outside of Highway 1, travel on Afghan roads was excruciatingly slow. The lead Stryker was equipped with the equivalent of a minesweeping snowplow, a steel harness that pushed thick concrete wheels. The harness was attached to the Stryker's front end, so the wheels rolled about a dozen feet ahead of the truck. They were supposed to set off bombs before the Stryker reached them.

But the wheels worked only on 'pressure-plate' mines, those that had a simple fuse set off by the weight of a vehicle. Lately, the Taliban were using more 'command-detonated' mines, which exploded when an insurgent set them off. So the driver of the lead Stryker stopped whenever he saw freshly dug dirt patches or suspicious pieces of roadside trash. The delays lasted anywhere from minutes to hours, if a mine was found. Meanwhile, the Strykers in the rest of the convoy idled. *How much farther now?*

Two hours after leaving Forward Operating Base Jackson, the convoy reached Hamza Ali. On the monitor inside Fowler's truck, low brick buildings replaced empty fields. 'Dismount in two,' Sergeant First Class Nick Rodriguez, the platoon's senior enlisted man, said.

Sergeant Coleman Young – one of the lucky guys, the ones

who slept – grinned at Fowler. Young was squat and muscular and as close to a friend as Fowler had in the platoon. 'Been watching that screen for us? Worst TV in the world. You know watching it makes no difference as to whether we hit a bomb. You do know that, right?'

'You missed out today.' Fowler didn't mind the ribbing. Not from Young.

'Yeah?'

'Two crazy Afghan chicks getting it on. Behind the burqa, you know.' *Behind the burqa* had become a catchphrase for 3rd Platoon. It meant everything and nothing.

The Stryker stopped. 'Ramp down in fifteen,' Rodriguez said. 'Blue' – American soldiers – 'left and right, so keep those safeties on.'

Fowler made sure his Kevlar vest was tight and checked his rifle. He stretched his legs and wiggled his toes inside his boots three times, *right, left, right*, his end-of-ride ritual. The Stryker's back ramp cranked down, kicking up gray-brown dust. One by one the men stepped out. 'Back to reality,' Young said.

'This is reality?'

'I hope not.'

The school was newly built, two stories with real windows and a chimney pumping a stream of black smoke into the sky. 'Hamza Ali Primary and Secondary School', a sign read in English. 'Funded by United States Agency for International Development.'

'Your tax dollars at work,' Fowler said.

'Not my tax dollars. Fowler, even you must know you pay no taxes as a member of the military serving in a war zone. You keep all twenty-five grand this year.'

'Plus all the chow I can eat.'

'Lucky you.'

'Heads up,' Rodriguez shouted to the platoon. 'Let's go!'

Rodriguez directed eight guys to stand sentry. The rest followed him and Lieutenant Tyler Weston, the platoon commander, to a dirt field behind the school. The low sun stuck in their eyes and turned them into teardrop shadows.

Weston had taken off his Kevlar and was wearing only his uniform. Soldiers called the practice *bucking*. Officers bucked at these events to prove that they trusted their Afghan hosts. Fowler thought bucking was idiotic. But then, he wasn't an officer, or much of a soldier either. He'd realized after a few weeks that he didn't belong in the Army. He got rattled too easily. He wasn't a coward, not exactly. He went outside the wire like everybody else. But he was scared a lot. The fear slowed him down. And being slow was dangerous. The guys who separated themselves from their fear, who moved fast and sure, those were the guys everybody leaned on. Fowler didn't like Rodriguez, the platoon's senior enlisted man. But he knew Rodriguez was a better soldier than he'd ever be. The Army had trained Fowler how to move, handle a radio, strip a rifle, but all the training in the world couldn't strip the fear from his heart.

So Fowler thought, and not for the first time, as an Afghan man stepped forward and shouted, 'Welcome, soldiers! Welcome, America!' He went on in Pashtun for a couple minutes, *baka-baka-baka*. The platoon didn't have an interpreter along, so none of the soldiers knew what he was saying, but the Afghans seemed to like the speech. When he was finished, Weston and Rodriguez stepped forward, holding a black bag. Weston opened it, tossed out a half dozen soccer balls.

'The United States is pleased to present this gift to the schoolchildren of Hamza Ali,' Weston said. He chipped one of the balls toward the school's back wall. Two boys took off after it.

'How is this nonsense winning a war for us,' Young said under his breath to Fowler. 'Giving them soccer balls? While they kill us with IEDs. Killing me *softly*.' These last three words delivered falsetto.

'With his song.'

'Cracker boy knows the Fugees.'

'Cracker boy, that's a compliment, 'cause I can roll.'

'Tell yourself that.'

'You think you're cool because you know the Fugees, Coleman? Everybody knows the Fugees. My grandma knows the Fugees and she's been dead five years.'

'I am the stupidest black man in the world, coming over here to fight this war. My uncle got two fingers blown off in Vietnam but at least he got drafted. What's my excuse?'

Fowler was spared from answering when two men and a boy stepped out of the school's back door. One man had thick black hair and wore a powder blue warm-up suit. The other carried a canvas bag and a sledgehammer. The boy was shirtless and wore nylon pants, canary yellow emblazoned with white racing stripes.

'A sledgehammer,' Young said. 'Stupid Afghan Tricks. Oh, *yes*.'

Without warning, the boy sprinted toward them and launched himself into a cartwheel and then three backflips. The man in the tracksuit followed with flips of his own. He finished beside the boy, picked him up, casually threw him in the air. The boy landed cat-quick and danced in a low furious whirl, kicking out his legs, the fabric of his yellow pants catching the sun. When the boy finished, the man raised his hands and said, in English, 'Please welcome to Parwan' – he tapped his chest – 'and Khost.'

He pointed to the boy. 'Famous father-and-son acrobat. Please like show.'

'How about some applause,' Sergeant Rodriguez said. The soldiers clapped as Parwan unzipped his jacket, revealing a tight black T-shirt. Afghan men insisted on modesty for women but showed off their own bodies at any provocation, Fowler had noticed.

When the applause ended, the man and the boy walked to opposite sides of the field. They turned and faced each other like cowboys about to duel. Then they sprinted at each other. Just before they were about to collide, Parwan ducked low and his son jumped. He flipped over his father's head and landed and spread his arms wide like an Olympic gymnast. Pure energy. Even Young clapped, though as a rule he was impossible to impress.

Parwan and Khost bowed to the crowd. The second man stepped forward and spun the sledgehammer over his head, an Afghan Thor. The hammer was handmade and brutal, a dull silver log flecked with red spots that hinted at a thousand atrocities. When he was finished showing off the hammer, he reached into the canvas bag and pulled out a board laced with nails.

Beside him, the boy leaned backward until his palms touched the ground. His head was upside down. His skinny stomach arched high into the air. The man lowered the board onto the boy's naked belly – nails first. The crowd was silent now. The man picked a flat brick out of the bag and placed it atop the board. He knelt and held the board steady as Parwan picked up the hammer—

'Oh, no,' Fowler said involuntarily—

And brought it down onto the brick. Which snapped gunshot loud. The nails quivered. The boy's stomach trembled. Parwan dropped the hammer, raised the two halves of the broken brick. The boy stood. A dozen crimson spots flecked his stomach, an instant case of chicken pox. Otherwise he didn't seem hurt. He touched his fingers to his stomach and raised them to show their crimson tips and kissed them. Father and son stood side by side and bowed as the men in the audience roared their approval.

'How do you win a war against people who break bricks on their kids for fun?'

Fowler had no answer for that.

Then the shooting started.

A short burst of AK fire, five or six rounds, a soft popping from the northwest. Sound traveled easily in the air here. Not much ambient noise. Fowler figured the shots were a way off. The threat wasn't immediate, if it was a threat at all. Fifteen seconds later a single shot followed. Then silence. Weston and Rodriguez murmured to each other. Rodriguez ducked his head to his shoulder, murmured into his radio. 'We're taking a walk,' he said to Fowler and the rest of 1st Squad. Fowler wished that they would let the Talibs come to them for once, instead of the other way around. But Rodriguez wasn't asking his opinion.

Back at the Stryker, Rodriguez grabbed his backpack and then huddled up the squad – seven men in all, since 1st Squad's driver and vehicle commander were staying in the village on sentry duty. 'Lieutenant wants us to take a look-see for those shooters. Rest of the platoon's staying here. It's probably nothing, and he doesn't want to mess up the show. What we know, there's a bunch of houses about a klick northwest. A canal runs that way. We'll go in dismounted. We're fishing for them, they're fishing for us. If there's somebody out there, let's take them out. Any questions?'

Rodriguez stepped up to Fowler, tugged on his Kevlar.

'No fear, Private. Say it.'

'No fear.'

Rodriguez looked over the men. 'Huddle up and *Hoo-ah!*' The two syllables were the all-purpose Army cheer – the sound of soldiers coming together.

'Hoo-ah!'

'Hoo-ah!'

'*Hoo-ah!*' Even Fowler felt his spirits rise.

They walked through the village's empty streets to the irrigation canal on the edge of town. Seven men. The tip of a sword that stretched halfway across the world. A hundred billion dollars a year to put them here, support them with drones and night-vision optics and ground-penetrating radar and every tool that the Pentagon's procurement managers could imagine, the more expensive the better. Now they walked, as soldiers always had and always would. They turned northwest, walked on either side of the dry irrigation canal, eight feet wide and four feet deep. A gray hole in this gray land. Their footsteps left no trace on the hard ground. They walked slowly. They didn't speak.

Rodriguez put four guys on the left side, three on the right. Fowler was second on the left, twenty yards behind the point. He didn't like the approach. Mud-brick walls dotted the fields around them, low and irregular, along with scrubby bare-branched trees. If they were walking into an ambush, the hostiles would have cover and a clear field of fire. But Rodriguez was gung ho as a rule, and the platoon hadn't sniffed a firefight in months. Fowler thought Rodriguez was probably hoping to engage.

They moved toward two shapeless clusters of huts, none more than ten feet high, protected by low walls. Donkeys and goats munched on garbage in a hand-built pen. No doubt everyone who lived here was related, a dozen families of kissing cousins.

Fowler kept his eyes up, looking for movement on the roofs. If any hostiles were hiding here, the ambush would start before 1st Squad got too close. For the most part, the Talibs used simple guerrilla tactics. They blew bombs at a distance and opened up with their AKs, trying to get American soldiers to chase them into fields of IEDs.

But the ambush didn't come. The soldiers stepped closer, their boots scrabbling along the canal's edge. On the left, one house had been painted bright blue. But sun and wind had bleached its paint until only a few snatches of color remained. All of Afghanistan felt drained of color to Fowler. Reduced to monochrome.

Rodriguez raised his left hand. The centipede of soldiers stopped. Rodriguez squatted low. Fowler followed his eyes toward a piece of metal that looked like the top of a soup can. He was trying to decide whether he was looking at a mine or a piece of trash. Finally, Rodriguez poked at the metal with the tip of his M-4. It flipped away harmlessly and skittered into the canal. Rodriguez stood, twirled his finger: *Keep moving*.

Two Afghans walked out of the hut that had once been blue. Both wore the *shalwar kameez*, the simple long tunic and pants that were standard for Afghan men. But one was wearing distinctly un-Afghan headgear, a black cowboy hat. 'Halt,' Sergeant Kevin Roman, on point, shouted in English, lifting his M-4. The two men stopped, raised their hands. The squad closed around them, forming a loose semicircle around the men.

'Gentlemen,' Rodriguez said. 'Why were you shooting?'

The men looked blankly at him.

'You have Taliban here?'

'Taliban? *La, la.*'

'Anybody speakee the English?' Rodriguez said. 'Come on.' He turned toward the huts, where little boys and girls peeked at them. 'Anybody home?' Rodriguez shouted. The kids disappeared. Fowler caught movement from a hut maybe fifty yards ahead and swung his rifle to cover. A man in a blue *shalwar kameez* stepped out, his hands high.

'Hello!' he yelled. 'Don't shoot! Everything is okay.'

The man walked toward them. Waddled, really. He was heavy, with a wide, rolling gait. He reminded Fowler of an Afghan they'd seen a couple months ago at a checkpoint they'd run maybe thirty miles from here. But he didn't seem to recognize them. Fowler stepped toward the guy, but Rodriguez shook his head. 'I got this, Private.'

'I feel like I've seen this guy before, Sergeant.'

'Yeah, well, they look alike.' Rodriguez was right on that. The Pashtuns had dark brown skin and brown eyes and thick beards and big noses and hands and feet. When the guy got close, Fowler saw he had a nasty scar down the right side of his neck, like somebody had just missed getting his head on a platter. Fowler was sure he'd seen that scar before. Weird.

'You are looking for Taliban?' Scar said.

'Always, my man.'

'No Taliban here.'

'Who was shooting at us?'

The guy shook his head. Rodriguez adjusted the plug of dip in his mouth with his tongue and spit a stream of brown saliva at the canal. His dipping and his temper had earned him the nickname Volcano.

'We heard shots.'

'No shooting.'

'Liar. Here's what we're gonna do. Roman, come with me. I

39

want to talk with this dude in private. In his compound. Fowler, Young, you stay here, keep an eye on the huts. B Team, you flare left, case we spook somebody out the side.'

'What about the right side?'

'Right side's going to have to look after itself. Can't do more with just seven guys.'

Fowler didn't like the plan. They were looking at only a few huts, but even so, they could be walking into an ambush. The Taliban didn't usually set up attacks inside villages, but there was a first time for everything.

'You steady, Private?' Rodriguez said.

Have to rub my face in it, don't you, Sergeant? Every time. Can't help yourself. An ugly thought flitted across Fowler's mind, an idea he couldn't have imagined having when this tour began. *I hope somebody lights you up. Mine, ambush, whatever. I hope you die, Rodriguez.*

'Like a rock.'

'Good.' Rodriguez walked toward the Afghan man in quick, confident steps. 'Quicker you show us around, quicker we're done.'

The other two Afghans tried to follow, but Young lifted his rifle fractionally and they stepped back. When Rodriguez and Roman were out of earshot, Fowler stepped toward Young.

'Coleman, I'm sure I've seen that guy before. At a checkpoint.'

'Like Rodriguez said, they all look alike.'

'They don't all have a scar like that.'

'More than you think.'

'I can't believe we've still got three months left. I can't do it.'

'You can. You will. And come home a hero.'

'Hero.'

'That's what they call us, isn't it?'

A hundred yards ahead, the scarred man pulled open a gate.

Rodriguez and Roman followed him inside. The way they were moving bothered Fowler. Rodriguez might be a dickwad, but he was a good soldier, always vigilant. Now he seemed relaxed. As if he were certain that nothing inside the gate would threaten. Fowler had the strange feeling that this patrol had been a sham, its only purpose to get Rodriguez to that compound. He watched the gate close and wondered why.

TWO

Missoula, Montana

The house at the end of the flagstone driveway was wide and brick and faced west toward the Bitterroot Mountains. It had two chimneys and a three-car garage. It looked . . . in truth, it looked like a nice place to live. Like it had a den filled with books that had actually been read and a refrigerator stuffed with leafy green vegetables. John Wells hadn't gotten inside and he was already feeling defensive.

Though the flagstone was a bit much.

Wells rolled up the driveway, which turned to asphalt beside the house. A thickly padded pillar supported a regulation-size basketball backboard. A teenage boy faced the hoop. He dribbled the ball between his hands like a three-card-monte dealer hiding an ace. He was maybe six-foot-two and, despite the cool fall air, wore only knee-length white shorts and a blue Boise State T-shirt. As Wells drove up the flagstone, the kid stepped back and launched a fadeaway jumper. It traced an easy arc and dropped through the net.

Wells parked his rental Kia a few feet from the boy and grabbed the bouquet of orchids and lilies he'd bought in downtown Missoula. He didn't want to open the door, but after a couple seconds he forced himself out.

The boy kept dribbling, skittering the ball between his legs. He was still growing into his body. His chest was flat, but his calves and forearms were thick with muscle. He had Wells's deep brown eyes and solid nose, and his hair was long and straight and pulled back in a ponytail. He launched another fadeaway jumper, this one just short. Wells collected the rebound.

'You must be Evan.' *You must be my son. Though I'm more or less guessing, since I haven't seen you since you were a baby.*

'I must be.'

'I'm John.' Wells stepped in for a hug, but the boy took a quick half step back and extended a hand.

'Nice to meet you.' Evan spoke softly, his words clipped flat. No hint of emotion. He sounded like a state trooper talking to a driver he'd pulled over for speeding. Without affect, the psychiatrists said. Though not without effect. Wells watched his son watching him. He supposed he'd earned that voice.

'Practicing your jumper.'

'Actually working on my dunks.'

'Right.'

Evan cocked his head at the flowers. 'Those for me? I'm more into roses as a rule.'

'Noted.'

Evan dribbled twice, threw up a fadeaway. This time the ball clanged off the front of the rim and bounced at Wells, who laid the flowers on the ground and corralled it.

'Coach tried to get me interested in ninth grade, but football was more my game,' Wells said. 'Now I wish I'd listened to him. All those hits add up. I still feel some of them.' Though Wells was lying. He wouldn't have traded football for anything.

He'd loved the sport's raw power, its velocity and contact. War without death.

He spun the basketball in his hands, dribbled once, flung up a jumper. The ball bounced off the back rim. Evan grabbed it and tucked it under his arm, an oddly adult gesture, as if he were in charge and Wells the teenager. His self-possession impressed Wells.

'You should probably tell my mom you're here.'

'Sure.' Wells turned to the house as Heather – his ex-wife – opened the door. Her hair, once a light honey brown, was streaked with gray and cut short, just above her shoulders. She and Wells had divorced barely a year after Evan was born, when Wells left them to go undercover in Afghanistan and infiltrate al-Qaeda for the first time. These were the prehistoric days before September 11. Wells had seen Heather only once since. Now he crossed the driveway and the stairs and hugged her. She hesitated and then reached for him and stretched her arms around his back. She was tiny, half his size. 'You look great,' he said.

'You lie.'

'Never.'

'Fairly often, I suspect. But come on in anyway.'

'What about . . .' Wells nodded at the side of the house, where Evan was once again shooting jumpers.

'Let him be. He'll come in on his own once he sees us talking.'

She led him through a house that was as handsome as Wells had imagined from the outside. The American dream alive and well in three dimensions. The pictures stung the most. Heather had remarried, a lawyer named Howard. They had two children, George and Victoria – Wells had looked up their names this morning. Family photos covered every wall. Victoria playing soccer. Evan spinning a basketball on his index finger. George standing on the Golden Gate Bridge. The five of them somewhere in Mexico or Central America, standing on a ruin, grinning.

Wells knew that the photos weren't for him. They'd been up long before he arrived. But he couldn't help feeling they were meant as an object lesson, a reminder of the life he'd traded away. Though he was probably fooling himself. Probably this life had never been open to him.

'They're beautiful. All of them.'

'Thank you.'

'And they get along?'

'You know, they're kids, they fight, but the fact that Evan has a different dad, that's never part of it. At least as far as I know.'

'That's great.' *What about me?* Wells wanted to ask. *Does he ever ask about me?* Even in his head, the question sounded impossibly self-centered.

Heather put Wells's flowers in a glass pitcher and they sat at a marble-topped island in the kitchen. She didn't ask whether he wanted anything to drink or eat, a reminder that he wasn't truly welcome.

'Howard's not around? Or the kids?'

'At the mall. And then a movie. I think something in three-D.'

'I'd like to meet them.'

'No, you wouldn't.'

'Give me a little credit.'

'I know you, that's all.'

Her certainty nettled Wells. 'What do you know?'

'You're very goal-oriented, John. "Must reconnect with son." ' Heather delivered that last sentence in a mock Terminator voice. ' "Building family ties, very important. Highest priority." '

Wells nearly flared up, said something like, *Still bitter after all these years*. But he hadn't come this far to argue. 'I don't

45

even think of you as an ex anymore, Heather. We've been apart so much longer than we were together.'

'Another way of saying you only called to see Evan.'

'It's another way of saying I hope we can be friends.'

'Sure, John. Friends.' She nodded at the absurdity of the idea. 'I want you to know I don't regret anything about us anymore, John. You gave me that boy and that's plenty.'

'Why'd you let me come, then?'

'Wasn't my choice. When you called, I asked Evan what he wanted, and he wanted to see you. And he's old enough to decide for himself.' She plucked out an orchid from the bouquet, twirled it in her fingertips so its delicate scent bloomed. 'So how's DC?'

'I haven't been there in months. Like I told you, I quit—'

'Officially. But that doesn't mean anything, right? And especially not for you.'

'It does and it doesn't,' Wells said, thinking about his last mission. Even though he'd been working privately, he'd used the CIA. And vice versa. 'It adds a level of complexity. But anyway I'm mostly up in New Hampshire these days.'

'With the new girlfriend.'

'Her name's Anne. And yes.'

'She's a cop, you said?'

'Correct.'

'You going to make an honest woman of her?'

'She doesn't need me to make her an honest woman.'

'Same old John. You must be bored. You always loved playing on the front lines of history.'

Wells couldn't tell whether she was being ironic. 'That's not how it feels.'

'No?'

'It feels like I'm putting my finger in a dike.'

46

'John Wells, the little Dutch boy.'

'More like a plumber. With a very specialized skill set.'

Evan walked into the kitchen, basketball under his arm.

'Hi, Mom.' He gave Wells a big fake grin. 'Hi, *Dad.*'

'Take a shower and lose the stink,' Heather said. 'And not just how you smell. John came a long way to see you.'

'Good for him.'

'And no girl showers today. Keep it short.'

'I thought you wanted me to get clean.'

'No need to wear out the plumbing. John probably gets himself clean in twenty-two seconds with a Brillo pad.'

'I'm in the field, I find a clean patch of stone and strip down and just scrape myself across it,' Wells said.

'And he waxes. Less hair to get dirty.'

'Every inch. Little-known Special Forces trick.'

'You two are *gross*,' Evan said. He backed out of the kitchen.

'Thank you for that,' Wells said, after Evan's footsteps had disappeared upstairs.

'For what?'

'Getting him to smile. He may have agreed to this, but it doesn't look like he's aching to bond.'

'You need to understand, John. All you can hope for at this point is to be a friend. Someone maybe he'll call if he's back east. And that's the absolute best.'

'I get it.'

'What were you expecting, John? You'd sail in and five minutes later everything would be cool?'

'I told you I get it.'

Upstairs, a shower kicked on. While they waited, Heather filled him in on Evan's life, his difficulties with AP Biology, his love of basketball, his dream college – the University of

California at San Diego. 'I don't know if he has the grades for it.'

'What about girls?' Wells said.

'Nothing serious. These kids don't really date. They text one another and sneak over to one another's houses and we can't do much about it unless we want to lock him in his bedroom all the time. Which would only make it worse. And I don't want to be a hypocrite either. Not like I was a nun in high school. So I told him to be careful, not to get anyone pregnant, and he looked at me like, "I'm not an idiot. I know."'

Evan reappeared freshly scrubbed fifteen minutes later. 'Ready, Pops?'

'Where to?'

'I figured you could take me into the backcountry, show me how to blow stuff up. Survival training. Make a *man* out of me, know what I'm saying?'

Wells looked at Heather. 'Please tell me he's joking.'

'Of course he's joking.'

'Of course I'm joking. We're going to this coffeehouse downtown. By the U. It's kind of a cliché, but the coffee's good.' Evan kissed his mother on the cheek. 'You were right. He doesn't have a great sense of humor.'

'I warned you.'

'I'm in the room,' Wells said. 'I can hear you. Both of you.'

Grizzly Coffee had overstuffed couches and grainy black-and-white photos of car accidents on the walls and a community corkboard with offers of rides to Seattle. The guy behind the counter had an ornate zombie tattooed across his right arm, its red-and-yellow eyes iridescent in the late-day sun.

Wells ordered a large coffee, skim milk. He was obscurely

pleased to see Evan do the same. The tables in the back were empty.

'Here we are, father and son, together at last,' Evan said.

'I want to thank you for seeing me, Evan. From everything your mom's said, you're an amazing young man.'

'I'm here because I figured you wanted to give me the key to a secret bank account with, like, a hundred million dollars.'

'If I had it, it would be yours. I just thought maybe we could get to know each other.' As soon as Wells said the words, he wished he hadn't. *Get to know each other*. Like this was a first date. A bad one, with no chemistry.

'I just threw up in my mouth.'

Wells sipped his coffee and waited for Evan to talk. To distract himself, he watched the barista make drinks, working the knobs and handles of the machines behind the counter as expertly as a nineteenth-century trainman running a steam engine.

'You're just going to stare into space until I start talking,' Evan said after a few minutes.

'Waiting is one thing I'm good at.'

'Fine. You win. *Ve have vays of making you talk.* So let's talk.'

'I just wanted to tell you face-to-face, I thought about you all these years. Wondered how you were, what your life was like.'

'You had a weird way of showing it. I know you were gone a long time. But you've been back five years now, more, and you never tried to see me.'

'Your mom didn't want me to, and I respected her wishes.'

'Yeah. You seem like the kind of guy who does what other people tell you.'

'I look at you, I don't see a stranger. I see how we're connected. And I know how you're feeling.'

49

'Of course you do, Dad. You know me so well—'

'Okay, maybe that wasn't the best way to phrase it—'

'Can we stop talking now?'

Wells played what he hoped would be his winning card. 'Is there anything you want to know about me? What I've been doing?'

'I know. You've been saving the world. *Call of Duty: John Wells Edition*. Only problem is, I don't see how the world's been saved. Looks like a mess to me.'

'Wait till you're my age.'

'Have you ever killed anyone?'

Wells was ready for this question, at least. He'd decided years before that Evan deserved the truth. 'Yes.'

'How many?'

'More than one.'

'More than one. What kind of answer is that? More than ten?'

Wells hesitated. 'Yes.'

'In self-defense?'

'That's not really a yes-or-no question.'

'I think it is.'

'What if Chinese cops are chasing you, and if they catch you, they'll turn you over to someone who's going to kill you? So you shoot them even though they're just doing their jobs? Or say it's 2001, after September eleventh, and you're undercover with some Talibs and you have to make contact with your side, the American side. But the only way to do that is to kill the guys you're with. So you do.'

'How come you put it in the second person? You mean I. "So I do. I killed them."'

'That's right. I killed them.' He'd executed them, no warning. Men he'd known for years. Their skulls breaking and exposing the gray fruit inside.

'Doesn't sound like self-defense.'

'It was necessary.' Wells leaned across the table, fighting the urge to grab his son by the shoulders. 'Evan. I'll tell you about what I've done. Everything I can, except the stuff that's classified and might get you in trouble. But I'm not going to argue the morality. Some things you can't understand unless you've been there.'

'That's what guys like you always say. That nobody else gets it.'

'These people we fight, they target *civilians*. Innocents.' Wells was arguing now, contradicting what he'd said just a few seconds before, but he couldn't help himself. 'They strap bombs to kids your age, and blow themselves up in crowded markets.'

'When we fire missiles and blow up houses in Pakistan, what's that?'

'I am telling you, I've seen this up close, and we make mistakes, but these guys are not our moral equivalents.' Wells wondered whether he should explain that he personally was certain that he'd saved more lives than he'd taken. But they weren't talking about him. They were talking about Iraq, and Afghanistan, and Vietnam. Those long, inconclusive conflicts that ground to a close without parades or treaties. Wars where the United States had a hundred different goals and the enemy had none, except to send American soldiers home in body bags.

'Let me ask you something, then, Dad. Suppose I told you in two years, "Hey, I want to join the Army. Enlist." Would you be in favor of that?'

'Not as an enlisted man, no.'

'But—'

'Soldiers follow orders. If you're concerned about the way we're fighting, you've got to be giving those orders. Be an officer. That's life. You wanted to go to West Point, get your butter bar' – the gold-colored bar that newly minted second lieutenants received – 'I wouldn't be against that.'

'But *you* quit. You left the agency.'

'Because I was disgusted with the politics inside Langley. But I'll always believe that the United States has the right to defend itself.'

'Oh, so that's what we're doing?'

The contempt in Evan's voice tore a hole in Wells's stomach real as a slug. Suddenly, Wells knew that Evan had agreed to see him for one reason only. Evan despised him, or some funhouse vision of him, and wanted him to know. Wells wondered what Heather had told Evan. Or—

'Is this because I wasn't around? Are you mad?'

'I have two real parents. I couldn't miss you any less.'

'Listen.' Evan stiffened, and Wells knew he'd said exactly the wrong word. Then he repeated it. 'Listen. You think you're the only one wondering what we're doing over there? Everybody who's been there asks himself whether we're doing any good.'

'But you keep doing it. They keep doing it.'

'Because those soldiers don't have the luxury of second-guessing their orders. They do what they're told, and when they're outside the wire, they have to figure out who's a civilian and who's the enemy, and if they guess wrong they die—'

'They're all volunteers. Right? They knew what they were getting into. Whatever we're doing over there, they're not bystanders. They're morally responsible.'

'That makes them heroes, Evan. Not villains.'

'Just like you.'

Wells pushed himself back from the table. He'd pictured meeting his son a hundred times: hiking in Glacier National

Park, rafting on the Colorado River, even driving to Seattle for a baseball game, an echo of the road trips he'd taken with his own father to Kansas City. He'd imagined Evan would want to hear the details of his missions, would ask him about being Muslim. Wells had converted during the long years he'd spent undercover, and he'd held on to the faith after coming back to the United States. He'd even wondered whether he might become something like an uncle who visited once a year. Ultimately, he'd imagined his son telling him, *I want you to be part of my life*.

But somehow he'd never imagined this particular disaster, this fierce, cool boy taking him apart as if they weren't blood at all. The bitterest irony was that Evan's dispassionate anger wasn't far from Wells's own casual cruelty. Wells didn't doubt that, with the right training, Evan would be a Special Forces-caliber soldier. He had the reflexes and the size. Though this might not be the moment to mention that career path.

'Evan. You're a strong young man, you're politically engaged—'

'Don't patronize me—'

'I'm *not*. But you think I'm a war criminal—'

'I didn't say that—'

'Close enough. And if not me, a lot of guys I know. And that's so far from the truth that I'm going to lose my temper soon, and I don't want that. You've got to be able to separate the war from the men who fight.'

'The war *is* the men who fight.'

'Let me take you home, and in a few years, when you have more perspective, we can try again. If you want.'

'I'm never gonna change my mind.'

'People your age always say that.'

'Let's go.'

*

Wells would have liked to ask Evan about basketball, or girls, or his classes, all the everyday details of life as a teenager. Surely high school hadn't changed, even if kids flirted now in 140-character bursts instead of whispered phone calls. But they'd left that conversation behind. They drove in silence. When they arrived, Heather waited on the front steps. Evan opened his door before the car had stopped. Wells sat in the car and watched him go. He'd lost his relationship with his only child without ever having one. Neat trick. After Evan disappeared, Wells stepped out of the car.

'Smart kid.'

'He is that.'

'Doesn't like the war much. Or me.'

She turned up her hands.

'You could have warned me.'

'I wasn't sure it would go that way and I didn't want to jinx it. I'm sorry.'

'I like him, you know. Politically aware, intelligent – he'll run for something one day. Something important. And win.'

'I hope so.'

'At least I don't have to worry that he misses me. He made that clear.'

'Would you rather he did? He felt some terrible lack in his life?'

She shoots, she scores. 'Maybe I'll try again in a few years. Meantime, if you or he want to reach me—'

She stood, hugged him. 'Good-bye, John.'

Wells drove. He'd booked a hotel for two nights, but now he just wanted to roll on 90, let its long twin lanes carry him east. He'd grown up in Hamilton, south of Missoula, and he'd planned to visit the graveyard where his parents were buried. He'd have to wait for another trip to pay those respects.

He wasn't angry with his son for questioning the necessity of war. *Blind faith in your leaders will get you killed*, Bruce Springsteen had said. But Wells could take only the coldest comfort in his pride. He'd lost any chance to connect with the boy. If Evan thought of him at all, it would be as a sperm donor, the man who'd contributed half his DNA and then disappeared.

Wells closed his eyes and counted silently to ten. When he opened them, the wide prairie on either side of the highway hadn't changed. Time to face the truth, leave his son behind.

And then his cell rang. A blocked number.

'John. You up in the woods, scaring the bears?' Ellis Shafer, his old boss at the agency. He was scheduled to retire in the spring. But Wells figured Shafer would work out a deal to stay. He claimed to have a happy life outside the agency, but he was in no hurry to get to it. Just like Wells. At this moment, Wells knew he'd buy whatever Shafer was selling.

'Montana. Visiting Evan.'

'Sojourning.'

'Is this call about the size of your vocabulary?'

'Master Duto has something for you. A mission, should you choose to accept it.'

Wells was silent.

'Before you say no—'

'I didn't say no.'

'Must have gone badly out there.'

Wells didn't answer.

'John?'

'I realize you enjoy demonstrating your cleverness at every opportunity, Ellis, but now is not a good time.'

'Duto wants you to go to Afghanistan.'

'He forget I don't work for him anymore?'

'He thinks there's a problem in Kabul, and I think he's right.'

'What kind of problem?'

'The kind better discussed in person.'

Sure as night was dark, Duto had an angle here. Angles, more likely. 'What's my excuse?'

'Officially, you'll be there on a morale mission. Also – and this will be shared privately with senior guys – you'll be making an overall assessment of the war. Nothing in writing, just impressions that you'll present when you get home. You go over, spend a couple days at Kabul station. Have dinner with COS' – an acronym that sounded like an old-school rapper but in reality stood for chief of station – 'then visit a couple bases, meet the Joes. Talk to whoever you like.'

'Pretty good cover.'

'Yes. Come to Langley, and Duto and I will fill you in on the rest.'

Wells wondered what Evan would make of this offer. No doubt he'd dismiss it as macho crap, a pointless exercise.

'Great,' Wells said. 'I'm in.'

THREE

Hamza Ali, Afghanistan

In the village, five minutes ticked by. The sun lost itself behind a cloud. Young pulled open a pouch on his Kevlar vest, extracted a pack of Newports.

'You have to smoke Newports, Coleman? I can almost see you on a billboard wearing one of those Day-Glo orange suits. Right above an ad with Billy Dee Williams sipping from a quart bottle.'

Young took a deep drag, blew the smoke in Fowler's direction. 'Menthol tastes good. Plus you people don't smoke them, so I don't have to share.'

'You people.'

'White people. You're the one who went there.'

'Lemme try one.'

'A white person?'

'Come on.'

Young tucked away the pack. Fowler surveyed the empty village.

'What are they doing?'

'Don't know. And not guessing.'

'Where's B Team?'

'Lighting up, probably. And nothing menthol. Nothing that comes in a pack.'

Fowler was embarrassed he hadn't realized. Of course. The three soldiers on the B fire team had turned into hash smokers the last couple months. Along with half the rest of the platoon.

'What are we doing here, Coleman?'

'You're tripping over your own damn feet. I'm trying to stay alive. Get home.'

'No, what are we doing here? Right now.'

'Maybe Rodriguez found himself a kebab stand.'

'Kebabs.'

'Or tacos. I don't know and I don't care. You're so curious, go check it out for yourself.'

Just that quick, Fowler decided he was tired of being scared. 'You know what? I think I will.'

'You find any kebabs, let me know.'

The street was filled with the random junk that was everywhere in Afghanistan, shreds of plastic and canvas, the stuff even the goats couldn't eat. No metal, though. Metal was valuable. The Afghans salvaged it.

The village looked as dismal up close as it had from a distance. In richer areas, Afghans lived in compounds hidden by ten-foot mud-straw walls. Here the walls were barely waist-high, exposing the battered homes behind them. The air was sweet and greasy, with a bitter tang underneath. A mix of wood smoke, cooking oil, and sewage.

Fowler heard the voices of women and children hiding in the houses. The words faded as he moved closer, picked up again once he passed. They couldn't see him and still they treated him like a leper. As if even their voices were a gift he didn't deserve. He wanted to hate them. But then, they hadn't asked him to come here. He reached the house where the Afghan had led Rodriguez and Roman. This was the fanciest place in town, the tallest midget, with seven-foot walls and a filigreed gate. He peeked through the filigree—

And a single shot cracked behind him. Fowler flattened himself against the wall, checked left and right. Chickens squawked wildly. Behind him, Young tossed away his cigarette and scanned the empty fields that lay between them and the rest of the platoon. Fowler wondered whether the Talibs had lured them out here to cut them off, trap them.

But nothing happened. Terror and boredom, the twin poles of infantry duty. The chickens chattered away. Fowler took advantage of their noise to pull open the gate. He slipped inside, two quick sliding steps.

The yard was empty aside from a rusty Weber gas grill, which didn't make sense, and a brand-new ATV, which kinda did. A diesel engine, probably an electrical generator, hummed somewhere in back. Electricity and an ATV. By local standards, whoever owned this place was living large. Fowler eased the gate shut and waited for someone to open the door, walk out of the house. But no one did.

Fowler stepped forward, then hesitated, holding his left leg off the ground with the exaggerated care of Inspector Clouseau. He could explain everything he'd done so far. He could say he'd come up for orders. But if he sneaked up to the house to see what Rodriguez was doing inside . . . Spying on a sergeant was definitely a no-no.

But maybe he wasn't spying at all. Maybe they needed him. Maybe the Talibs had captured Rodriguez and Roman. Fowler imagined them tied back-to-back. They looked up in awe as Fowler picked off the insurgents one by one, with the practiced double taps of a Special Forces lifer. Fowler saluted them casually: *No need to thank me. Just doing my job.* The vision was ridiculous. Still, it spurred him. He crossed the yard, pressed himself against the house.

And heard a voice. A woman. Moaning quietly. Had he stumbled on a brothel? Impossible. The Afghans stoned women to death just for talking to men. Fowler inched along the side of the house to a window covered by a wrought-iron grille. He lowered himself to his knees, peeked in—

And found himself watching porn. The video was playing on a television propped against the back wall. Rodriguez and Roman had come here to *watch porn*? Fowler didn't get it. Then he looked around the room and—

Everything made sense. Roman sat against the wall, a glass pipe in one hand, lighter in the other. He flicked the lighter to the pipe and sucked, greedy as a newborn. He exhaled a gray cloud and rubbed his stomach happily. 'Good smoke,' he said to the ceiling. 'Steep and deep.'

Rodriguez ignored the commentary. He stood next to a wooden table as the Afghan with the scar put two plastic-wrapped bricks on a digital scale. 'Two point zero exactly. Sixteen kilos total.'

Rodriguez pulled a Ka-Bar, a knife, off his belt. He carefully sliced the plastic around one of the bricks. 'What is that?' the Afghan said.

'Testing, one, two, three.' Rodriguez pulled a pouch from his backpack. 'Soon as this powder in here turns green, we're ready to go.'

'I promise you, it's good.'

'From the factory to you,' Roman said. 'Buy direct and save.'

Rodriguez stepped to the television and kicked over the DVD player hooked to it, stopping the show. 'Stand post at the front door, Roman. Lemme finish, get us out of here. We wasted too much time already.'

'Sir, respectfully point out that I am stoned to the gills and not at full combat readiness—'

Rodriguez snapped the pipe from Roman's hand. 'Now. Before I jam this down your throat.'

Fowler picked up his helmet, pushed himself up, inched along the wall. Then he heard Roman's gear rattling inside the house and his composure broke. He ran for the gate.

Back on the street, he closed the gate as smoothly as he could. He checked over his shoulder. The house's front door was just opening. Fowler squared his shoulders and walked back to Coleman Young. He didn't look back. He was proud of himself for that much anyway.

'I miss anything?' Young said.

'No kebabs. The door was closed and I couldn't decide whether to knock. I stood there until I felt stupid and left.'

'That's it.'

'That's it.'

'Huh. What happened to your pants?'

Fowler looked down. His knees were covered with a dark brown splotch that stank of diesel. He must have knelt in a puddle without realizing. It was the porn's fault. The porn had distracted him. He wiped madly at the stain and succeeded only in covering his hands with a greasy film. Might as well be wearing a sign that said 'I've been spying on you, Sergeant'.

'It was a drug deal. A big one. They had a scale.'

'Don't tell me.'

'Kilos. It's true.'

Young grabbed Fowler's Kevlar, pulled him close. 'I don't care if it's true. I don't want to hear it.'

'What do I *do*, Coleman?'

'You keep your mouth shut, Private.' Young pushed Fowler back so hard that he nearly fell on his butt. 'Be cool. They coming now.'

Fowler turned. Rodriguez and Roman walked toward him. The Afghan in the blue robe was gone. Probably still in the house, watching porn. A real good Muslim. Dealing smack to the infidels.

Roman grinned at them, pointed a finger pistol at Fowler. Fowler's mouth went dry. If he didn't calm down, he feared he might cry. 'I'm not built for this, Sergeant,' he muttered.

'It's all right, Ricky. Nothing's gonna happen now. I'll watch your back and we'll talk later. Back at the FOB.' Young tapped out two Newports, handed one to Fowler. Fowler wiped his mouth, lit up, puffed away.

'Tastes like an air freshener.'

'Good for you. Makes your lungs all minty. Smile and salute.'

B Team rounded the corner as Rodriguez reached them. His backpack sat snug on his shoulders, Fowler saw. All that extra weight. 'Anything to report?'

'That one shot,' Young said. 'Nothing else.'

'All right. We're done here then. Got a couple names. Probably junk but Weston'll like it. He can give it to the G-2.' The battalion intelligence officer.

'They'll give him a pat on the head and a present with a big red bow.'

'When Daddy's happy, everybody's happy.' Rodriguez poked at Fowler's knees with the muzzle of his carbine. 'What happened there, Private?'

'Sir. Figured I'd look over the left side of the villa. Fell in a puddle of diesel. I think it was diesel, anyway, sir. Smells like it.'

'Excellent soldiering. We get home, I'm signing you up for the Very Special Forces, where everybody's a winner.'

'I think of myself as a very special soldier, sir.'

'Yes, you are. You see anything over there around the corner? Besides the puddle?'

Fowler held Rodriguez's eyes. 'Goats, Sergeant. Nothing but goats.'

'All right then. For showing that initiative, I'm giving you point on the way back, Private. Look alive. Do me proud.'

'Yes, sir.'

They shuffled back toward Hamza Ali. For once, Fowler wasn't worried about mines. He couldn't stop thinking about the scale, those plastic-wrapped bricks. He'd seen drugs before. Heck, he'd grown up two hours from the Mexican border. He'd smoked pot like everyone else in the universe.

But buying heroin by the kilo was a different game. Fowler couldn't figure what Rodriguez was doing with the stuff. He wasn't selling it on base, that was for sure. And where did he get the money for it? Fowler didn't know what a kilo of heroin cost, but even here at the source it had to be a couple thousand bucks.

Next question: Did everybody know what was going on? Was Fowler the only sucker in the squad? Young hadn't seemed surprised. Although Young always acted so cool. No, if everybody knew, Rodriguez wouldn't have bothered to hide the deal. So Fowler had a choice: keep his mouth shut, ride out the last couple months. Or go to the CID – the Army's Criminal Investigative Division – which had offices at the big base at Kandahar. But if the CID officers came poking around, Rodriguez would probably guess that Fowler had snitched.

Maybe Young would have the answer. Fowler was almost embarrassed to be leaning so hard on Young, who was barely two years older than him. But Young got along with everybody. He had that black-guy way of being cool without working at it.

The squad was stretched out, moving slowly, half-assed. Fowler slowed down to let them catch up. Rodriguez was directly behind him, Roman on the other side of the canal. Fowler was glad that Young was watching.

When they got about three hundred meters outside Hamza Ali, Fowler saw clumps of men and boys walking toward him. The show at the school must have ended. Fowler had forgotten all about the Stupid Afghan Tricks. The kids made a game of jumping across the canal, their gowns ballooning around their legs. A boy kicked one of the soccer balls that the platoon had handed out, his steps as precise as Fowler's mom dicing an onion, back home in the kitchen. Fowler wished he could be there now.

The boy popped the ball into the air and headed it to himself. Kids were kids everywhere. Fowler smiled. 'Hey,' he yelled. Fowler pointed at himself. 'Kick it here. Me.' The kid hesitated and then kicked a perfect curling strike that soared out of the canal toward him—

And exploded.

Fowler heard the shots after he saw the ball disintegrate. They came from the right side of the canal, away from the village, an AK magazine fired on full auto.

Fowler jumped into the canal for cover and spun to find the shooter. To his right, the rest of the squad followed. They were stretched in a line, rifles at the ready. The fields in front of them looked empty. Then Fowler saw the shooter. It was the Afghan with the scar, the one who'd sold the drugs to Rodriguez. He was a long way off, at least four hundred meters, and sneaking along a low wall perpendicular to the canal. He was doubled over like he had a bad case of the runs.

For once, Fowler wasn't afraid. His training took over. He

grabbed the rough stone at the edge of the canal and pulled himself up to get a clean shot. He didn't squeeze too tight and he led the target. He thought he had the guy.

But he missed. The dude was just too far off and too low and too many walls were in the way. Fowler aimed again, tightened his finger on the trigger—

He never heard the shot that cut his spinal cord in half. Didn't feel it either. The pain faded as quickly as it bloomed. The earth rushed up to him and caught his chin. He didn't understand what had happened to him, couldn't frame this new place he'd gone. This lost country.

Pure confusion. He stood up, but he didn't. His legs didn't work, or his arms. The dark trickled into his eyes and his brain got thirsty and he needed air. So he took a breath but nothing happened. He had to breathe. Breathing was easy. Everyone could breathe. But not Fowler. Then the fear, panic, a pure white panic that flared against the black, but the black came on, stronger and stronger, and the white shrank to a pinprick and then nothing at all and—

He died.

Young was closest to Fowler and the first to realize what had happened, that he'd been shot from behind, from somewhere in the fields between the canal and Hamza Ali. Young ran to Fowler. The others followed. They pulled his body into the canal and set up a perimeter and screamed at the villagers to get back, back, back.

Rodriguez got on his radio, called Weston. The rest of the platoon arrived minutes later. But the shooter was gone by the time they reached the huts behind the canal that were the most likely firing point. None of the villagers had anything to say. No one had seen anything. And so the Lost Boys of Bravo

Company could do nothing but carry Fowler's corpse back to their $2 million Strykers.

The guys didn't talk much on the ride back to FOB Jackson. When they did, they cursed Hamza Ali and the Taliban, and Fowler, too, for his bad luck. Everybody figured he'd died in a freak ambush. He was the kind of guy who worried so much that he attracted his own trouble. Bad karma. Coleman Young didn't say a word. But as he sat on the bench next to the empty space where Fowler should have been, he wondered who had killed Fowler. Rodriguez and Roman couldn't have. The shot had come from behind the squad. Which meant someone else in the platoon was involved.

Young went through the likely suspects in his mind. One name stood out. He wondered what he should do. If anything. Three months left on this tour. Coleman Young closed his eyes and thought of home.

FOUR

Langley, Virginia

The floors at CIA headquarters were not created equal.

Take the third floor of the New Headquarters Building, home to the unit once called the Directorate of Administration and now known as the Directorate of Support. On its public Web site, which existed mainly as a recruiting tool, the CIA did its best to make the DS sound exciting: 'Our job is to ensure that all our mission elements have everything they need for success . . . while the support we provide may be invisible – the results certainly are not!'

Invisible indeed. The agency's more glamorous divisions hardly noticed the DS's existence. But the directorate's employees soldiered on, administering health plans, making sure the agency wasn't overcharged for printer paper, and approving the world's strangest expense reports: *Six vials cobra antivenom: $360*. No one but DS employees ever went to the third floor of the NHB.

Which made it the perfect place for a sterile room.

BC1-3-114 had once been a supply closet. The evacuation plans that the DS so meticulously maintained still identified it as one. The only clue to its new use came from the keypad and thumb reader that opened its magnetic door lock. Inside, it held a steel desk, two battered chairs, a phone – and a computer that with the right passwords could access any agency database. Even ones that were supposed to be available only on much more important floors.

Shafer had just explained the setup to Wells, who was back at Langley for the first time in almost a year. He'd come directly from Montana, not even stopping in New Hampshire for a change of clothes.

'Doesn't a room like this violate every rule of computer security ever created?'

'*Every* and *ever* are redundant, John. And have you been studying network architecture in your spare time?'

'Seriously, Ellis?'

'Seriously. First, you need passwords. Both on this end and for the database you're accessing. Second, the mirroring software works only in this room. Third, and most important, nobody knows it's here.'

'Who exactly is nobody?'

'Me, Vinny, a couple others. We installed it last year, and it's been used only twice, in situations like this, when we want to get somebody up to speed quietly. This way, you can read every file from Kabul station and nobody will know.'

'I *get* it, Ellis.' Despite all Wells had done, Shafer still sometimes treated him like a quarterback who needed extra time in the video room.

'Okay, you get it.'

'What I don't get is what I'm looking for.'

'Just read.'

*

68

The case files from Kabul painted a bleak picture. The station was the ultimate hardship post. Officers left their families on another continent and risked kidnapping and assassination every day. Unlike the Army or Marines, the CIA was a civilian organization that couldn't order its employees to take dangerous jobs. Most officers stayed a few months, just long enough to put an Afghan posting on their résumés.

Building real relationships with the tribal chiefs who ran Afghanistan took much longer. That work fell to a cadre of hard-core operatives who lived in Kabul for years. By mid-2009, their efforts were paying off. They were a long way from the leaders of the Taliban or al-Qaeda, but they were moving up the ranks.

Then Marburg showed up.

The Marburg reports covered sixteen hundred pages and included scores of photographs, everything from the first surveillance shots of Rashid to the carnage at Camp Holux. A separate file contained the video from the Karachi hotel where Marci Holm had met Ahmad Rashid. The file ended with the eighty-nine-page after-action report from the agency's internal investigation.

The report's language was passive, but its meaning was clear. The agency blamed Manny Cota and Marci Holm for the disaster.

SUMMARY/CONCLUSIONS
MARBURG penetrated Holux due to avoidable operational error. It is true that some agents initially reject physical searches. The successful case officer must overcome those doubts and convince the agent that a pat-down protects both CO and agent. Holm never established those ground rules with MARBURG. Holm did not explain

in her case reports why she did not insist that MARBURG be searched. Other officers recall that Holm said she found MARBURG personally charming.

Both Holm and Cota believed that MARBURG had extremely high-value intelligence. In their eagerness, the officers missed warning signs, most notably the ease with which MARBURG supposedly penetrated AQ. It is simply not credible that an outsider such as MARBURG would meet Ayman al-Zawahiri so quickly.

Once the officer who picked up MARBURG questioned whether he might be wearing an explosive vest, prudence and protocol dictated a physical search. Either Holm or Cota should have insisted on such a search.

RECOMMENDATIONS

1) Case officers must inform ALL sources/agents that they will be patted down before being allowed onto any secure facility. If an agent protests, his or her officer will explain that the rule must be followed without exception.

2) No more than five agency officers/contractors shall be present at any meeting with an agent. A closed-circuit video link may be provided for additional officers. Authorization at the DD or higher level shall be required to override this rule.

3) Case officers shall encourage agents to take regular polygraph tests. If an agent resists, cash compensation may be offered.

The recommendations continued for several pages. Some made sense, like limiting the size of meetings. Others were irrelevant, like the suggestion that all spies should be polygraphed. That idea might have sounded good at Langley, but it had nothing to do with the way case officers actually worked.

All in all, the report was what Wells expected. The agency had to hold someone responsible for this disaster, if only so that it could tell its political masters what it had learned from its mistakes. Holm and Cota couldn't defend themselves, so they'd taken the blame. The nastiest line in the report was a throwaway, that Holm 'found MARBURG personally charming.' The implication was obvious.

In the video from Karachi, Rashid had impressed Wells as smooth and convincing, right down to his supposed concerns about his family. Wells wasn't sure that he would have known Rashid was a double. But he would have searched Rashid before letting him inside Holux. Pat-downs were a part of life these days. For whatever reason, Holm had let him through. Two-plus years later, Kabul station was still recovering.

Duto had appointed Jimmy Wultse to replace Cota as station chief just seventy-two hours after the bombing. The choice had seemed solid. Wultse, the chief for Tajikistan, knew Afghan politics intimately. Unfortunately, he also had a drinking problem. He'd managed it in Dushanbe, but the stress of Kabul turned him into a full-blown alcoholic. After four months, Duto ordered him back to the United States for rehab.

Duto's next choice was Gordie King, an agency veteran who'd spent most of his career in South America. Wells understood the choice. King had a reputation as an old-school butt-kicker. Unfortunately, King didn't speak Pashtun and disliked Afghanistan intensely. He rarely left his office when he was in Kabul. Making matters worse, he refused to choose a deputy.

Under King, the station slipped into crisis. Case officers cut their tours short and were not replaced. Senior officers in Afghanistan's intelligence service began skipping their weekly meetings with the agency. Two top sources in eastern Afghanistan were assassinated. Fifteen months after Marburg, the CIA's intelligence-gathering effort in Afghanistan existed mostly on paper. Its operations consisted of drone strikes and payoffs to supposedly friendly tribal chiefs.

In the medium term, the problems made little difference to the war. The soldiers and Marines in Kandahar and Helmand provinces didn't need the CIA's help to kill Taliban guerrillas. But in the long run, the CIA's role was crucial. Military intelligence officers weren't supposed to spy on the Afghan government or explore the relationships between the insurgents and Iran and Pakistan. Those jobs belonged to the CIA. But as the agency slipped, the Defense Intelligence Agency began recruiting its own sources in Kabul and all over Afghanistan.

Duto faced an unpleasant choice. Replacing King would mean admitting a big mistake, and Duto hated admitting mistakes. But he hated losing turf even more, especially since Afghanistan had always belonged to the CIA. The agency had helped battle the Soviets in the 1980s. After September 11, while the Pentagon dithered, CIA operatives helped push the Taliban from power.

And so Duto sent King home barely eleven months after naming him as station chief. In his place, Duto appointed Ron Arango, a solid officer who had served in Pakistan and Russia. As deputy, he chose Peter Lautner, who had been in Kabul for seven years. Lautner was known as especially aggressive. He had reason to be. He'd lost his wife and his brother to Marburg.

Under Arango and Lautner, the station seemed to be recovering. Lautner had rebuilt relationships with tribal leaders. Arango had taken five top Afghan intelligence officers to a counterinsurgency conference that was a thinly disguised bribe, an excuse for a vacation in Paris.

But despite the activity, the station was still foundering. Some of its recent intel had proven flat wrong. A month before, one of its best sources had reported that a senior Taliban commander wanted to defect. The 'defection' was a hoax, leading to an ambush that killed an Afghan general. The station still didn't know whether its source had lied or been used to pass along disinformation. Worst of all, the station had just lost another top agent, the deputy interior minister. A bomb hidden in a fuel tank had blown apart the minister's armored 4Runner.

With all the problems, Wells wasn't surprised that the station had largely been left out of the hunt for bin Laden. Langley and the Pentagon had directed the operation, with help from the NSA. Kabul had barely been involved.

Shafer had offered to let Wells stay in a spare bedroom while he waded through the reports. But Wells wanted to read the files without having Shafer quiz him like an annoying high school teacher. So Wells was staying a few miles from Langley in a Courtyard by Marriott. He liked Courtyards and Hilton Garden Inns and the other three-star hotels that sat on suburban feeder roads, bland, efficient boxes where every room was identical and no one noticed anyone. Every day he woke at six and worked out in the Marriott's underwhelming gym for ninety minutes. He reached the agency by nine o'clock and read files for twelve hours, until his eyes burned. Then he headed back to the hotel.

Wells had converted to Islam more than a decade before, but in the last few months he'd hardly prayed at all. He wondered whether he'd ever regain his fervor. Perhaps he'd grown permanently weary of battling jihadis born into the religion he wanted to claim as his own. He kept his Quran on his bedside table, but he didn't pray. Instead he watched baseball until he fell asleep, rooting for close games and miracle finishes, trading one faith for another.

After a week reading files, Wells had grown to sense the station's different personalities. Arango, the chief of station, wrote in a businesslike, slightly bureaucratic tone. Lautner had an aggressive edge. Gabe Yergin, the number three, was hurried, almost sloppy, as though he were perpetually behind schedule, running between meetings.

By Friday night, Wells had nearly finished the files. His mouth was dry, his eyes scratchy from the closet's stale air. Office work left him tired, but not in an honest, muscle-sore way. He wanted to put a pack on his back and hike for twenty-four hours straight. He looked up as the magnetic lock clicked open and Shafer stepped in.

'You look dazed.'

'I thought we were trying to reduce the amount of paperwork the stations generate.'

'That's a work in progress. Plenty of memos going around about it, though.'

Wells laughed.

'You caught up?'

'Pretty much.'

'Duto wants to see you, talk about it.'

'He works this late?'

'You kidding? He's got some fancy dinner tonight. With Travers and McTeague, I think.' Congressman Raymond Travers and Senator Hank McTeague were the chairmen of the House and Senate committees that oversaw the CIA. 'Duto will tell them stories about Sarkozy and Carla Bruni, make them think they heard something that they couldn't have read on Page Six.'

'Sounds like fun.'

'Better him than us. Anyway, he's coming by your hotel at ten tomorrow. I'll be there, too. Try not to sleep late.'

'Yes, Your Highness.'

Wells stepped out of the Courtyard's freshly mopped lobby at ten the next day, just as a black Chevy Tahoe rolled up the driveway. Inside the Tahoe, Duto and Shafer. Duto wore the weekend uniform of the powerful, gray windbreaker, blue shirt, pressed khakis. He was nearly sixty, and his hair had thinned since Wells had seen him. Otherwise he hadn't changed. His handshake was firm. His smile was all lips and no eyes.

They rolled out, turned left toward D.C. Two identical black Tahoes followed.

'Subtle pickup,' Wells said. 'You should just paint "CIA Taxi" on the doors.'

Wells and Duto didn't get along. Their mistrust wasn't playful. It wasn't a light banter that hid mutual affection. They simply disliked each other. Wells had quit the agency because of Duto. Yet they seemed to need each other. Several months before, the CIA had helped Wells on his mission to Saudi Arabia. Now it was Duto's turn to ask for a favor.

'How are you, John?' Duto's voice was quiet. Almost silky. Wells wondered whether Duto was taking vocal training. He had once been famous for his temper. But years as director had taught him restraint. *Let others squabble. The ultimate decision belongs to me. No need to show my claws.* Wells wanted Duto to go back to being a screamer, but so far Wells hadn't managed to provoke him.

'Fine.'

'And Anne?'

'She's fine, too.' Wells wondered whether Duto remembered

her name or had been briefed. 'Though my son seems to have decided I'm a war criminal. Never wants to see me again.'

'That's too bad.' Duto didn't exactly sound torn up.

'I'm sure he thinks even worse of you.'

'They have no idea what we do for them. What it takes to keep them safe.'

'We're five miles from the Pentagon,' Shafer said. 'Around here, most of them are us.'

'You know what I mean. Civilians.'

'They know exactly what we do,' Wells said. 'That's the problem.'

'We killed Osama. And no civilian casualties in the op. Not one. Ten years since nine/eleven and no real attacks on American soil. Not even jerks with AKs lighting up a mall. We've kept our people safe. Tell me that doesn't count for something, John.'

They turned onto the Chain Bridge. Wells watched the Potomac rush by. Knowing he'd have to answer. Knowing Duto was right. 'Okay. You win. You sound like you're planning to run for something—'

A smile curled Duto's mouth and then was gone, brief and shocking as lightning in a cloudless sky. Suddenly, the good suits and voice lessons and personality transplant made sense. *Impossible*, Wells almost said. *You're only fooling yourself.*

Duto was more powerful than any senator or congressman. Only one elected office would be worth his effort. But the presidency was off-limits to anyone too deeply involved with the agency. The first George Bush was the only director ever to have won the presidency, and he'd served at Langley barely a year. Duto had spent most of his adult life at the CIA. His fingerprints were on the agency's most controversial programs. His record couldn't possibly bear public scrutiny.

But if his smile was any indication, Duto thought it might.

'Anyway,' Wells said. 'Unless you want more awkward small talk—'

'You read the cables. What do you think? Operationally speaking.'

'You already know the answer. It's a mess. Been one since Marburg. Wultse was a drunk, Gordie King was burned out. The new guys, Arango and Lautner, they look good, they're saying the right things and maybe doing them, too, but they've been there awhile and so far they haven't made progress. If Kabul ran half as well as Islamabad, we'd have won the war by now.'

'Can they? Make progress?'

'I'm not going to pass judgment from seven thousand miles away on guys I've never met.'

'So you'll go see them then?'

'Vinny. What is it you're not telling me?'

'Right now, Kabul's our most important station. More than Moscow, Beijing, whatever. If I have to change it up again, I will. But that would be the fourth new chief since Marburg. And it's not like I have great options. I don't want to move anyone from Islamabad now that they're getting traction. I don't want to bring someone else in from outside the region unless I have to. I want an outside opinion and I know you'll tell me what you think.'

Wells looked at Shafer. 'Okay, I'll ask you. What is it he's not telling me?'

'That there might be a leak inside the station.'

'To the *Taliban*? Come on.'

'About a month ago, a source told one of our Pak officers about a rumor that, quote unquote, "A CIA officer is helping the Talib."'

'That could mean anything.'

'I know. We asked him for more. He didn't have it. He's a

good source, though. A Frontier Corps general.' The Frontier Corps was the Pakistan Army unit that guarded Pakistan's North-West Frontier province.

'That's all you have?'

'I know it's thin—'

'It's not thin. It's nothing.'

'It isn't all,' Duto said quietly. Wells and Shafer both swiveled toward Duto. Duto was smiling again. Shafer wasn't. His mouth had opened a half inch, like an ATM machine about to spit cash. Apparently Duto hadn't told Shafer about a second source either. 'About ten days ago, I got a call from Mike Yancy.'

'Should I know that name?' Wells said.

'Deputy director of the Drug Enforcement Agency.'

'Their motto: A palace for every kingpin.'

'Thank you for that wit and wisdom, Ellis. So the DEA has offices in Kandahar and Helmand. They try to convince farmers to stop planting poppies, switch to food crops like wheat. It's tough. You can imagine. Opium's much more profitable.'

'Sure,' Wells said.

'Anyway, the DEA guys were in a village – and before you ask, Yancy didn't say which one, told me he couldn't – and this farmer takes them aside and says to them, "Why should I work with you when the CIA is buying opium?" The DEA guys say, "No, that can't be right." But he insists. Tells them that he knows that the CIA is working with the Talibs. But no specifics.'

'How would it work?' Wells said. 'A CO goes outside the wire, comes back with a suitcase of junk? How does he make sure he doesn't get blown to bits or kidnapped? And what does he do with the stuff then? Put it out at the Christmas party?'

'Yancy said his agents felt this farmer was credible. He talked to them alone, didn't want anyone to hear.'

'Let me walk through this,' Shafer said. 'A farmer in Kandahar whose name we don't know told a DEA agent whose name we don't know about a dirty CIA officer whose name we don't know. Now you're telling us. That's a lot of telephone, don't you think?'

Duto turned to Wells. 'He's right. It's all smoke. Only we're having an awful lot of trouble over there.'

'It's Afghanistan, Vinny. And they're rebuilding the station on the fly. In the middle of a war.'

'I'm going over in a month,' Duto said. 'With Travers and McTeague. They've been asking me to go and I've been putting them off, but finally I had to say yes. So it's set and I can't change it, not without a really good excuse. I would like to introduce them to the fine men and women of Kabul station without wondering whether one of the people they're meeting is working for the other side.'

'No wonder you're taking time from your busy Saturday to beg John for help,' Shafer said.

'It would be a disaster. And not just for me. All I'm asking, you go over, see what you find.' Duto squeezed Wells's shoulder. Another new move. His handlers must have told him that real politicians weren't afraid to touch. Though Duto still needed to work on his technique. His grip was too strong. Like he was trying to tear Wells's arm off. 'Sniff it out. You don't come up with anything, fine. Still be a good trip. The speeches you give to the Joes, those guys will be happy to see you.'

Wells removed Duto's hand from his shoulder. Wells knew that, as director, Duto had broken more than a few laws. Yet for that very reason, Wells trusted Duto's instinct about Kabul. *Set a thief to catch a thief* . . . If Duto thought the station had been corrupted, he was probably right. Why he'd chosen to involve Wells was a question Wells would consider later.

'A poorly defined counterintelligence mission without official authority? Based on rumors from an anonymous Afghan farmer? Where do I sign?'

'Thank you, John.'

'Don't thank me yet. *Inshallah*' – God willing – 'I won't find anything.'

FIVE

Forward Operating Base Jackson

The folding chairs were cheap and gray and lined up in tight rows. Before them, a framed photo of Ricky Fowler sat on a homemade plywood table. The picture had been taken at the beginning of the tour. Wearing his uniform, his floppy camouflage hat low on his head, Fowler smiled shyly. He seemed almost hopeful.

Wartime memorial ceremonies at combat bases followed a rigid formula. The dead couldn't just be forgotten. Their buddies needed to say good-bye. But the ceremonies couldn't be too long or mawkish. At home, the death of a healthy twenty-something was rare, an occasion for waterfalls of grief. In Afghanistan, healthy twenty-somethings died all the time. Fowler's family and friends in Texas would have time to mourn. His platoon mates could not afford the luxuries of grief and depression. Not when they would be back outside the wire in a day or two.

So the Army focused funeral ceremonies on the fact that the fallen had died as *soldiers*. Fowler's empty combat boots stood beside his photo. His rifle was placed behind the boots, muzzle down and stock up. His helmet and dog tags topped the rifle. The combination of boots, rifle, and helmet symbolized his corpse, which had already been sent back to the United States. They were as important as his body. They were the reason he'd died.

The chairs were set up in a quiet corner of the base, behind the brigade aid station. But life at FOB Jackson didn't stop for a funeral. Behind a blast wall a hundred yards away, Stryker engines roared to life as another platoon got ready to go outside the wire. A pair of Kiowa helicopters circled low, their turbines thrumming. Meanwhile the soldiers of 3rd Platoon bowed their heads and sang the national anthem. Then Lieutenant Weston stepped behind the plywood podium and unfolded two sheets of paper.

'Private First Class Richard Edward Fowler. Ricky Fowler. All of you knew him. In a unit this size, after this many months together, we all know each other. He was a good kid. A good man. If it was hot, he'd share his CamelBak. For some reason he liked the Dallas Cowboys and I could never convince him he was a darn fool for that. He loved his mom and dad and he wasn't afraid to tell them so. Every night you could find him at the MWR talking to them. I know we gave him grief for that, but it was the right thing to do. Day after he got killed, I called my folks and told them I loved them. I hadn't said that to them for a long time. Too long. And I was thinking about Ricky when I did it.

'I'm not going to lie to you. We all know that Ricky wasn't necessarily our top soldier. But the truth is that he improved a lot over the tour. Every day, he made himself stronger. A few weeks ago, I asked him to stand point on a motorcycle registration. You all know that's a crummy job. Hot and dangerous and you've got to deal with a lot of hajjis pretending they don't understand when they know exactly what you want. But someone has to do it. I think a few months ago, Ricky would have bitched about it. But I saw the soldier in him take over and he said, "Yes, sir," and he went right up there for four hours and got it done, registered, like, fifty motorcycles. I was proud of him then for being a man, proud of the Army for making him one.

'In the movies, these stories have happy endings. This war is tough but we get through, and when we're home, our families and wives and girlfriends put their arms around us. But Fowler didn't get the happy ending. His trip ended too soon. We have three months left on this tour. We owe him the honor of keeping up the fight. Taking it to the guys who did this to him.'

Weston folded up his papers. It was a good speech, he thought. Better than Ricky Fowler deserved. The platoon's soldiers looked up silently. Captain Mark Field, a logistics officer who served as the battalion's chaplain, stepped forward to read a benediction and the Lord's Prayer. 'The Lord is my shepherd, I shall not want . . .'

Then Sergeant Rodriguez stood for the final act, roll call. One by one he read the names of the platoon's soldiers. 'Private Acosta—'

'Present.' Acosta stood.

'Specialist Alexander—'

'Present.'

Until Rodriguez reached Fowler's name. 'Private Fowler.' Silence. 'Private Fowler.' Silence.

'Priv-ate Fow-ler!' Angry this time, almost desperate. Rodriguez let the silence hang, giving Fowler one last chance to return to his buddies. And when the truth of his absence could no longer be ignored—

'Sergeant Gentry—'

'Present.'

The man, gone. The platoon, alive.

When Rodriguez finished calling roll, Weston connected his

iPod to speakers beside the podium and played the long, mournful notes of Taps. The soldiers of 3rd Platoon shuffled their feet and stared at the boots and rifle and helmet and waited. Finally the song ended and the men drifted away in ones and twos, murmuring to one another.

Weston turned to Rodriguez. 'Thank you for that roll call, Sergeant. Well done.'

'Your speech, too, sir.'

'I'd like to speak to you in private.'

Soldiers called the northeast corner of the base Zombieland. Here, maintenance units dumped vehicles that couldn't be salvaged and garbage too toxic to burn. A blown-out Stryker and three Humvees sat together, their wheels missing. The vehicles were less than two years old, but already they looked prehistoric, their paint flecking off, bits of rust creeping in.

Weston peeked inside the trucks, making sure they were alone. Most soldiers considered Zombieland bad luck and avoided it, but some guys came here to smoke hash. 'You know, a couple years, we're gone, these'll still be here,' Weston said. 'Hajj kids playing jungle gym on them. We should get rid of 'em. They're bad for morale.'

'You know what's bad for morale, Lieutenant?'

'What's that, First Sergeant?'

'Shooting your own fucking men.'

'You see an alternative? Or did you want him to come back here and narc?'

'I would have handled it.'

'How? Told him that buying smack by the kilo was the new COIN program? How did this even happen, Rodriguez? That pickup should take five minutes. Even if you're testing the stuff. You guys get a circle jerk going?'

'All of a sudden, out of nowhere, he got some balls, decided to snoop. Improving as a soldier, Lieutenant? I had to bite my lip so I didn't laugh when you said that. As a soldier, he sucked. Truth is the unit's safer without him. Puta.'

'Rodriguez—'

'Tell me I'm wrong.'

'Enough, Sergeant.'

'Don't make like you care about him any more than I do, Lieutenant. You're even colder than me, only you're better at hiding it.'

'It's not about whether I feel sorry for him, Sergeant. It's a *problem*. Don't you get it? A KIA means my after-action report gets read all the way up to brigade. Losing a man on a routine patrol looks bad. Worst case, somebody decides the whole thing sounds weird, sends a couple guys to ask the squad what really happened. Maybe even goes over to the village, starts trying to figure out how a shooter just vanished into thin air. It's unlikely, but it's possible. You want that?'

'I'm not the one who shot him, Lieutenant.'

'Thanks for that insight. Long as nobody talks, we should be fine. I used an AK, so even if there's an autopsy nothing's going to show up.'

'Nobody's going to talk. Not when we're out there every day.'

'All right then.' Truth was that neither Fowler's family nor anyone else had any reason to suspect what had happened. Guys died over here every day. A standard two-paragraph press release marked their deaths.

The Department of Defense announced today the death of a soldier who was supporting Operation Enduring Freedom.

Pfc. Richard Edward Fowler, 20, of Midland, Tex., died in Zabul province, Afghanistan, of wounds suffered when enemy

*forces attacked his unit with small arms fire. He was assigned to
the 1st Battalion, 17th Regiment, 7th Stryker Brigade Combat
Team, 2nd Infantry Division, Ft. Lewis-McChord, Tacoma,
Wash.*

Fowler's hometown newspaper back in Texas would add a
few paragraphs, throw in quotes from Fowler's parents, maybe
a buddy or two. Not a girlfriend. Fowler didn't have one. The
guy might even have died without breaking his cherry. Too
bad for him. His friends would update his Facebook page for a
few weeks. Then Ricky Fowler would be forgotten. One day his
name would wind up on a memorial somewhere.

'You're right,' Weston said. 'Fowler shouldn't be a problem.
You sure nobody's going to talk.'

'Coleman's the only one who might, and I'll keep an eye on
him.'

'Good. What about the stuff?'

'I'm no chemist, but it looks good. When's your high-speed
buddy coming?'

Weston shrugged.

'Sooner we get rid of it, the better.'

'Agreed.'

'Kinda weird, isn't it, Lieutenant?'

'What?'

'We're partners now. Blood brothers. White boy from Florida
and a gangbanger from Chula Vista. Might as well get each
other's names tattooed on our asses, because there's no going
back.'

Rodriguez was right, Weston realized. Together they'd
committed crimes that could land them in jail for life. Whether
they liked each other was irrelevant. 'You sorry we did this,
Rodriguez? Got involved in this shit?'

Rodriguez shook his head.

'Not even after this, you know, hiccup?'
'Nope.'
'Me neither.'

Coleman Young sat on his bunk in the back left corner of 1st Squad's hutch. He put in his earbuds and turned up his music. Didn't help much, but at least it gave him a chance to think. The bunk above him, Fowler's bunk, was empty now. His stuff had been inventoried and bundled into a green footlocker. Soon enough, Weston would come by with Fowler's helmet and tags and boots. He'd wrap them up, put them in the footlocker. They'd ship it back to Texas, and Fowler would be gone for good.

Young opened the footlocker. Fowler didn't have much in the way of personal effects: *The Stand* by Stephen King, DVDs of *The Office*, a cheap laptop, last year's Cowboys cheerleaders calendar. And a packet of letters from his folks. Fowler had saved them neatly in a Ziploc bag. He'd been a mama's boy, no doubt. The letters were written in a cheery red scrawl on sheets of pink paper. Fowler had told Young that his mom was a teacher. For sure she had teacher's handwriting, that *I believe in you, you can do better if you just apply yourself* handwriting. Must have been fifty letters. Young didn't think anybody could have that much to write about, much less Ricky Fowler's mom from Nowhere, Texas, but the letters kept on coming. One had come yesterday. Posted weeks ago. Posted before Fowler died.

Before Fowler got murdered.

Maybe Fowler hadn't been cut out for soldiering, but he'd been a decent enough guy. The whole thing put a knot in Young's stomach. He didn't believe for a second that Fowler's death was a coincidence. He'd wondered for a while whether Rodriguez was buying drugs. But he'd figured on a few ounces of hash. What Fowler had said was kilos of heroin. Industrial-strength. Young was from Oak Cliff, a tough part of southwestern Dallas. He knew guys who dealt. But nothing like this. You had to be seriously connected even to think about that kind of weight. Otherwise the dudes on the other end took it from you and put a bullet in you so you didn't come back on them.

Young was sure that Rodriguez wasn't keeping the stuff at FOB Jackson for long. Too risky. Some of the minesweeping dogs around here had been drug sniffers back home before they got retrained. What was he doing with it? Had to be a bigger gang involved. Or maybe helo pilots. They could go from base to base easy enough.

Young wished he could bust Rodriguez, and whoever was working with him. But Young had nothing but smoke for evidence, and not the good kind. Sure, he could protect himself better than Fowler. But outside the wire, anything could happen. He didn't know whether he could afford to have Rodriguez on his back.

He looked once more through the footlocker, Ricky Fowler's sad legacy, and snapped its top closed. Coward, he whispered to himself. Maybe he was. But unless he could be sure that an investigation wouldn't come back to bite him, he was keeping his mouth shut as tight as that locker.

SIX

C-17 Globemaster,
One hundred miles west of Bagram Air Base, Afghanistan

The Globemaster was a four-engine Air Force jet built for carrying capacity, not for comfort. Two hundred fifty soldiers sat packed like a tin of well-armed sardines in rows five across and benches on either side.

Wells was on the right aisle eight rows back. He'd come to Afghanistan on a flight like this years before, but the mood had been different. Better, to be precise. Back then, the war had been younger. Wells had landed with a unit arriving at Bagram for the first time. On this flight, the soldiers were heading back from their two-week midtour leaves. The ones who'd had good trips home missed their families and friends already. The ones who hadn't were upset they'd blown their shot at freedom. All of them knew that they wouldn't be leaving again until their tours were finished.

Mostly they wanted to catch up on sleep. Before takeoff, the soldier next to Wells tapped three tiny white pills from a bottle of generic drugstore ibuprofen. He had a teenager's moustache, wispy and brown, and a teenager's faith in the power of chemically induced happiness.

'Ativan,' he said, when he noticed Wells looking. 'Girlfriend get 'em to me. Knock you right out. You don't even dream.' He offered Wells the bottle.

'No, thanks.'

'Your loss. Wake me when it's over. And if I slobber on you, don't be afraid to stick an elbow out.'

The soldier dry-swallowed the pills and closed his eyes as the engines spooled up. Ten minutes later, as they leveled off, he grunted, 'What,' to no one and fell into a head-forward trance. Every so often, his thick pink tongue edged out of his mouth.

Wells closed his eyes. His years in Afghanistan and Pakistan had taught him patience, how to escape the world around him. As the jet winged east and the voices around him wound down, he thought about Anne.

They'd had mostly good months since his mission to Saudi Arabia. One night in late March, he'd made himself tell her what happened over there. They were walking their dog, Tonka, in the woods north of her house, first-growth New Hampshire forest that had never faced an ax. After months of cold, the night was unseasonably warm, shirtsleeve weather. Thick chunks of snow slid down the firs as the forest crackled awake from the winter. Wells spoke slowly, wanting to get every detail right. He even told Anne about the jihadi he'd shot in the back in Jeddah, probably the lowest moment in all his years in the field. She wrapped her arm in his and didn't interrupt.

'Feels good to open your mouth, doesn't it?' she said when he was finished. 'And the world didn't end.'

'I'm sticking you with something you don't deserve.'

'I'm glad to have it.'

'Do you think I should go after them?'

'Saeed and Mansour?' The Saudi princes who had created

the terrorist cell responsible for the mayhem Wells had tried to stop. They were near the top of the royal family, untouchable and living in luxury in Riyadh. 'If you think you can get them and get away with it? Eight ball says yes.'

Wells hadn't expected that answer. Anne worked as a cop in North Conway. She was even-keeled and not inclined to vengeance. Unlike him.

'What about the rule of law, all that good stuff?'

'Yes. All that. Under normal circumstances. This time, it's you or nothing.'

They walked for a while, listening to branches crack under the snow.

'No one's going to touch those guys for years,' Wells said eventually. 'They've got too much protection. But eventually they'll relax. Everyone does.'

She looked at him. 'Almost everyone.'

They went home and made love, and life fell into the best kind of groove for a while. Wells spent his days volunteering at an animal shelter in Conway. The shelter workers put down any dogs judged as a threat. Wells worked with the ones who had escaped the first culling, dogs who let themselves be petted even as they pulled back their lips to show their big yellow teeth. He soothed them in a low, reassuring voice and knelt beside them in their pens, waiting for them to relax.

A lot of them couldn't be saved. There was Nick, a black pit bull with cigarette burns cratered across his belly, docile with men but uncontrollable around women. Jimmy, a one-eyed German shepherd who cowered hopelessly in a corner of his cage. Rabbit, a slobbery husky who seemed ready for adoption until he attacked a pug, tearing off half her ear before Wells pulled him away. As much cruelty as Wells had seen, he couldn't understand the sheer wickedness of people who tortured animals for sport.

Even so, working with the dogs soothed him. He saw that the most vicious were the most frightened. He learned to retreat from their attacks without even raising his voice. And he saved a few.

'I'm going soft in my old age,' he said to Anne one night, back from the shelter.

'I don't think so.' She stretched her legs over his lap as they sat on the couch watching *Jersey Shore*. On-screen, orange-tinted women tore at one another's shirts. An addiction to reality television might have been her greatest flaw. 'We should go down there next summer,' she said, nodding at the television. 'You could beat some sense into those morons.'

'Probably the worst idea you've ever had.'

'Actually my ex reminds me of the Situation. My first husband. Though he's considerably less charming than Sitch.'

'Which one is the Situation again?'

'Like you don't know. And did you notice the hint I dropped? My *first* husband, John. Like maybe it's time for a second.'

'Very subtle. I'm not sure I got it. Now that you've explained.' Wells turned off the television. 'Would you believe me if I said I'm worried you might get hurt? I don't mean emotionally either.'

'I'm a big girl. And a licensed peace officer in the state of New Hampshire.'

'I've always liked that expression.'

'Big girl?'

'Peace officer. Like you were hired by the city of peace. The opposite of a police officer is a criminal. So would the opposite of a peace officer be a war officer?'

'You're avoiding the topic at hand, John.'

'Not avoiding it. Outrunning it with wit and wisdom.'

'You should know better than to rely on those.'

'And you know what happened to you-know-who.' Years before, Wells's former fiancée, Jennifer Exley, had been wounded in an attempt on his life. 'These guys, when they decide to come at you, they don't care about collateral damage. Up here, it seems like a long way from that, but it's not.'

Anne was silent. Wells stood, looked out the window. The warm months were almost gone. The easy months. The oaks and maples had shed their leaves and were waiting for winter.

'I believe you when you say you're worried about my safety,' she said. 'But it's my choice, too.'

'Yes and no.'

'Sooner or later, the excuses won't matter. Even if they're true. Why don't you go see Evan, at least? You've got a lot to sort out and that's a good place to start.'

The next day, Wells called Heather, told her he wanted to see his son. A week after that, he headed west to Montana. Now the wheel had swung again, and he was on this jet, bound for the war zone where he'd spent half his adult life.

He wondered if the job – not necessarily this job, but *the* job – would cost him Anne. Experience said yes. It had cost him everyone else. Though she was still cutting him slack, for now. When Wells told her what Duto wanted, her first words were, 'When do you go?'

He'd gone up from Washington to visit her for a night before flying out. In the morning she gave him a present, a neatly wrapped box about the size of a hardcover book. 'Should I open it now or later?'

'Now. I want to be sure you'll like it.'

'I'll like it.'

In fact, Wells wasn't very good at getting gifts. He was so self-contained that he wanted very little. Not that he insisted on living like a monk. He'd given away most of his money, but he still had plenty saved. And if he found something that he thought he would use, like a new motorcycle, he would buy it. But he had no interest in accumulating possessions for their own sake. Brand names and new clothes meant nothing to him. He didn't want much, and what he wanted, he had.

In other words, buying presents for him was a nightmare.

Anne spun her finger, *Stop stalling and open it*. Inside, Wells found a pair of aviator sunglasses, gold Ray-Bans. 'They're vintage. That means they're old.'

'They're great. Thank you.' Wells put them on, went into the bathroom, and checked himself out. 'Nice,' he said. 'I look like the sidekick in an eighties action movie. The guy who gets killed a half hour in.'

'I think they're very Dirty Harry. You really like them?'

'I do.' He came back into the bedroom and picked her up.

'They're sexy.'

'You're sexy.' He kissed her, chastely at first and then openmouthed. He laid her on the bed as Tonka grumbled and jumped off. She was wearing only a T-shirt and sweatpants.

She smirked. 'I want you to leave them on.'

'That's kinda creepy.'

She ran her tongue across her upper lip, intentionally lewd. 'Remember I'm from the generation that grew up with Internet porn.'

'I thought nice girls didn't watch porn.'

'All girls watch porn.' She reached up, pulled him down onto the bed. 'You'd better leave them on.'

He left them on.

The jet eased into a slow descent. Then the overhead lights kicked on and the speakers crackled. 'Captain Hawes here.

Beauty sleep's over. We're about a hundred miles from Bagram. Buckle up, stow your gear, turn off anything with a battery. Should be on the ground in about twenty-five minutes. Though if you send a few bucks to the cockpit, I could be convinced to stay up here longer.'

The soldier next to Wells jerked awake. He was a specialist, an E-4. On his sleeve he wore a big yellow patch with a dark black horse's head – the insignia for the 1st Cavalry Division, the famous 1st Cav, whose history dated to 1921. 'I miss anything?'

'Nope. You're with First Cav?'

'Yeah, Second Battalion. You?'

'I was a Ranger once upon a time. A while back. Then I worked at Langley for a while.'

'Now you're a contractor? You guys usually fly commercial.'

'I get off on leg cramps and the smell of ten thousand farts. How's business?'

'Ever been to Afghanistan before?'

'Yes.'

'Then you know. The problem with these guys we're fighting is they like it, you know. After all these years they got a jones for it and they won't ever stop. How it feels anyway. Only good thing is they're lousy tactically. They're not scared, but they can't shoot straight, and half the bombs they make don't go off. Otherwise more of us would be coming home in bags.'

'People have been fighting over these mountains for a long time.'

'I got six months left in my tour, and a year after that on my contract, and then I'm done. I thought I wanted to be a lifer, but one round is gonna be it. Lucky me, I only signed a four-year bid, I'll only be twenty-two when I get out, so I can still do something else.'

'And how's morale?'

'The PR is not the best time to ask.'

'PR?'

'Parole Revoker. What we call these flights back from leave. That's why you're not hearing any hoo-ahs or singing or anything to get us chunked up. But, you know. Guys hang in. My sarge and loot aren't too bad, so I can't complain. And on my base, we live okay. Hot food, showers, laundry, free Internet at the MWR.' The Morale, Welfare, and Recreation Office.

'Not everybody's got it so good.'

'Heck, no. The small outposts, firebases, it's MREs, cold showers, no coms. They live like dogs. Every so often, you hear about a platoon that's got real messed up.'

Not exactly what Wells was here to investigate, but he was intrigued. 'Messed up how?'

'Drugs. Target practice on civvies. Ugliness. But it's just rumors.'

'It always is. Till it's real.'

'Anyway. I'm Howard Gordon. Specialist Gordon.' The guy extended a hand.

'John Wells.'

'John Wells. Why do I know that name?'

'I did something interesting once. A few years back.' Wells had been a celebrity after his first big mission. Since then, he'd kept his head down. Most civilians had forgotten him. Wells saw that the amnesia had spread to the military. At least the junior guys. Not that he minded. He didn't have an ego. Anonymity worked to his advantage.

Okay, maybe he minded a little.

'That bomb – in New York—' Gordon said.

'Yeah. That was me.'

'You don't mind my asking, what are you doing here?'

'Somebody asked me to come check things out.'

'You want my opinion?'

'Sure.'

'I say we bring in a pile of AKs, RPGs. They got plenty already, but let's make sure everybody has one. And some bigger stuff, too. Then you know what we do?'

'Tell me.'

'Build a wall around the whole country, twenty feet high, concrete. Then we leave. We set up outside, watch the perimeter, make sure none of them get out. And we let 'em have at it. Because they will, man. If they don't have us to kill they'll just take turns popping each other. Like checkers, jump, jump, double jump, clearing out the board. Until there's only one left. When we see that one guy, you know what we do?'

'Kill him?'

'Too easy. Let him have it. He earned it. He's King Turd of Asscrackistan.'

'Asscrackistan.'

'Never heard anyone call it that?'

Wells shook his head.

'You will.'

The jet came in hard and fast and stopped quickly, tossing Wells forward in his seat. A drawn-out sigh rose from the soldiers, air leaking from a punctured tire, not a groan but not a cheer.

'Welcome home,' the captain said. Specialist Gordon raised twin middle fingers to the front of the cabin. Wells wished he had room to stretch. His hamstrings felt especially tight. Anne was pushing him to take up yoga. He might have to give in.

Gordon didn't seem bothered. He was a head shorter than Wells and narrow shouldered, but he shouldered his pack easily, rolled his neck. 'You look tired, man.'

'Wishing I were twenty again, instead of twice that.'

'I'll be twenty-one next month. Get to celebrate here. Woo-hoo.'

'Should be fun.'

'I can't believe that back home I'm not old enough to get a beer without sneaking around. When I get out of here, I'm going to Myrtle Beach with my boys, make up for lost time, drink until I can't stand.'

The unspoken part of the sentence went, *If I'm still alive.* 'Sounds like a plan.'

Gordon extended his hand. 'Be seeing you, Mr Wells.'

'John.'

'John. You get home, you tell those big boys my idea. About the wall.'

'Roger that. Watch your six, Specialist.'

'Always do.'

Outside, Afghanistan. The air was crisp and cold, the sky thick with stars. White-capped mountains loomed over the hangars around them. Most Afghans didn't live in those mountains. The fiercest fighting happened in the south, the scrublands of Kandahar and Helmand. But the Hindu Kush was as central to the *idea* of Afghanistan as the desert was to Saudi Arabia. Its peaks had defeated invaders for centuries. They could be occupied, but never truly conquered.

A wiry man in jeans and a light green windbreaker walked toward Wells. 'John? I'm Pete Lautner. Good to meet you.' They shook. Lautner had close-cropped gray hair, piercing blue eyes, and a coiled awareness of everything around him. Losing your wife and brother to a suicide bombing would have that effect, Wells thought.

'The same.'

'Ready for the beautiful Ariana Hotel? We've got a room with your name on it.'

Lautner led Wells to a black Suburban parked fifty yards away. The air base at Bagram had been built up since Wells's last trip. Hangars and concrete bunkers stretched along the main runway.

'Wonder what we'll do with it when we leave.'

'MOAB.'

'Never heard of 'em.'

'You know daisy cutters?'

'Sure,' Wells said. Daisy cutters – officially called BLU-82s – had been the largest non-nuclear bombs ever built. Six tons of ammonium nitrate with a sprinkling of artificial flavors. The Pentagon had created them to cut through the jungles of Vietnam.

'Like those. But bigger. Nine tons of explosives, give or take.'

'The daisy cutter wasn't big enough.'

'I guess not.'

'Wonder what the Air Force is compensating for.'

Lautner smiled. 'Who said we're leaving anyway?'

They stopped beside a four-seat helicopter, black, with a bubble canopy. The pilot stood a few feet away, cigarette in hand. He was Hispanic, with thick black hair. He was maybe twenty-six. Everyone in this war seemed to be younger than Wells. The pilot tossed aside his smoke, sending embers across the tarmac.

'One of these days you'll hit some jet fuel and we'll be screwed,' Lautner said.

'Stop, drop, and roll,' the pilot said. He extended a hand to Wells. 'I'm Mike Hernandez.'

'John Wells.'

'Mike is the best,' Lautner said. 'We can land Black Hawks

at the Ariana, but these work better. And that glass is thicker than it looks. It'll stop anything up to a .50 cal. And with the headphones, we can actually talk inside.'

'Good enough for you is good enough for me.'

'You will want to wear your Kevlar, though. And your Nomex.'

Wells pulled on his black fireproof gloves, strapped on his vest, climbed in, buckled up. Hernandez went through two minutes of clicking switches and consulting the computer screens in the center console. 'Ready?' Without waiting for their agreement, Hernandez twisted back on the throttle until the helicopter vibrated with its power. He pulled back on the collective and they leaped into the night and rode low and fast onto the Shamali Plain.

Beneath them were the scars of three decades of war. Bomb craters pockmarked the earth. The houses that had survived were dark and shuttered against the world. Few Afghans had electric generators. Those who did rarely used them after dark. Noise and light attracted thieves. Faint plumes of smoke from the chimneys offered the only proof of life.

The helicopter swung south toward Kabul. Five miles away, headlights appeared below them, cresting a hill and speeding north. 'Afghan police,' Lautner said. 'This is probably the safest stretch of road in the whole country.'

'But we're not driving.'

'Flying's still safer. You're a VIP, Mr Wells. My ass if anything happens to you.'

'Generally I can feed and clothe myself. I do need a little help on the toilet.'

Lautner snorted, a half laugh. To the south, the yellow glow of Kabul appeared. 'Brighter than I remember.' The embassies and aid groups have their own generators. 'You don't mind my asking, anything in particular you're looking for on this trip?'

'Vinny asked me to come over, tell him what I thought. About the war and the station, both.'

'Is there a problem with the station?'

'You tell me.'

Lautner hesitated. 'It's tricky. Maybe a conversation we should have on the ground. So the director asked you himself.'

'Correct.'

'Rumor is that you and he don't get along. Rumor is that's why you quit.'

So the story of his struggle with Duto had spread all the way here. Wells didn't see the percentage in denying the truth. 'We don't. But this is too important.'

'And you're gonna be speaking to soldiers, too.'

'I'm set for a couple speeches in Kandahar. Honestly, I'm not sure they even know who I am. But it's a decent excuse to hear what the frontline guys think.'

'Look, I'm glad to talk to you, and so's everyone else. You know, there's going to be specific programs and intel we can't discuss. I hope you're not offended, compartmentalized stuff that you're not read in for.'

'I figured as much.' Though Wells hadn't. He was here with Duto's direct support. He was surprised Lautner was pushing back. He was glad now to have read the station's files at Langley, and doubly glad that no one in Kabul knew.

'But in terms of questions about morale, how we're putting the station back together—'

'Since Marburg—' As Wells said the word, Lautner's lips tightened slightly, but he had no other reaction.

'Since Marburg. It's been a struggle, but we're getting traction. I don't have to tell you it's a very tough environment. Traditional rules of intel and counterintel don't apply. There's no ideology, no consistency. They'll switch sides instantly for a better offer. Tough to build anything lasting. Especially since they know we won't be here forever.'

'But we've got the money.'

'That we do.'

Lautner hadn't lied, Wells thought. Instead he'd given Wells generalities about Afghanistan that had been true twenty years ago and would be equally true twenty years from now. Nothing about the station's real problems. Lautner obviously saw him as an outsider, sent by Langley to second-guess. The attitude didn't mean Lautner or anyone else was a mole. Quite the opposite. A mole would be more welcoming, Wells thought. He decided not to press Lautner any further, at least for now. Maybe Arango, the chief of station, would be more willing to talk.

Wells looked out the window toward Kabul. A quilt of shacks and mud houses and garbage mounds covered the land. During the civil war in the 1990s, refugee camps had sprung up on the outskirts of the city. Now the refugees didn't want to go home. The camps had food and water and basic sanitation, all luxuries in rural Afghanistan.

The helicopter swooped left. For a few seconds it seemed to be flying almost sideways. If a double-rotor, forty-passenger Chinook was a bus, and a twelve-passenger Black Hawk was a sports car, this little chopper was a motorcycle. A racing bike, not an overpowered Ducati, but a Honda CBR600 with sticky tires that gripped the pavement.

A low hill loomed ahead, topped by a mound that looked at first like a funeral pyre. The sour stench of a garbage fire filled the cabin. The chopper hopped over the hill and down the back side and turned right, following a narrow two-lane road that headed toward the center of Kabul. They were no more than forty feet off the ground, so low that Wells could count potholes on the road beneath them. Each turn blended into the next. Even if someone had an RPG on them, hitting them would be impossible.

The pilot leaned forward in his seat, his helmet almost touching the canopy, his hands loose. 'Looks like he could do this with his eyes closed,' Wells said.

'Mike's got those nice video-game reflexes.'

Two minutes later, the helicopter approached the Ariana Hotel. 'Home sweet home,' Lautner said. The hotel was unlit and painted dark gray so it would be a tougher target for RPGs. The concrete blast walls around it glowed under arc lamps. The combination turned the hotel into a devil's flower, a black hole ringed by light.

The helicopter's engines revved down abruptly. For a moment, they hung motionless. Then they descended gently and touched down in the very center of the painted white cross that marked the hotel's landing zone. Hernandez nodded to their thanks and went back to checking the chopper's displays. Wells realized that he and Lautner were nothing but cargo to the kid, an excuse for him to play a real-life video game. Even so he was a great pilot.

Lautner led Wells to a room on the fourth floor, in a part of the Ariana used by contractors rather than CIA employees, another none-too-subtle reminder that Wells was no longer part of the club. After the flight from Washington, Wells was happy just to have a bed. He fell asleep with his shirt and pants still on. He woke once, in the deepest part of the night. He didn't know where he was.

When he finally realized, he found himself strangely comforted.

SEVEN

Moqor, Ghazni Province, Afghanistan

The dented Toyota pickup crept down Highway 1, past the gray blast walls of Forward Operating Base Moqor, which stretched for a half mile along the road. The guys in the Toyota's front seat looked Afghan. They were actually a Delta sniper team. Daniel Francesca, the sniper, drove. William Alders, his spotter, sat next to him.

After a week outside the wire, Francesca and Alders were ready for a shower and a hot meal, but the traffic refused to cooperate. Despite being called a highway, the road was only two lanes wide. An accident outside the entrance to the base had snarled traffic, and they were stuck in a line of diesel-belching trucks.

On the opposite side of the road, Afghan boys waved bags of peanuts and candy at the truckers. After every sale, the boys brought the money to a fat man sitting in a rocking chair beside a closed gas station.

'How often you think one of them gets snatched?' Alders said.

'Snatching is unnecessary. I think the portly gentleman takes any reasonable offer.'

'Fresh six-year-olds. We will not be undersold.'

'Eat all you want. We'll make more.'

'That was Fritos?'

'Doritos. Jay Leno.'

'Good old Jay.' Now the traffic was starting to flow and the kids were running into the road, playing chicken with the trucks. 'This country.'

'This country.'

Five minutes later, they reached the base's entrance, which was really just an opening in the blast walls. Francesca turned inside, but stopped short of the concrete hut that served as the external checkpoint. Hescos, four-foot-tall wire-and-cloth baskets packed with dirt, ringed the hut. A machine gun sat on the roof, surrounded by layers of sandbags.

The outer checkpoint was the post most exposed to suicide bombers and thus the riskiest guard position. Here – as at most bases – the post was manned not by soldiers but by contractors, Nepalese Gurkhas. They were in Afghanistan for the money and nothing else. They spoke little English and even less Pashtun and knew exactly how much danger they faced.

So Francesca kept his hands high and his Common Access Card visible as he stepped out of the pickup. He knew the guards wouldn't make him for American, not right away. He wore a gray *shalwar kameez* and had black hair and olive skin, thanks to his Sicilian ancestry. He couldn't pass for Pashtun, of course. The Pashtuns looked like no one else, with their nut brown skin and giant hands. But he could easily have been from northern Afghanistan. Off base, looking local kept him alive. Here, not so much.

A Gurkha in a tan flak jacket stepped out of the hut, pointed an M-4 at Francesca's chest. The man raised his left hand, palm out: *Stop.*

'I'm American. Special Ops.' The Gurkha came forward, looked over the access card, the identification all soldiers carried. The guard motioned with his rifle at the pickup, where Alders sat in the front passenger seat, his hands flat on the dash. 'He's American, too.'

The Gurkha disappeared into the hut with Francesca's identification. He came back a few minutes later and waved them through.

'Home sweet home.'

Francesca and Alders had been operating in the mountains in the southeastern corner of Zabul province, just inside Afghanistan's border with Pakistan. The United States had only a couple thousand troops in all of Zabul, part of the same Stryker brigade that included Tyler Weston. Most American forces were farther west in Helmand and Kandahar provinces, which were more heavily populated and strategically important. The Taliban had taken advantage, making Zabul a major route for smuggling weapons and men from Pakistan.

So Francesca and Alders had set up watch on a ratline, a trail the Talibs used to bring in weapons. They lived at Kandahar Air Field in a base within a base, a compound restricted to the Delta elite. Delta and Special Forces teams usually ran missions by helicopter, flying on modified Black Hawks that had nozzles for midair refueling jutting out of their front ends like steel straws. But Black Hawks attracted attention, and Francesca needed absolute camouflage to succeed. At his best, he killed quietly and precisely, and then disappeared. *Take nothing but shots. Leave nothing but bodies.*

Instead of a Black Hawk, Francesca and Alders took a Toyota, with civilian Afghan plates, and joined the stream of civilian traffic leaving Kandahar. At Kharjoy, they left the highway and wended their way southeast on the one-lane tracks and dry riverbeds that passed for roads in Zabul. Ten miles before the border, the hills turned into mountains and got too steep for them to drive at all. They left the Toyota near an abandoned hut and humped up to the ridgeline of a nine-thousand-foot mountain that overwatched the trail. The mission was hugely risky. They had no backup. If the Talibs found them, they would have to call for a helicopter evacuation that would take hours. By then they'd probably be dead. Or, worse, captured.

For a week, they lived rough. They ate bread and dried fruit and rationed their water and slept under the thorny bushes that offered the only cover around. But the mission turned out to be a bust. Maybe the Talibs had guessed that the route had been discovered. Maybe they'd used other trails this month. Either way, Francesca and Alders saw nothing but a couple of kids herding goats.

But they had a second, unofficial reason for the mission. On the way into the mountains, they'd picked up a bag of tightly wrapped blue bundles from Lieutenant Weston at FOB Jackson. They'd hidden the bag along with their rifles and uniforms in a special compartment that was welded under the bed of the pickup.

Now they were back on friendly territory. Francesca wanted a shower and contractor-cooked chow. Forward operating bases had the best food in the military. The giant headquarters bases like Kandahar focused on quantity. But the dining halls at the forward bases offered chicken, steak, ice cream, fresh vegetables, and unlimited Gatorade and PowerBars.

'Starving,' Francesca said. 'You?'

'Sure.'

Francesca and Alders didn't need to talk much. They were close as husband and wife. Closer, maybe. Neither man's marriage had survived this war. They had worked together as sniper and spotter for three years.

On one calm day the previous summer, Francesca sighted, held his breath, gently squeezed the trigger on his rifle – a four-foot-long .50 caliber Barrett M107. Across a rock valley, a fat Afghan clutched his chest and dropped. He tried to stagger up and then lay down and didn't move again. 'Nine hundred yards,' Alders told him.

'Always wanted to bust somebody at half a mile.'

'Now you have.'

Francesca would be bummed when this tour was finished. It was his third and last. Not his choice. The Army gave you only three. In the three tours, two in Afghanistan and one in Iraq, he'd racked fifty-six kills, a good number, especially with the drones doing so much work these days. Maybe *good* was the wrong word. Francesca wondered whether all that killing had changed him. Course it had. Back home, civvies called guys like him serial killers. The more he pulled the trigger, the easier it came. He'd given up waiting for God or anyone else to punish him. He hadn't been hit by lightning or gotten cancer or gone blind. He was in the best shape of his life. Plenty of money in the bank, and more coming. The Joes treated him like a minor god.

He wasn't too worried about payback in the next world either. He'd watched close through his scope for souls leaving the men he'd killed. Hadn't seen a single one. Only the red mist, the cloud of blood and tissue that shrieked from the body when a bullet cut through. The afterlife was a fable for little boys and girls. Not real men like him.

So when an old friend in Kabul reached out a few months before, told him about a scheme he had, Francesca said yes right away.

'What about your spotter?' his friend had said. 'He gonna be okay with this?'

'He does what I tell him.'

'That simple.'

'He knows the difference between shooting and spotting.'

Sure enough, Alders agreed. Working out the pickups was the tricky part. At first his friend wanted him to pick the stuff up himself. But the Talibs hated snipers. Francesca couldn't risk meeting them directly.

Instead he reached out to Tyler Weston, a platoon leader he knew in Zabul. Tyler's brother had been a good friend of Francesca's, back in the day. Weston bought in quick once Francesca explained, quicker than Francesca had expected. He got it. He saw how everybody was getting rich over here. The companies, the contractors, the locals. Only the Joes got the shaft. This deal was a way to get them a piece of the money they'd been missing. He and Alders split ten grand a kilo, two-thirds for him, one-third for Alders. More than a million dollars already. Francesca had parked his share in a bank in Germany while he figured what to do with it.

Inside the base, Francesca called Kandahar, explained they'd hit a rut on the way back from the mountains. 'Blew the right front tire. We got the spare on. But it put a leak in the left, too. And maybe some damage to the axle.'

'Where are you now?'

'FOB Moqor. We'll be stuck here tonight. Mechanics say they don't have time to check the axle until the morning.'

'All right. But do me a favor. Get back by tomorrow night.'

'Yes, sir.'

Francesca turned into a giant parking lot filled with armored trucks and pickups. Thousands of vehicles were parked on this base. No one would notice, much less check, a random pickup truck. He found a spot and hopped out. He and Alders took off the right front tire and replaced it with the spare and tossed the tire a couple hundred yards away.

'Let's eat. Where's the chow hall, Alders?'

'How'm I know that?' Alders had grown up on the side of a mountain in eastern Kentucky. He had a hillbilly accent that made him seem a lot stupider than he was. 'Thought you could smell it.'

They walked past a grove of Porta-Potties and a line of blast walls that hid a dozen steel trailers. Francesca guessed they were home to the base's midlevel officers. Lieutenants and captains usually bunked in pairs. Majors and above lived alone. The Army was extraordinarily hierarchical, although it made exceptions for Special Forces guys. In a low-intensity war like this one, the regular Joes often had to hold their fire for fear of killing civilians. Francesca didn't have that problem. He killed more Talibs in a year than the average forty-man infantry platoon. So the Army put up with him. Even so, he knew regular officers viewed guys like him as a necessary evil. Their casual refusal to wear uniforms or salute discouraged regular soldiers from following orders.

'Want to go over there, ask for directions?'

'You know what I want?'

'What you always want. A nice cold Dr Pepper.'

'Read my mind. A nice cold Dr Pepper. Wouldn't mind a shot of Jim Beam right next to it, but I guess that ain't happening.'

'Funny, isn't it. We can't get a drink, but we got a million bucks of junk back there—'

'Junk in the trunk.'

'Had to go there. You ever think about trying it?'

'Nope,' Alders said firmly. 'It's just Oxycontin without a

prescription. Half my cousins are addicted to Oxy and they lie around on their asses doing nothing 'cept talking about how high they are. From what I can see they can't even get out of bed. Don't look that great to me. You ever done meth?'

'Only the greenies.' One secret of the Special Forces was that a lot of guys had stashes of amphetamines tucked away. All the training in the world couldn't prep you for two hours of sleep a night. A little chemical help went a long way.

'Yeah, meth is that times ten. The greenies give you energy, keep you up, but being on meth changes your whole attitude. You feel like you could lift a car. Unstoppable. You find some chick on it, too? You gonna tear each other up. If I'm going to get high, I want to feel *high*.'

'That's the longest speech you've ever given me.'

'You asked, man.'

'So I did.'

They found the mess hall, and Francesca ate plates of crab legs and barbecued chicken and drank two Fantas. He wanted a third, but the mess hall regulations said two. These tiny rules had somehow kept a hold on him. Maybe following them helped him pass as normal, instead of the Shadow he was. Take care of the pennies, and the pounds will take care of themselves. He'd read that somewhere growing up. Take care of the Fantas, and the kills will take care of themselves.

He laughed a little.

'What?' Alders said.

'Nothing.'

'That creeps me out.'

'What?'

'That laugh. That high-pitched crazy-man laugh. *Hee-hee-hee*. You been doing it a lot. And every time I ask you what you're thinking about, you say, "Nothing."'

'Just thinking.'

'Three tours is enough,' Alders said.

Francesca got himself two slices of Oreo pie. Alders had ice cream. The conversations eddied and flowed around them, but none of the other soldiers talked to them. Everyone knew enough to leave them alone. The mess hall had a television that played the Armed Forces Network, a mix of live sports and shows like *House*. During the commercial breaks, the channel played military public-service announcements instead of the usual back-home ads. The announcements were targeted at rear-echelon administrative types at bases in Europe. Tips for dealing with sexual harassment, that kind of thing. They had less than nothing to do with the reality of the war over here. Lately, Francesca could hardly watch them. He wanted to shoot everyone in them, especially the whiny chicks who didn't like being told their asses looked good. *What you just said to me makes me uncomfortable, Sergeant. I suggest— Oh—* Whomp. She doesn't even get a hand up. Dead before she hits the floor. Two points.

Francesca felt that high-pitched laugh rising in his throat and stifled it. When had he started thinking about shooting his fellow soldiers? 'I guess it is,' he said aloud.

'What?'

'Enough. Three tours.'

'I'm starting to think it's too much.'

Francesca laughed, for real this time.

Back at the pickup, Alders slid under the back bumper, opened the hidden compartment, came out with the dope and a thick plastic bag that held their uniforms and toiletries. 'Showers?'

'I don't know,' Francesca said. 'I think I smell pretty good.'

'You smell like a wild animal.'

Francesca had gotten into the habit of taking the hottest showers he could. Today, he turned the handle left until the water scalded his skin. He closed his eyes and smiled. Two minutes later, he stepped out, feeling almost human.

He brushed his teeth and ran his hands through his black hair and looked himself over in the mirror. He was an okay-looking guy. His nose was a little bit of a bulb and his ears stuck out. Growing up in Orlando, fifteen minutes from Disney World, he'd inevitably been nicknamed 'Mickey' in elementary school. He pulled on his camouflage, laced his boots. The pants and blouse looked clean and crisp. And even if they hadn't . . . the tag on his left arm was all he needed: *Special Forces*. Anyone who had one of those didn't have to wear a name tag or rank insignia.

He packed the bricks of heroin into his pack and headed over to the airfield, a giant gravel square where the helicopters landed. Moqor was the next big base past FOB Jackson, more or less halfway between Kandahar and Kabul. But only a few helicopters were permanently stationed there. The Chinooks and other big passenger birds were mostly based at Bagram and Kandahar.

Francesca stepped into the oversize wooden shack that housed the soldiers who ran the airfield. Inside, hundreds of heavily thumbed paperbacks testified to the countless hours of waiting for flights. When the wind and dust kicked up, helo rides got canceled. *Slide it to the right*, guys said. Meaning, block off another day on the calendar, because this one's gone.

'Got anything heading east today?' he said to the private behind the counter. The kid was so young he still had teenage acne, the pimply, oily kind.

'There's a Presidential' – a contractor helicopter – 'to Kabul at seventeen hundred. Also the Canadians are running a Chinook to Kabul and then Bagram at 2030. Guessing you don't have an

AMR.' The letters stood for 'air mobility request.' Having one meant a confirmed seat.

'You are correct. Flying Space-A.' Space-A meant 'space available,' the military equivalent of standby. Flying Space-A sometimes meant waiting for days. But Francesca much preferred it, because it left no record. Space-A requests were logged by hand on a paper chart. Once a flight landed safely, the records were tossed. He had flown all over Afghanistan on a Space-A basis and left no trail. Which made him feel more confident about the thirty-plus pounds of heroin in his pack.

'They're stuffed,' the private said. 'Chinook looks a little better.'

'I can wait for the Chinook. Long as I get out tonight.'

'I'll jump you to the top of the list. But I still can't guarantee it.'

Francesca put his elbows on the counter and leaned forward. 'Can I trust you?' The kid's breath was terrible. 'I don't want to say too much, but I have got to get to Bagram tonight. I got something in RC-East and it can't wait. Way east. You see what I'm saying.' Francesca knew he was laying it on thick, implying he had a mission in Pakistan. He also knew he looked seriously high-speed with his beard and tags. He thought the private, who probably had never gotten outside the wire, would bite.

The private's eyes widened. He nodded once and backed away like a kid who'd walked in on his parents going at it. And Francesca got on the 2030, the last man on, when a half dozen guys got dumped. As he walked toward the Chinook, ducking the gravel caught in the backwash from its double rotors, Francesca smirked to himself. Too easy. He pressed his way into the Chinook, took the last seat on the bench, tucked his million-dollar bag between his legs. Better make sure it didn't slide out the back.

The engines whined and the chopper's front end rose and then its rear end lurched up into the night. The Chinooks were so big that sometimes they gave the illusion that they were moving in pieces, like accordion buses, instead of all at once. Francesca couldn't see much, but he didn't need to. He'd killed people all over this damn country.

He untied his boots and put in his earplugs and closed his eyes and let the Chinook's vibrations put him to sleep. Strange but true, these rides were the only place he truly relaxed anymore.

In Kabul, only a couple guys got off, so the copter stayed stuffed. Fifteen minutes later, the Chinook touched down at Zebra Ramp in Bagram. Francesca's job was almost finished. Though this last bit was the trickiest.

The Chinook had landed north of the airport runway. The passenger and cargo jet terminals were on the south side. The runway was supposed to be impassible. Anyone connecting from a helicopter to a jet was supposed to leave the tarmac and reenter through the passenger terminal.

But Francesca didn't have that option. Bags at Bagram were examined before they were allowed on the tarmac. The screeners were mainly looking for explosives, but the plastic-wrapped bundles of heroin in his pack bore an uncanny resemblance to bricks of C-4. Francesca couldn't put the bag through an X-ray machine. Fortunately, he was on the tarmac already. He just needed to cross the runway to get to the passenger side.

Francesca stepped out of the helicopter, looked around. Unlike civilian airports, Bagram never slept. Planes took off and landed twenty-four hours a day. Even now, close to midnight, the air was thick with jet fuel. As he watched, an F-18 pulled off the runway almost vertically and disappeared into the night. A minute later, a Reaper drone took its place on the runway, slowly gaining speed, finally rising from the earth. Compared to the F-18, the Reaper looked like a hobbyist's creation, spindly wings and a long, narrow nose. Yet the Reaper was a far cheaper and more effective weapon.

Around Francesca, the Chinook emptied like a clown car, passengers pouring out the back, glad to leave the noisy bird behind. They grabbed their bags and made their way toward the gate that separated the helicopter landing area from the rest of the base. Francesca lit up a cigarette, an excuse to wait on the tarmac.

'You need a ride somewhere?' a white-haired guy in a General Dynamics jacket said.

'Thanks. I'm good.' Francesca smoked until he was the last guy by the bird. When the cigarette was finished, he edged toward the gate. After a few steps, he bent over and tied his boots. The pilots were finishing their final postlanding checks. All the passengers were close to the gate. No one was within a hundred feet of him. No one was looking at him. Chinooks weren't exactly loaded with classified technology. They'd been around forty years. And nobody cared too much where passengers went after a helicopter touched down.

Francesca turned, walked purposefully away from the gate. Sure, somebody could have run back to ask him whether he was lost. But folks had rides waiting and didn't want to be late. The Special Forces tags helped. He ducked behind a hangar and waited. A few minutes later, he heard the pilots joking with each other as they left. He waited fifteen minutes more. Now he was alone for sure.

He headed for the gate, which had been closed and locked. An all-terrain vehicle was parked beside it. The mechanics rode them around the airfield. A lucky break. Even better, the key was in the ignition. Francesca rolled east along the outer taxiway, leaving the Chinook behind. He passed an enormous hangar filled with fighter jets. Mechanics stood by an A-10 Warthog, the ugliest and arguably most useful plane the Air Force had. The Warthogs flew low and slow and fired rounds the size of Coke cans. They could slice through tank armor or reduce a house to rubble. The mechanics looked over as if wondering who he was. He nodded, didn't say anything, kept driving.

Finally, Francesca reached the northeastern edge of the runway, where dozens of old Russian Mi-8 helicopters slept in a fenced-off pen, as if to prevent them from contaminating American choppers and jets. Contractors flew the Mi-8s, which were rickety and slow but famously indestructible. The finicky turbines that powered American helicopters needed clean fuel or they seized up in midair. Mi-8s ran on practically anything.

At the edge of the tarmac, Francesca turned south and steered the ATV to the end of the runway. 'No Trespassing. Emergency Vehicles Only,' a sign warned. To his east, a fence blocked the end of the runway from the perimeter road that circled the base. This far over, planes would be hundreds of feet above him on takeoff. A C-130 lumbered overhead, giving him some cover, as he headed across the runway to the southern taxiway.

Now he just needed to find the big jet to Frankfurt. One left every night, usually around two a.m., filled with soldiers heading home for their leaves. The departure time seemed lousy, but it got guys to Frankfurt in time for morning connections to the United States.

Unlike big civilian airports, Bagram didn't have jetways. To board, guys walked out a fenced area at the back of the terminal and across the tarmac and up a mobile staircase and into the jet. Francesca planned to park the ATV near the terminal. When the guys left the terminal to board, he'd join the line. In the darkness, he would be just another soldier. No one would notice him or question his presence.

Before he got to the stairs, he'd find a cargo handler and ask whether he could stow his bag in the hold, because it was so big and heavy. The handler, most likely a contractor, would take the bag and give him a gate check. Francesca would put it in his pocket and walk back into the terminal and disappear. Tomorrow he'd catch a Space-A back to Moqor. No one would ever know he'd been here. What happened to the bag in Frankfurt wasn't his concern. He had never asked, but he imagined someone on ramp duty there would pick it up.

He didn't register the headlights until they were almost on him. An SUV had edged onto the taxiway, blocked his path. Now he saw the black letters on the side: *Military Police*. He wondered whether he'd popped up on the ground radar the controllers used to track the taxiway, or if the stop was just bad luck.

No matter. The military police at Bagram were basically crossing guards. He'd make sure they saw he was Delta, be on his way. The cop on the passenger side got out, put a flashlight on him. Francesca raised a hand to shield himself from the glare and started to stand. The cop put a hand on his shoulder.

'Don't move. What's your name?'

'Chief Warrant Officer Daniel Francesca.'

'You come over the runway just now?'

'The far edge over there, Officer. I thought I was okay. I'm sorry.'

'Bet you are. Did you see the sign?'

'Sign?'

'The *big* sign that says emergency vehicles only. No trespassing. That sign. Did you see it?'

This guy was a real hard-ass. Francesca felt his anger rising.

Another jet soared into the night. He cooled himself down, waited until it passed.

'Like I said, I'm sorry. Even us bug-eaters make mistakes. I'm supposed to be going to Frankfurt tonight, start my leave, and my ride was delayed and I didn't think I would make it.'

The cop moved his flashlight to Francesca's backpack. 'What's in the bag?'

'The usual.'

'I'm going to need to see it.'

'You don't want to do that.'

The cop's hand was on his holster now. 'What did you say?'

'I said, sure, Officer.'

Francesca knew what was going to happen. He should have been looking for a way out, but he wasn't. The knife on his leg would do fine. He'd never killed anyone with a knife. He was looking forward to it. Military, civilian, friend, enemy, he didn't care anymore. *Let's do this.* He felt his pulse beating down to his fingertips. He had the sensation whenever he put a target in his sights.

He tossed the bag on the ground. The cop bent down for it. Francesca dropped his hand toward his knife—

And the Tahoe honked, long and loud.

The officer wagged a finger at Francesca, *Don't move*, and hurried back to the Tahoe. The two cops had a short conversation, and then the first walked back to him. 'Your lucky day. A Gator' – an armored vehicle – 'just pancaked two joggers. Even stupider than you, running at night. We got called to find witnesses. I told my partner you're full of it, you don't belong out here and I want to take you in, but I got outvoted. So good-bye and get lost.'

The cop hustled back to the Tahoe. It rolled off, lights

flashing. Francesca watched it disappear. He touched the gas, headed the four-wheeler toward the passenger terminal. The cop was right. *His lucky day.* Even if he had killed both officers cleanly and ditched the bag, he'd have left a trail. His fellow passengers on the Chinook would have remembered that he hadn't left with them. The mechanics had seen him on the cart. The military investigators would have pulled the Space-A files at Moqor from the trash and his name would jump out.

So, as he steered along the south taxiway, Francesca knew he should have been relieved. Instead, as his pulse slowed and the electricity in his fingertips faded, he felt nothing but disappointment.

EIGHT

Kabul

Wells rode in the front passenger seat of a crew-cab pickup in the shark-tooth mountains east of Jalalabad. The man beside him had a long black beard, a Talib beard. Wells had a beard, too, dyed blue. He wondered whether he was a prisoner. But the other man ignored him. In the distance explosions thumped hollowly. The pickup came over a rise and Wells saw an M1 tank blocking the road. Its turret swung toward them. The pickup's driver grinned at Wells. *Are you ready?* He gunned the engine—

And Wells opened his eyes and found himself at the Ariana. The explosions were knocks on his door. 'John? It's Gabe Yergin.' The station's operations chief, its third in command. 'Wondered if you wanted lunch.'

Wells dragged himself up, saw a bloodshot-eyed zombie in the mirror. *Getting too old for this.* That thought came to him more and more. 'I'll come by your office.'

'Sure.'

The station's senior officers worked on the second floor. A thick-necked guard buzzed Wells into a corridor whose walls were lined with high-res satellite maps of Kabul and Kandahar

– as well as the Pakistani cities of Quetta and Peshawar. Proof, not that any was needed, that this war didn't stop at the border.

'Here.' Yergin poked his head from a doorway like a ground-hog checking for his shadow. He was thirty-five going on fifty, a small man with a deep widow's peak and puffy black circles under his eyes. Even after he sat beside Wells on the couch, he seemed to be in motion. He rocked forward, drumming his fingers against his jeans. He produced a pack of Marlboros from his jacket, lit up, dragged deep. The nicotine worked its magic immediately. Yergin relaxed, sat back against the cushions.

'Let me guess,' Wells said. 'You didn't smoke until you got here.'

'Been smoking since college. Every six months or so I quit, but it never takes. Hasn't anyone ever told you? There's something very satisfying in meeting an addiction over and over. You like the posters?' Posters for *Transformers* and *The Godfather* hung behind Yergin's desk.

'Sure.'

'*The Godfather*, best movie ever made.'

'And *Transformers*?'

'I could tell you it's a metaphor for the way we can never trust the Afghans, they're always changing. Truth is, it's an excuse to put up a picture of Megan Fox.'

'I'm sure the women in the office love that.'

'You'd be surprised. So Vinny sent you.'

'So much for small talk, huh?'

'My ADD can't tolerate it.'

'The director wants my take on how it's going.'

'We must be doing a terrible job.'

'Finger-pointing isn't my style. I'm trying to help. But I promise you this about Duto: If he thinks you guys are in trouble and that the problems could come back at him, he'll make sure he's insulated. If that means ending your career in the ugliest possible way, he will. So if there's an issue, it's talk to me now or talk to somebody else later. Maybe under oath.'

The speech left plenty of questions unanswered, but it seemed to satisfy Yergin. 'First off, understand the strategic situation's a mess. We're playing Whac-A-Mole here. First we had our guys in the east, and the south went to hell. Now we've moved everybody south, and the east is going to hell. And by the way, the south isn't great either. This quote-unquote government we're working with, it's beyond corrupt. Everything's for sale. You want to be a cop? That's a bribe. Five to ten grand, depending on the district.'

'Ten thousand Afghanis?' That was four hundred dollars.

'Ten thousand American dollars. To become a *patrolman*. You want to be a district-level police chief? Twenty, thirty thousand. At the national level, the cabinet jobs are a quarter million and up.'

'That seems crazy.'

'You have to remember, this country has African-level poverty. Average income is six hundred dollars a year. Total economy, maybe twenty billion. We come in, we're spending a hundred billion a year. Think about that. Five times the Afghan GDP. And the locals make sure they get their share.'

'How so?'

'Three main buckets. The military spends billions on base construction, supply convoys, local guards. Second, we fund reconstruction projects, roads, dams, schools, et cetera. Third, we give direct subsidies to the Afghan government to pay for their army, police, judges, toilet paper for all I know. Combine the buckets, probably close to twenty billion.'

'The money we funnel in is equal to the rest of their economy put together.'

'Correct. So the Afghans, they can keep living on two dollars a day, or they can get onto our gravy train. If they have to pay bribes to do it, they will. And lots of this money sneaks back into the Taliban's pockets. The contractors we hire to deliver fuel, they bribe the Taliban not to attack them.'

'We're paying for both sides of the war.'

'More or less.'

'You don't sound optimistic.'

'It is what it is.'

'What would you do if you were in charge?'

'I'd pull out. But barring that, I don't have a good answer.'

'So the war's a mess,' Wells said. 'What about the station? Marburg knocked you guys down for a while.'

'Knocked us down? Marburg lit us on fire and threw us off a cliff. Seeing those coffins at Bagram was as bad as watching my parents get buried. Nine dead. And it was so avoidable. Marci and Manny wanted al-Zawahiri so bad they didn't pat Marburg down. Basic blocking and tackling. Not that we talk about it.'

'Because of Peter?'

Yergin's eyebrows lifted so high they nearly fused with his widow's peak. 'I didn't say that. But yes. Hard to believe, but our deputy chief doesn't want to hear about how his wife got herself and his brother killed. And since then, you know the history.'

'The outlines, sure.'

'Jim Wultse turned out to be a grade-A boozer. I remember walking into his office once around noon, seeing him spike his coffee. Nice silver flask, had a dragon inscribed on it. His hand shook when he saw me, and whatever he was pouring wound up on his desk. He looked down like, "Sweet manna of heaven, I've lost you." If I wasn't there, I swear he would have started licking the wood.'

'That bad?'

'No joke. I thought I was watching an after-school special on the dangers of alcoholism. And when Wultse left, Gordie King came and we were excited for about two minutes. Thought he was going to kick ass and take names. But he just didn't have the stones anymore. He hated Kabul. Refused to live here. This is where the war is. It's not moving to Switzerland.'

'You lost more than a year.'

'It was brutal. We covered for it. Getting bin Laden took a lot of heat off. We didn't have much to do with that – it came out of Pakistan and then the CTC took over. But it had a halo effect, made everybody look good. Plus we kept running the drones, and that's basically a military op. Runs off tactical intel. So we blasted lots of low- and midlevel guys. A lot of the intel for those hits comes direct from the insurgents, by the way. They use the drones to settle scores with one another, and we let them.'

'What about civilian casualties?'

'We're careful. We see kids around, anything like that, we won't shoot. And the optics these things carry are amazing. You ever seen them?'

'Not really.'

'You should. You know how in the movies they show the bad guys' faces and you see every pore crystal clear? It's even better than that.'

'Too bad you can't read their minds.'

'Too bad. So yeah, even in the worst days, we blew up a bunch of guys carrying guns over the border, that kind of thing. But they're totally replaceable. There's an infinite supply of them.'

'We kill their drones with our drones.'

Yergin laughed wheezily. He sounded like a flooded lawn

mower engine trying to start. 'More or less. And that's not what we're here for.'

'What are you here for?'

'You know full well.'

'I want to know how you see the job.'

'If we're doing it right, we're getting into the top of the government, assessing who's trustworthy. Figuring out which Talib commanders we can buy off and which we can't. Offering an independent view of how the war is going, so the White House isn't relying only on the military.'

'And finding al-Zawahiri and Mullah Omar.'

'Ron and Pete haven't emphasized that as a goal. And I agree. The logic is that (a) they're probably in Pakistan and it's Islamabad's job, and (b) al-Qaeda doesn't have much to do with the insurgency here.'

'Makes sense.'

'Glad you approve. Can I have my promotion now?'

Wells smiled. More and more, Yergin reminded Wells of Shafer. He probably wasn't as cynical, not yet. Give him thirty years.

'So how many officers do you have?'

'We're close to full strength now. Six hundred in country.'

'Six hundred?'

'But you have to remember, only a few are case officers. More than two hundred handle security. Then we have the coms and IT guys, logistics and administrative – just keeping this hotel running is a massive job – and the guys at the airfields, handling the drones. Fewer than forty ever get outside the wire to talk to the locals. Of those, most are working with Afghan security and intelligence forces. If you're looking at guys recruiting sources on the ground, it's maybe a dozen.'

'The few and the proud.'

'But unavoidable. The security situation is impossible. Only the very best officers can work outside the wire without getting popped, and even then only for short stretches.'

'You oversee them.'

'Correct. There're few enough of them that they can all report directly to me.'

'Do you report to Lautner or Arango or both?'

'Mainly Peter. Arango's more of an administrator.'

'And Peter? What's he like?'

'He's—'

A knock interrupted him. Lautner walked in.

'Like I was about to tell you, Peter's the best boss anyone could have.'

'Sorry to interrupt,' Lautner said to Wells. 'I think a Predator just went down outside Jalalabad.'

Wells didn't want to get paranoid, but he wondered why Lautner had shown up at the very moment Wells asked about him. Was he sending Wells a message: *I'm watching you?* Probably not. Probably Lautner's appearance was pure coincidence. Wells hated coincidence. 'Drones go down a lot?' Wells said.

'Not too often,' Yergin said. 'Main thing is to blow it up before the Afghans can get their hands on it.'

'I can come back,' Wells said.

'No, it's okay. I'll finish up with you fast, and then if you have more questions, find me.'

'Another day in paradise,' Lautner said. 'Carry on, Captain.' He saluted Wells and turned and walked out.

'I get the feeling he doesn't like me much,' Wells said.

'He doesn't like the fact you're looking over our shoulders. Neither do I. I hide it better.'

'So you and he and Arango took over a little more than a year ago.'

'About that. For a while, things went really well. Recently, not so much.'

'Vinny said you've lost some of your best agents.'

'Did he tell you what happened?'

'No.' Technically, Wells wasn't lying. Duto hadn't told him. Wells had read the reports himself, in the files.

'One of our best sources got hit by a truck bomb. Trust me when I tell you it was an occupational hazard. Not necessarily because anyone knew he was ours. Another source, he told us a Talib commander was ready to defect. It was pure smoke. And now he's gone. Either he got caught and he's about to get his head chopped off, or he was playing us all along.'

'So that's two of your best sources gone.'

'Listen, we know the rumor, John.'

'What rumor?'

'You insist on acting like some jarhead with more muscle than brains and I'm not sure why. Rumor is, somebody back home thinks we've been penetrated.'

So much for keeping the mission secret. Wells was surprised that Yergin had revealed so soon that he knew the real reason Wells had come. Forcing the issue into the open put Wells on the defensive.

'Nobody seriously thinks that's possible,' Wells said.

'Then why are you here?'

'Let me rephrase. I don't seriously think that's possible. How could the Taliban turn one of you? What could they offer?'

'Devil's advocate, maybe they bought somebody. Money knows no ideology.'

'Suppose they came to you, Gabe. Would you trust them to

pay? And the truth is, money's not a good motivator for treason. Money is the icing on the cake.'

'And the cake is—'

'Ideology or blackmail.'

'What about Aldrich Ames?' The worst traitor in the CIA's history. 'He did it for money.'

'Money as ideology. Ames convinced himself it was nothing but a game on both sides and he should get paid while he could.'

'So there's no mole, John? You're just here for your health.'

'Is there something you want to tell me?'

Yergin lit a fresh cigarette with his silver-plated Zippo. He flicked the lighter into the air and snapped it shut one-handed. 'What if there is?' He sucked down on the cigarette, obviously enjoying the moment. But when he exhaled, he said only, 'Course not. We were dealt a bad hand, but all in all I think we've played it pretty good. Duto should leave us alone, let us do our jobs. Anything you want to ask me?'

Wells decided to press. 'Suppose you're wrong. Suppose we're both wrong. Any obvious candidates? Anybody acting strange?'

'Everybody's acting strange. We're all stressed beyond belief.' As if to punctuate his words, the hollow drum of an IED sounded somewhere beyond the blast walls.

'Anybody find excuses to get outside the wire without backup?'

'No, but that doesn't mean much. Somebody senior like me could easily get to Kandahar or a big FOB and then go from there.'

Wells felt Yergin was almost winking at him, hinting he was guilty. 'I'd like to look over your entry and exit logs.'

'Sure.' Yergin looked at his watch. 'I have to figure out this drone that went down. Talk to anybody you like.'

Wells stood to leave. And played his last card. 'What about drugs?'

'What about them?'

'Do you monitor the trafficking networks?'

'Around the edges. We're not the DEA.'

'But it's a source of funding for the insurgency.'

'You can overstate its importance. The Taliban run cheap. I mean, they literally pay fifty dollars to these kids to plant IEDs. If the drug money disappeared tomorrow, they'd still have cash from the charities, Iran, the ISI. But sure, we try to watch it.'

'Who specifically?'

'Right now an analyst named Joanna Frey. She's been here seven months, leaving next month.'

'Where's her office?'

'On five. She's quite nice.'

'I'll try not to scare her.'

'I wouldn't worry about that.'

Frey was maybe forty-five, with a corona of long gray hair and wire-rimmed glasses. She looked like a college librarian. She didn't look like she belonged at the agency, much less in Kabul.

'Ms Frey?'

'Joanna.' She waved him in. 'Sit.'

'I'm John Wells.'

'Of course. We got an e-mail you'd be visiting. Said we should cooperate.'

Another curiously passive-aggressive move. *Cooperate* somehow implied that Wells was not to be trusted. 'So your tour is almost done?'

'Next month.'

'Looking forward to getting out of here?'

'I am. I volunteered to come, but I'm ready to go. Sick of being cooped up.'

'What did you do at Langley?'

'Counternarcotics analysis. Mainly stats, estimates of coca planting and refining all over South America. Where the stuff went. How big the business was start to finish. Lots of looking at satellite imagery, reviewing seizure reports and cables from Colombia and Bolivia.'

'Big picture.'

'We were interested in the big traffickers, their relationships with the government, the police. A lot of ELINT.' Electronic intelligence could range from wiretaps to cell phone traces to bank transfers. 'Though we had trouble getting the NSA's help. If it's not terrorism or WMD, it's not a priority for them.'

'What about the DEA?'

'They didn't always share. Didn't view us as such a reliable partner. Thought we had different priorities.' Put another way, the CIA sometimes traded information with the same cartels the DEA was trying to break.

'So then you came here.'

'Yep. It's similar to what I was doing back home. Only the politics are even more complicated. Understand, if we wanted, we could kill every poppy plant in Kandahar and Helmand. There's no technical obstacle to spraying. This isn't Colombia. No jungle canopy. But if we did that, two million Pashtuns would go to war with us.'

'Without opium, there's no economy down there.'

'Correct. So the DEA mainly tries to interdict a couple of levels past local. It lets the farmers sell the poppies and get paid. But even then, it's tricky. The Afghan police move a lot heroin and opium. We're not touching them. Then som tribes in the north, the friendly ones, are in the

And it might be tricky if Congressman X starts complaining we're in bed with known traffickers.'

'But what we don't know—'

'Correct. When I came here, my predecessor told me my job was, quote, to give policymakers the overall trends in drug trafficking. Not to play detective. End quote. I suspect that on the second floor they may get intercepts that I don't. Ones with names like Karzai in them. But I don't ask. I keep my head down and do what I'm told. I'm just a little church mouse, even if I do keep a SIG Sauer in my nightstand back home.'

'You have a SIG in your nightstand?'

'A nice little nine. Fits right in my palm. Better safe than sorry. I used to lock it in the closet so I wouldn't be tempted to shoot my philandering husband, but I live alone now.' Wells's face must have revealed his disbelief. 'I may look like an overage hippie who belongs in the Haight, but as far as I'm concerned the Second Amendment's the one that pays for all the others. Out of my cold dead hands, mister.'

She was smiling, but she wasn't joking. Wells liked her. And he thought that she'd give him straight answers if she had them.

'You'll be glad to get home to your SIG.'

'Got that right.'

'Ever seen any intercepts about anyone from the agency buying dope from the Talibs?'

'No.'

'What about other coalition forces, the military or someone else?'

For the first time she hesitated. 'Not really.'

Wells folded his hands together and waited.

'It's like this. I don't have to tell you the Pashtuns aren't just . There're really dozens of subgroups, every one different province or region or village. One that we watch is called the Thuwanis. They also move a lot of dope. Nasty bunch.'

Suddenly Wells was in Kowt-e 'Ashrow, west of Kabul. The years were blurry, but he thought it was 2000. October, maybe. Somewhere far away, Bill Clinton was president. But in the Afghan hills, summer was over and winter was closer than it seemed. And a Talib named Alaa Thuwani had ordered two Shia prisoners to run through a minefield where rotting goat carcasses lay like the devil's own mascots.

Thuwani told the Shia they had a choice. They could run through the field, which stretched about two hundred meters. Or he could shoot them in the back of the head. He promised that if they got through he'd set them free, let them go back to their homes in the north. They were small men, Wells remembered. One had a little belly that poked out of his gown. They didn't argue.

Wells wasn't with the Thuwanis. He'd been riding in a convoy of Talib guerrillas. When they heard about the prisoners, the fighters wanted to stop and see the show. The five-tons pulled off the road and everybody jumped off.

'It was practically a party,' Wells said now, at the Ariana. 'We just needed fireworks and a band.'

'What was?'

'I tell you apostates, go to Allah and beg for His mercy!' Thuwani fired his AK into the air. The Shia ran. The one with the potbelly got fifty yards before the ground exploded around him, clumps of dirt spraying high in the air. When the dust settled, he lay on the ground, moaning and begging. Thuwani shot a couple of rounds in the air from sheer joy. Then he and the other Talibs opened up with their AKs.

The other Shia didn't zigzag or look down or back. He just ran straight through like he expected to levitate over the mines. And somehow he did. He crossed onto the path at the far edge of the field. He dropped to his knees and touched his head to the earth and shouted, '*Hamdulillah!*' Thanks be to God. Thuwani said something low and dark to the men around him. They laughed.

'Now come back!' Thuwani yelled. 'Then I promise you'll really be free.'

The Shia stood and looked across the field. 'Back!' Thuwani yelled. Like the Shia was a misbehaving dog. The Shia ran hopelessly away toward a cluster of mud homes. Thuwani and his friends lowered their AKs and sprayed long bursts, one-handed on full auto. They shot so badly that for a few seconds Wells thought the guy might get away. But then one stepped back and took careful aim.

'The Thuwanis,' Wells said. 'Nasty. The chief's a guy named Alaa.'

Frey looked puzzled at his knowledge, but she said only, 'Alaa died a few years ago. Replaced by a guy named Amadullah. Cousin or half brother, I'm not sure. Anyway, we've been up and down on them.'

'Meaning?'

'Meaning we have a few phone numbers for them, and Amadullah's canny. But some of the younger guys aren't too smart. So we get a ping from them every so often. But I don't want to overstate their importance, tell you their names come up a ton.'

'But they are Talibs. They're connected to the central leadership.'

'Yes. And they move enough weight to be worth watching. Anyway, a couple months ago a wiretap transcript popped up with one of their old phones. A Pak cell one of Amadullah's nephews uses. He was calling an Afghan cell and he told the guy on the other end, "Tell your men to have twenty packages at the house by the river in the red field. The infidels will pick them up. Tomorrow afternoon. The usual procedure." Now, a package usually means a kilo, so that would imply twenty kilos.'

'That sounds like a lot.'

'It is. As for a river in the red field, that could be anywhere. They use simple codes for locations. River could mean mosque, red field could mean a specific village. Nothing complicated about it, we just don't know what it means.'

'And what did the guy on the other side say?'

'Just, "The same Americans." The first guy said, "I think so, yes." I wondered if the translation was wrong, but translation from the NSA is pretty good, and anyway, American is an obvious word. Then they said good-bye and hung up. Nothing else. It seemed clear they'd done this before.'

'He said Americans.'

'That's right.'

'And this was when?'

Frey pulled up a screen on her computer, paged through the wiretap database. 'Ten weeks ago today. After I got it, I cross-checked to see if the number on the other end had ever come up. But it hadn't. It was an AWCC phone, a burner.'

'AWCC?'

'Afghan Wireless. Almost all their phones are cash prepaid. Not too many credit cards here. So we had no idea who was on the other end. And the Paki cell never popped up again either.'

'And no one ever found Amadullah's nephew.'

'No. Truth is I can't even be sure he was the one making the call. Anyway, I'd never heard any reference like that before. I told my boss – that's Julianna Craig, she's in charge of all analysis for the station. She agreed it was interesting, told me to chase it.'

'So there was no interference.'

'The opposite. Julianna told me the guys on the second floor were interested.'

'Did she say who, specifically?'

'No.'

'Back to the call. Can you check the database, see how many times that Paki cell was used in the year leading up to it?'

After three quick clicks, she had the answer. 'Five,' she said. 'But never to that Afghan number. A couple of times to other Thuwanis, and I'm not sure about the rest.'

'And afterward it was never used again.'

'Correct.'

'One last thing. Can you print me a copy of the transcript?'

'That's a real no-no.' But she clicked the screen, printed him a copy. It was barely a page long.

'Thanks.'

'Do me a favor. Burn it before you leave.'

'Will do.'

'And one day when we're both back home, you can come over and teach me how to use that SIG.' She winked.

Wells edged out the door. 'Your first impression is deceptive.'

'So they say.'

Wells tucked the transcript away, went back to the second floor. He spent the rest of the afternoon talking to Arango, the chief of station, and Julianna Craig.

Craig confirmed Frey's story about the wiretap. Lautner and Yergin had encouraged her to have Frey pursue it, she said.

Arango was a Marylander from the Eastern Shore, polite, distant, and soft-spoken. He deflected Wells's questions, swallowed them up in inspirational clichés that offered no hint of what he was thinking.

'So Gordie King left the station a shambles?'

'I wouldn't say shambles. But we had to put up our sleeves and get to work and that's what we did.'

'It must be difficult for Pete Lautner to work here after what happened.'

'I wasn't here for Marburg, although of course I know what happened. Pete came highly recommended. He's done fine work. I don't think it's my place to ask him how he feels about his family. We all have different ways of coping with grief.'

'Do you think Duto made a mistake sending me here?'

'I'd never second-guess the director. Of course I've instructed everyone to answer whatever questions you might have . . .'

And, finally: 'Do you remember a wiretap that indicated US military forces might be purchasing large amounts of heroin from the Taliban?'

Arango didn't hesitate. As if he'd expected the question. Wells wondered whether Frey or Craig had tipped him. 'Yes. Lautner mentioned it. This was a couple months ago. I asked him if the intercept had any actionable details. He said no. I told him to keep me informed.'

'So you had a particular interest in it?'

'I imagined it could be a sensitive issue for the military. I wanted to be sure that if it progressed further, I'd know, so I could inform the right people. But no, it wasn't of particular interest. As far as I know, there's been nothing since then.'

A sensitive issue. And Wells thought of a question he should have asked before.

'Did you ever pass the intercept to military intel? Or tell them about it?'

'I don't believe so, no.'

'Or the DEA?'

'You can imagine how many intercepts this station sees in a month, Mr Wells. Not to mention HUMINT and surveillance reports. This was vague, didn't touch on our ongoing operations. As far as I can recall no one even suggested to me that we make it an action item.'

After ninety minutes of this thrust-and-parry, Wells begged off. *You need anything, you let me know*, Arango said, as Wells left.

I'll be sure to do that.

Back in his room, Wells lay on his bed and tried to make sense of everything he'd learned. He hadn't expected the officers here to treat him like a hero. But their unconcealed hostility surprised him. He wouldn't want to be first through the door with only Lautner or Arango behind him. The conversation with Yergin perplexed him, too.

In truth, Wells much preferred having a trail to chase. Instead he was looking for an enemy who might not even exist. So he did what he had done before at these moments. He called Shafer.

From outside, on the Ariana's helipad. On his own sat phone. He wondered whether he should have left the compound entirely. The sun had set and the floodlights outside the blast walls were up. Diesel smoke smudged the stars. Wells hadn't liked Kabul a decade ago and he didn't like it now. During the civil war, the city was overrun more times than anyone could count. By 1999, half its houses were rubble. Amputee children begged on every corner, surrounding any Westerner foolish enough to have stayed. In the mountains Wells saw flashes of a gentler – and certainly more beautiful – Afghanistan. Never here.

Now NATO and Western donors had rebuilt the city. But the new offices and houses looked cheap and tacky. Billions of dollars in reconstruction money had been siphoned to bank accounts in Dubai and Lebanon. *Why bother to rebuild it properly?* the Afghans seemed to be asking. *When you leave, we'll just have to destroy it again.*

Only the mosques had survived. Wells wondered when the calls to prayer would sound. He wanted to get into a mosque and tip his head to the floor and see whether his faith could find him. Behind these blast walls he felt divorced from Islam. On the flight over, he'd looked forward to coming back to Afghanistan. Now he saw that he hadn't returned, not really. The Ariana wasn't the United States, but it wasn't Afghanistan. It was purgatory.

He called Shafer. 'Ellis.'

'John. How's it feel to be home?'

'Kabul was never home.'

'I didn't expect to hear from you so soon.'

'They've all gone native, Ellis.' Wells explained what he'd found so far, finishing with the intercept. 'It doesn't add up. They said the right things about investigating it, but they didn't, as far as I can tell.'

'You have it? Can you read it to me?'

Wells did. 'There's no unit name or number. No village or district. Not even a province. A hundred thousand suspects. How do we narrow that down?'

'I don't know. But I'll tell you someone who does. Amadullah Thuwani.'

NINE

Quetta, Pakistan

David Miller was still alive.

Mere survival hardly qualified as an achievement for most people. But Miller was a heroin dealer and a sometime user, too. He was married to two women on two continents. He had been arrested in Chicago and Karachi, snitched for the DEA and the CIA. He had reason to be proud of his continued existence.

Now Miller was again putting his life on the line. He wished he had a choice in the matter. He was headed for a meeting with Amadullah Thuwani, the chief of a tribe of Pashtuns who lived on both sides of the Afghan-Pakistan border. Miller knew Amadullah's reputation for mindless viciousness. For a generation, the Thuwanis had fought – against the Soviet Union, other Afghans, and now the United States. During the 1990s, they'd locked prisoners in steel shipping containers without food or water, then let the containers cook in the desert. These days their main income came from drug trafficking.

Miller figured the Thuwanis didn't like him much either. His dad was a Pakistani from Karachi, but his mom was African-American. He'd grown up in Chicago. Like all Pashtuns, the Thuwanis were obsessed with bloodlines. They viewed his lineage as impure. But they dealt with him, because he helped them move a lot of heroin.

Miller's birth name was Daood Maktani. His dad, Omar, had always wanted him to think of himself as Pakistani. Every summer, Omar packed Daood off to Karachi to stay with his grandparents. The trips backfired. Daood liked the First World comforts of the United States, air-conditioning, televisions, his own bedroom. He got sick in Karachi, nasty intestinal bugs that glued him to the toilet. He couldn't wait to leave. The longer he spent in Pakistan, the more he considered himself American. A few months after he turned eighteen, he changed his name to show the world how he felt. Daood Maktani became David Miller.

Miller's preference for the United States extended to its police. In January 2002, DEA agents busted down the door of his apartment and found six ounces of heroin wrapped neatly on the kitchen table. Miller expected to go down hard. He didn't. He turned out to be triply lucky. He was lucky that the feds and not the Chicago cops had arrested him. A six-ounce haul was a good day's work as far as the locals were concerned. They would have gladly sent him downstate for ten years. The feds had bigger ideas. They wanted to bust kingpins who trafficked by the ton. They saw Miller as nothing more than a way to move up the supply chain.

He was lucky, too, that he'd been using at the time they busted him. He convinced the DEA he was a college kid who'd turned into a junkie and then a dealer to finance his habit. Please. In reality he'd gone to Harold Washington City College for a semester before he figured out he could make a lot more money dealing. And he was no junkie. He got high on the weekends, coke when he was out late, H to chill. Never more than a couple times a month. He'd seen what the stuff could do if it got away from you. But the feds, they believed their own frying-pan hype. They believed that casual users didn't exist. When he said he wanted to come clean, they lapped up his story.

Most of all, he was lucky to be a Muslim arrested after September 11. A nonpracticing Muslim, that is. About two weeks after his arrest, after he made clear to the DEA that he would cooperate, a CIA officer showed up for his interviews. I'm not DEA, he said. *Not FBI either*. He introduced himself as Mr Blue. He was white, late forties, with pale skin and freckles and thinning red hair.

Blue didn't say where he worked, but Miller understood. He sensed that the man wanted him to know without saying so. Blue was smarter than the DEA guys. He didn't fall for Miller nearly as hard as they did. Miller could tell Blue was looking him over, deciding whether he was a true believer. He wasn't. Miller drugged and drank and ate pork fried rice every chance he got.

Maybe six weeks after Miller got busted, Blue came to see him alone. He took Miller to a wood-paneled conference room instead of the usual windowless interview cell. He unlocked his briefcase and pulled out a bottle and two glasses.

'Courvoisier,' Miller said. 'Nice.'

'Didn't want to insult you with anything cheap.' Blue poured two generous glasses, pushed one at Miller. 'Drink up. No cameras in here.'

Miller glanced at the clock on the wall. Eleven-thirty. Blue followed his eyes. 'You know what they say. It's five o'clock somewhere.'

Miller picked up the glass, sloshed around the golden liquid inside. If this was a test, he was happy to pass. He took a long swallow. Blue followed.

'Daood Maktani, you're an infidel start to finish.'

'Am I under arrest for that, too?' The warmth of the cognac glowed inside Miller. He hadn't had a drink since getting locked up. He'd missed the feeling. He finished the glass. Blue refilled it.

'Could you fake it?'

'It.'

'If I have to explain, I may have the wrong guy.'

Miller raised a hand in apology. 'Those guys and I don't exactly socialize, understand. I couldn't even tell you where to look. You'd have to tell me.' But he was exaggerating a little bit. He knew the mosque behind the barbershop on South Marcy where the believers in his nabe hung out.

'But you've got the right pedigree. Spent summers over there growing up.'

'Mostly in the john,' Miller said before he could stop himself. The cognac had hit him hard. 'The water over there, it's nasty.'

'Focus, Daood—'

'My name's David. And I'm telling you, you probably know more about Islam than me.'

'Best start reading up then. You speak Urdu and you've got a Paki passport, and if you grow yourself a beard I'll bet they'll be happy to have you in the local prayer group. You help me, I can help you. The place I work doesn't give a rat's ass how you pay your bills.'

'Help you how.'

'You want me to say it? Okay. I will.' The CIA officer took out a business card. It was blank. And light blue. He wrote a phone number and e-mail address on it and pushed it at Miller. 'Find me some genuine jihadis, this is your get-out-of-jail-free card.'

'You can do that?'

'You know, they're still finding bits of bodies at Ground

Zero. At this moment, guys like me, we have the full faith and credit of the United States government on our side. Six ounces of heroin doesn't mean jack.'

Miller raised his glass. 'I'll drink to that.'

Two months later, the prosecutors sealed the charges and cut Miller loose with probation. He kept up his side of the bargain. He became a regular at underground mosques in Chicago. He wormed his way into prayer groups that fed money to Islamic charities that recruited suicide bombers for the war in Iraq. Meantime he kept on trafficking. The jihadis never complained. Like the CIA, they didn't care where he made his money.

Miller earned enough chits at the agency over the years to get sprung from two federal drug indictments. His biggest slip came when he tried to avoid paying a three-thousand-dollar bribe to a police colonel in Karachi. He was arrested and stuck for two weeks in a nasty jail there before he bought his freedom for three times the initial asking price.

He didn't make the same mistake again. He had a nice run, making a couple hundred grand a year shipping heroin from Pakistan to Chicago, mostly inside brass lamps and other trinkets. To launder the profits, he bought low-end apartments in Dubai with the cash. Then he hired a local property management company, a legit business, to rent them to the laborers building skyscrapers in the desert. The management company forwarded the rent to Miller's Citibank account. Simple as that, Miller had cash he could legally spend in the United States. He even paid American taxes on the income, like any honest citizen.

A decade after that conversation in the conference room, Miller had houses and wives in Chicago and Dubai. He looked a little like Malcolm X, six feet tall and dark skinned. His clothes were simple and expensive and suited him. He could honestly say he appealed to women of all ages, creeds, and colours. Life was good.

Then the bill came due. In a way he didn't expect. He was sipping a glass of Heineken Light in a business-class lounge at Terminal 1 at Heathrow when his phone rang.

A blocked number. Miller didn't like blocked numbers. He sent it to voice mail. A minute later, the phone rang again. This time the caller ID came up as *Daood Maktani*, his own long-lost name. Miller decided he'd better answer.

'David Miller.'

'Daood.'

'This is David.'

'Same difference.'

'Who is this?'

'Your new best friend.' And the man explained why he'd called.

'Tell me something,' Miller said when he was finished. 'This thing you want, is it official or unofficial?'

'Both. But don't you worry about that.'

'I guess I shouldn't ask your name either.'

'You can call me Stan. As in Afghani-stan.'

Clever, Miller thought. 'It's impossible. The Thuwanis will never trust you. You've hit them too many times.'

'Enemies today, friends tomorrow. Like me and you. Anyway, I'll have you on my side, making the introductions.'

'I don't know them. They're on a different planet. A much heavier planet.'

'Same solar system. You can get people to vouch for you. And I hear that lately they've been looking for a new connection. Their buyers got stung.'

Miller had heard the same rumor. He didn't bother to ask where the man had gotten that information. 'It's impossible.'

'No is not an option here, David. Over the years, you've made a whole lot of people guests of the government. Don't you think they'd like to know who's responsible for their change of address?'

Miller hung up. His phone rang again. He hesitated, then clicked on.

'Let me explain something to you, *Daood*. Something you need to understand. Are you listening?'

The man waited. Miller had never felt so powerless, not even in that windowless cell in Karachi. There he'd known that eventually they'd ask him for money and he'd pay and they'd let him out. But the man talking to him didn't want money, and Miller had no idea how to manage him. 'Yes. I'm listening,' he finally said.

'Good. So, please understand, nobody at my shop likes you. We've dealt with you for a long time because that's what we do: we deal with guys like you.'

'And I've worked with you. I've helped you—'

'That's true. You have. But you got paid in full every time. You figured you were being smart, making sure that you didn't leave anything on the table. But the truth is that's straight ghetto logic. Short-term thinking. Problem with playing that way is that at a moment like this, when you really need help, somebody who can help you with me, you don't have anyone. You don't have any favors in the bank. Not even a primary officer. Because nobody trusts you. It's all transactional. You see?'

Miller kept his mouth shut, but he knew the guy was right.

'I'll take that as a yes. So now, you go to anybody with this, ask about some guy named Stan and the favor he wants, nobody's gonna care. Especially since you don't even know my name. But I know yours. And when the word gets back to me, and I promise it will, I'll jam you so hard you'll wish you were back in that hole in Karachi. You don't think I can find you? I'll tell you where you are *right now*. You're in Heathrow, waiting for a flight to O'Hare. Three-thirty p.m. You're in seat two-A. Business class.'

Miller looked around the lounge, half expecting the man to wave to him.

'I upgraded.'

'Congratulations.'

Knowing when he was beaten was one reason Miller had survived. 'I'll try to do what you want.'

'You'll do more than try. I'll be in touch.' *Click*.

Miller couldn't see a way out. Unless he just left everything behind, took his hundred grand in emergency cash and ditched everything, including his women. Bought a ticket to Lahore or some other Pakistani slumhole and melted away. Turned himself into Daood Maktani. He didn't think this guy Stan would bother to chase him. He'd find some other pawn to do his work. The problem was that Miller would have to stay in Pakistan if he ran. He'd have to keep his head down, since even if the agency wasn't actively after him, it would probably give his name to the Pakistani police. It wouldn't even have to give a reason, just say he was an American citizen on a watch list. Miller would wind up in a crummy two-room apartment, watching his money dwindle, cut off from everything and everyone.

No. He'd take his chances, play the game. He knew how to survive.

Miller had never visited Quetta before, but he knew the place from the moment he landed. Like Peshawar, three hundred miles northeast, Quetta was old, overgrown, dirty, and filled with secrets. The cities were twins, trading and commercial centers that sat on caravan routes between Russia, India, and Africa.

Today, most goods traveled by jet or ship. But Quetta and Peshawar remained true to their history. In their bazaars and mosques and mansions, smugglers, jihadis, merchants, tribal chiefs, generals, diplomats, and spies drank tea together and practiced the art of lying for fun and profit. Truths might be told in Quetta, but never on purpose.

Arranging the meeting that Stan had requested took Miller a month, every favor he had in Pakistan, and eighteen thousand dollars in 'friendship payments' spread among the lesser members of the Thuwani clan. But finally he was blindfolded and tossed into the back of a van and driven into the mountains outside Quetta. He didn't know exactly where. Geography wasn't his strong suit, even where he could see where he was going. He was dumped inside a concrete-walled compound where four guys with AKs watched him without much love.

Hours passed before Amadullah finally arrived. He was tall, with a thick black beard. He chewed the bright green tobacco that Pashtun men favored. Miller imagined that his teeth glowed green in the dark, like a monster in a sci-fi movie.

Amadullah didn't bother with the usual Pashtun pleasantries, offers of tea or sweets. He extracted a wad of tobacco from a gold tin and pressed it into his mouth and said through fatted lips, 'What is it you want?'

Miller was so tired of having to navigate *Pashtunwali* codes – the baffling and sometimes contradictory set of rules that governed life in the mountains – that he actually appreciated Amadullah's lack of respect. Without further ado, he presented the offer. Which was met as he'd expected.

'The Americans wish us to sell them drugs?'

'This man and the ones who work for him, yes.'

'And who is he?'

'He's a CIA officer named Stan.' Miller had figured that 'Stan' wouldn't want to be identified with the CIA. But Stan had insisted that Miller mention his connection with the agency. Miller didn't know why.

'He must think we're fools. What we bring, they'll take it and capture us. I should cut out your tongue for wasting my time with this.'

'You won't have to bring him anything. He'll send soldiers to pick it up.'

'From here.'

'In Afghanistan. The soldiers will pay the usual price to your men and then I'll pay, too, directly to your men here. So you get double.'

'Why would he do this? Pay so much.'

'He can bring the drugs directly to Europe. On a military plane.'

'Then he sells it himself?'

'Someone there buys it from him. I don't know who.'

'And he can take as much as I produce.'

'At first just ten kilos, make sure the arrangement works. After that, more. Maybe twenty kilos a month.' To his surprise, Miller saw that Thuwani was interested.

Thuwani spit a long stream of green tobacco onto the ground. 'You say that American soldiers will pick it up.'

'After you and I choose the locations. In Kandahar and Zabul. The soldiers come on patrol to a village. Your men meet them.'

'Always the same soldiers?'

'I don't know, but I think so.'

Amadullah stood. His calf muscles were as big as grapefruits. For such a big man, he moved quickly. He leaned over Miller, tipped a thumb under Miller's chin to push up his head, close enough for Miller to see the creases in his green teeth. 'The price is six thousand dollars a kilo. Three thousand to my men and three thousand to me.'

'That's too much.' Pure heroin cost twenty-five hundred a kilo or less in Afghanistan.

'That's the price.'

Considering that a kilo of heroin sold for seventy-five thousand dollars in Europe, Miller figured that 'Stan,' whoever he was, would be okay with the deal. Anyway, Miller didn't have a lot of leverage. Not surrounded by guys with AKs.

'That's the price, then. Ten kilos okay to start?'

'Very good.'

They sketched out the details of the transfer. 'You are sure these soldiers can do this?' Amadullah said.

'Yes.' In truth, Miller didn't know how Stan would arrange the pickups on the other end. But that wasn't his problem.

'All right. Give me your mobile number. My men will tell you when they're ready.' And – again without the usual pleasantries – Amadullah swept out.

They hadn't met face-to-face since then. Miller arranged the pickups with Amadullah's nephews. They'd run five drops so far, roughly one every six weeks. In all, the soldiers had picked up about a hundred kilograms of pure heroin, worth six hundred thousand dollars to Amadullah and his men, $8 million to the gangs back home that bought by the kilo and cut the stuff for sale, and $40 million on the street.

The math went like this: a ten-dollar bag, a single dose, held about twenty-five milligrams of pure heroin. So a gram translated into forty dime bags. One kilo equaled a thousand grams. And a hundred kilograms meant four million dime bags. Figure twenty million hours of empty dreams for the lost souls putting needles into their arms.

Not bad, considering the stuff came out of the ground for free. Poppy plants hardly even needed watering. As every Afghan farmer knew, they were tougher than food crops like wheat.

Stan treated Miller as a conduit to Amadullah, nothing more. Miller didn't know the names of the soldiers who picked up the stuff, though he had figured out that they had to be part of the Stryker brigade in eastern Kandahar and Zabul province. He knew that Stan was moving it to Germany, but he wasn't sure how. Still, Miller couldn't complain. He was making more money than he ever had. Stan paid him twenty-five hundred dollars a kilo. A quarter million dollars so far, for a few days of work. He was wondering whether the call at Heathrow hadn't been a lucky break after all.

Then Stan called with a new request.

'You need to see our friend. Now.'

'I'm in London.'

'I don't care. Get over there. E-mail me after you set the meet and I'll tell you what I need.'

Stan's tone brooked no argument. Miller hung up and booked his flights to Quetta and reached out to the Thuwanis. Fortunately, the successful deals had bought him goodwill. By the time he reached Quetta, Amadullah agreed to a meeting. Miller e-mailed Stan with the news.

Stan's response came a few hours later. After he read it, Miller wanted to disappear. Until now, he'd convinced himself that Stan might be making these deals as part of a larger CIA mission he couldn't see. Maybe they were connected to a trade with the Thuwanis to get Mullah Omar.

But now Stan wanted Miller to tell Amadullah that a Special Forces squad was going to raid a farm in Kandahar province where two of Amadullah's nephews were hiding. Miller was no lawyer, but he figured that giving the enemy advance warning about an attack spelled treason. He wrote back, one word: *Can't*.

His phone rang ten minutes later. 'What's the problem?'

'People get executed for this kinda thing.'

'You're only seeing a piece of this. Trust me. It's all right.'

'What about the guys going in? It all right with them?'

'It is.'

'I don't believe you.'

'Too late for that.'

'I do this and I'm done.'

A sigh on the other end of the line. 'Daood. This isn't some movie where you do one last deal and then get out. Let me know when you've set the meet.' *Click*.

Miller wished he could see a way out. But he didn't.

Now he sat in the backseat of a Toyota Crown wedged between two stinking Pashtuns. He wore Hugo Boss cologne and a black cashmere sweater and two-hundred-and-fifty-dollar Diesel jeans. He was pissed off and in no mood to wear local threads. He wasn't pretending to be one of them today. Anyway, they knew he wasn't. Though they trusted him enough not to handcuff or blindfold him.

The road ran northeast out of Quetta toward Peshawar. After an hour, the Toyota pulled into a garage. The men led Miller down a spiral staircase and into a concrete tunnel so low that Miller had to duck his head. The tunnel opened into another garage, this one empty except for a Pakistani police van. One of the Thuwanis put on a police uniform. The others piled in the back with Miller.

The van's cargo compartment had no windows, so Miller couldn't see where they were headed. His companions talked of people he didn't know, villages he'd never seen. They made no effort to include him in their conversation and he didn't press.

Finally the van stopped. The back door opened. 'Stay,' the men said to Miller. They stepped out. A minute later, to Miller's surprise, Amadullah lumbered in. The door shut and the van rolled off.

'What is it you needed to tell me?'

Miller explained the raid. Amadullah rubbed his big brown hands down the sides of his face, like a primitive sculpture come to life. 'When does this happen?' he asked when Miller finished.

'In the next few days. I can't be sure exactly. But you should tell your nephews to leave. Or be ready to fight if they stay.'

Amadullah stroked his beard. Long, careful strokes, as if he were petting an ornery dog. The van drove slowly now, on rutted roads. 'Why do you tell me this?'

'I do what I'm told. Stan said it would be valuable to you.'

'What does he want in return?'

'Nothing.'

'He tells me about an American operation and asks for nothing.'

Stan had once used the word *cutout* to describe Miller's role in this operation. For the first time, Miller really understood what Stan meant. He was as disposable as construction paper that little kids used in art class. He wondered which parts of him would get cut out if Amadullah lost his temper.

'That's what he says.'

'Does he think I'm a fool?'

'I do what I'm told,' Miller said again.

'Then I want to talk to him directly. Maybe he should come to Quetta. Tell him I promise he'll be safe.' Amadullah smiled, but his eyes stayed cold.

'He said you would say that. He said he wants to talk to you, too. Give him a phone number and he'll call you.'

Amadullah yelled, 'Stop!' to the front of the van. He leaned over, latched a thick brown hand around Miller's neck. 'I give you my mobile and a missile blows up my house. Give me his phone number.'

'I don't have it.' Amadullah's rough fingers tightened around Miller's neck. Miller smelled sweet tobacco and something else, a heavy perfume. 'I swear to Allah.'

'If you're smart you won't mention Allah again. How do you reach him without his mobile?'

'We e-mail. When he wants to talk to me, he calls me. I've never called him.'

'Give me the e-mail address.'

Miller croaked out Stan's address. He decided afterward that Stan had expected him to give up the e-mail all along – and had simply wanted to provoke Amadullah by telling Miller to ask for Amadullah's phone number. Stan was a perverse dude. Without ever having met him, Miller was certain of that.

A few minutes later, the van stopped. Amadullah kicked Miller out. Literally. He put his big Pashtun sandals in Miller's rear end and shoved him onto the road. Miller found himself outside a sweetshop in some lousy Paki village in Balochistan. He couldn't even guess how far he was from Quetta, or how long he would need to get home.

Even so, he'd delivered the message, as he'd been told. He could add treason to his list of crimes. But he was still alive. For now.

TEN

Islamabad, Pakistan

The Kingdom of Saudi Arabia had deep connections to the Islamic Republic of Pakistan. Hundreds of thousands of Pakistani men worked in Saudi Arabia. Hundreds of thousands more visited Mecca every year for the Hajj, the sacred pilgrimage that all Muslims are supposed to perform at least once. Saudi charities built religious schools and mosques across Pakistan to spread Wahhabism, the conservative version of Islam practiced in the kingdom.

The Saudi embassy in Pakistan reflected the importance of the relationship. Set inside Islamabad's diplomatic quarter, not far from the American embassy compound, the embassy was a handsome beige building, wide and solid. The kingdom's green-and-white flag flapped from a half dozen poles around a fountain in the driveway. Hidden behind the embassy, a figure-eight-shaped pool allowed diplomats and their families to relax during Islamabad's scorching summers.

To maintain security, the embassy had only two entrances. A small back gate was open only to employees and diplomats. Everyone else came through a guardhouse beside the front gate. The embassy opened to visitors at noon, but the line for entry formed hours before. Saudis were not known for their work ethic, and the kingdom's bureaucracy meant that visas could require several visits. Now, at 11:30 a.m., six men stood outside the gatehouse, waiting for its windowless front door to open.

Wells was first in line. Patient and quiet. He wore a white *dishdasha* and *ghutra* – the long gown and headdress favored by Saudi men. The men around him, all Pakistani, chattered about how long they'd been waiting, about the earthquake that had ripped through Kashmir a week before, about whether Kuwaitis or Saudis were more likely to beat their servants. Life's white noise. Wells had nothing to say, and said nothing.

A few minutes after noon, the guardhouse door opened. A Saudi soldier motioned Wells inside. He passed through an X-ray machine and down a corridor that ended in a steel door and Plexiglas window. A Saudi man in a suit sat behind the glass.

'*Salaam aleikum*. My name is Jalal Haq.' The alias tasted unfamiliar on Wells's tongue.

'*Aleikum salaam*. Your business, please?'

'I'm here to see Mr Naiz.'

'You will look up to the camera, please.' A security camera was mounted over the door. The security didn't surprise Wells. Al-Qaeda hated Saudi Arabia as much as the United States.

Finally, the door clicked open. Inside, Wells found an office with cheap plastic chairs and a scratched wooden coffee table. The only reading material consisted of in-flight magazines from Saudi Arabian Airlines. The Saudis obviously preferred that visitors not be too comfortable. A narrow window at the back of the room offered a view of the fountain and the main embassy buildings.

A few minutes later, a black Land Rover with smoked-glass windows and diplomatic plates came down the drive and stopped outside the guardhouse. A tall Saudi in a tailored blue suit stepped out and walked into the office.

'*Salaam aleikum*, Mr Haq. I'm Saeed Naiz. Please come with me.'

Wells followed Naiz to the Land Rover. A minute later, they'd left the embassy and were rolling through the manicured streets of the diplomatic quarter. They passed the military checkpoint that split the district from the rest of Islamabad. Finally, Naiz parked alongside a newly built two-story strip mall that included a bridal store and a flower shop. If the signs had been in English, the place could have passed for Los Angeles.

'I'm honored to meet you, Mr Haq. I thought it best we speak outside the embassy. In the back, those are yours.' A briefcase and suitcase sat side by side in the backseat.

The briefcase was buttery black leather, slightly nicked. Inside, Wells found two envelopes. The first contained a Saudi passport and identification card, both in the name of Jalal Haq, both with Wells's photograph. The second, a platinum AmEx card and two rubber bands of cash, ten thousand dollars in hundred-dollar bills, and twenty-five hundred in Saudi riyals. A BlackBerry. And a Quran, its green cover embossed with gold filigree.

'It was all the money I could get on such short notice. I hope it's enough.'

'If it's not, I'm doing something wrong.' Wells thumbed through the passport and found a proper Pakistani entry stamp. 'It's real?'

'It's in our system. You could fly to Riyadh with it, no problem.' Naiz sounded almost offended.

'I hear Riyadh is nice this time of year.'

'Yes. The summer heat is done and it's pleasant. Have you ever been?'

'Only Jeddah.' Wells looked over his identification card. It said he lived in Umm Khutut. 'And where is Umm Khutut?'

'The northern Najd, the high desert. You're the first son of the fourth wife of a tribal leader there.'

'First son, fourth wife. And my father, he'll vouch for the story?' Though the odds that anyone would ask were extraordinarily slim. The men Wells planned to meet didn't have spies inside Saudi Arabia.

'Of course.'

'Thank you for all this.'

'There's no need to thank me. I have a guess who you are,' the Saudi said, switching to English.

Wells didn't bite. 'Tell me something,' he said, staying with Arabic. 'Do I sound Saudi?'

'Maybe to these Pakistani peasants. Not to me.'

Not the answer I hoped to hear, Wells thought.

'I have my own question. You're going into the mountains?'

'Balochistan.' Balochistan was a Pakistani province that stretched for hundreds of miles along the Afghan border. Its biggest city, Quetta, was just 125 miles southeast of Kandahar.

'And, I am imagining now, you will tell the men you meet there that you are a wealthy Saudi and want to donate money to a good cause?' The cause being jihad.

'Something like that.'

'I won't ask why you're doing this, but is there someone in particular you want to meet? You understand, sometimes our charitable organizations ask me about aid recipients. Will the Americans mind if they give to this village or that madrassa? Will they wind up on any unpleasant lists that will make it hard for them to put their children in school in New York?'

'Are those donors hoping you'll say yes or no?'

'Depends on the donor.'

Wells wondered whether getting Naiz's advice was worth the risk of the potential double cross, and decided it was. 'I'm looking for a man called Amadullah Thuwani. He's the leader of a Pashtun tribe that lives on both sides of the border. He's hiding near a town called Muslim Bagh. Maybe a hundred kilometers northeast of Quetta.'

'The Thuwanis, yes. They're definitely on the American lists, not that you need me to tell you.'

'Has any donor ever asked about Amadullah?' Wells couldn't afford to meet real Saudis on this trip. They would almost surely see through his con.

'No.' Naiz reached for the suitcase. 'I'll show you the clothes and shoes I brought. They're authentic.'

'I trust you.' Wells didn't plan to wear the clothes. No Saudi in Balochistan would advertise his presence so overtly. But they'd aid his cover if the Thuwanis checked his bags. 'Thank you for all this.'

'One more thing.' Naiz opened his jacket, revealing a shoulder holster. 'I have one for you if you like.'

'I'm hoping these men will be happy to see me. And even happier to see my money.'

'Go with God, then. When you come back to Islamabad, look me up.'

'I'll do that, *inshallah*.'

Wells had considered several disguises to approach the Thuwanis. He could have gone in as a would-be jihadi from Lebanon hoping to join the fight in Afghanistan. Or a drug trafficker from London looking for new sources. He even wondered whether the tribe would accept an overture from an American reporter or photographer.

But those covers felt wrong. The Thuwanis were part of the

Taliban, but they didn't train foreign fighters, at least as far as the agency could tell. They were already selling all the heroin they could produce. And as for going in as a journalist . . . Wells could hardly trust the Thuwanis to keep their promises of safe passage. They'd kidnap him, and after they squeezed as much ransom as they could out of him, they'd make a souvenir of his head.

So Wells decided to present himself as a wealthy Saudi eager to support the Taliban. The Saudis had financed jihad for a generation, through the same charities that built schools and mosques. They bought weapons and gave money to the families of suicide bombers, so-called martyrdom payments.

Of course, Wells would have a tough time asking about heroin trafficking if he came in as a Saudi financier. But meeting the Thuwanis would give him a fix on where they lived – and get him cell phone numbers and e-mail addresses for the NSA to trace.

After his mission the previous year, Wells knew he could count on the Saudis for help. He called Amadullah's half brother, Prince Miteb. The explanation took a few minutes, since Miteb was nearly ninety and half deaf, but eventually the prince understood. 'It will be done.' Miteb coughed into the phone, the gasps of a man whose heart was nearly finished pumping. 'Mr John, if you have any other favors, I suggest you ask them now. I don't expect to be alive much longer.'

'I pray you're wrong.' *And not just for you. For your country.*

'Save your prayers for something else.' The sharpness in Miteb's tone reminded Wells of Amadullah.

The next day, Wells was told to report to the embassy in Islamabad. Now he had his cover, and it was as real as could be. But having the right passport didn't guarantee that Wells would convince Thuwanis to open their not-entirely-friendly arms to him. Wells was one-quarter Lebanese. He could pass for Jordanian or even Syrian. But most Saudis were a shade darker than he was, and – as Naiz had told him – his Arabic couldn't fool a native Saudi. Wells didn't doubt the Thuwanis had seen their share of Arab jihadis over the years. Wells would have to keep his story simple and tight and hope that greed blinded Amadullah.

The hard work was just beginning.

At the Islamabad airport, Wells rented a 4Runner. He wanted to come across as wealthy, not gaudy. If he seemed too rich, the Thuwanis would suspect a trap, or simply fleece him. He headed to the highway that ran west toward Peshawar and called Shafer with the BlackBerry Naiz had given him.

'Nine-six-five area code,' Shafer said when he picked up. 'I see the Saudis came through.'

'It's nice to have friends.'

'Any idea how long you'll be gone?'

'A week or two at most. More than that and you should send a search party.'

'Put your face on a goat milk carton.'

Wells laughed. 'Did you tell Duto where I was going?' To make sure the mole couldn't alert the Thuwanis he was coming, Wells had lied about his plans, claiming that he was going to Moscow to follow a lead.

'No. But he's wondering. He reminded me that his trip with the congressman is only three weeks out. Did you want me to?'

'Let him wonder.'

Wells hung up, called Anne. 'You may not hear from me for a couple days. I'm going into the hills.'

'The hills? Sounds relaxing.'

'Like a spa.'

'Next time you go on vacation, I'm coming.' She sounded resigned rather than angry. Resigned was worse.

'It's a deal.'

'You're lucky to have me.'

'Don't I know it,' Wells said.

'I'm not sure.'

'You're trying to decide if you can put up with a lifetime of this, aren't you?'

She didn't bother to answer.

'If I told you I loved you, would it make any difference?'

'If you actually loved me, it would make a difference, John.'

She hung up. When he called back, she didn't answer. So he made his way west. He tuned the 4Runner's radio to an all-Arabic network, and as the miles rolled on he left himself behind. He became Jalal Haq, a middle-aged Saudi eager to support jihad any way he could. At Kohat, a cramped city on the edge of the mountains, he turned south. Tractors puttered along the side of the road, pulling carts loaded with sacks of cement. Sheep twirled on spits outside one-room restaurants, their dead eyes staring at the trucks rolling by.

The sun was low in the sky when Wells reached Dera Ismail Khan, halfway between Islamabad and Quetta. He would have to stop for the night. The roads in Balochistan weren't safe to drive alone in darkness. Ahead, a highway sign advertised the 'D.I. Khan Guesthouse for Muslim Men, Clean and Safe.' 'Perfect,' Wells said aloud in Arabic.

His room at the guesthouse was simple and spare. Four thin walls, a single bed, a sink, a stand-up shower. The call to the *Maghrib*, the sunset prayer, sounded a few minutes later. Wells hurried down to the simple mosque attached to the guesthouse. He hadn't prayed alongside other Muslims in more than a year.

The mosque had threadbare carpets and concrete walls

stenciled thickly with Quranic verses. The men around Wells touched their foreheads to the floor as fervently as if they were in the Grand Mosque in Mecca. In this room, Wells remembered why he had become a Muslim, the power and simplicity of the faith. Jalal Haq belonged here, and Wells, too. As much as he belonged anywhere.

In the morning, he woke early, fueled up, and turned onto the N50, which connected Dera Ismail and Quetta. At first the road was smooth and straight. Then, in typical Pakistani fashion, it turned without warning into a potholed track barely one lane wide. The heavy trucks that dominated the highway hardly seemed to notice. They barreled along, creeping so close to Wells's back bumper that their grilles filled his mirror like the faces of unsmiling gods. He had to edge off the road to let them by.

He came over a hill to find a tractor blocking the road, two men with AKs beside it. A dozen more men in *shalwar kameez* stood nearby, along with a firepit where a goat was roasting. The mood seemed festive rather than angry. But the roadblock was real and so were the AKs. Wells stopped and one of the tribesmen waddled over. He wore a long gown that might once have been white but was now stained with grease and what Wells hoped was goat blood.

'*Salaam aleikum*,' Wells said, opting for Arabic.

'*Aleikum salaam*.' The man said something else to Wells. Wells knew Pashtun, and even a few words of Dari. But the tribes up here had their own dialects, and he'd never heard this one.

'*Saudia, Saudia*,' Wells said in Arabic. 'I don't know what you're saying. Do you speak Arabic?'

'*Arabiy! Arabiy!*' The man waved to the other tribesmen, who clustered around the Toyota. Another man, this one wearing sunglasses despite the gray clouds above, leaned over and yelled in Arabic, 'We're collecting a toll.'

'All right, my brother.' Wells had put a few hundred rupees in the glove compartment for just this reason. He reached for them.

'But first, what is your name?'

'Jalal.'

'And where are you headed, my brother Jalal?'

'Quetta.'

'Quetta, Quetta!' The man couldn't have seemed more excited if Wells had announced his next stop was Tokyo. 'And what shall you do in Quetta?'

'I have gifts for our brothers fighting the jihad.'

The man translated to his fellow tribesmen, who roared their approval. A long, excited conversation followed. Finally the man said, 'You must feast with us! And then target practice!'

Long as I'm not the target. 'You've made me an offer I can't refuse.' Wells probably shouldn't have made the joke – Jalal Haq wouldn't have – but it escaped unremarked. Wells pulled the 4Runner off the road and spent the next hour eating goat with the tribesmen. The meat was tender and tasty, long strips with a sour yogurt sauce.

'Young goat,' the man in the sunglasses said.

'Young goat.'

The men lived in a village on the other side of the ridge. They weren't Talibs, just Baluchi tribesmen who wanted nothing to do with any central government, whether in Islamabad or Kabul or Washington. After lunch, they led Wells through a ravine into a dry streambed. Three oil drums sat in a row two hundred meters away. The first was wrapped in the American flag, the second in the Pakistani flag, the third in the Israeli flag. The man in sunglasses unstrapped his AK and then shoved the rifle at Wells muzzle-first – not exactly safe firearm handling.

'As our guest, you go first, *Arabiya.*'

'You do this during the day? What about the police, the Army?'

'Do you see them? We don't fear them. They fear us. Our only enemy is the American planes, and we know when they're coming. We can hear them.'

Wells wasn't so sure about that, but he didn't argue the point.

The AK was nicked and worn, but Wells didn't doubt it would work. A decade before in Afghanistan, Wells had seen a Talib drop an AK into a well that must have been a hundred feet deep. It rattled off the walls the whole way down and splashed loudly at the bottom. No matter. The Talib hustled up a boy who couldn't have been more than six and told his father that he'd be riding the bucket down after it. The man tried to argue. The Talibs told him that if he didn't shut up, they'd send him down the well, too, and not in the bucket. He shut up. In the event, the kid came back up with the rifle. Without bothering to strip the AK clean, or even dry it off, the Talib pointed it in the air and pulled the trigger. Sure enough, it worked.

Now Wells checked the rifle he'd just been given. Full. He had a moment's fantasy of playing Rambo and taking out his hosts, but he reminded himself that these men had never fought the United States and weren't exactly high-value targets. He settled for wasting the magazine on full auto, missing the flags wildly.

'You Arabs shoot like donkeys,' his new friend said.

A few minutes later, the tribesmen sent Wells on his way. They didn't even ask for a bribe. The rest of the trip was uneventful. The land opened into a high plateau, dry and arid, with only a few spindly trees to break the monotony. To the west, a dusty range of mountains rose along the Pakistan-Afghanistan border. The road improved as suddenly as it had worsened, opening into a four-lane divided highway that was empty of traffic. Wells arrived at Muslim Bagh in late afternoon and found a guesthouse. He prayed that night in a two-room mosque down the street.

In the morning, he rose before dawn. He showered and slicked back his hair and pulled on a blue *shalwar kameez*. The town was still dark when the calls to prayer sounded. The center of Muslim Bagh had a limited electric grid, but the plains and hills around it were dark. Wells walked along the town's dusty main street, looking for the busiest mosque. Only the most fervent believers would rise for the dawn call. They were the men he needed to find.

A pickup truck drove by, a Toyota, with two men in the front seat and two more standing in the bed of the truck. The two in back carried AKs, with bandoliers of copper-jacketed ammunition draped across their chests. A thick layer of grit covered the Toyota. These had to be men Wells wanted to see. The Thuwanis. Advertising their power, reminding villagers here that they and not the Pakistani police ruled this region. Wells raised a hand and the truck pulled over beside him.

'My brothers,' he said in Arabic. '*Salaam aleikum.*' The men in back vaulted over the side of the cab and flanked him. Their rifles weren't quite pointed at him, but they weren't relaxed either. Without knowing how, Wells had angered them.

'Yes, yes, *aleikum salaam*,' the man closest to Wells said. His beard covered most of his face, but the exposed skin was discolored. Frostbite, possibly. December through March, deep snow covered the border mountains. 'What do you want?' he said in Pashtun. 'What are you doing here?'

Until he knew more about these men, Wells didn't plan to let them know he spoke Pashtun. 'I don't understand,' he said in Arabic.

'I said, what do you want?' the frostbitten man said, in Arabic this time.

'Do you live here, my brothers?'

'What's it to you?'

'I'm looking for a place where I might find the men who live on both sides of the border.'

The man raised his weapon a notch. 'Speak clearly. No riddles.'

The hostility confused Wells. Had these men made him as American? Had someone from the Saudi embassy betrayed him somehow? 'My name is Jalal Haq. From Saudi Arabia. I'm looking for men who live in the hills around Muslim Bagh. Fierce Muslim warriors who have fought jihad for years.' *Flattery never hurts.* 'They're named the Thuwanis.'

The man nodded and leaned into the pickup's cab for a whispered conversation with the men inside. He returned smiling, a hollow smile like a sinkhole in the forest of his beard. Wells would have preferred a frown. He'd made a mistake. Whoever these men were, they had no love for the Thuwanis.

The sinkhole closed as the frostbitten man's smile became a sneer. 'Tell me, Mr Haq, you wish to join these fierce warriors?'

'I'm sorry to have bothered you.' Wells tried to sound meek. 'I'll find these men another way.'

'Do you have a gun?'

'What, brother?'

'We're not brothers. I ask again, are you carrying a weapon?'

'No.'

'Then you'll do what I tell you, Jalal Haq.' The Talib stepped back, pointed his AK at Wells's chest. 'And I'm telling you to get on your knees.' The sun had just emerged over the low hills to the east. It lit the Talib's face, his ruined skin and hard black eyes. Wells didn't doubt this man would kill him in the street. Without a weapon of his own, he was trapped.

He went to his knees.

'If he moves, shoot him,' the man said in Pashtun to the other Talib who'd come off the truck, a tall man who stood three steps back.

'Yes, Najibullah.'

The frostbitten one, Najibullah, stepped around Wells and reached into the bed of the pickup and grabbed a black hood.

And that was all Wells saw.

ELEVEN

Forward Operating Base Jackson

This was a week earlier. Coleman Young rested on his cot watching *Terminator* on his computer for the hundredth time. Arnold was shooting his way through the Los Angeles police station like the pumped-up badass he was. Across the barracks, Roman lay on his own cot, playing a driving game on his Sony PSP. Roman loved driving games, Young knew. He knew more about the guys in his platoon than he ever would have expected, and more than he wanted. Bunk with dudes for a year, eat with them, ride with them, burn through ten thousand rounds with them, and sooner or later their secrets came out. PFC Battis picked his nose and ate the snot when he thought nobody was watching. The whole platoon ragged him, but he couldn't stop. Specialist Corlou had a big Z tattooed across his left pec: it stood for something in Greek that translated into 'He is risen,' meaning Christ but also Corlou's brother, a Marine who had died in Iraq five years ago. Sergeant Taz jerked off in his bed even if the lights were on and everybody was still awake. But Taz was the best around when the bad guys came to play.

'Wanna work out?' Roman said to Young across the barracks. Young ignored him. Roman had been looking for excuses to stick close to Young since the memorial. He wasn't even crafty about it.

Roman's Roshan – his local cell phone – rang. He answered, listened. 'Right. I got it.' His eyebrows puckered as he concentrated. 'No, I got it.' He had to be getting orders from Rodriguez, Young figured. Nothing else would make him think so hard.

'Who was that?' Young said.

'Nobody. Sure you don't wanna go lift? Or grab chow?'

Suddenly, Young got it. Rodriguez must have told Roman to keep a close eye on Young for the next few minutes. The handoff must be happening right now. Young turned off *Terminator*.

'Yeah, let's work out. Lemme just drop one.'

'You sure?'

'Am I sure I have to take a dump?'

'I'll go with you.'

'No, you won't.' Young walked out of the barracks. He was probably making a mistake. In a minute or two, Roman would come looking for him. But Young thought of those stupid pink letters Fowler's mom sent every week. He kept walking.

He turned left, toward the Porta-Potties, and checked over his shoulder. Sure enough, Roman was peeking out the front of the barracks. Young kept going until Roman couldn't see him and then cut through the shower trailers and followed a blast wall north. The base was so big and so chopped up with walls and barracks that there were a hundred different ways to move across it, and a thousand different places to hide stuff.

But Young guessed that the handoff was happening at the junk pile at the northeast corner of the base, the area everybody called Zombieland. He kept his head down, didn't break stride when a couple guys grunted hellos at him. He reached the big road that ran past the brigade aid station, where docs worked on guys whose wounds didn't rate evacuations to the hospital at Kandahar.

He crossed the road and circled north past a rubber reservoir that held millions of gallons of water for the base's showers and toilets. The thing looked like an overgrown water bed, forty feet square and three feet thick. Finally he came to a two-room concrete shelter marked 'Casualty Holding Point' in no-nonsense black letters. Young ducked into the shelter. It was empty and dark and had never been used. Fortunately, FOB Jackson had never faced a ground attack, only the occasional rocket. Young peeked through a firing hole. From here he could see along the flight line to the blast walls that marked the outer edge of Zombieland. Sure enough, Rodriguez leaned against the wall, alone, smoking. Watching to be sure nobody was headed his way.

Five minutes passed. Then Rodriguez whistled and two men walked out of Zombieland. The front man carried a big backpack. Young didn't recognize him. He was a couple hundred feet off, too far for Young to see his face clearly. He was tall and wore a uniform and had a black beard and non-reg boots. He had to be a Special Forces operator, maybe even a Delta. Nobody else could get away with the boots, much less the beard. And nobody else had the walk, the loose don't-mess-with-me strut.

Tyler Weston followed. Young's lieutenant. His platoon commander. Young had always suspected Weston of Fowler's murder. He'd hoped he was wrong, but the truth was obvious. Weston ran the platoon. Of course he'd known about the deal. He'd probably been the one who'd actually pulled the trigger and killed Fowler.

The SF guy and Weston walked his way, Rodriguez following like a guard dog. *Man, oh, man.* Young leaned back, away from the firing hole. The shelter was unlit. Young didn't think they could see him unless they stopped and looked directly inside. He hoped they'd get close enough for him to see the SF guy's face clearly. But about a hundred feet from the shelter, the SF guy jumped into a pickup truck parked on the side of the road. The pickup rolled off. Weston and Rodriguez kept walking, past him, past the shelter. Young waited until he was sure they were gone and headed over to the DFAC for chow. Roman found him a few minutes later.

'Thought we were gonna work out.'

'I changed my mind. Got hungry.'

'You should have told me.'

Young ignored him, went back to his barbecued chicken. That night, he poked around Zombieland, looking for places Rodriguez and Weston might have hidden the stash. But nothing stood out in the piles of broken metal and plastic parts. Anyway, Young figured they'd given the stuff to the SF guy.

He wanted to push on Roman. Roman was the weak link. Roman had started talking about how he was buying himself a farm when he got home. Finally, Sergeant Taz asked him how the heck he was going to buy a farm when he had two kids by different moms and he'd been so broke he filed Chapter 11 three months before they deployed. Roman mumbled something about how he'd been saving his money. The next morning, Roman and Rodriguez went for a walk and after that Roman didn't talk about buying a farm anymore.

Young figured that he'd wait until they were a couple days from going home and then try to bluff Roman into giving up the truth. It wasn't a great plan, but he didn't have anything better. And at least he wouldn't be giving Weston and Rodriguez much chance to come back at him.

*

A week later, Young was headed to the gym when he felt a tap on his shoulder. 'Sergeant Young.' He turned to see Rodriguez.

'First Sergeant Rodriguez.'

'How you been, Coleman? Good workout?' Rodriguez clapped a hand around the meat of Young's biceps and squeezed. 'Damn, Sergeant. You got some guns on you.'

'You like that, Rodriguez? Didn't think you went that way.'

'Take a walk with me, Coleman.'

Young followed Rodriguez to the big lot where Strykers that needed minor repairs were kept. The mechanics weren't up yet. No one was within a hundred yards.

Rodriguez was short and broad shouldered and cocky. He stood close to Young, making sure Young could feel him. Trying to back Young up. Typical Mexican crap, Young thought. He'd dealt with plenty of them in south Dallas. Dealing with them didn't mean he liked them.

'What's up, First Sergeant?'

'Wanted to be sure you were okay, Coleman. I know you and Ricky were good friends.'

'Yeah? You seen us holding hands, First Sergeant?' Young knew he should keep his mouth shut. But Rodriguez had been under his skin even before Ricky got juiced.

'You saying you weren't friends.'

'Friends, sure.'

'So it's only natural to be depressed.'

'Let me ask you something, First Sergeant.' Rodriguez liked to be in charge. Giving it back was the way to play him. Young wondered whether he should speak up about the SF guy he'd seen, decided to keep that bit to himself for now. 'It strike you as odd, what happened to Ricky?'

'Odd like how?'

'Like once he got hit, the enemy disengaged right away. Almost like he was the only target.'

'I think the shooter figured he got lucky, decided not to push. Dropped his gun and ran, knowing we couldn't touch him.'

You and Weston would tell CID that exact story if I went to them, Young thought. *All I got on my side is the word of a dead man.*

'The lieutenant and I are worried about you. We feel you've withdrawn from the rest of the platoon.' Rodriguez put a hand on Young's shoulder. Young brushed it off.

'I prefer to keep my thoughts to myself.'

'That's your choice.'

'I think it's safer for everyone.'

'Could be. Anyway, the lieutenant and I, we were thinking if you wanted to get out of here, chill at KAF for a couple weeks, get your head on straight, we'd get that. Maybe even finish out the tour over there. You know we got barely two months left.'

So Weston and Rodriguez wanted him gone. They didn't know what he knew, what he'd guessed, what Fowler had told him. They didn't know what he might have told his family or his buddies in other units. They figured that trying to take him out might be tricky. It wouldn't look good if another soldier in the platoon went down in some suspicious way. So they were offering him a deal. KAF, Kandahar Air Field. Young was more likely to get shot back home in Oak Cliff than at KAF. He'd be more or less certain to finish his tour in one piece.

Too bad I'm not looking to run. Young stepped close to Rodriguez, chest-to-chest, so Rodriguez had to tilt his head up to make eye contact.

'I appreciate that, Sergeant. That's a generous offer. Thoughtful. But I'll pass.'

'All right.'

'And know this, too. Ricky wasn't much of a soldier.' Young stared at Rodriguez until the first sergeant nodded. 'Me, I take care of myself. I'll engage and destroy any threat outside the wire. Any threat.'

Rodriguez didn't say a word, and they stood looking at each other for what seemed like a very long time. Finally, Young got tired of the staring contest and put his hands on Rodriguez's shoulders and shoved, shoved hard—

And Rodriguez stumbled back and landed on his ass on the Stryker gravel. He muttered something under his breath that Young couldn't hear. He popped up like he was on springs and took a half step toward Young.

'You're gonna regret that, Sergeant.'

'Am I now? Whyn't you show me?'

But Rodriguez stepped back and smiled. 'I don't have to. Somebody else will.'

'Listen to me, Rodriguez. Soon as I get back to my bunk I'm gonna write my brother and my best friend some thoughts I been having. I'm going to put them letters in envelopes. I'm gonna write on the outside, "Only open if I die", and then I'm gonna mail them off.'

'Yeah? Good luck with that.'

'Wanna know what it's gonna say? Just your names, you and the lieutenant, and a note that says, "These two did me. Whatever the Army tells you, don't believe it. And you come back on them." And I can promise you that they will.'

'Never seen you scared before, Coleman. Telling fairy tales about how your best friend's gonna come at me. How's he even know where I live? He a detective or something? And then he's hunting me down? Please.'

'I got letters to write, Rodriguez.' Young turned away.

'You go ahead.'

Young went back to the hutch and wrote his letters. For all the good they'd do. He might just have gotten himself killed this morning and he couldn't see how to get clean. He had no evidence against Weston and Rodriguez. And not only did he not know the name of the SF operator he'd seen with them, he hadn't even gotten a clear look at the guy's face.

Nothing else to do, so Young went to breakfast. It was still early, and he was one of the first inside. He loaded up with eggs and hash browns. Normally he was careful about what he ate. Today he didn't care. He grabbed a couple of Cokes and found a seat by himself in a quiet corner and leaned his head over his plate and did something he hadn't done in years. He said grace.

PART TWO

TWELVE

Muslim Bagh, Pakistan

The hood over Wells's head gave off a funky odor, sweat mixed with dried blood. If the devil sold perfume, it would smell like this. *Taliban. The New Fragrance from Mullah Omar.*

'Stand,' Najibullah said. Wells stood. Najibullah patted him down through his *shalwar kameez* and grabbed the passport and the money from his pockets and tied his wrists behind his back with rough plastic twine. Then Najibullah and the other man frog-marched Wells to the back of the pickup and shoved him in.

'Lie down.' Wells did. The truck rolled off. It had been headed northeast when it stopped. Now it made a U-turn, back toward Quetta. Wells turned so he was lying against the sides of the pickup bed. With his arms hidden against the walls, Wells flexed his hands and rubbed his wrists together to test the knot. It was loose and the twine was cheap. Wells thought he could cut it on a sharp rock. He stopped moving and closed his eyes and tried to eavesdrop, but the pickup was moving too fast.

The truck swung off the highway and slowed and rattled over an unpaved road. The air cooled. They were rising into the mountains. The road noise lessened, and Wells heard Najibullah.

'Won't Amadullah be surprised? We'll make him pay if he wants this one.'

So these men were fighting the Thuwanis. Maybe they were Afghans who had moved into territory Amadullah didn't want to share. Or local bandits defending a smuggling route. Or they blamed the Thuwanis for a drone strike. Whatever the reason for the feud, Wells was caught in the middle. With better information he might have avoided this mess, but the CIA had almost no firsthand knowledge of this part of Balochistan. Americans had barely operated here in decades. The good news was that these men weren't after Wells. They had no idea who he was, or how dangerous he could be.

The truck turned onto a bumpy track that seemed to be little more than a streambed. After half an hour, it stopped. 'Get up,' Najibullah said. Before Wells could move, Najibullah kicked at Wells, dragged him up, shoved him out of the back of the truck.

Wells stumbled on a rock, let himself fall. As he hit the earth, he rolled sideways so his arms were hidden. He worked the twine around his wrists over a rough rock, cutting at the strands, feeling them come loose.

'Stupid cow,' Najibullah said. He kicked Wells. Wells grunted underneath his hood and squirmed up. Najibullah grabbed him and dragged him forward. The ground was uneven, and after a few steps Wells stepped into a ditch and stumbled again.

'Take off his hood,' one of the men in front said. 'He'll slow us down.'

'I don't trust him.'

'He's no threat. He's a stupid Saudi. Take off his hood.'

Najibullah grabbed the top of the hood and pulled it off, snapping Wells's head back. He found himself on a stony hillside, the sky a bright morning blue, the sun rising to the east, casting long shadows. Wells checked the positions of his captors. The pickup's driver and passenger walked a few yards ahead. They carried holstered pistols, not rifles. Najibullah stood behind Wells. The thin one, Najibullah's partner, brought up the rear.

Wells turned to walk and Najibullah caught him with a rifle butt in the side, over his right kidney. This time Wells wasn't faking when he went down. He rested on his knees, his breathing ragged, the pain swelling with every heartbeat. *Enjoy yourself, my friend, because the end is nigh.* But Wells pushed the thought from his mind. No anger. Angry men made mistakes, and he couldn't afford another mistake this morning.

'There's no need for this. I only want to *help*.' Let them think he was pathetic. A pathetic prisoner was no threat.

Najibullah smiled down at Wells. A generation of war had bred countless men like him, sadists pure and simple. 'You Arabs come here and play at jihad and then you go back to your fancy houses. And Saudis are the worst. At least Iraqis can shoot. You're only good for strapping bombs on. Blowing yourselves up. If Allah gives you the bravery to go through.'

'My brother—'

Najibullah cuffed Wells on the shoulder with his AK. 'I warned you about calling me that. My cousin went to Riyadh to work. And you know what happened? The man who brought him over said he was stealing. So he locked him in a cage. For a *month*. Like he was a dog. No court, no *sharia*. Just locked him and beat him. He still doesn't walk right. I'll put you in a cage, see if you like it. "My brother." Call me "my brother" again and Allah will have you.'

'Najibullah,' the man in front said. 'Enough.'

'It's true,' Najibullah said sullenly.

*

They walked. The hills were quiet, no evidence of humans or any living creatures. Not a squirrel or a sparrow. Wells wanted to make his move soon. He didn't know how many men would be waiting at the camp. He kept his pace slow, widening the gap with the two jihadis ahead. 'Faster,' Najibullah said, jabbing at him.

Ten minutes later, the hills around them narrowed into the beginnings of a canyon. The trail angled right, along a pile of scree, loose rocks and boulders that had slid down. Wells pretended to stumble, kicking rocks back toward Najibullah. The jihadi slipped, sending a minor avalanche down the hill.

'You oaf—'

Wells flexed his shoulders and biceps, pulling at the knot, trying to split the ragged twine. The knot tensed and stretched and then it tore. His hands came free. He spun backward. Behind him, Najibullah was lifting his AK.

But before he could get the rifle into position, Wells stepped toward him. Wells wrapped his right arm around Najibullah's back and pulled him close so the AK was trapped between them. Then Wells reached up with his right hand and grabbed Najibullah's hair and pulled his head back. Before Najibullah could even open his mouth to scream, Wells raised his left forearm and forced it under Najibullah's chin and drove his head up and back and up and back—

And Najibullah's neck snapped as sharp and sudden as a branch breaking. The hate and the anger and everything else left Najibullah's eyes. He fell away from Wells, dead, and his rifle came free. Wells grabbed it before it hit the ground and pulled it up and dropped the safety. All this in a single breath. As a linebacker in college, Wells had never been the biggest or the strongest player on the field, but he'd always had the quickest first step.

The tall jihadi behind Najibullah fumbled for his rifle. He looked at Wells, his eyes pleading for mercy. '*La*,' he said. *No*. Wells shot him, three in the chest, knowing that he would have to deal with the two in front. Knowing that he couldn't risk leaving an armed man behind him, even one who wanted to surrender. The jihadi tore at his chest and grunted and pitched backward. Wells forgot him and turned and looked up the hill.

The two men ahead were grabbing for their pistols. They were maybe sixty feet up the trail, four car lengths, only a few scrubby trees and bushes between them and Wells. Wells went to a knee as the jihadi farther away fired three rounds high and wild. The shots echoed off the hills, and behind Wells, a branch broke. Wells sighted and steadied the AK, putting the stock against his shoulder. *Make haste, not hurry*. He squeezed the trigger three times. He was a good shot, not great, but he didn't need to be, not with a long gun at this range. Two neat holes tore into the jihadi's gown and he fell backward and didn't move.

The fourth jihadi fired twice. He had a clean shot, but he was nervous and rushed it, and sixty feet was much more difficult for a pistol than a rifle. The rounds clicked against a rock a few yards to Wells's right. Wells put the AK on him. The jihadi turned and fled up the hill, shooting wildly across his body as he ran, all his discipline gone. Wells squeezed the trigger twice. The jihadi yelped and spun down, hit in the right shoulder. He pushed himself up and stumbled to his feet. Wells fired again, catching him in the gut this time. The man screamed and dropped his gun and pressed his hands over his stomach. He slipped to his knees. The echoes of the scream faded into a hopeless grunt, the sound of a hungry baby with no tears left to cry.

Wells ran up the hill. 'Leave the gun,' he said. The jihadi didn't answer. The front of his gown was black with blood. Wells put a hand over the man's and pushed down. The blood kept coming, covering Wells's palm, spurting through his fingers. The shot had torn open the jihadi's intestines. Surgery might save his life, but they were a half day from even the most basic hospital. 'You'll be all right,' Wells said in Pashtun.

The man tilted his head, looked at Wells. *I know you're lying, and you do too*, his eyes said. He said something and Wells leaned close to hear him. 'Allah forgive me for screaming. But it hurts.'

Wells almost had to admire the insanity of these Pashtuns. This man would be dead within the hour. Yet his biggest fear was that Wells would think he was weak for showing pain. 'Where can I find the Thuwanis?'

The man's head drooped. *You waste my last minutes with this?* his eyes said. 'They pray at a mosque east of town. Near the turnoff for the mines.' He licked his lips. 'I'm thirsty.'

'Why do you hate them? Why do you fight with them?' Even as he asked, Wells realized the answer didn't matter. Men here fought for a thousand reasons. Over slights to honor, real and imagined. To prove their strength and amuse themselves. Because they'd always fought and always would.

'I don't hate them. They're not the ones who killed me,' the man said. 'Now finish it. Before I dishonor myself.'

Wells heard shouts, distant but closing. The firefight must have echoed a long way in these hills. 'Your men are coming.'

'Finish it. Don't pretend you can't.'

'*La ilaha illa Allah. Muhammad rasulu Allah,*' Wells said. The words were the *shahada*, the Muslim declaration of faith, the first pillar of Islam. *There is no God but God, and Muhammad is the Messenger of God*. Pious Muslims hoped that the shahada would be the last words they heard.

'*Allahu akbar,*' the man said. '*La ilaha illa Allah. Muhammad rasulu Allah.*'

He squeezed his eyes shut and crossed his hands over his chest. Wells put three shots into him and he twitched and stilled. Then Wells reached into the front pocket of the man's shalwar and plucked out the keys to the Toyota and a cell phone and a Pakistani identification card smeared with blood. He jogged back down the hill to Najibullah's body. The corpse's head was twisted at a grotesque angle, jaw loose, tongue flopped out. It seemed to be leering at Wells. 'You started it,' Wells said. He grabbed Jalal Haq's passport and money.

He knelt beside the fourth Talib, the thin one, the one who hadn't wanted any part of this mess. The man lay facedown on the scree. A fist-size hole punctured his back, and bright red arterial blood sopped through his gown. AK rounds were supersonic and big. At close range, they tore through guys. The man's rifle was trapped under his body. Wells flipped the corpse over and closed its eyes. Then he ran down the hill, his bloody gown flapping.

The pickup was parked in a clearing alongside two others. Wells put the AK on single-shot and blew out the tires of the other two. He switched to semiauto and fired a half dozen shots into their engine compartments. His pursuers would have a tough time following him.

He heard distant shouts and screams. They must have found the bodies. Wells started the pickup and wheeled it around and bounced down a narrow but serviceable track. The dead man's phone showed no service. Which meant that the men behind him couldn't call anyone to come up the hill and block him. Probably. Maybe.

The track wound east, into the rising sun. Wells raised a hand to shield his eyes and found it sticky with blood. In the bright white glare, he saw the fourth jihadi, the one who'd tried to surrender. He hadn't wanted to kill these men. They'd left him no choice. He wondered whether his son would call what he had done self-defense.

Probably not.

The track had no intersections or gates. It dead-ended at the main highway, which was empty. Muslim Bagh lay to the left, a few miles down. Wells wanted more than anything to turn right, southwest toward Quetta. He could ditch the pickup there, catch a bus to Islamabad. He would be in the United States in forty-eight hours. He would wash his hands clean and lie in bed with Anne.

He turned left. To Muslim Bagh.

THIRTEEN

Wells ditched the Toyota behind an empty mosque on the edge of town. He washed the blood from his hands and face with a trickle of brown water from a rusty irrigation pipe. At the guesthouse, he changed into a clean gown and grabbed his things and rolled out.

Twenty miles northeast of Muslim Bagh, he pulled over and called Shafer at home. He didn't like breaking cover so soon after starting the mission, but he needed to tell someone what he'd done, and Shafer was his only choice.

'Hello?' Shafer's voice was scratchy. It was close to midnight in Virginia. 'John?'

'You in the situation room?'

'Naturally.' After years of encouragement from his wife, Shafer had installed a giant flat-screen television and a couple leather couches in his basement. Shafer called it the situation room. He was threatening to add a hot tub. 'Trouble already?'

Wells explained. At the end, Shafer sighed. 'Four guys.'

'That's right.'

'You should come with a warning label. You want my advice? Get out of there. Amadullah Thuwani isn't the guy you went over there to catch. He's a stepping-stone. Go. We'll find another way to find the mole.'

'Just leave?'

'Have you thought maybe Amadullah won't like an outsider messing with his business? He might hand you over to the families of the guys you killed. Trade you to settle their feud.'

'You think so.'

'Probably not. Most likely he'll give you a big Thuwani high five for getting rid of them. But who knows? And you're a stranger, not a guest. All that Pashtunwali junk doesn't apply to you. And you know it's more than a little elastic anyway.' According to the *Pashtunwali* code, hosts were responsible for the safety of their visitors. But some tribes took their obligations more seriously than others, as more than one outsider had found out too late.

'I have to see this through.'

'All right. Then when you see the Thuwanis, just play scared. Tell them you got caught and the guys who had you started fighting about what to do with you. Then they started shooting at each other and you took off.'

'Will they believe that?'

'No one else is alive to tell them different. They're more likely to believe that version than that some random Saudi took care of four locals.' Shafer paused. 'You sound like you're having a hard time with this one, John.'

'I'm all right.'

'Try to remember. You don't want to do it anymore, you don't have to. You can always get into alligator wrestling, free-climbing, something safe like that.'

'Sure. Anyway. When I get back, we're going to sit on that couch and watch football until we fall asleep.'

'Can I rest my head in your lap?'

For the second time in five minutes, Shafer had made Wells smile. 'I thought you'd never ask.' He hung up, tossed the AK in a ditch, and turned around, back to Muslim Bagh. About five miles from town, Wells saw a rutted road, blocked by a chain and marked with a small sign that read 'East All-Balochistan Mines Company.' He'd taken no notice of it the day before. Chromium and nickel mines studded Balochistan's hills.

The mosque lay a hundred yards past the turnoff. It was new, with fresh white paint and a fifty-foot minaret. Wells parked beside a minibus. *You're Jalal Haq. You've just had the most terrifying experience of your life. But you lived, and now you want to find the men you came here to meet.*

The mosque was high-ceilinged and carpeted with new wool rugs. It could hold a couple hundred men, but Wells saw only three, Pashtuns squatting against the back wall. They looked to be in their twenties, though Wells couldn't be sure. Men aged quickly in these mountains. A silver teapot and a bowl of grapes sat on the carpet before them. Breakfast in Balochistan.

'*Salaam aleikum.*'

The man nearest Wells popped a half dozen grapes into his mouth and chewed noisily. '*Aleikum salaam,*' he mumbled. 'Please sit.'

Wells sat. 'I hardly speak Pashtun. Do any of you know Arabic?'

'Certainly I speak Arabic,' the grape-chewing man said proudly. Up close, he was maybe eighteen.

'I'm seeking a famous tribe that lives in these hills. The Thuwanis.'

'My friend. You've come to the right place,' the man said. He tapped his chest. 'I am Sangar. My uncle, Amadullah, he leads our tribe. I am the youngest of all his nephews.'

Wells supposed he was due for a break. He gave Sangar his cover story, not mentioning what had happened in the mountains that morning. Sangar was friendly and a bit dim. When Wells finished, Sangar asked him to wait. He waddled out, returning a few minutes later with an older copy of himself. The second man introduced himself as Jaji, another of Amadullah's nephews. Jaji waved Sangar away and sat across from Wells, his legs crossed, feet tucked away. 'So Daood sent you?'

Wells hid his surprise. Daood was a Pakistani name, not Saudi. Was he an ISI agent? 'I don't know any Daood,' he said truthfully.

Jaji frowned. 'Then tell me why you've come.' Again Wells explained. Jaji listened intently, leaning forward, hands on his knees. 'And you chose our tribe,' Jaji said, when he was finished. 'Who told you of us?'

'His name was Faisal, the friend of a friend. He said the Thuwanis were great warriors. He told me of a time in Afghanistan, years ago, when you made two Shia run through a field like the dogs they are. It was a special field, he said. The kind that grows explosions and reaps arms and legs.'

Jaji smiled. 'I remember that day. They cried and begged, but it did them no good. But tell me something, Jalal. Why come now?'

'I wanted to help my brothers.'

'You could have joined the cause long ago.'

'A year ago, a cousin of mine, my age, really my best friend, was feeling poorly. A bad cough, sweating at night. He went to the doctor, expected that he'd be given some pills, be fine. Instead, he learned he had cancer of the lung. Two months later, we buried him. And then a few weeks later, another cousin, he died in his sleep, lying next to his wife. His heart. You're too young to understand that these things happen. Even men who don't die in war can die suddenly.'

'*Inshallah*. We live and we die as God sees.'

'Yes, we live and we die. But all these years, I've thought of joining the jihad and I've always found an excuse. I see now I've been trying to protect my little life. But it's vanishing anyway, so why shouldn't I come? When I meet Allah, I'd like him to know that I tried to fight for him, at least.'

Wells had offered the jihadi version of a midlife crisis. The story seemed to satisfy Jaji. 'I'll tell my uncle you've come,' he said.

'Before you do . . .' Wells explained what had happened that morning, finishing with a false version of his escape. 'When we were on the trail, they argued with each other as to what to do with me. Then they shot at each other. I couldn't believe what I was seeing. Truly Allah must want me to fulfill this mission, because he was protecting me.'

'And then what happened?'

'Three of the men died. I took a rifle and shot the fourth. Then I ran away.'

'These men, you know their names?'

'One was called Najibullah. Another was this man.' Wells passed over the identity card. Jaji looked it over, and a smile that Wells couldn't read curled his lips. Wells wondered whether he'd made yet another mistake, whether he would have to kill the men in this mosque and race for Islamabad with half of Balochistan chasing him. Then Jaji grinned. He stood, reached a hand to Wells, pulled him up. Wrapped his arms around Wells and hugged him so close that Wells could smell his oddly perfumed hair.

'Oh, I think my uncle will be glad to see you.'

Later, Wells learned that a cousin of Najibullah's had raped a niece of Amadullah's two years before. So the Thuwani men said anyway. Najibullah's clan no doubt had its own version. The cousin denied the rape and refused to pay compensation.

The two sides had feuded ever since. Four men had died so far around Muslim Bagh. Family values, Pashtun-style. The Thuwanis were so overjoyed to hear Wells had been responsible for the deaths of four of their enemies that he probably could have told them who he really was and still been treated as an honored guest.

Jaji took Wells to a big concrete house on the high plateau east of the main road. A feast awaited him there, raisins and grapes and pomegranates, rice and flatbreads flavored with garlic, heaping platters of lamb and chicken. Black ghosts in burqas brought out pitchers of sweet mango juice and tart lemonade and thick yogurt shakes. The tang of roasted meat filled the room, and Wells realized he was famished. He hadn't eaten that day. His hunger unsettled him – *kill and eat and eat and kill* – but he followed his appetite and ate until he was sated. As the honored guest, he sat beside Amadullah, a big, boisterous man, the center of the room, with the deepest voice and the loudest laugh. He chewed the green tobacco that the Pashtuns favored, spitting into a cup that shone with the buttery sheen of pure gold. On his wrist he wore a thick gold Rolex. The killing of Najibullah had put him in high spirits. But Wells could imagine his mood darkening instantly if anyone challenged him. The alpha male in a tribe like this could never afford to show weakness.

Afterward, the chief dismissed his nephews and brothers and sat with Wells. 'I hope you enjoyed our lunch,' he said. 'Of course, we're poor peasants who have nothing like the wealth you Saudis have at home—'

'There's no need for modesty. I couldn't have eaten another bite. I'd always heard of the famous hospitality of the Pashtuns. Now I've seen it myself. When you come to the kingdom for your Hajj, my family will host you. We'll do our best to match your feast.'

'The men who took you this morning weren't so polite. Allah smiled on you, to survive those thieves.'

'He saw the rightness of my mission.'

'So now do you want to be one of us? Live in these mountains?'

'I'm not a warrior like you. I can do more good raising money for you.' From his pocket, Wells offered the bundle of hundred-dollar bills Naiz had given him in Islamabad. 'It's only ten thousand dollars, but if I can show everyone at home that the money is going to jihad, I should have no problem getting more.'

Amadullah played cool. 'I understand,' he said gravely. 'Please come with me.' He led Wells through the compound to a windowless room. A laptop sat on a desk.

'MacBook Pro,' Amadullah said. 'Top of the line.' He rubbed his fingers over the laptop's shiny brushed aluminum case as if he were stroking a prized Persian. 'Let me tell you, we always need money. For trucks, rifles, explosives, to give to the families of the martyrs.' And MacBooks, Wells thought.

Amadullah opened the laptop and clicked through a photo-and-video gallery of an IED attack, start to finish. A Chinese 120-millimeter mortar shell was turned into a bomb, taken over the border in the back of a minibus, and buried on a dirt road that crawled along the edge of a steep hillside. A blurry video of an explosion and a smoking Humvee followed.

'My nephews did this. Three years ago.' Amadullah clicked forward to an image of eight young men pointing AKs at the camera. Another photo showed the same men smiling at American soldiers on patrol. 'You see. They have no idea. We cross the border as we like, we live in the hills or in the villages with our cousins. When the moment is right, we strike. When it's to our advantage, not theirs.'

'Will you send me these photos? It'll help me raise money.'

'Of course, Jalal. I'll have my nephew give you one of those little things—'

'A flash drive—'

'Right. But anyway, you see how it is. We learn more about the Americans every year, while they know nothing about us.'

'Still, it must be hard to know how they think. Have you ever captured one?' Wells was fishing now, hoping to get Amadullah to talk about the drug trafficking ring, though he wasn't sure Amadullah would.

'No, but—' Amadullah broke off. He flipped to another photo, lower resolution than the others. Taken from a cell phone camera, Wells thought. It showed three American soldiers standing in front of a high mud-brick wall. Unfortunately, the soldiers were too distant and the photo quality too low for Wells to see details of their faces. But he could tell that one looked Hispanic while the other two were white.

'You see these men?' Amadullah said. 'We corrupt them.'

'I don't understand.'

'We sell them drugs. Heroin.' Amadullah flipped forward to a photo of a bag of grayish powder being weighed.

'My brother. You're a genius.' So Amadullah was presenting his drug trafficking as a plan to corrupt American soldiers in the service of jihad. 'So – if you don't mind my asking – how does it work?' Wells decided to take a blind shot. 'Is Daood involved?'

Amadullah snapped the MacBook shut. The good cheer on his face disappeared. At this moment, he reminded Wells of Vinny Duto, only bigger and browner and much more dangerous. And Wells knew he had his answer. Daood, whoever he was, connected the Thuwanis with the mole in Kabul.

'Who told you about Daood?'

Again Wells found himself playing the frightened Saudi. 'No one. I mean, Jaji. But he didn't tell me anything. When I met him, he asked if Daood had sent me. So I thought—'

'Thought what?'

'Allah forgive me, when you showed me these pictures, I wondered if Jaji thought these drugs were the reason I'd come here. I'm so very stupid. I'm sorry.'

'No. Jaji should never have mentioned the name. Daood is no one for you to worry about.'

'I won't then.'

As quickly as that, Amadullah's anger passed. He smiled and went back to playing the gracious host. He took Wells to an outbuilding to see his arsenal, AKs and RPGs and even a rusted-out Stinger.

After the weapons tour, Amadullah didn't seem to know what to do with Wells. He obviously wanted to prove his jihadi credentials to keep the money flowing. But Wells could see that the Thuwanis weren't exactly on the front lines this fighting season. Wells suspected that Amadullah was making so much money from the drug ring that he didn't want to take chances.

They had another feast that night. Amadullah's men regaled Wells with stories of attacks on American and Afghan units. Wells felt a little like a visiting dignitary, a member of Congress who had come to a forward base to be told how well the war was going. He promised that on his next trip to Muslim Bagh, he would go on a mission.

'Yes, come with us. Watch us kill kaffirs,' Jaji said. 'Slit their throats and make them wish they'd never come to our country.'

'God willing,' Wells said. He wondered whether he could steal the laptop and decided not to take the risk. He had gotten Daood's name and the photos. He would have to hope that would be enough.

The next morning he left. He carried a flash drive with photos and video of the attack, a Gmail address for Amadullah, and a mobile number for Jaji.

'You don't have a phone, Amadullah?'

Amadullah circled a finger over his head as if to say, *They're listening*. 'To reach me, call Jaji. Or just come back to the mosque.'

'Very good.'

They said good-bye and hugged. Then Wells walked out with Jaji, headed for the mosque and his 4Runner. The last twenty-four hours had been among the strangest of his life. He had killed four men – and then been treated as an honored guest. He couldn't help feeling that he'd gotten off easy.

Seven hours later, at Dera Ismail Khan, he stopped at a gas station and called Shafer. 'Daood,' Shafer said, when Wells finished. 'First name is all you got. How about an age? Physical description? Nationality?'

'None of the above.'

'Because that's a little bit vague.'

'Why don't you come out here and try doing your own detective work?'

'You're sure he was connected to those soldiers, the dealing?'

'I can tell you Amadullah was seriously unhappy that I made the link.'

'Okay. I'll start looking. So what's next? Are you heading back to the Ariana? See if anyone will admit knowing Amadullah or Daood?'

Wells had considered that idea. But going back to Kabul was unappealing. The mole would have his defenses ready, and Wells didn't have the leverage to break them. The Ariana felt like a trap.

'I think I'm better off staying away. So I'm going to Kandahar, shake some hands, maybe see if I hear anything about drug smuggling.'

'Long shot.'

'I know, but that was half my cover for coming over here anyway. I might as well stick to it. Until you find Daood. Get that big brain in gear, Ellis.'

FOURTEEN

Daood. Dawood. Daud. Daoud.

Bad enough that Ellis Shafer couldn't find the courier, didn't have a hint of who he was. Almost a week after talking to Wells, Shafer couldn't even be sure how to spell the guy's first name.

Like many Muslim names, such as Ibrahim and Yusuf, Daood was a Quranic version of a Jewish Biblical name, in this case David. Muslims chose names from a relatively small pool. Their favorites included Abdul, Ali, Hussein, Khalid, and the always popular Muhammad, a name given to tens of millions of Muslims worldwide – and a few unlucky Christians, too. Daood and its variants weren't quite as popular. Still, Shafer had hundreds of thousands of potential targets.

He wouldn't be going door-to-door.

After his talk with Wells, Shafer's first call went to Fort Meade. He asked the NSA to track the e-mail address and phone number that Wells had gotten, and search its e-mail and voice databases for references to men named Daood. But his hope for a dose of technological magic didn't pan out.

The agency started with an e-mail to Amadullah's Gmail address. The e-mail looked like a standard account-maintenance message, but opening it would infect the host computer with a virus that would broadcast the IP address of the server connecting the computer to the Internet. The agency could use the virtual address to pin down the computer's physical location. But the plan was a bust. As far as the NSA could figure, Amadullah never used the Gmail account. As for the cell number, the NSA was already tracing it as part of its surveillance of the Thuwanis.

The broader e-mail and phone searches Shafer had requested also came up dry. The name Daood appeared hundreds of times in the agency's databases. But after two days of combing through suspect messages, Shafer found nothing that appeared remotely related to trafficking or the Thuwanis. He wasn't surprised. The CIA officer running this plan would know just how good the United States had become at tracking Internet traffic.

The voice records had their own problems. The NSA's voice database was spottier than its e-mail counterpart. Nearly all e-mails worldwide passed through a handful of electronic junctions that the United States tapped. But phone companies tried to keep calls inside their own systems to avoid paying interchange fees to other phone companies. A phone call from Islamabad to Peshawar might never leave Pakistan, making it harder to trace. And even if the NSA did have the calls in its databases, finding them in a blind search would be extraordinarily difficult. The agency couldn't possibly hire enough Arabic and Pashtun speakers to go through all the calls in its databases. It had spent hundreds of millions of dollars on voice recognition programs that listened for obvious words like *bomb* and *martyrdom* – as well as more subtle ones like *container* or *antibiotic*. The NSA could also query the software to track specific words. Calls pegged as suspicious were passed to human analysts.

But the software was spotty. Computers had a hugely difficult time parsing and recognizing human speech, as anyone who'd ever called an airline 800 number knew. And the agency particularly disliked blind searches, which used huge amounts of computing power and generally came up dry. So Dr Teresa Carter, who oversaw the programs, told Shafer.

'You're telling me it's impossible,' Shafer said.

'We can try. But I need to know, will finding this man Daood stop an imminent threat to American civilians or military personnel?'

Shafer hesitated. 'I can't guarantee that.'

'In that case, given the other projects we have queued up, we can't treat this request as a top priority.'

'A medium priority?'

'It'll be on the list.' Her voice was cool. 'Mr Shafer, we're currently tasked on other searches that have a direct probability of saving lives. You may not believe me, but I want to help. If there's an imminent threat, call me and I'll push.'

Shafer hated being reminded how much the CIA relied on the wizards across the Potomac. The Luddite in him was almost happy to find out that technology wasn't totally infallible. But he needed a new way to shrink the target pool. He decided to flip the search, look from the inside out instead of the outside in. Specifically, he would assume that Daood was already connected with the agency, that whoever was running the trafficking hadn't recruited him cold.

If Daood had ever worked for the agency, his real name would be kept in a database at Langley, Shafer knew. Even before they were officially recruited, agents received code names – Sparrow, Gemstone, Medallion. Case reports and files always referred to them by those names. Under normal circumstances, only a handful of people would know an agent's real name. But all agents also had their names and biographical information sent to Langley and saved. The reason was simple: the CIA mistrusted everyone, even the agents it recruited. Most especially the agents it recruited. If they were suspected of being doubles controlled by their home governments, counterintelligence officers and desk officers at Langley might need to know who they really were. So each regional desk kept a database of biographical information.

But keeping the names at Langley came with its own risks. In 1985, a disgruntled counterintelligence officer named Aldrich Ames had given the real names of the CIA agents in the Soviet Union to the KGB. Several were executed. After the Ames scandal, the agency tightened access to the databases. They were no longer stored at each regional desk. Instead, the Directorate of Security stored them on encrypted hard drives in a vault that could be opened only upon a written finding signed by an assistant deputy director. Once a database was pulled, two 128-digit key codes were required to unlock it.

Given the importance of the databases, Shafer understood the precautions. But they meant that he couldn't search the databases quietly. Word of the search for Daood would likely leak to Kabul. Shafer didn't know what the mole would do if he heard.

He did have one other option: the 'Kingdom List.' Even inside the CIA, the existence of the Kingdom List remained a closely held secret. It contained the name and basic biographical information of everyone that the agency had ever recruited, active or retired, dead or alive.

The list was stored in a cavern in West Virginia, part of the underground complex where the president would be evacuated if Washington faced a nuclear attack. A written finding from the president, vice president, or national security advisor was required to see the Kingdom List. It could be decoded only in the presence of the agency's director or most senior deputy director. Theoretically, it provided the ultimate backup in case of a catastrophic nuclear attack on the Langley campus.

In reality, a nuclear attack big enough to destroy Langley would probably destroy all of Washington. In reality, the list served as the last defense against a top-level mole. For example, if the director suspected that an agent in Russia could prove that his deputy was a spy for the FSB, the list would give him a way to contact the agent directly without anyone else inside the CIA knowing.

Shafer wondered whether Duto would give him access to the list. Probably not, especially since they still had no hard proof that the mole existed. But it was worth asking. He called the seventh floor, Duto's direct line.

'Director's office.' The voice wasn't Duto's.

'Where's Vinny?'

'This is Joseph Geisler. May I help you?'

'It's Ellis. I need to talk to Vinny.'

'Ellis who?'

'Ellis Shafer, you nimwit.'

'I'm afraid I don't know that name.'

Shafer closed his eyes and counted to ten. His doctor had warned him about stress. He was closer to seventy than sixty now, and learning the aging process was just growing up in reverse. Every time he went to the doctor, another pleasure was taken from him. And those were the good trips, the ones where he wasn't poked and prodded and snipped.

'Sir?'

'Joseph. How old are you?'

'Twenty-nine.'

Shafer had worked for the agency longer than this guy had been alive. He wished he could be happy about that fact. 'And how long have you worked for Vinny?'

'I've had the honor to be a member of Director Duto's personal team for three months.'

'Please tell someone who is not in diapers that Ellis Shafer is coming up to see Vinny, and it's urgent.'

'Sir, the director is in meetings all morning—'

'Ellis,' Duto said when Shafer walked into his office. Duto's eyes looked up, but his thumbs didn't. He had his legs on his desk and was texting away furiously. 'You hurt Joe's feelings, you know.'

'Every month you have more of these guys. What's next? Food taster?'

Duto didn't rise to the bait. He rarely did these days. 'I'm glad you came by. I was wondering about John. Kabul said he's disappeared. Left the station one morning and went to Moscow. Funny thing is that no one in Moscow seemed to get the message.'

'Went to Pak to chase a lead. Now he's back in Afghanistan, at KAF.'

'He's in Kandahar.'

'Correct.'

'What's he doing there?'

'Talking to soldiers, shaking hands.' *Avoiding that snake pit in Kabul.*

'What about his cover?'

'Junk. No one at the Ariana believed it. They told him they knew he was after a mole.'

Finally, Duto stopped texting. 'Did they now?'

'They did.'

'And did he get what he was looking for in Pakistan?'

'Progress as promised, Vinny.' Shafer recounted Wells's trip to Muslim Bagh, leaving out only the way Wells had killed the four men. Duto wouldn't mind, but Shafer figured that Wells should decide whether to tell that part of the story.

'So now we're trying to find Daood. We figure he'll lead us to the mole. Though the theory does have one weak link.'

'What's that?'

'Aside from that story you initially gave us from the DEA before John went over, we still have no evidence connecting the trafficking with the mole. John and I both think it's likely. These soldiers making the pickups can't have found Amadullah on their own. Somebody at a high level has got to be directing all this, somebody who can operate on both sides of the border. But that somebody isn't necessarily one of ours. We think it is, but thinking it isn't the same as proving it.'

'Amadullah Thuwani,' Duto said. 'Would you believe that two nights ago an SF team raided a farm in Kandahar where a couple Thuwanis were supposed to be living? Guys in their twenties, Amadullah's nephews. We suspected that one was connected to a bombing on Highway 1 that cooked an MRAP and everybody inside. We helped develop the intel, so JSOC kept Kandahar station informed.' The letters stood for the Joint Special Operations Command, the group that oversaw Delta Force, the Green Berets, and other elite units.

'And what happened?'

'Special ops had satellite recon for weeks, had their patterns down. Everything. Locked down. And guess what? When we hit, we didn't find one military-age man on the compound. Not one. Kids and old men only. Which is the reason I know about this. JSOC intel's chief and our guys in Kandahar can't figure out how it leaked.'

'Could be a coincidence.'

'You think so?'

'No.' Thuwani's men wouldn't have left without good reason,

and operational security on night raids was extremely tight. Someone had tipped them. The mole was real.

'Me neither. Now tell me about Daood. Why you're so sure he's one of ours.'

'Our mole is too smart to take a chance on a courier he doesn't know. He wants somebody he can leverage. Somebody he can own. But at the same time, he wants somebody who doesn't have an active case officer, because in that case the guy might go running to his CO.'

'What if the mole is actually Daood's CO?'

'Our guy's too smart to use anyone who could be connected with him that easily. No, Daood is an occasional.' CIA jargon for a low-grade informant who provided tips but didn't merit full-time management by a case officer. Since they weren't officially on the CIA payroll, the agency paid limited attention to them. 'I'm afraid Kabul will hear if I start fishing for him. Now that we're certain the mole's real, is there any chance I can use the Kingdom List?'

'That's national emergencies only, and this doesn't qualify.'

'Meaning you don't want the White House to know you may have a mole.'

'I'm not debating this.'

'Vinny—'

'Forget it, Ellis.'

Shafer gave up. Duto's tone brooked no argument.

'Then what do you suggest?'

'What about the DEA?'

'What about them?'

'Maybe he's in their system, too. Maybe he's one of these guys who bounces around, us and the feds and the DEA. Soon as we figure out he's giving us a big bag of nothing, he gets a new daddy.'

Duto's words gave Shafer an idea. The DEA would be in no hurry to do the agency any favors. But occasionals weren't protected like real agents. Sometimes their names spread wide. Especially if they were problem children, the type who did business with more than one agency. Shafer stood to leave. 'Thanks for all the help, Vinny.'

'Should I ask what you're doing?'

'What I should have done all along.'

'What's that?'

I'm giving up on a silicon-flavored miracle. I'm doing my job the old-fashioned way, the right way. I'm calling somebody who can answer my questions. 'I'm going home, breaking out the Dewar's, raising a glass to your health.'

'In that case, make it a double.'

Back in his office, Shafer unlocked his safe and pulled out his Rolodex, an antique like him. He had thousands of case officers and station chiefs and desk heads in here, decades of contacts scratched in pen and pencil. Maybe two in five were still active. The rest had retired or quit to work for contractors. Or died. Just in the As, Shafer recognized Henry 'Argyle' Aniston, an old-school agency type who'd worn the ugliest sweaters known to man and dropped from a heart attack three months before he was scheduled to retire, and James Appleston, whose prostate cancer had spread to his brain. Shafer thought he'd take the heart attack.

Thousands of names, but nearly all useless for this call. He needed an officer who'd served on the Af-Pak desk in the last decade but hadn't been a star. The stars had spent their time chasing bin Laden and al-Zawahiri. They wouldn't have been interested in Daood. Also, he needed somebody gossipy. But not so gossipy that he'd whisper to Kabul that Shafer was poking after an occasional. And he needed somebody who liked him enough to be honest.

Shafer had to get to the *R*s before he found someone who might fit. Mark Ryker had retired five years before. If Shafer recalled correctly, he lived somewhere in southwestern Virginia. A lot of agency guys wound up in that area, far enough from Washington to avoid the dangers they'd spent their lives fighting, close enough to feel like they were still part of the world.

Shafer punched in Ryker's number. To his mild surprise, the phone was picked up after one ring. 'This is Mark.'

'Mark. It's Ellis Shafer.' He heard a sitcom's canned laughter in the background.

'Ellis. Ellis Shafer.'

He wasn't quite slurring his words, but his tone was as bright and artificial as the dye for a kid's birthday cake. Pharmaceutical enhancement for sure. 'I'd like to talk to you about something.' Shafer figured he'd need to draw out Ryker. He was wrong.

'Mr Ellis Shafer wants to talk to me? About *something*. Must be important. I assume this is a face-to-face business, tête-à-tête, too superclassified for an open line?'

'You are correct.'

'And urgent?'

'Life-and-death.' Shafer vamping now, getting into the spirit.

'Life and death. Death and life. I know about those. All right. Tell you what. Shoot down 81 tonight, and I'll meet you in Lexington. You know where that is?'

'I can find it.'

'I suppose you can. There's an Applebee's there, and I promise you nobody'll bother us. Say, eight.'

'Eatin' good in the neighborhood.'

'Are you too fancy for Applebee's, Ellis?' Pause. 'That wasn't a rhetorical question. I want an answer.'

'No. Sorry.'

'See you at eight then.'

Shafer called his wife and told her he probably wouldn't be home that night. She didn't ask why, or where he'd be. One of the virtues of being married as long as he had. He got his usual late start and had to fight through the suburban DC traffic, but 81 was as beautiful and open as ever, running southwest through the lush Virginia hills. He pulled into the parking lot at 8:05.

The Applebee's was bright and three-quarters empty and the server was a purty little bleached-blond thing who greeted him too eagerly. 'Table for one, sir?' Shafer ignored her and found Ryker sitting alone in a booth. He was drinking a bright green concoction that Shafer would swear was an appletini. Ryker didn't look good. He was skinny and weirdly tan and his shirt hung loose. Shafer didn't get it. He hadn't known Ryker well at Langley, but he remembered the guy as just another Central Asia desk officer. During the 1990s, Pakistan and Afghanistan hadn't been glamorous posts. The action was elsewhere.

'Mark. Good to see you. It's been too long.'

'You, too.'

'How's Lois?' Shafer kept the names of wives in his Rolodex, an old trick.

Ryker laughed low and ugly. Everything about him made sense now. Shafer had better update his index cards. People kept dying. Shafer wondered how he'd do as a widower. Probably no better than Ryker. Maybe worse.

'When?'

'Three months ago.'

'I'm sorry. I didn't know.'

'Why would you? It's not like we were friends.'

'You want to tell me about it?'

'No. Instead let me tell you why I agreed to see you, knowing that you're going to ask me to give up something classified, something I shouldn't tell you, or why else would you have driven all the way out here on four hours' notice?'

'Sure.'

'Because who cares?'

Maybe this isn't the time, Shafer almost said. But he kept his mouth shut. He needed to know about Daood. Ryker was his best bet. So he flagged a waitress and ordered a Bud Light and popcorn chicken and told Ryker he was looking for a guy who might be an occasional and might have been running drugs, too

'A hundred guys fit that profile,' Ryker said. 'More. You want to tell me why you need this one?'

'No.'

'That's all you have? You have a name?'

'A first name. Daood. Though I'm not sure how to spell it.'

Ryker sucked down his appletini and licked his lips. 'I am. D-A-O-O-D. Last name Maktani. Daood Maktani. Though he prefers to call himself David Miller.' Just that quick, something woke up in Ryker's face. For the first time all night, he looked to Shafer like a case officer instead of a man waiting for the clock to run out. 'Half the desk knew his name. No OPSEC on an asshat like him. One of those guys. Running drugs out of Pakistan the whole damn time. Didn't even try to hide it, really. The DEA bitched at us for using him, but they used him, too. He was a smart guy and he gave us just enough that we kept him around, but nobody liked him.'

'Tell me about it.'

So Ryker did.

FIFTEEN

Kandahar Air field, Afghanistan

The Drone Home, aka the Unmanned Aerial Vehicle Center, occupied a couple acres on the south side of the Kandahar runway. A high-security fence backed with green netting hid hangars and concrete workshops from prying eyes. Inside, Air Force mechanics and CIA engineers and General Dynamics contractors worked on the drones so crucial to the Afghan war. The Predators and Reapers were well-known. Less so the agency's newest baby, the 'Beast of Kandahar.'

The Beast was a miniature single-wing plane that looked like a hobbyist's model of a B-2 stealth bomber. It didn't carry weapons. It was designed solely for surveillance, the stealthiest plane ever built. It was invisible to radar or the naked eye from more than a couple hundred yards away. It carried ground-penetrating radar and color cameras sensitive enough to distinguish eye color from a thousand feet up. It had spent hundreds of hours in the air above Osama bin Laden's compound in Abbottabad. Neither bin Laden nor the Pakistani military had ever guessed at its presence.

Now the agency was trying to add microphones to the Beast. Picking up voices from an aircraft circling hundreds or thousands of feet in the air was a monumental technical challenge. But the payoff would be just as big. The CIA would hear the other side's plans in real time. And it would make fewer targeting errors, a euphemism for *civilian deaths*.

Francesca, who was waiting for his buddy Stan in the parking lot outside the Drone Home, knew all about the Beast. He and Alders did most of their work in the border areas where the drones were busiest. To reduce the chance that he'd be mistaken for a Talib, Francesca carried a transponder. When on, it emitted an electronic signature identifying him as American. He'd been briefed on what to do if the transponder failed. The advice basically boiled down to, *Get out of the hot zone as quickly as you can, because you don't want to be on the incoming end of a Hellfire*.

The briefings had come from an Air Force colonel. Francesca had never met any of the guys who actually piloted the drones. He wondered about them. From what he'd heard, they were mostly contractors in their twenties and thirties, some ex-military, some civilian. Were they normals, or Shadows like him? Did they see the red mist when they closed their eyes?

Probably not. Probably they pushed a button when their bosses gave them the okay. A few seconds later, they watched a house disappear on-screen in a little puff of smoke. Like a video game. Shift work. When they were done, they drove home from Nellis AFB to their families in the Vegas suburbs. Without their toys and their satellite links, they were nothing. They hadn't earned any of the power they'd been given, hadn't paid for it in any way. Did they think they were tough? They were nothing, and he'd gladly show them—

The front gate opened, pulling him out of his homicidal reverie. Stan walked out and slid into the pickup's passenger seat and they rolled off. No rush. The roads at KAF were dirt and gravel, and traffic was heavy. Francesca had no idea what all these inside-the-wire dudes did, but driving around the base seemed to be a big part of it.

'My man. My man Afghani-stan.' Of course, Francesca knew Stan's real name. But he liked the alias. It was pretty funny.

'Danny. Long time no see.' They bumped fists. Neither was the hugging type.

'What's going on in there?'

'At the home of the drones? The usual. GD promises that for just a few hundred million more they can give the Beast ass-wiping functionality. They did a PowerPoint and everything.'

'If technology could win guerrilla wars, we would have ended this nonsense a long time ago.'

'Yeah, I suspect you're not going out of business anytime soon. Bang, bang, you're dead.' Stan sighed. He looked like he'd aged ten years in the last two. His hair had gone from jet-black to mostly gray. He'd lost weight, too. Of course, he had good reason.

'You look good, my friend,' Francesca said.

'That's a lie.'

'Come on. Let me buy you a cup of coffee. The Brits have a new girl working the counter.' KAF had a half dozen privately staffed coffeehouses. By common agreement, the British had the best-tasting drinks, and the best-looking staff.

'Wish I could, but I have to meet the J-2' – the intelligence chief for all military operations in Kandahar – 'at noon. And I ought to be there on time.'

'Aren't you fancy?'

'You tell me to come down and see you, I need an excuse. Meeting the J-2's a pretty good excuse. So no crap. Let's just take a spin around the perimeter, put the windows down, breathe our fill of that Kandahar dust. 'Cause I'm glad you called. I have something to tell you, too.'

*

Until now, Francesca had kept Ricky Fowler's killing to himself. He figured Weston and Rodriguez had their platoon under control. Stan had enough to worry about. But with this douche Coleman Young making trouble, he figured he had to tell.

'My Strykers may have a problem,' Francesca explained.

'Wish you'd told me before,' Stan said, when he was finished.

'Didn't want to bother you.'

'Didn't want to mess up the gravy train, you mean. This guy Fowler, anybody actively looking into his death?'

'Weston says no.'

'You believe him.'

'I do. Weston even called Fowler's mom and dad, talked to them for a while, told them what a great guy their son was. Checking to see if he would get any vibe from them that they were making noise, calling the battalion to complain that they didn't understand what had happened. Because Fowler was real close with his folks. But Weston said when he was done, he was sure they weren't doing anything like that.'

'I'm glad he checked.'

'Didn't really surprise me.' In Francesca's experience, the families of the dead went one way or the other. Some wanted to know every last detail, to *understand*, whatever that meant, get *closure*, whatever that meant. But most, especially the Southerners and Texans and the ones from small towns, they didn't want to know. They figured that all the questions in the world weren't going to bring their kids or husbands back. They accepted whatever story the military told them.

'So the family's no problem. And the sergeant, Young, hasn't gone to CID or the battalion chaplain or anybody else?'

'Not as far as Weston knows, and I think he'd hear. Either

formally or somebody would tap him on the shoulder and tell him, "Watch out."'

'So it's just these letters Coleman sent, or claims he sent. Protecting himself.'

'Correct. After it happened, I told Weston to make Young a deal, send him here for the rest of the tour. But Young said no. Fowler was his buddy. It's like he's too scared to do anything about it, but he can't let it go either.'

'I can see that.'

'But since then, Weston called me, asked me if I'd take care of it.'

'Not very sporting of them.'

Every so often, Stan got on with that kind of nonsense, like he was the second coming of James Bond. 'They think I can do it, no muss, no fuss.'

'Can you?'

'Obviously I can't use my rifle. Would look a little strange if an American soldier got taken down with a .50 cal. I'll have to get a Dragunov from somewhere—'

'I can handle that.' The Dragunov was a long-range Russian rifle that Taliban snipers favored.

'You can?'

'I think so.'

'That would be handy. Sooner you set it up, the better. No way will I be as accurate on it as on the Barrett. But it would help to have a couple chances to practice. Plus Young's going to be wearing Kevlar and a helmet every time he goes outside the wire. Inside, too, for all I know. Weston said he's being real careful. And I'm only gonna get one shot. I miss, he goes running to his battalion commander, CID, whoever. They'll pay more attention to him if he's got a round stuck in his Kevlar. Even best case, it's a clean kill, it looks weird, he's telling people his own guys are threatening him. Then he gets hit.'

'Is there any way that he could know your name?'

'Not unless Weston or Rodriguez told him. And they wouldn't. They know better.'

'Then here's what I think. Forget Young, unless he seems to know you. Sit tight. Those Stryker units will be home in two, two and a half months. After that, Young can squawk all he likes. He's got no evidence. Not even enough for CID to open an investigation. And if Weston and Rodriguez get brought in somehow, they just have to keep their mouths shut. They smart enough to do that?'

'No doubt.'

'That's it then. And Young must have figured that, too, because if he thought he could get an investigation opened, he'd try.'

'All right. I'll tell them.'

'And tell them not to freelance, in case they have any ideas.'

Francesca nodded. 'Something else I wanted to ask. We gonna keep this going after those guys leave?'

Stan grunted, like he hadn't given the question much thought. Which surprised Francesca. Stan was making more money than anyone. 'Your tour's up, too,' he said after a few seconds.

'Sniping, yeah, but I can stay in if I like.'

'Didn't know you were thinking that way.'

'The money's right. And it's not like I got anything waiting at home.'

'Then maybe we will.'

They made their way around the northern perimeter and now turned left, to the west side of the base. Dirt fields stretched for miles. In the distance, a farmer grazed goats on scrub and garbage. The airfield didn't have blast walls here, only barbed wire and a few warning signs. The apparent lack of security was deceptive. Plastic alarm wires snaked through the fence, and a blimp overhead watched the fields. Anyone who tried to sneak close would be seen long before he reached the perimeter. Cutting the fence would trigger an immediate alarm from the quick-reaction force at the northwest corner of the base, a platoon of Humvees armed with .50 cal machine guns. Even suicide bombers needed better odds than that.

'Fortress Kandahar,' Francesca said.

'We should just spread the perimeter mile by mile until it goes all the way to the borders, kick all the Afghans out. You know a guy named John Wells?'

'The name, sure.' Wells was legendary in the Special Forces. He'd been involved in a couple ops so highly classified that they were rumor even among the Tier One guys. Word was that one involved a nuclear weapon.

'Wells is sniffing around our thing.'

'How do you know?'

'Because he came to Kabul asking about it. He freelances now, thinks he's some kind of do-gooder, and he got interested in this.'

Francesca didn't get why John Wells would care about a few kilos of heroin. He suspected Stan wasn't giving him the full story, but he didn't want to push. 'So what do we do about it?'

'For now, nothing. I think he's been chasing the source, but that won't do him any good. Guy's never met me. I've used a cutout. You're the only one who knows my real name.'

'I'm honored. What about the cutout?'

'I'll worry about him. But I wanted to let you know about Wells. If you hear his name, see him sniffing around, assume it's not a coincidence.'

'But why would I see him around? How could he get to me?'

'I don't think he can. But if he does.'

They had circled back to the southern side of the base, just a couple hundred feet from the heavily fortified headquarters of Regional Command South, which oversaw the war in Kandahar province. 'I'll hop here,' Stan said.

'Good to see you. Next time I'm going to make you have that coffee, okay?'

'Okay.'

Francesca pulled over. 'You know what we are, Stan? Shadows. Come and go as we like, do what we like, and the normals can't touch us.'

'Be safe, Danny.'

'You, too, my man.' They bumped fists and Stan walked away.

John Wells, Francesca thought. Ever since Alders had made fun of him at lunch, he'd been keeping his high-pitched giggle under control. Now he let it loose. *John Wells*. This whole deal had just gotten a lot more interesting. Enough Talibs in manjamas. Finally, Francesca would have the chance to play against a man worthy of his respect.

Stan made sure that Francesca's pickup truck had disappeared before he headed to the RC South headquarters gate. He'd almost blown it. He should have known Francesca would ask whether he wanted to keep smuggling after the Strykers left. Francesca was making a lot of money. Plus he liked the game. He was getting weird, all that talk about shadows and normals.

So no more mistakes. Stan had worked too hard, come too far. He'd convinced Amadullah of his sincerity. In a few days, he would cement that trust. Then he'd be only one step away from his true and final goal, the one that he'd told nobody else, not even Francesca. The revenge that belonged to him, and him alone.

SIXTEEN

Chicago

After meeting Ryker, Shafer did what he did best. He sped back to Langley and spent the night mining databases as ferociously as a prospector who'd glimpsed a vein of pure gold. By noon, he'd tracked down addresses and arrests and immigration records for Miller. Curiously, Miller's American passport showed only three visits to Pakistan in five years. Shafer figured Miller had another passport, probably Pakistani, probably in his birth name. He'd use that for trips to Pakistan to save himself trouble at American immigration.

Since the NSA had *everything*, it probably had Miller's Pakistani passport records in a database somewhere. But no one had bothered matching up the files. Miller wasn't an agent and he wasn't a terrorist. He was a sleazebag occasional. The CIA had plenty of those. Ergo, no one paid much attention to him or his travels. Until now.

Flight records showed that Miller had left Chicago for Dubai about a month before. He was scheduled to return to O'Hare two weeks later, with a one-day stopover at Heathrow. His usual pattern. Miller often stayed in London on his way home from Dubai. Maybe he had an English girlfriend.

This time, his plans changed. Miller never got on the London–Chicago flight. He turned around, went back to Dubai and then Quetta. He was so eager to reach Pakistan that he used his American passport the whole way instead of taking the time to book flights under different names. Shafer didn't see any clues to explain Miller's haste. His Chicago cell phone didn't have the answer. Miller seemed to use it exclusively to order takeout and call home. No doubt Miller had other cell phones in Dubai and Pakistan. And the mole would have insisted on burner phones and single-use e-mail accounts. Short of using human couriers, constantly shifting numbers and e-mail addresses was the best way to stay ahead of the NSA. Though even couriers had risks, as Osama bin Laden had learned.

After arriving in Quetta, Miller disappeared. He wasn't using his credit cards or phone. Maybe Amadullah was holding him captive in Muslim Bagh. Maybe he'd gone over the border into Afghanistan. Maybe he'd gone back to Dubai on still another passport. Shafer wasn't too worried about him. *The guy's a cockroach*, Ryker had said. *A survivor. He'll still be here when you and I are sucking down dust.*

Shafer called Wells to fill him in, tell him to head for Dubai.

'You sure this is the guy?'

'My source thinks so. And I've confirmed the arrests, the name change, everything.'

'I'm sick of Kandahar anyway.'

'You get anything yet?'

'It's tough to sit in the mess, start asking guys if they know about big-time heroin dealing. Kind of a conversation stopper.'

'So that's a no.'

'That's a no.'

'Miller can take us straight to the mole if we find him.'

'So you want me to go to Dubai. I've got the perfect cover.'

'You're about to make a joke, aren't you, John? I can tell because you get all out of breath, like it's your first time on a bike with no training wheels.'

'Jehovah's Witness.'

'That's funny.'

'I'll go knock on his door. See if anybody's home.'

'I want more than that.' Shafer explained.

'B-and-Es aren't my specialty.'

'The DST boys have amazing gear now. Idiot-proof.'

'I appreciate the vote of confidence.'

'Book a room tomorrow night at the Grosvenor House under the Saudi passport. I'll FedEx you what you need.'

'And what about Chicago? Who's going to handle that?'

'Me.'

'You.'

'I can talk to a drug dealer's wife without you backing me up.'

'It's foolish, Ellis.'

'Call me from Dubai.'

It was nearly eight p.m. when Shafer shipped Wells the equipment he'd promised. He drove home, booked the night's last flight to O'Hare. He packed a garment bag with his best blue suit. Then went to the safe in his basement to grab the FBI identification that he wasn't supposed to have and the 9-millimeter he never used. He had just opened the safe when he heard footsteps on the stairs. He turned—

And saw his wife. Who wasn't smiling. 'What are you doing?'

'I thought tonight was your book club.'

'Tomorrow.' She was standing at the foot of the stairs, holding Costco bags she hadn't even put down. He went to her and kissed her and took the groceries.

'What are you doing?' she said again.

'I have to go to Chicago. Be back tomorrow.'

Normally that would have been enough for her, but this time she folded her arms and looked at the safe. 'Why do you need that?'

'I'm not even gonna load it.'

'You're carrying a gun with no bullets.'

'It's a prop.'

'Ellis, you're too old for this. You think it's cute, these little adventures—'

'I'll be fine. I have to go. Flight leaves in an hour.'

'You're behaving like a *child*, Ellis.'

He couldn't even meet her eyes. 'Forget it, will you.'

'At least load it. If you're gonna carry it, load it.'

The next morning Shafer parked his rental car, a dark blue Chevy Malibu, at a hydrant outside a tidy brick house on the Near North Side, practically in the shadow of the John Hancock Tower. David Miller had done well for himself. Real estate records showed he'd paid eight hundred and forty-five thousand dollars for the place five years before, an all-cash deal. Shafer slipped an FBI placard on the dash, smoothed out his suit, tucked his pistol in his shoulder holster.

A television played faintly upstairs. Shafer knocked heavily on the front door, peeking through a frosted window. The door opened to reveal a heavy black man wearing a White Sox T-shirt and jeans. Asha Miller was keeping busy.

The guy folded his arms across his gut, which was nearly as big as Shafer's body. 'Help you?' His voice was high, almost Tyson-esque. He didn't look like he wanted to be particularly helpful.

'I'm with the FBI.' Shafer flashed his badge. 'I'd like to talk to Mrs Miller.'

'Who is it?' a woman yelled from upstairs, over the *Today* show. 'Tell him we don't want any.'

'Man claiming to be an FBI agent. By himself, though.' To Shafer: 'You boys usually travel in pairs. Like roaches.'

'I'm here about Daood Maktani,' Shafer shouted up the stairs.

'Nobody here by that name,' the man said.

The television muted. The man opened the door and Shafer glimpsed Asha Miller walking down the stairs, a pretty black woman, but tending toward fat. Oprah had ruined a whole generation, Shafer thought.

'Shoo, Bernard,' she said.

'Look at him. He look like an FBI agent to you?'

'He knows that name, he is FBI. Federal something anyway. Now shoo.'

Bernard trudged down the hall. 'I'll make coffee,' he said over his shoulder. Keeping his dignity. Asha took his place at the door and looked at Shafer. She had merry eyes. Or maybe she was just amused by the sight of him in his blue suit.

'What's your name, Mr FBI?'

'Ellis Shafer. May I come in?'

'You may not. Unless you have a warrant. First thing Daood taught me.'

'Daood went to Dubai a month ago.'

She didn't ask how he knew.

'He hasn't come back.'

'That a question?'

'When was the last time you heard from him?'

She sighed. 'Somebody arrest him again?'

'I don't know. But I think he's in trouble. And you didn't answer me.'

'He's always in trouble, always gets out. The last I heard from him was in London.'

'Two weeks ago.'

'Sounds about right. He said something had happened and he had to go back to Dubai.'

'Do you know how he made his money?'

'This is how it went. We were together when he got arrested the first time, and I stuck by him, and he liked that. Didn't expect it, I think. Couple years later, we got married. Maybe 'cause I told him I was leaving him if he didn't. Maybe so he could be sure I couldn't testify against him. Maybe he just liked the idea of getting married. It was an excuse for a party and he loves parties. But I was never under any illusions that I was his only woman. That wasn't his style.'

'So you knew?'

'Please. Man never had a job in his life, and look at this house. But I figured he was playing both sides. He was too lucky for too long in terms of not getting arrested. Nobody's that lucky. Plus every so often, I'd see cars at that same hydrant you parked at. American cars with tinted windows and two men in suits inside. Never came to the house, never knocked on the door, just sat and watched.'

'Letting you know they knew.'

'Something like that. And also that's just how David is. Playing both sides, he thinks that's style.'

'I understand.'

She smiled. 'Bet you grew up just that way. So, yes, I knew that he wasn't any Boy Scout, but I never asked any details.'

'Anything change the last year or so?'

She shifted her weight and some of her spirit creaked out. 'You out to get him?'

'No. Truth? I think he got into something deep and I might be able to help.'

She looked him over, weighing his sincerity. Finally, she

nodded. 'I think you're telling at least half the truth. But it don't matter, because I don't know anything. Just recently he seemed more stressed out. Drinking more, too. But I don't know why.'

'He ever mention anyone in particular from the FBI, the DEA, the CIA? Anyone leaning on him?'

She shook her head.

'Could he have left anything important on a computer here?'

'Not here. He was careful about that.'

'You have a phone number for him? E-mail?'

She gave him both. Shafer was happy to hear that the cell wasn't the one he'd already found. But he sensed she was keeping something back. 'What aren't you telling me?'

'When I said I hadn't heard from him since London. That's true, I mean actually hearing his voice. But about a week ago, he e-mailed. Said he was in Pakistan and might be there awhile, and he didn't know when he'd be back and he wanted to tell me he loved me. Wasn't like him to write that. Like he wanted me to understand that he was in deep.'

'Thank you. You get anything from him, please let me know.' Shafer handed her his card.

'Long as you promise to do the same.' She lowered her voice. 'I know what you're thinking about Bernard, but if you look close, you'll see he's just a big old queen who keeps me company when David's not here. My husband's not a one-woman man, but I'm stuck with him and him alone.'

Everybody overshares these days, Shafer thought. He blamed Oprah for that, too. 'Call me anytime, day or night,' he said, and backed away from the door.

SEVENTEEN

Dubai

Wells was happy to leave Kandahar Air Field. Even in war zones, the military needed big, well-defended bases to house its planes, coms networks, all the stuff that made the guys on the front lines so effective. But the guys at KAF sometimes seemed to forget that their job was supporting the soldiers outside the wire, not the other way around. Massive resources went into making sure that the airfield's forty thousand inhabitants had plenty of creature comforts. Meanwhile, some infantry units lacked basics like showers.

KAF's size was part of the problem. The people who worked there could be forgiven for forgetting that Afghanistan even existed. Almost no Afghans lived or worked on the base. The Taliban fired rockets blindly from the ugly brown mountain that loomed over the base to the north, but they rarely did much damage. Like bases back home, KAF even had a full complement of military police officers who wrote parking tickets and enforced other petty regulations, like making soldiers wear reflective belts after dark.

The Air Force didn't run flights from Kandahar to Dubai, so Wells booked a ticket on Gryphon Air, a Pentagon-approved charter service. Most of Gryphon's passengers worked for DynCorp, a contracting company that filled thousands of jobs at Kandahar.

The contractors at Kandahar split into two broad groups. The English-speaking ones were mostly ex-military, soldiers and Marines who'd cultivated special skills like training bomb-sniffing dogs. When their contracts expired, they jumped to private contracting companies that paid a hundred and fifty thousand or more a year.

'Same job, but three times the money and a tenth the risk,' one said to Wells over lunch at the giant Kandahar mess hall called Luxembourg. 'PMCs' – private military contractors – 'never go outside the wire. No such thing as desertion or dereliction of duty. No brig. Worst they can do is fire you and tell you they won't pay. Plus I got no sergeants telling me what to wear or how to salute or what time to be in bed. Course, back when I was wearing the uniform, I bitched about the contractors, said they all were useless as tits on a bull.'

'You feel differently now.'

'I do and I don't. Not saying I work like a Joe. But how was I gonna turn this deal down? Hundred and sixty K. My wife doesn't work and we got three kids. I put in my time, spent five years getting shot at. Fair's fair. I don't make the rules.'

Wells had had several similar conversations. He figured that the contractors were honest guys who felt guilty about their windfall. So they overexplained, justified themselves. Wells wanted to tell them not to worry, that Alex Rodriguez got paid as much to play one baseball game as they did in a year. But he thought that kind of reassurance would just piss them off, so he kept his mouth shut.

The second set of contractors didn't talk to Wells. They hardly spoke English. They were the Filipinos and Indians who cooked and scrubbed and took out the trash, the scut work that the United States military no longer did for itself. Wells supposed that they freed up American soldiers to fight. They weren't making a hundred and fifty thousand a year, either, so they might even have been cost-effective.

Still he found their presence disconcerting. They made Kandahar feel like an old-school colonial occupation. Brown men taking care of white men who were fighting other brown men.

The Gryphon jet flew southwest over the empty desert that dominated southern Kandahar province and then swung over Pakistan and the Persian Gulf. It landed in late afternoon at Dubai's massive airport. Wells grabbed his bag and joined the parade of unshaven contractors thirsting for Dubai's bars.

But along the way to the immigration hall he disappeared into a men's room. When he walked out, he was wearing a *dishdasha* and *thobe*. Once again he was Jalal Haq, Saudi adventurer. Wells had considered entering Dubai on his real passport, setting a lure to see who at the agency was tracking his moves. He and Shafer decided that the plan had too much risk. They couldn't be certain of finding whoever was tracing him. Better for Wells to use the invisible Saudi passport.

Saudis were favored travelers in Dubai. The immigration agent barely bothered to look at Wells before waving him through. Two minutes later, he stood in the humble-jumble at the front of the airport and listened to deals being made in English and Arabic and a dozen other languages. Pakistani taxi drivers and Indian hotel hawkers competed for business from Russian tourists in velour sweat suits. Dubai was a long way from anywhere, a six-hour flight from Europe and Russia, twelve from the United States. Despite the jet lag, everyone seemed excited.

By rights, Wells should have disliked Dubai. As much as anywhere in the world, the city represented the triumph of empty consumer culture. Yet he found the city strangely compelling. It had no natural advantages. Its weather was miserable most of the year. It lay thousands of miles from the major cities of Europe and Asia. It didn't have a good natural harbor. Unlike the rest of the region, it didn't even have oil. Yet since the 1980s, Dubai had grown as fast as anywhere on earth, sprouting thousand-foot-high sand castles built with cheap labor and cheaper money.

Americans didn't have a good word for cities like Dubai, or the buccaneers who made and lost fortunes in them. The English did: *flash*. Flash was the shiny toy that broke the day after its warranty expired. Flash was the drunk buying rounds for everyone with a credit card a buck short of its limit. Flash was the late-night investment guru promising to give up the stock market's secrets at a $799 weekend seminar. Act now and save $100.

At their worst, flash men carved misery into the lives around them. They lived high and skipped town, leaving behind thousand-dollar suits and unpaid child support. But mostly they meant no harm. Mostly they were lazy dreamers who couldn't multiply or divide any better than their customers. Every so often, almost by accident, they came up with something great. As they had in Dubai with the Burj Khalifa, which Wells saw from the cab taking him to his hotel.

The Burj was the tallest skyscraper ever built, a half mile high, an incredible feat of engineering. To withstand the desert winds, the Burj was built of a dozen rounded towers that buttressed one another as they rose. One by one the supporting towers fell away until only the tallest remained, impossibly long, a fingerclaw puncturing the sky. Most of the Burj was empty, and as a business venture the tower was no doubt a disaster. But who cared? Like Notre Dame or the Hoover Dam or the Great Wall, the Burj would awe visitors long after its architects were gone. It was a hundred-and-fifty-story monument to flash, with an almost magnetic pull. Wells stared at it until lesser skyscrapers nearer the highway blocked his view. 'Have you been to it?' he asked his driver.

'Not me, no. Very expensive. One hundred dirhams.' About twenty-five dollars. 'Also I am afraid of heights.' The driver sounded sheepish. To prove he wasn't a coward, he cut in front of a tanker truck.

The Grosvenor was a five-star hotel, marble and sleek. Wells used one of his Saudi credit cards to take a high-floor suite that overlooked the gulf. Dubai was located on a western-facing shoreline of the Arabian peninsula, so the dusky red glow of the setting sun echoed in the waters of the gulf.

Wells wondered what Shafer was doing in Chicago, ten time zones behind. Probably about to knock on Asha Miller's door. Wells hoped he didn't get himself in trouble. He supposed Shafer qualified as his best friend these days. An atheist Jew and a Christian turned Muslim. But Wells trusted Shafer as deeply as he'd ever trusted anyone. He had lied to Shafer over the years, and Shafer had done the same to him. But never out of malice, on either side. Shafer had his back. Wells wondered whether he could ever build similar trust with Anne, if he had the strength to open himself to her that way.

In Dubai, the calls to prayer sounded more quietly than in most Muslim cities. The hotels and nightclubs didn't want to remind Western tourists that Dubai wasn't really Las Vegas East, that a different set of laws applied. Even so, as the sun descended into the gulf, Wells heard faint calls for the *Maghrib*. He knelt before the sunset – for Mecca was almost straight west of Dubai – and lowered his head. He prayed to an Allah who might accept him and Shafer and Anne alike, for forgiveness for the blood he had shed and would shed again. His more orthodox brothers might find his prayers wanting. But in the end only Allah could judge. And He was keeping His thoughts about Wells – and everything else – to Himself.

After his prayers, Wells showered, brushed his teeth, opened the FedEx box that the concierge had given him. He found a black leather carrying bag with a shoulder strap. Anne would have called it a man purse. The thought made Wells smile. The bag held what looked like the leftovers from an estate sale: a flash drive, a Zippo lighter, two garage door openers, two strips of white plastic, two handkerchiefs, a flat gray rock, high-resolution satellite photos of David Miller's house in Dubai, and a credit card-size Sony camera. Only the camera and the photos were what they appeared to be. Everything else came from the basement labs at Langley, the Directorate of Science and Technology.

When Wells trained at the Farm, these toys hadn't existed. He needed to give them a dry run. He looked through the online Dubai real estate listings until he found a target. Then he called the Avis office in the Grosvenor's lobby and rented a Toyota. Nothing fancy. Nothing memorable.

He drove east through the Dubai night, away from sky-scrapers on the coast, toward the industrial neighborhoods near the airport. The roads stayed fantastically wide, eight- and ten-lane boulevards, but the traffic steadily lightened. Wells saw a sign for 'Dubai Oasis Super East' and turned right onto a long, curving boulevard. Suddenly he entered a ghost city.

Beginning in 2008, developers abandoned housing projects all over Dubai, especially in the unsexy neighborhoods far from the gulf. These developments were the tinsel side of flash, paid for with 100 percent borrowed money. Now the banks had stopped lending, and these half-built houses literally could not be given away. Finishing them would cost more than any buyer would pay. They sat empty, waiting for cheap money to start flowing again, or the desert to retake them.

The boulevard narrowed and then turned left into a cul-de-sac. Eight lanes into none. Urban design at its worst. One finished house and three shells were scattered around the teardrop. Halfway down the block, a single street lamp leaned drunkenly over the asphalt. The winds had tilted it, or the summer heat had buckled its base. Or both. To the east, helicopters fluttered around the Burj Khalifa. But the cul-de-sac occupied another universe, postapocalyptic in its desolation. Wells half expected to see a sentient robot scuttling by.

He parked outside the wire fence protecting the lone finished house. 'No Trespassing/Alarmed Response,' signs warned in Arabic and English. Wells pulled himself over and trotted for the house. The front door had two locks, a dead bolt up high and a standard knob below. Inside, a red light blinked on an alarm box.

Wells turned the door handle. Locked. As he'd hoped.

He flipped open the Zippo lighter Shafer had sent him. Where the metal cage around the wick should have been, the lighter had a notch that looked like a USB port. Wells slipped the head of the flash drive into the port. Then he pulled off the plastic casing at the back of the drive, revealing two narrow metal picks with oddly shaped tips. When Wells plugged the flash drive into the Zippo, a light on the side of the drive blinked green.

Wells lined up the tips of the picks with the deadbolt's keyhole. He pushed a tiny button next to the light, and the picks slid into the keyhole. Metal scraped on metal inside the lock.

Then the flash drive made a quarter turn sideways, and the deadbolt slid back with a solid thwack.

Wells repeated the procedure with the bottom lock. He reached for the handle and the door opened smoothly. Wells stepped inside, let his eyes adjust. The rooms were empty. The house was hot and stale and stank of varnish and something sharp, maybe mold. The windows and doors hadn't been opened in years, but grit and sand covered the floors.

Ten seconds after Wells walked in, the alarm beeped frantically, as if it were guarding a nuclear weapon, not an empty house. Wells pulled out the device that looked like a garage door opener, a black plastic box with a single black button. He peeled a plastic sheet on the box's back, revealing a sticky adhesive, and pressed it on the wall next to the alarm system. He pushed the button on the front.

Shafer had promised him that the device would beat any standard household alarm. Something about a short-range electromagnetic pulse powerful enough to disrupt circuits. The pulse caused the software inside the alarm to run very slowly. An alarm that normally sounded thirty seconds after a break-in would instead need an hour or more to go off.

'Just make sure you give the thing a couple of feet when it's on.'

'Why?'

'Just make sure.'

So Wells pressed the button and stepped away. The response was immediate and gratifying. The alarm no longer warned of the end of the world. Now it sounded like a heart monitor, with long pauses and dignified single beeps. Incredible. Wells walked through the empty rooms for a few minutes. The house was nearly finished. The bathrooms even had sinks, though when Wells turned the taps he heard only a faint hiss.

He took one final look and walked out, grabbing the alarm

disruptor. The device did have one flaw. It stopped working once it was removed. An operative who used it had to pull it and run, or leave it and prove that he wasn't an ordinary thief. But the advantage the device offered was worth the trouble. The next time he came home, Wells wanted to meet the engineers who'd built it – and the lock picker.

A half hour later, he was driving through the neighbourhood where Miller lived. He didn't plan to hit Miller's house this night, but he wanted to case it. The technology was new, but the fundamentals of surveillance hadn't changed.

'Always see the target before you make your move,' Guy Raviv, Wells's favorite teacher, had told Wells and the other eager beavers in his training class at the Farm. Raviv was dead now, and the class a lifetime away. 'If you're not sure about something, go back again. Once. No more. You don't want them wondering who you are before you get there. And never spend more than fifteen minutes inside, whether it's a home or an office. Five is preferable. Ten is trouble. Fifteen is the limit. People turn around, double-check that they haven't left the air-conditioning on. Janitors change their schedules, work the floor you're on instead of the one below you. Time is not your friend on these missions. Never. So do what you came to do, whatever that may be, and get out quick.'

Easier said than done, then and now.

Miller lived in an area called Al Barsha South, closer to the gulf than Wells's last stop. 'Welcome to ABS,' a billboard proclaimed in English. 'A great place to live. An even better investment.' But Al Barsha hadn't escaped the bust. Its streets were named after European landmarks, Hyde Park Street and Trevi Fountain Drive, names that sounded even sillier in Arabic. Most houses were dark. On one lot, a blue tarp flapped over a

Caterpillar earthmover, its treads sinking into the earth. A fence and 'No Trespassing' signs blocked off an unfinished playground, complete with a slide that didn't reach the ground, a half-remembered dream. East of the playground, the only evidence of life came from the distant headlights along the outer Dubai ring road.

Miller lived in Al Barsha's wealthier western end, which had been built first and avoided the crash. Here, eight-foot walls protected concrete mansions. Miller's house stood two stories tall and nearly filled its lot. The satellite photos from Shafer revealed that it had a small oval pool in its backyard, a bright blue tear. In Dubai, as in Beverly Hills, pools were closer to a necessity than a luxury. Wells rolled by slowly, peering through the bars of the front gate. In their last conversation, Shafer had told him that Miller had a girlfriend, or possibly a second wife, in Dubai.

'You don't know?' Wells said.

'There's some evidence in the records for both. Anyway, it doesn't matter. Point is, figure probably somebody's home. The electric records show use consistent with an occupied house the last few months, even when Miller's in Chicago.'

As usual, Shafer was right. As he passed the front gate, Wells heard the rumble of a garage door rising. He tapped the brakes, stopped long enough to glimpse the icy headlights of a luxury sedan inside the garage. Before the gate could swing open, Wells rolled on. At the end of the street, he turned left, onto the eight-lane avenue that connected Al Barsha South with the main Dubai highway. If the car was leaving the neighborhood, it would come this way.

Wells pulled over, put on his hazard lights. He popped the hood and got out and pretended to fiddle with the battery. Ninety seconds later, a Lexus rolled by, nearly blinding Wells with its xenon headlights. A man drove, with a woman in the back. The lights stopped Wells from seeing her clearly. But she was Arab. She wore a long-sleeved gown and a loosely tied head scarf that let her hair flow freely, the uniform of the cultured gulf elite outside Saudi Arabia. The wife/girlfriend. She was having dinner with friends. Getting her nails done. Shopping. The malls in Dubai stayed open late. Wells didn't care, as long as she stayed out at least a half hour.

He quickly made a U-turn and drove back to Miller's house. He grabbed his man purse. In a perfect world, he would have had gloves, pliers, a grappling hook and rope. Maybe a knife or pistol. But Wells couldn't pass up this chance to get inside. Once the woman got back, he didn't know when she'd leave again. A stakeout would be difficult and conspicuous in this neighborhood. Anyway, Wells wasn't too worried about leaving evidence. Let the Dubai police dust all they liked. Jalal Haq hadn't been fingerprinted at immigration.

A door was notched in the concrete wall beside the driveway gate. It had a simple knob lock that Wells thought the picker would handle with ease. He reached for the buzzer to check that no one was home – and stopped as a car turned onto the road. It was a white Nissan sedan with a blue light bar across its roof. Neat Arabic script along the side of the car proclaimed, 'Al Barsha Private Security.'

Wells willed the Nissan to drive by. Instead, it pulled over beside him. The driver's window slid down. '*Salaam aleikum.* Excuse me, sir.' Wells stepped toward the car. Two men in blue uniforms sat in front. They had the dark skin of men from the Indian subcontinent. Wells decided being aggressive was the best play. Saudis demanded deference, especially from anyone from Pakistan or India.

'What do you want?'

'May we see your identification, sir?'

'Is this good enough for you?' Wells pushed his Saudi passport through the window.

The driver paged through it. 'Mr Haq, sir – is this house yours?'

'*You're* questioning *me*? I could buy this whole street if I wanted. Buy you, too, and put you in a suitcase and send you home tomorrow. Would you like that?'

The driver glanced at the other guard and back at Wells. 'Sir. I don't mean to disturb you.' His voice quavered a little. 'We received a call that a strange car was driving around the area—'

'You speak Arabic like a dog. My language. You mangle it. And it's not a strange car, it's *my* car, and these people are friends of mine, which is why I have their key. Please, go ahead, call the police.'

'There's no need—'

'No, perhaps you should. Real Emirati police. Let them see the way you treat Saudis. They'll be impressed.'

'We're sorry to have bothered you.' The guard handed over his passport. Wells snatched it back.

'You should be.'

But they didn't leave. As Wells went back to the gate, he realized he would have to open it while they watched. The passport and his fit had cowed them, but they obviously had to make a report. The longer he waited, the stranger his story would seem. They would wonder why he hadn't parked inside. He couldn't risk buzzing either. He'd told them he had the key, so why would he buzz? No, he'd just have to pick the lock and walk in. The house should be empty. The woman and her driver were gone. If Miller happened to be home, Wells would be happy to find him.

Wells stood at the gate, so his body blocked the cops' view of the keyhole. He took the picker from his pocket and lined it up with the hole. Three seconds later, the gate was open. The guards couldn't have seen what he'd done.

Wells walked into the yard and slammed the gate. At the front door, he saw an alarm, its light flashing green. A lucky break. He wouldn't have to fiddle with the disruptor.

He heard footsteps and realized too late that he hadn't been lucky at all. The alarm was off because someone was inside. Probably a housekeeper. Wells should have known. In a neighborhood like this, full-time housekeepers were practically mandatory. She'd heard him and was coming to investigate. He checked the doorknob. It was unlocked. He opened it, stepped in.

A woman stood on the staircase that rose from the front hallway. She was dark skinned and almond eyed. Ethiopian or Somali. She wore sensible black shoes and a white uniform that reached her ankles. She screamed and he ran up the stairs for her. She turned and took a step and tripped and he grabbed her before she fell. She punched at him wildly, like a child, but he wrapped his forearm over her mouth and pulled her down the stairs.

At the bottom of the stairs, he turned and dragged her down the first-floor hallway. The floor was polished marble and didn't give her much purchase. She bit at him, her teeth scraping through his robe. He handled her roughly, squeezing her wrists, trying to make her understand his strength so she wouldn't resist. He pushed open the first door he saw. A guest bathroom, with a toilet, sink, and fancy pink soap. He dragged her inside and felt her panic increase.

'I won't hurt you,' he said. He spun her so they were face-to-face, shifted his grip so his right hand was over her mouth, pushed her against the wall. Their eyes met and her head vibrated sideways in panic like a metronome on high. He raised a finger to his own lips and then lifted his hand off her mouth. She twisted her head, drew her breath to scream. Again he covered her mouth, her lips pressed wetly against his palm. He put a finger to his lips for the second time. This time, she nodded. He lifted his hand a few inches from her mouth.

'Please, sir,' she said in heavily accented English.

'I'm not going to hurt you.'

'No rape.'

Wells's heart clenched. No wonder she was terrified. 'No rape. I want to . . .' He swung a finger around. 'The mister? Does he have an office?'

'The mister not here.' She shut her mouth as if she realized she'd made a mistake by admitting she was alone.

'I need his office. His papers.'

She shook her head, her face uncomprehending. He grabbed her and turned her so she was facing the wall and reached into his bag for the flex-cuffs – the wide white plastic strips Shafer had sent. She started to scream, and he made a fist and belted her in the side of the head hard enough that her knees sagged. He twisted her arms tight and cuffed her wrists together. He grabbed a handkerchief from the bag, wound it over her mouth, tied it tight. He turned her around and sat her on the toilet. Their eyes met and her mouth worked on the kerchief. She couldn't speak, but her eyes told him what she thought of him.

I'm doing the right thing. I'm one of the good guys. One day you'll thank me. Someday we'll look back on this and it will all seem funny. Springsteen. Maybe he really was losing it. He'd have plenty of time to hate himself. Not now, though. Now he had to get on with the search.

He went to a knee beside her and pulled back her right ankle and used the second flex-cuff to tie her leg to the narrow pipe behind the toilet. 'All right,' he said. 'Stay calm.' He left her in the bathroom, took the front stairs two by two. He had to find whatever papers or computers Miller might have left. At least he didn't need to worry about being subtle. Not anymore. Not with the evidence of his home invasion bound and gagged in the bathroom.

He opened doors along the second-floor hallway. Master bedroom, second bedroom, bathroom, closet. At the end of the hall, a locked door. Wells lowered his shoulder and ruined it, splintering the wood, tearing the lock from the frame. Happy for the chance to hit something instead of someone. The room was dustier than the rest of the house. Wells guessed the housekeeper wasn't allowed in here. A shaded window overlooked the pool. A framed photo of the Chicago skyline dominated one wall. On a coffee table, a laptop and a legal pad. Wells grabbed them. He tossed the couch cushions and pulled books off a shelf beside the couch, looking for keys, flash drives. He found a miniature notebook, palm-size with a black leather cover, and grabbed it.

All along, Wells heard the housekeeper thumping like an angry ghost in the bathroom downstairs. He didn't think anyone outside could hear her through the thick concrete walls, but these homes were awfully close. He finished ransacking the room, looked once more through the rooms upstairs. From the bedroom, he grabbed a silver-framed picture of Miller.

Downstairs, he glanced through the kitchen, the dining room, the living room. Nothing. The worst search ever. Barely ten minutes after he'd entered the house, he walked out the front door. Guy Raviv would have been happy about his speed, if nothing else. He left the housekeeper locked up. He wasn't worried about her. He would call the Dubai police in the morning and tell them to check on the place. But the cops were likely to find her long before. The lady of the house would be home in a couple hours. And the housekeeper might be able to beat the flex-cuffs even sooner. She was strong and angry and Wells hadn't bound her very tight.

The private security car was gone when Wells emerged on the street. Good. He would have to leave Dubai on the first flight he could book. He had left a trail that even Mr Magoo could follow. The Dubai police would call the local security guards as soon as they got inside the house. In hours, Jalal Haq would be a wanted man.

So Wells headed for Dubai International. Along the way he made two phone calls, one to Air India, the other to Singapore Airlines. Getting out at this hour was easy. Most long-haul, fully fueled flights took off from Dubai after dark to avoid the desert heat. The airport was as busy at midnight as at noon. Reserving seats was no problem, once Wells explained that he would be happy to buy a first-class full-fare ticket.

At the airport, he dumped the Toyota in a short-term lot and checked into the one a.m. Singapore Airlines flight under his Jalal Haq passport. He headed straight for passport control. He'd left the house barely forty minutes before. Even if the police had already arrived and gotten Jalal Haq's name from the guards, Wells couldn't believe the immigration agents would have it yet. 'You didn't stay long, Mr Haq.' The agent was polite, vaguely puzzled. Nothing more. Dubai was the ultimate stopover. Plenty of visitors stayed only a few hours.

'I'll be back.'

'Please do.' Then Wells was through, down the escalator and onto the moving walkway that ran to Terminal 1. The place was as absurdly diverse as a Coke ad. Two blue-eyed Russian hookers in miniskirts stood next to a half dozen women in full burqa. An African man, tall and thin and ebony dark, towered over three Japanese tourists who were, yes, taking pictures of one another. A cliché in three dimensions.

The police would be looking for a Saudi in a robe. Wells stopped at a duty-free store and bought an overpriced button-down shirt – long-sleeved, to hide the bruises on his arm where the housekeeper had bitten him – and a pair of jeans and reading glasses and a blue baseball cap with the logo of the Burj Dubai. He found a men's room and went back to being John Wells. At a newsstand, he bought a copy of Michael Connelly's newest paperback. A trick from the Farm. Books hid their readers' faces almost as well as newspapers, and were a far less obvious disguise.

He found the gate for his Air India flight to Delhi and presented himself to the agent. 'Name's John Wells. Wanted to double-check my seat. Think it was two-A, but I lost my boarding pass.' The no-nonsense American businessman, skipping pronouns to save time.

'I'm sorry, Mr Wells. You haven't checked in.'

'Sure I did.'

She tapped her keyboard doubtfully. 'I can't find it in the system. But I guess you must have or passport control would have stopped you. No matter. I'll recheck you.'

Wells took his boarding pass and settled in to read Harry Bosch's latest adventures. Connelly was always reliable. A half hour later, he looked up to see three airport police officers walking briskly past. The Singapore flight boarded ten gates down.

Five minutes later the Air India flight opened for boarding. Wells was first in line. As he walked onto the jetway, he heard the terminal's loudspeakers announce, 'Mr Jalal Haq, please report to security. Mr Jalal Haq, please report to security.'

Wells would have to remember for future reference that the Dubai police didn't waste time. Jalal Haq had managed to clear passport control, but he'd have no way to get on a plane. Without the spare passport, Wells would have been stuck. When cops looked over the surveillance videos, they would realize that Jalal had gone into a bathroom and hadn't come out. Meanwhile, though, the police weren't about to shut down one of the world's busiest airports to look for one Saudi who'd tied up a housekeeper.

Delhi was supposedly a fascinating city. Wells didn't care. He checked into the hotel closest to the airport, a Radisson. As soon as the door to his room closed, he booted up Miller's laptop and scanned its files, which consisted mainly of photos of Miller with different women. Plenty of the pictures were what Internet gossip sites called Not Safe for Work. Wells also found spreadsheets and tax returns. For a drug dealer, Miller kept good financial records. Wells didn't see any hint of Miller's drug trafficking or his connection with Thuwani. Of course, he was no expert at recovering hidden files. He would send the laptop to Shafer and hope the Langley geeks could find more.

The miniature black notebook held a handwritten list of figures and dates that stretched back years. Wells guessed he was looking at Miller's record of his drug deals. On the last page of the notebook, Wells found three phone numbers, another crumb for the NSA.

Finally, Wells turned to the legal pad. Its top sheet was blank. Wells wasn't even sure why he'd taken it, except that it had been directly under the laptop. He flipped through it, not expecting anything.

But there it was. About three pages from the end, Miller had written, *Stan???* and an e-mail address. *Real name??? Find him? HOW? Strykers. Dragon. Make a Deal/Treason/Authorized mission? $$$!*

Everywhere else, Miller's handwriting had been careful and precise. Here he'd swiped the words across the page. His desperation was obvious. Wells puzzled over the sheet for a while and then called Shafer. Who answered on the first ring, though it was midnight now in Virginia.

'What are you doing in Delhi?'

Wells didn't ask how Shafer knew the city code for Delhi, much less the country code for India. 'Long story.'

'You all right? Did the stuff work?'

'Yes, but I had some trouble.'

'Anybody die?'

'No.' Wells hesitated.

'Out with it.'

'I had to punch a woman in the head. A civilian in the house.' Wells couldn't bring himself to say *housekeeper*.

'As long as you didn't kill her.'

'I'm comforted to hear you think I'm capable of killing a random woman. How was Chicago?'

'Not much. The wife hasn't heard from him in a while. Besides punching women, did you get anything?'

'His computer. I didn't see anything on it, but I'll send it to you. And I want to fax you something he wrote. There's some kind of code on it.'

'Code.'

'You'll see.'

Ten minutes later, Shafer called back. 'Where's the code?'

'Dragon? Stryker?'

'You never heard of Strykers? Big armored trucks? Badly designed, lots of problems, but the Army bought them and by

God it's going to use them even if they get guys killed. Ring any bells?'

'Now that you mention it.'

'And guess what. The 7th Stryker Brigade Combat Team, also known as Task Force Dragon, is based east of beautiful Kandahar City in Zabul province at Forward Operating Base Jackson. About four thousand soldiers there. Now all you have to do is figure out which of them are big-time heroin smugglers. Don't worry. I'm sure they have a big sign over their cots.'

'Four thousand is better than a hundred thousand,' Wells said. 'What about Daood?'

'You've got ideas on where to find him, I'm open. But I suspect he's up in the mountains with Amadullah, and I think you'd be pushing your luck to go back there.'

'I can't disagree.'

'Plus, the way I read this note, Daood was trying to figure out who was running him just like we are.'

'Stan?'

'There's no one with that first or last name at Kabul station. I checked. And doesn't it strike you as awfully coincidental? Like, Afghani-stan?'

'Nice.'

'Nice. So I'll put the NSA onto the new phone numbers and e-mail addresses you got. But I'm betting they won't go anywhere. Anyway, soon as Miller comes out of the mountains and hears what happened in Dubai and Chicago, he'll know we're looking for him. He'll know the game is almost over. I'll bet he reaches out to us.' Shafer talked fast when he was excited, and he was talking fast now. 'Even if he doesn't, I'll bet we find him pretty damn quick. We have his real name, his bank accounts. We know where he lives.'

'And in the meantime?'

'In the meantime, I'm gonna look at that brigade. Check out its 15-6s and 32s and after-action reports in the files for its tour.' A 15-6 was a military record of an investigation into suspected criminal behavior by a soldier. An Article 32 report was similar, but used for serious crimes, the military counterpart of a grand jury indictment.

'And I'm supposed to go to that base and start asking guys if they know about a massive heroin trafficking ring.'

'You laugh, but I have an idea.' Shafer explained his plan.

'That can't work.'

'You have anything better?'

Wells was silent.

'Then I suggest you get on it.'

'Okay. But there's one thing you're going to need to send for me to have any shot at all. A secret weapon.'

'What secret weapon?'

Wells told him.

'Not bad, John. Maybe you have learned a few things.'

'Still. It'd be nice if we could find David Miller. I bet he can move us up the chain.'

'My concern is that whoever's running him is thinking the same.'

Wells didn't have to ask Shafer what he meant.

EIGHTEEN

Paktika Province, Afghanistan

Roads in Afghanistan came in two categories: bad and worse. The fifty-mile track from Sharan to the Pakistani border belonged in the second group, less a road than a dashed line on a map, washed out and littered with stones big as beach balls.

Down this uncertain path bounced a Ford Ranger, four doors, nearly new, a gift to Afghanistan from the American taxpayer. Amadullah Thuwani drove, David Miller beside him. Amadullah sat low and steered one-handed, fingers draped over the steering wheel. He reminded Miller of a South Side gangbanger. He just needed a Bulls cap tilted low on his forehead and a fat gold chain along with his Rolex. Fortunately, his driving style posed no danger. The Ranger was moving barely twenty miles an hour. Any faster and rocks would tear up the chassis.

Without warning, Amadullah reached across the seat, pinched Miller's cheek like an unfriendly grandfather. 'You're sure this is the way,' he said. They'd been driving for three hours and Amadullah's patience looked to be wearing thin.

'Of course.' Miller wasn't. He wondered what Amadullah would do if they stumbled into an American convoy. As usual, Miller was the only one in the truck who didn't have a weapon.

Come to think of it, he was probably the only adult male in the whole province who didn't have an AK within arm's length.

· The road passed through a loose group of mud-walled compounds, and Miller saw the abandoned schoolhouse Stan had told him to look for. Against its wall, three empty oil barrels were stacked in a pyramid. *Side by side means no meeting*, Stan had said. *Pyramid means keep coming.*

'That's it,' Miller said, nodding at the barrels. 'We're close.'

Five minutes later, Amadullah stopped the Ranger beside a wash of scrubby pine trees. He lowered the windows and killed the engine.

'Now we listen for mosquitoes,' Amadullah said, Talib slang for drones. 'They won't face us like men. They use this science instead.' In Amadullah's mouth, science sounded like a curse. He spit out the window into the dust. Amadullah's son Azim wandered off and took a long piss against a mud wall.

They sat and listened. But the air was still. So was the land, no cars or trucks. Not even any donkey-drawn carts. The mountains in Paktika were shorter than the famous peaks of the Hindu Kush but equally unforgiving, crumbling hills with soil too rocky for farming.

'You see my watch?' Amadullah raised his wrist to show the gold Rolex.

'Are you giving it to me? That famous Pashtun hospitality?'

'If I give it to you, you'll wear it around your neck.'

'Sounds uncomfortable.' Miller knew he should take what Amadullah dished out, but the boasting and threats had worn thin.

'It was a Saudi who gave me this. Many years ago.'

'Osama bin Laden?' The Talibs loved to brag about how they'd fought alongside bin Laden, especially now that he was dead and couldn't contradict them. Osama would have had a million-man army if they were all telling the truth.

'Not Osama. Though I did meet him once. Skinny and full of love for himself. No, this man, when he came here, I had just come back from Kandahar, a very good mission. We bombed Russian tanks, linked the explosives and set them off all at once. The whole road was on fire. Killed four tanks. Boom-boom-boom-*boom*! The wrecks stayed on Highway 1 for a month, and after that the Russians left us alone down there. Thanks be to Allah. Those T-72s had heavy armor all over, but underneath they didn't. Stupid Russians.'

'But the watch.'

'Yes, the watch. So the Saudi came, and we had a feast. And they were calling me the lion of Zhari, that's the western part of Kandahar province. And the Saudi, he said to me, "What can I do for you, lion? I want to be part of this jihad." And I said, "Give me your Rolex."'

Miller could imagine the look on the Saudi's face. 'Not what he was expecting.'

'You know, I can't even remember his name. Probably Abdul. All of the Saudis who came here were named Abdul or Saud or Faisal. The Saudis. They pretend they hate the princes, but they fall to one knee when one passes within ten kilometers.' Amadullah spit again into the dirt.

'So he gave you the watch.'

'Of course he did. He was far from home.'

'What became of him?'

'Only Allah knows. But I still have the watch. My second wife polishes it every week and it still works perfectly. Do you see what I'm telling you?'

Miller saw. The visitors from Saudi Arabia and Russia and the United States came with their gifts. But sooner or later, they left the warriors in these mountains to their business. Amadullah had spent his whole life within a hundred miles of here. He didn't have a passport or a bank account. He'd never seen a skyscraper or flown on an airplane. As far as Miller knew, he couldn't even read or write. Yet he and his people could never be broken, not in this land. Killed, but not broken.

Miller had forgotten most of his single semester at Harold Washington City College, but one class had stuck with him: Philosophy 101. At first he'd done the reading mainly to impress his teacher, this cute white girl from the University of Chicago. He never did work up the guts to ask her out. The U of C might have been on the South Side, but it was in a different universe from his. Anyway, a few weeks into the semester, he'd seen her boyfriend picking her up. But by then he was into the class, and he kept on reading.

He wasn't interested in Plato and the Greeks, debating the mysteries of existence, shadows on the cave wall. No, he liked the political philosophers, the ones who talked about power in the real world, where it came from, how to use it. Especially this English guy, Hobbes: *the life of man, solitary, poore, nasty, brutish, and short.* Amadullah surely felt the same. Or would have, if he'd ever heard of Hobbes.

Miller wondered whether the watch's backstory was bloodier than Amadullah had said, whether the Saudi who'd given it to him had been taken on a mission that didn't have a way out.

'A very nice watch,' Miller said aloud.

'Real gold. Swiss-made.'

'I'm sold.'

They fell silent. Miller found himself intensely conscious of the ticking of the Rolex. Finally, Amadullah muttered, 'Enough.' He shoved a plug of tobacco into his mouth and started up the Ranger. The road rose slowly, following a dry streambed around the flank of a brown mountain, an unpoetic stretch of land, a place to grind through. Behind the mountain, the road forked.

'Left or right?'

'Right.' The marker was reflective tape stuck low on a lightning-scarred tree.

The right fork turned back into the mountain, rising in the shadow of a ridgeline. The pines here were sheltered from the prevailing easterly winds and stood thicker. The road dead-ended at a man-made clearing, the trees cut to stumps. At the far edge, two horses stood riderless, a mare and a gelding, both saddled and tied to a tree. They stamped their hooves and whinnied as the Ranger rolled in. Miller relaxed a little. He'd brought them to the right place.

The CIA officer who called himself Stan had done an extraordinary job of winning Amadullah's trust, Miller thought. A year before, the United States had created a most-wanted list of forty-seven Taliban commanders, including Amadullah. Thirteen of those men were now dead, and seven more captured. Even so, Amadullah had agreed to leave the safety of Muslim Bagh and come to Afghanistan to meet Stan. He was taking an enormous chance. The Americans could have a company of Special Forces operatives waiting.

But Miller understood why Amadullah was taking the risk. Miller had delivered hundreds of thousands of dollars to Amadullah, money Amadullah could use to control his tribe and build a private army. When the Americans left Afghanistan, Amadullah would be ready to govern a province, maybe even bribe his way into a cabinet position. Then Stan had cemented his relationship with Amadullah by tipping him about the Special Forces raid. Amadullah had told Miller earlier today that Stan had been right, that helicopters had raided the farm a few days after their meeting.

Amadullah slung a short-stock AK over his shoulder. 'You've never been here before,' he said to Miller.

'All I know is that we're supposed to follow the path.'

'Then let's follow it. Find this man I've come to see.'

'Father,' Azim said. 'Let me come, too, guard you.'

'You think I need to be guarded from *him*?'

Amadullah walked over to the taller horse, the gelding, and mounted him in a single smooth leap that belied his size. Miller put a hand on the mare's flank. She was skinny and swaybacked, white except for the gray blaze on her chest. She turned her head, fluttered her big lips at him. She seemed friendly enough, but Miller hesitated. He'd never ridden before. The South Side of Chicago wasn't exactly horse country.

'Come on,' Amadullah said.

Miller awkwardly stepped into the stirrup and swung himself over the saddle. The horse swayed. For an unpleasant moment, he thought he might fall. Then he jammed his left foot into the other stirrup and grabbed the reins.

'Not too hard,' Amadullah said. 'She knows what to do if you'll let her.' He turned his horse up the trail. Miller followed. The path rose in short switchbacks. The forest was thicker than Miller expected, and crusty branches whipped at his legs. He ducked low, leaning over the mare's back. To his surprise, he found the ride relaxing. The mare moved at a steady walk and didn't seem to mind carrying him. Miller looked for a trap, broken branches or footprints made by men waiting to capture Amadullah. But the trees appeared undisturbed.

'Your friend planned this meeting well,' Amadullah said. 'Even if I wanted to take him, I couldn't.'

Amadullah was right, Miller realized. The path could be followed only in single file. No doubt it circled around the mountain and reached another clearing where Stan had hidden his own vehicle.

After twenty minutes, they crossed a notch in the ridge, emerging on the mountain's north face. The trees stopped suddenly. Patches of snow were scattered in the shadows of the boulders above them. The trail passed through a rock slide, squeezed between two house-size boulders, and opened onto a stretch of flat rock.

And there he was. The CIA officer who called himself Stan. Miller had expected a big guy, a military type. But Stan was skinny. He wore an olive green North Face jacket and a 9-millimeter Glock strapped to his hip, but no armor or sunglasses or beard. At first, he didn't look like a soldier. More like a lawyer. But his eyes gave him away. They were blue and hard and flat, the eyes of a man who had been shown no mercy and would show none. In Miller's experience, white folk rarely had those eyes. He wondered where Stan had gotten his.

'Amadullah,' he said in Pashtun. 'Meet Stan, the man with the plan.' Like he knew Stan. Like they were friends. Stan didn't blink. Miller hoped he couldn't speak Pashtun. Miller would have a better chance of continuing his unbroken winning streak in the life-versus-death sweepstakes if he could play translator, tweak the conversation to his advantage. He knew that he might never get off this mountain. Even so, he couldn't help feeling weirdly privileged to be here. How often did Talib commanders and CIA operatives meet face-to-face?

Amadullah slid off his horse and offered a hand to Stan. Miller waited for the trap to spring, for soldiers to jump from hidden positions. Instead, the American put his left hand on Amadullah's arm and patted his own chest with his right hand to show his respect. 'Tell him I'm glad he came,' Stan said to Miller in English. 'I know it's dangerous. For both of us. I'm glad he trusted me enough to come.'

So he doesn't know Pashtun. Good. Miller translated.

'I wanted to see you with my own eyes,' Amadullah said.

'Here I am, then. I wish I could have seen your country fifty years ago, when there wasn't a war. When we could have met in your home and feasted like men instead of hiding here like beasts.'

'I don't know anything about you. Not even your name. You know my name and I don't know yours.'

'My name wouldn't mean anything to you. I'm not famous like you.'

'Still I need a name for you.'

'Call me Stan, then.'

Amadullah considered. 'It will do. Tell me why you've done all this, at least. You're a believer?'

'A Muslim?' A gray smile crossed Stan's face. 'No.'

'For money, then?'

'The money's nice, but not the main reason.'

'Then why?'

'I'm tired, that's all.' Stan tipped his head up, directing his explanation to the heavens. 'The agency I work for, it's corrupt. My country, my government, this whole war, corrupt, corrupt, corrupt. We tell you we've got the answers, but we don't have anything at all. We lie to ourselves as much as everyone else. It's time for us to leave here, leave you alone.'

'What do you think,' Amadullah said to Miller, when he'd finished translating. 'Is he telling the truth?'

Miller was surprised Amadullah had asked his opinion. 'I don't know why he'd lie. Maybe there's more to it, but I don't know what it is.'

'Did he say anything to you about it?'

253

'I told you. He treats me as a courier. Nothing more.'

'Ask him, then, why he's brought us here.'

Stan smiled, a real smile this time, when he heard the question. He led them to his horse, a thick-legged white stallion tied to a mulberry tree. A white wool blanket was draped over the horse's flanks. Stan pulled off the blanket with a magician's flourish, revealing twin boxes. They were about six feet long, a foot square, and covered with Cyrillic lettering.

'You know these?'

'SAMs,' Amadullah said in English. 'Russian Stingers.'

'A new model. SA-24s. The Russians started making them about three years ago. The Russian Army says these can take out a Black Hawk, and I think they're right. Especially if I give them some help. You think you might have use for these, Amadullah?'

Amadullah grinned.

'Now I'm going to tell you something,' Stan said. 'The director of the CIA is coming to Afghanistan soon. In only a few days. And American politicians, too. Important ones.'

'You're certain of this.'

'Yes. I'll have their flight schedule.'

Amadullah tapped one of the steel boxes. 'And what do you want for this?'

'Nothing. It's a gift.'

'I don't like that sort of gift. Not even stones are free, we Pashtuns say.'

'All right, Amadullah. If you insist, you can give me something in return. Information. Tell me, have any Americans come to see you recently?'

'Aside from this one, no.' Amadullah spit green spit at Miller's feet.

'Anyone else? Has anyone come to Balochistan? Not necessarily American.'

Amadullah pursed his lips. 'Almost two weeks ago, yes. But he was Saudi. He wanted to help fund the jihad. These men appear every so often. They never make any trouble. If they do, we send them home. One way or another.'

'You're sure he was Saudi.'

'He had a Saudi passport. He came for a day and left.'

Stan reached into his pocket, handed Amadullah an envelope. Amadullah flicked it open with his dirty yellow thumbnail, extracted a photo. He looked it over, grunted in surprise, handed it to Miller.

The photo showed a tall man, handsome and square shouldered. He had wavy brown hair and a crooked smile that was more lips than teeth. Miller didn't recognize him.

'This is the Saudi. How did you know?' Amadullah said.

'That's John Wells. One of our agents.'

'He wasn't American. He couldn't have been. He spoke Arabic, Pashtun. And he killed four men. Troublemakers. Enemies of my tribe.'

'Sounds like Wells. What did you tell him?'

Amadullah chapped a new plug of tobacco in his mouth. *Buying time*, Miller thought. 'Nothing. I didn't trust him.'

'Did you give him any phone numbers or e-mail addresses?'

Amadullah nodded slowly.

'Destroy all those phones. Burn them and then burn the ashes and then drop them off the side of a mountain. Never use any of those e-mails again. Destroy all the computers where you've ever checked those e-mails. And probably plan to move.'

'The computers, too? My new Apple from Dubai.'

'All of it. Did you tell him about me?'

'No.'

'This is important, Amadullah. That we'd been in contact? Anything?'

'No. I swear to Allah.'

'Did you tell him about the drugs?'

'I told him that we sold drugs to Americans, nothing more.'

'Did you tell him what unit?'

'No.'

'Did you tell him about Daood?'

'No, but one of my nephews did.'

'But no,' Miller said in English, pretending to translate. 'I didn't tell him about Daood. And he didn't know anything about Daood.'

Miller did not want Stan to hear that John Wells knew his name. He was as certain of that as he'd ever been of anything.

Stan was quiet. His dead blue eyes shifted from Amadullah to Miller. In the silence, Miller heard the wind rustling down the mountain. 'You think I don't speak Pashtun?' Stan said to Miller. In Pashtun.

Stan pulled his pistol. 'On your knees, hands behind your back.' Miller had looked at pistols before. He'd pulled them himself. An occupational hazard of the drug business. Usually folks were playing, showing off. This time, Miller felt a sick certainty that Stan would blow his brains out. He went to his knees, feeling the stones scrape his shins through the thin fabric of his gown.

'What did you tell Wells about Daood?' Stan said to Amadullah.

In answer, Amadullah swung his rifle toward Stan. Miller kept his breathing steady. *Maybe they'll kill each other and I'll walk away.*

But Stan said, 'I'm no danger to you, Amadullah. We're partners.' He pulled the magazine from his pistol and dropped it. It clapped against the stone and skittered away. 'Just one round in the chamber. For him, if we decide so.'

Amadullah lowered his AK. Miller felt his hope fade.

'What did you tell Wells?' Stan said again.

'Nothing. In truth, my nephew Jaji mentioned Daood to this man Wells, that's all. Then Wells asked me about Daood and I told him it wasn't his business.'

'See,' Miller said. 'Wells doesn't know anything about me. You know how many guys are named Daood in Pakistan?'

Stan turned toward Miller. 'Has he tried to contact you? Don't lie.'

'No. I swear. I promise, if he finds me, I won't say a word. Anyway, Stan, I don't even know your name, your real name, I mean.' Miller was sputtering, trying to find the magic words.

'You promise.'

'I promise. I'm sorry I didn't translate right, I should have told you what Amadullah said, but I thought—'

'I know what you thought. If it makes you feel any better, Daood, I probably would have had to kill you anyway. Now that Amadullah and I have gotten to know each other, you're a liability.'

'Wait. If I hear Wells is after me, I'll let you know. That way, you'll have some warning. Besides, if I disappear, my wives will look for me. I'm more useful to you alive.'

For a moment, Miller thought his offer might work. Then Amadullah walked next to Stan, and together they looked down at Miller. Judges from hell.

'The Russians, when they came here, they had a saying,' Amadullah said. 'Death solves all problems. No man, no problem.'

'From Stalin originally,' Stan said. 'He had another saying, too. The death of one man is a tragedy. The death of one million is a statistic.'

'I think this one wouldn't even be a tragedy.' Amadullah

pointed his AK toward Miller, and Miller knew the time for begging was done. He had to distract them long enough to get to a horse. He looked down, saw two gray rocks on the stone slab in front of him. One was as big as a cell phone, the other an oversize egg. His best chance. Only chance. They could quote Stalin all they liked. Miller would stick with 2Pac.

Wonder how I live with five shots /
Niggas is hard to kill on my block.

'Let me pray, then. Please.' Miller began to murmur the first surah of the Quran. *Bismillahi-rahmani-rahim* . . . All the time he'd spent infiltrating mosques had taught him the words.

He leaned forward, and as his head touched the stony ground he grabbed the rocks, the bigger in his right, the smaller in his left. He came up throwing, aiming a sharp sidearm right that caught Amadullah on his left cheek. Amadullah grunted and twisted away and fired high. The shots cut rock from the slab behind Miller.

With his left hand, Miller threw the smaller rock at Stan's chest. It caught him full in the stomach. Stan grunted and fired low and wide. The round sliced across Miller's right biceps, doing no real damage. Stan cursed and bent over, looking for the magazine he'd dropped.

Miller stood and ran for the big white horse. He didn't want to go back the way he'd come, not with Amadullah's son waiting for him. Anyway, the stallion looked fast.

Behind him he heard the stutter of metal on metal and wondered whether Amadullah's AK had jammed. He heard Amadullah curse and knew it had.

Miller reached the stallion and pulled the reins from the mulberry tree and jumped onto its back. But this horse was taller than the filly he'd ridden, and stronger, and didn't like him. Miller found himself sprawled across the saddle, perpendicular to the stallion's body, the missile boxes pressing into his legs and chest. The horse neighed and tossed his head in the air and stepped sideways.

Miller grabbed the stallion's reins and pulled himself around until he faced forward. Somehow he kicked his right foot and then his left into the stirrups. Blood trickled down his arm onto the stallion's back. Behind him, Miller heard the hard snap of a 9-millimeter magazine being jammed into a pistol.

Miller pushed his legs into the horse's heavy flanks. '*Go!*' he yelled. The stallion took a half step forward and he slapped its neck with his right hand. Miracle of miracles, the stupid thing started to trot. Miller ducked low and slid his arms around the stallion's neck. He wondered whether Stan would shoot his own horse. If he could get out of the clearing, they'd have to chase him—

He heard three shots, loud and close. The stallion whinnied and jumped and reared up. Miller grabbed at the reins and tried to hang on, but his feet slid out of the stirrups and—

He fell, landing on his right shoulder. He heard as much as felt his collarbone crack. When he tried to sit up, a highway of fire flew down his arm and across his chest. He knew he should run, but instead slipped onto his left side and cradled his right arm in his left. Stan grabbed the horse. Amadullah walked over to Miller and grabbed his right arm and tugged. The pain was so intense that Miller couldn't even scream. He must have passed out for a few seconds, because when he opened his eyes Amadullah and Stan stood in front of him. Miller felt the blood trickling down his skull and getting caught in his hair, and he knew he wasn't going anywhere. *Maybe 2Pac wasn't the best role model. Considering he got gunned down when he was twenty-five.* Miller smirked.

Stan knelt down and looked at Miller. Miller raised his head to make eye contact, an effort that sent a shiver of agony through Miller's arm. 'I'm only going to ask you one more time. If I think you're not telling the truth, I'm going to let Amadullah do what he likes with you. Did John Wells ever call you, e-mail you, anything?'

'No. I swear.'

Stan looked at him with those cold blue eyes and finally nodded. Miller bit his tongue so he wouldn't beg, and Stan put his pistol under Miller's chin. Miller closed his eyes and tried to pray again, for real this time. But it was no good. He couldn't remember the words, Arabic wasn't his language and had never been, and he'd never been the churchy type anyway. All he could think of was Biggie Smalls, Tupac Amaru Shakur's Brooklyn twin, standing onstage, a microphone to his mouth, singing, *Biggie Biggie Biggie, can't you see*—

And Stan squeezed the trigger.

NINETEEN

Forward Operating Base Jackson

The soldiers formed neat lines on the airfield, a camouflage rectangle of men and women fifty wide, forty deep. About two thousand soldiers in all, half the brigade. Wells looked them over from a makeshift wooden stage, as Colonel Sean Brown, the base commander, stepped to the podium.

'Soldiers of the 7th Strykers, I have the pleasure of introducing John Wells. I'm sure all of you remember how he stopped the attack on Times Square a few years back. Took a bullet doing it. What you may not know is that Mr Wells spent years in Afghanistan both before and after September eleventh. He knows the Taliban and al-Qaeda from the inside out. He's a hero, plain and simple. Join me in giving a Dragon's roar to Mr Wells.'

Arranging the speech at FOB Jackson proved easy. The Strykers had turned into the Army's ugly and unloved stepchild. Their soldiers ranked last on the list for everything, including celebrity visits. Wells wasn't Carrie Underwood, but he was better than nothing. Colonel Brown was happy to have him.

'Why don't you come in two days?' Brown said. 'We can

have dinner and I'll give you a tactical briefing. You can talk the next afternoon. I'll make sure the whole base shows, bring in the guys from the outposts, too.'

The night before he arrived, Shafer filled him in on the brigade's records. 'They're spread pretty thin, across eastern Kandahar and Zabul. They spend a lot of their time playing defense, having to react.'

'You see any specific platoons or companies that I should focus on?'

'One or two, sure.'

Wells waited for more, but Shafer stayed quiet. 'Gonna tell me which ones?'

'I'd rather not, not right away. Better for you to give this speech fresh.'

'What if the company's on patrol when I get there, doesn't even hear what I'm saying?'

'Let's try it my way first. I have a feeling about this. Let them come to you.'

'And a speech is going to make them do that?'

'If it's the right speech.'

The next afternoon, Wells rolled out of Kandahar with a platoon Colonel Brown sent to pick him up. At the base, Brown waited. He had a ropy neck and a strong handshake. He led Wells to the brigade's Combat Operations Center, a house-size wooden building surrounded by satellite dishes and filled with high-res flat-screen monitors. His office had four laptops and three corkboards covered with maps and Excel spreadsheets and letters to and from the Pentagon. Even without fighting the Taliban, running a brigade was a full-time job.

'Looks like you have a lot of downtime.'

'You should have seen it before we got organized. Coffee?' Brown had an expensive coffeemaker on his desk, well away from the laptops. 'My wife sent me this thing and I've finally learned how to use it.'

Wells nodded, and Brown poured them two cups. 'You came a long way to see us.'

'Hadn't been here in a while. I missed it.'

'And has it changed?'

'I think I have. Maybe I'm just older.'

'I don't think any of us thought this war would last this long.'

'Except the Taliban.'

'True enough. You enjoy your first Stryker ride?'

'I guess you get used to not having windows after a while.'

'Not everybody. I suspect the next generation, if there is a next generation, will have that V-shaped hull that you see on the new trucks, the Cougars and the Gators. Turns out that's a pretty good way to keep guys alive.'

'How's morale?'

'I assume we're just talking. This isn't going into a report.'

Wells nodded.

'It's been a long tour and the guys are ready for it to be over. In just the last two months, we've had three guys evaced to Landstuhl for mental health problems. Lot of home-life stress. At least a hundred divorces.'

'Are you in line with other brigades?'

'Little bit worse. This tour hasn't been great for my career. No way around the fact that these vehicles we ride in are not ideal. Compared to a Humvee, you can argue for them. Okay, they're not as maneuverable, but they're better armored and they carry a whole squad. But the debate isn't Stryker versus Humvee anymore. It's Stryker versus MRAP. MRAPs have as much armor as the Stryker and the safer hull design. And they're more maneuverable than Strykers, too. And cheaper. So all the Stryker really gives us is the chance to put a whole squad in a single vehicle, instead of two or three. Which is nice when we come out under fire. But mostly we don't.'

'And the guys know it.'

'Doesn't take long to figure out. So that's bad for morale. And they hear about the Marines fighting in Helmand and the airborne getting busy in western Kandahar and they know that we've been stuck off to the side driving Highway 1. That said, I believe we've done a solid job here, given the constraints. We've kept the highway clean. We've found tons of caches. We've supported the ANA and ANP.' The Afghan Army and police. 'Have we degraded the Taliban directly as much as I'd like? No, but we've been directed to keep civilian casualties to a minimum and that hurts our ability to engage. We leave the high-value targets to SF, and those guys operate independently.'

'How many confirmed kills does the brigade have?'

'About a hundred fifty since we arrived.'

Wells controlled his surprise. This brigade, which had five thousand soldiers and occupied vital territory, had killed only a hundred and fifty enemy fighters in nine months?

'What about our casualties?'

'Forty-eight American KIA. About a hundred thirty wounded who needed evac out of theater. Some have come back, fortunately.'

They talked for a while about the tactical situation, and then Wells casually asked about drug use in the brigade.

'I hope I don't come across as naive, but I don't think there's much of it,' Brown said. 'I do worry about the ANA. Walk through the Afghan tents on base, you'll smell hash and pot. Nothing we can do. Those guys have their own command-and-control and I'd catch all kinds of crap from my higher-ups if I tried to interfere. No doubt some of my guys have picked up bad habits from the Afghans. But mostly these are solid kids. And the ones going outside the wire, they know it's bad for readiness.'

'So you've never heard about any kind of large-scale smuggling? Opium or heroin?'

'No.' Brown frowned. 'Have you?'

'Not really. Just that a soldier on the plane over mentioned it. And, of course, this province is one big poppy farm.' Wells didn't want to lic, but hc didn't scc an altcrnativc.

Brown looked at his watch. 'Hate to pass on dinner but I have an eight p.m. pretargeting meeting and I have to talk to my XO.'

'So overall what do you think of our chances, Colonel?'

'Not touching that, Mr Wells. Not with a ten-foot pole. I may have gotten stuck commanding the maxivan brigade, but I'm still hoping for a star.' He nodded at the door. 'One of my sergeants will find you a rack.'

Wells saluted. 'Good to meet you, Colonel. Can I ask you one favor?'

'What's that?'

'You won't interrupt me tomorrow when I start to roll.'

'Will it be that bad?'

'Nothing your guys don't already know.'

Brown considered. 'Let's do it. Long as you don't tell anybody to shoot me.'

Now Wells stood on the podium as the soldiers on the airfield cheered. But their applause fell off fast. No doubt they were expecting Wells to mouth the usual clichés. Good. He'd surprise them.

'Thank you, Colonel, for those kind words. You made me sound a lot more heroic than I am.' Pause. 'What the colonel didn't tell you is that it was the New York City police who shot me back in Times Square.' Polite laughter. 'Anyway, I want to thank you all for being here. Now, probably I should give the talk you're expecting. Tell you how you're all heroes, everyone back home is grateful to you. Throw in a bunch of clichés about how you're building a new Asscrackistan.' A murmur went through the crowd as Wells offered the forbidden word.

'But you deserve more than that. You deserve the truth. So first let's talk about the Taliban. We tell folks back home they're brutal, uneducated, hate women, they won't let kids go to school. And that's true. They're bad guys. But then we say the Taliban oppressed the Afghan people and we've set them free. We are saving Afghanistan from the Talibs. And you know the reality is trickier. You know that around here, most people support the insurgents, or at least don't oppose them.'

'Bull,' a soldier near the front yelled.

Brown stepped forward and waved his hands sideways like an umpire calling a runner safe. 'This man's come a long way to talk to us. Let's show some respect.'

'I'm not saying that's true everywhere. Not in Kabul, at least among the educated people who don't want to get whipped for watching television. But plenty of these Pashtuns, they'll happily raise that white Taliban flag. If we hadn't invaded after September eleven, the Taliban would have taken complete control of this country. They had the Northern Alliance pinned practically back to Tajikistan. And you can believe me on that, because I was here. And if we left tomorrow, the Taliban would take over around here pretty damn quick.'

'So what do we do?' the soldier yelled. 'Pull out, let them have their way?'

'I can promise you that won't happen. The powers that be have decided that Afghanistan is too important to be left to the Afghans. I guess we could come in here with a Vietnam-size force, a half million guys, and own the place. But that's not happening either. We don't have the money or the stomach for that war. So we've got limited options. Believe it or not, I think the plan the four-stars have come up with isn't too bad.'

'Can you explain it, then?' somebody yelled from the safety of the middle of the crowd. 'Because I don't get it.' A few soldiers laughed. Wells was glad to see them loosen up.

'Put a bunch of guys into Helmand and Kandahar to kill any Talib dumb enough to come at us. Push their midlevel commanders into the mountains, so the SF can pick them off with minimum civilian casualties. Use drones to get after the high-level guys in Pakistan, make them negotiate with us. And I mean negotiate, not surrender, because they aren't surrendering. Basically get them to see that they can't have the whole country, so they might as well join up with the government and get what they can.'

'What about destroying them?' the soldier yelled.

'Destroying them isn't going to happen. Let me tell you something. You should be proud of the fact that you've put these guys on their heels even a little bit. The Russians couldn't, and they had way more men. Now I want to talk about what's going on back home. Ninety percent of Americans can't find Afghanistan on a map. They think about you twice a year, Veterans Day and Memorial Day. You see it when you're on leave. You go to a bar, guys buy you a round, ask about what you're doing. But if you tell them, their eyes glaze over. It's too far away, confusing. Plus, they're ashamed to hear about it because they're getting drunk in college, mommy and daddy paying the bills, and you're putting your butts on the line for them every day. They don't want to think about it. They just want to buy you a beer and tell you you're a hero.'

'Amen!' somebody yelled.

'And let me tell you, it sounds cheap when they say it, but

they're right. You are *heroes*. You didn't come here on your own. Nobody in this brigade said, "It's time to invade Afghanistan." You didn't hold a bake sale and charter a C-17. Presidents from both parties have signed off on this mission. Whatever is right or wrong about what we're doing here is on them. Not you. You're doing what your country has asked. And I know you'll keep doing it. You'll fight because you gave your word and you don't break promises. You'll fight to make the lives of the people here a tiny bit better. And you'll fight for each other. The folks back home will keep sleeping, and you'll keep fighting.'

'Hoo-ah!' someone cheered. The chant spread through the crowd, melding, until two thousand voices shouted as one: '*Hoo-ah! Hoo-ah!*'

Wells looked out at them. For the first time, he understood the lure of politics. He had connected with these soldiers. Roused them. For a moment, he felt a thousand feet tall. And he came to the hidden point of the speech, the reason he was here.

'Hoo-ah. Yes. But there's one more thing to say. I know you care about your fellow soldiers. I see it. I heard it just now, when you brought your voices together.'

Another cheer.

'But not every soldier is worthy of the name. Some guys don't respect the uniform. I'm speaking from experience here. Once I was one of you. Before I was in the agency, I was a Ranger. And I feel duty-bound to say this to you. If you see guys crossing the line, dishonoring your service, you have to stand up to them.'

The crowd, so enthusiastic a few seconds before, turned sullen. No matter. He pushed on, hoping someone on the field understood what he was saying.

'I'm not talking about crying to your sergeant because

somebody steals your flip-flops in the shower. I'm talking about the guys who are taking out their frustrations by shooting locals, smuggling drugs. If you're going to be safe outside the wire, you have to be able to trust the soldiers in your unit. Soldiers who behave that way are soldiers you can't trust.'

Wells looked over the airfield, hoping for nods, signs of life. But his sermonizing had taken the air out of the crowd. He'd taken his shot and he'd have to see whether anything came of it.

'Anyway. That's what I've got. I wish I could sing, or play the guitar. Do something to put a smile on your faces. But believe me, you don't want to hear me sing. If anybody wants to hear about how I got myself shot by New York City's finest, or anything else for that matter, come on over to the trailer where I'm staying and I'll tell you. I might even have some beer over there, the non-nonalcoholic kind. First come, first served.' Wells looked at Brown. 'The colonel's just going to have to pretend he didn't hear that.'

A cheer roared through the crowd. *The secret weapon.* Shafer had packed four cases of beer in bubble wrap and overnighted it to Wells at Kandahar.

Brown took the microphone back. 'I didn't hear a thing,' he said. 'I can tell you one thing, John. Nobody's ever given a speech like that to this brigade before. Let's give Mr Wells a big round of applause.' And they did.

When Wells got back to his barracks, a dozen guys were waiting. 'Here's what we'll do,' he said. 'I've got two cases of Bud and two of Bud Light for those of you watching your girlish figures. There's some ice cream and Cokes, too, from the DFAC. I'm just going to bring them out for everyone to share. I ask you to keep the beers to one per person, 'cause there're so many folks who'd like one.'

The beer didn't last long, but somebody set up an iPod and a pair of speakers. Guys, and a few women, hung around and chatted and pretended they were anywhere but FOB Jackson. Nobody mentioned what Wells had said near the end of the speech. After about ninety minutes, the crowd thinned. As a morale raiser, the speech had worked pretty well. As a backdoor approach to an informant, it was looking like a bust. Wells would have to get potential targets from Shafer and go at them directly.

Then a guy Wells hadn't seen before walked up. He was black and stocky. The sun had disappeared behind thick clouds, but he wore a floppy hat low on his head. He had the triple chevrons of a sergeant. His name tag read 'Young.'

'Sergeant. I'm afraid we're all out of beer.'

The guy leaned in. 'I was thinking about what you said back during your speech.' The words slid out the side of his mouth, a low mumble. 'About bad guys. Almost sounded like you had something in mind. Like a particular situation.'

'That's a possibility.'

'I'd like to talk to you in private, Mr Wells.'

TWENTY

Langley

For two days, Tyler Weston and Nicholas Rodriguez had stared at Ellis Shafer. Their headshots were pinned to a corkboard in his office. Shafer had tried to amuse himself by drawing a handlebar mustache on Rodriguez and giving Weston a thought bubble that read 'I love the smell of poppies in the morning.' Still, their two-dimensional lips smirked at him.

Assuming Coleman Young was telling Wells the truth, Rodriguez and Weston were drug traffickers and killers. Wells believed Young. And if Wells believed him, then so did Shafer.

But he couldn't find the link. Weston and Rodriguez weren't connected with anyone at the CIA, in the United States or Afghanistan. According to their personnel records, neither man had been to Kabul on this tour. Their platoon was based hundreds of miles from the Afghan capital.

Shafer did notice that Weston's platoon had split from the rest of Bravo Company early in its tour. In theory, it provided extra protection for supply convoys on Highway 1. In reality, the trucks ran once or twice a week. On other days, the platoon was given scut jobs like guarding detainees. Basically, the unit operated on its own. As long as Weston's guys did the work no one else wanted, his commanders wouldn't bother him. Even Fowler's death – which should have raised red flags because of Weston's decision to send just seven men to investigate a potential enemy position – rated only a three-page after-action memo. Weston and Rodriguez couldn't have asked for a better setup.

The personnel files for 3rd Platoon showed that Weston came from central Florida, near Orlando. He'd played second-string quarterback in high school and gotten good grades. He'd joined up after serving in the ROTC program at the University of Florida. In other words, he was indistinguishable from most junior officers, except for his family's surprising criminal history. His father had served eleven months for insurance fraud in a minimum-security prison near Tallahassee. And his brother Jake had also been arrested as a juvenile. The court records were sealed, but the case had taken months to process, and the family had brought in a prominent defense lawyer to represent Jake. Nobody did that for a vandalism misdemeanor. Tyler Weston had seen more criminal behavior growing up than the average Army first lieutenant.

Rodriguez had his own problems. His file showed two arrests for gang fights. His criminal record should have disqualified him for military service. But he'd enlisted when the Iraq war was at its worst and the Army was missing its recruiting quotas. He scored in the ninety-third percentile on the intelligence test for new soldiers and was granted a waiver.

The only hint of a connection between Weston or Rodriguez and the agency was the fact that two case officers had gone to the University of Florida at the same time as Weston. But the U of F had forty thousand students. Shafer saw no evidence that the three had met one another. Plus the officers worked at Langley and had never been to Kabul. When Shafer surprised them with visits to their offices, both denied knowing Weston. He believed them.

Other potential trails also petered out. Bank records for Weston and Rodriguez showed no evidence of large deposits. Maybe they were buying gold with their drug profits, or hiding it in safe-deposit boxes. Most likely they hadn't brought it back from Afghanistan yet. Cell records were another dead end. Neither man had used his American phone since arriving in Afghanistan. Their military e-mail accounts revealed only official communications, nothing personal. They were careful, and someone even more careful was helping them.

Shafer had also checked out Kevin Roman, the third guy Young accused of being involved. But Roman's bank and e-mail records were as clean as the other two. Young had told Wells that Roman wasn't much more than a lookout. Shafer believed him. His IQ was thirty points below Rodriguez's and Weston's, according to the Army's tests. He was taking orders, not giving them.

Wells wanted to go at Weston and Rodriguez directly. But Young had blocked him. He was worried what might happen outside the wire. *You talk to them after you figure out who the Delta dude is*, he'd told Wells. *Not before*. Young had also said that no one could talk to people who knew Weston and Rodriguez back home. Doing so would risk tipping them off. So Shafer was stuck looking for clues in the electronic world.

Wells and Young were missing something else, too, maybe the most important piece. Motive. Shafer wanted to understand the why along with the *who* and *how*. Money was a possibility, of course. But money rarely told the whole story.

Shafer's phone trilled. Not a number he wanted to see, but he picked up anyway.

'Vinny. To what do I owe this pleasure?'

'So John's at a forward base, I hear.'

'FOB Jackson, yes.'

'And made a speech there.'

'Why are you pretending to be surprised by this?'

'I've had a complaint. About the speech. Reg told CENTCOM that Wells was encouraging insubordination.' Gregory 'Reg' Nuton was the two-star general who commanded the tens of thousands of soldiers who occupied Kandahar and Zabul.

'He didn't encourage anything. He talked about the war. At the end he made a coded plea to anyone who might know about the trafficking.' Shafer didn't plan to tell Duto that Coleman Young had come forward. Not yet.

'He gave out alcohol.'

'He had a couple cases of beer.'

Duto laughed, an unexpected sound. 'All right. I did my duty. Some three-star at the Pentagon called to moan about this and I promised I'd make sure I'd make it clear the behavior was unacceptable. And now I have. Like we don't have better things to do. Like a war to fight. From the way they're whining, you would think that Wells showed up with a tanker truck of vodka and called for a mutiny.'

'No one ever got stars on his collar by taking chances.'

'That said, Wells is going to have to leave the base. Nuton is insisting.'

'He can't. Not yet.'

'I'll buy you a couple days, but – are you close, Ellis?'

'Not sure. You leave in a week, right?'

'Six days.'

'Can you push it back?'

'Congressmen don't like it when you mess with their

schedules on short notice. Not without a good excuse. Which I don't have. No, I'm going.'

Pride made men strange, Shafer thought. Duto was willing to put himself and his congressional paymasters at risk, simply to avoid admitting a problem. 'Your call. But there's something you should understand.'

'Do tell.'

'Whoever this guy is, he's smart. And he's gone to a lot of trouble to stay unfindable. I just have a feeling that it's not about the drugs for him, or even about destroying our networks. I think he has something bigger in mind.'

'Spit it out, Ellis.'

'You going over there, it could be his chance. I'm not saying don't go, but—'

'Ellis. You don't like me, true?'

'I can't see the percentage in answering that question.'

'You can say it. We're grown-ups, and I know it anyway.'

'Not particularly.'

'But have you ever known me to be a coward?'

Shafer didn't need to answer. Duto was arrogant, power-hungry, and vain. But no one had ever accused him of being afraid, not physically anyway. As a case officer in Colombia, he'd been captured by leftist rebels, held for two months. In the pre-al-Qaeda days, the jungle rats were the agency's worst nightmare. When a Special Forces team finally hit the camp and pulled him out, Duto had lost twenty-eight pounds and two teeth.

Normally, after that kind of ordeal, officers went to Langley for at least a year of recovery. Many never went back to the field. Duto? He took his wife and kids to Barbados for two weeks, stayed at a five-star hotel on the agency's dime. Then he went back to Bogotá. A year later, he was station chief.

'I'm going. I'm counting on you and your boy to sort this out before I get there. If not, maybe the congressman and the senator and their aides will get a more honest view of the war than they bargained for.' Duto hung up. For the first time in a long while, Shafer felt something like respect for the man.

Shafer had barely cradled the phone before it rang again.

'Ellis?' The voice belonged to Jennifer Exley, once Shafer's deputy. A blue-eyed tornado, irrepressible and good-hearted and a brilliant analyst. She and Wells had nearly gotten married. Shafer supposed he'd loved her, too, in his own way. Though he'd never given his feelings the slightest space for fear they'd explode into the open and destroy his marriage. She was the steadiest member of their troika. But she'd quit years ago, after nearly dying in a botched assassination attempt on Wells. Now she was in exile. When they'd last talked, a few months before, she'd claimed to be at peace with the world. Raising her kids and getting on with her life. Shafer wasn't so sure. Being on the inside, knowing the world's secrets, left an itch that civilian life could never really scratch. Maybe Exley was different, but Shafer didn't think so.

'Jennifer.'

'Ellis. How are you?'

'My feets is tired, but my soul is rested.' Shafer winked at the photos of Weston and Rodriguez. They didn't wink back.

'Lies both ways.'

'Not like I believe in human perfectibility or anything, but do we have to make the same mistakes over and over?'

'I believe we do.' She laughed her deep, throaty laugh. 'And speaking of making the same mistakes, how's John?'

Oh, my. Just as Shafer had never entirely believed that Exley was through with spying, he'd never been certain that she and

John wouldn't get back together. They had connected with an almost electric force.

'In Afghanistan.'

'In the mountains?'

'Believe it or not, he's at a base of ours. Though not necessarily safer.'

'Is he okay?'

'He's John. He went to see his son a few weeks ago and it didn't work out and he was disappointed.'

'I'm glad he went. Anyway. He needed to.'

'How are yours?'

'David's looking at colleges. He applies next fall.'

The last time Shafer had seen Exley's son, he'd been playing thirteen-and-under youth soccer.

'We're all getting old. He have anywhere in mind?'

'Dartmouth, believe it or not.'

'John can give him the tour.'

'They want him to play soccer. Though he's thinking about UVA, too, and I have to admit I wouldn't mind that.'

'You'd save a few bucks.'

'There's that. Plus it'd be two hours to see him instead of ten.'

'No doubt he views that as a disadvantage.'

'But I don't think he'd get to play soccer at Virginia. They recruit from all over the world.'

'Be good for him. Teach him that disappointment starts early and never stops.'

'Life lessons from Ellis Shafer.'

'Not playing soccer would give him more time to get laid.'

'You're talking about my little boy.'

'I'll bet if you check out his Facebook page, his Twitter feed, you'll find plenty of evidence he's all grown up.'

'Precisely why I've resisted the urge so far.'

And then Shafer realized he might have another way to find the connection between Weston and Rodriguez and the SF officer. He would need them to be a little bit gullible, and a little bit horny – but then, they'd been in Afghanistan for ten months. The horniness wouldn't be a problem.

'Jenny. I have to go.'

'Something come up?'

Shafer could hear her disappointment. No doubt she'd love to know what he was working on, but she was too much of a pro to ask. 'You could say that.'

'Knock 'em dead. Literally.'

'Come on by sometime for a cup of that famous Langley coffee.'

'Tell John to be safe, okay?'

'You want to tell him that, tell him yourself.' Though Shafer wasn't sure that he wanted her to follow through. Sometimes the past was best left undisturbed.

'Bye, Ellis.'

He hung up, got to work.

TWENTY-ONE

Eastern Zabul Province, Afghanistan

In rural Afghanistan, AK 47s were as cheap and easy to find as cell phones. The Pashtun family that didn't own at least one rifle was poor indeed. American soldiers quietly tolerated the weapons. They'd learned the hard way that confiscating them caused unnecessary trouble.

But they treated Dragunov sniper rifles very differently. Dragunovs were costly and rare, and soldiers would detain anyone caught with one as an insurgent. Even Amadullah Thuwani didn't have one. He ordered his clansmen to find one, and after two days a half nephew came back with a never-used Dragunov, still in its crate. The price was two thousand dollars. Amadullah grumbled and paid. He had no choice. He had to have it. Though not for himself.

Since picking up the surface-to-air missiles, Amadullah had stayed in Afghanistan. He was living now with his half brother Hamid in a village in Zabul so small it didn't appear on maps. He'd trimmed his beard and taken off his Rolex, trying to stay anonymous. Still, he kept the cell phone Stan had given him. He knew he was taking a risk. The Americans could track the phone

279

when it was on, and for all Amadullah knew, when it was off, too. But after seeing Stan kill Daood, Amadullah had decided to trust him. His lies, his venom, were aimed at other Americans. Why else had he killed Daood and given Amadullah these SA-24s? Amadullah had even brought his bomb-making cousin from Muslim Bagh to look over the missiles. They were real. Amadullah thought now that the drugs had been an excuse, a way for the CIA man to reach him.

Three days after their meeting, Stan called and asked him to buy the Dragunov. 'And what shall I do with this?'

'Bring it to Kharjoy on Saturday. At noon. On Highway 1. Park at the petrol station by the bazaar.'

'I know where Kharjoy is.'

'Of course. Someone will meet you.'

'How will I know him?'

'He'll know you.'

'An American?'

But Stan was gone.

Amadullah had understood the Soviets. They were kaffirs and unbelievers, brutal men. In the early years of their invasion, when they still believed that they could win with sheer force, they had bombed whole villages into dust. They had killed two of Amadullah's brothers. Even now Amadullah hated the single star of the Red Army. But he'd understood what they wanted. They wanted the Afghans on one knee, serving the Kremlin. They had come from the north over the Amu Darya River and tried to break the Afghans. But Amadullah and his people had broken them instead. The Russians were hard, but the Afghans were harder. All the Soviet jets and tanks weren't enough. Finally they turned tail and went home.

The Americans were different. They had come here to rid themselves of Osama bin Laden and the Arabs. Amadullah didn't blame them. After all, the Arabs had attacked them in their own country. And the Arabs were troublemakers. Amadullah didn't like them. The rich ones looked down on the Pashtuns. The poor ones made a competition of prayers, as if Allah cared how many verses of the Quran they knew. None of them respected these mountains.

So the Americans came and broke up the camps where the Arabs trained. They had even killed bin Laden. They'd taken a long time, but they'd killed him. But still they hadn't left. Their soldiers were everywhere. Even the birds couldn't escape their helicopters and their big white balloons filled with cameras that watched the whole world.

The Americans said they were friends. Maybe they believed their own words. They hired men by the thousand to dig ditches and clean fields. Their officers met village elders each week to drink tea and talk about building canals and schools. At first, Amadullah thought that the meetings were a trap and the Americans would arrest anyone who came to their bases. But no. The safe-conduct privilege was real. The Americans wanted to hear what the elders had to say. They didn't rape and murder like the Russians either. Amadullah knew of a boy who had fallen down a well and broken his legs and arms. His brothers dragged him out and carried him to an American base near Kandahar City. The doctor there helped him, put him in a cast and gave him medicine. The boy's brothers had been Talibs. But the doctor hadn't cared.

So Amadullah couldn't hate the Americans as he hated the Russians. Maybe they were telling the truth when they said they didn't want to rule Afghanistan. Even so, he and his men would fight them as long as they stayed. They didn't belong in his country any more than he belonged in America. No matter how hard they tried to prove they meant well, their very presence stirred up trouble. On patrols, they gave candy to children and made them disrespect their fathers. They brought Tajiks and Hazaras down to the Pashtun lands and gave them rifles and told them they were soldiers. Even worse, they caused problems between men and women. The Americans talked about giving rights to women, but the truth was the opposite. The women wanted the Americans gone most of all. They wanted to know why their husbands and fathers couldn't stop soldiers from coming into their houses and looking at them, disrespecting them, humiliating them.

If the Americans would just leave, then Amadullah and the other Pashtuns would make sure that al-Qaeda never came back to Afghanistan. Amadullah himself would slit the Arabs' throats. He had fought his whole life. He wanted a few years of peace, a few years of living in a country that wasn't just a battlefield for outsiders. But the Americans didn't trust the Pashtuns to do that work. They didn't understand. And so every day, more Americans died. Amadullah had no sympathy for them, no pity. He'd kill as many as he could. But still he couldn't help but feel that the war was a waste.

Now he'd run across this strange CIA man. Amadullah thought the man must be mad, that something had happened to twist his reason. He supposed that one day he'd learn what. The mountains exposed every secret.

Amadullah didn't want to carry the Dragunov in his Ford. The Americans and Afghans sometimes put roadblocks on Highway 1. He stowed the crate in the back of Hamid's old Nissan pickup and covered it with sacks of bricks and told Jaji to follow him in the Nissan. Jaji ran his hands through his thick black Pashtun hair and looked vaguely sulky at the order but didn't dare disagree. In any case, the roadblocks were off that morning.

They reached Kharjoy at eleven a.m. A cold rain had fallen the night before, but the swift autumn wind had moved the clouds away and left the sky bright and blue.

They parked near the petrol station and walked through the bazaar, stepping over the mud puddles the storm had left. Merchants and their boys sat under plastic tarpaulins outside one-room stores. They sold potatoes and pomegranates and flour, plus chips and batteries and brightly colored candy from China. These days they also had music and movies. Some merchants had gone back to selling pornography, too. During the Taliban's time, a merchant caught selling regular movies was supposed to get twenty-five lashes. One selling the sex videos could get a hundred. Of course, plenty of the Talibs liked pornos. They would watch the DVDs they took from the merchants.

At the edge of the bazaar, Amadullah bought himself a Coke. As he did a patrol of American soldiers walked past. 'Good morning,' a soldier said. He was young, like all of them, and broad in the shoulders and wearing the sunglasses that they favored and the heavy armored vest. A child who hoped that hiding his eyes would make him a man. He walked with a loose, proud gait, as if he believed he belonged here. Just as Stan had named Kharjoy for the meeting and then told Amadullah it was on Highway 1. As if Amadullah hadn't lived here his whole life. As if he didn't know every village and all the chiefs within a hundred miles.

Amadullah hated the soldier and felt a strange shame, too. Living in Pakistan had kept him safe. But it had also let him avert his eyes from these American boots everywhere on his soil. *Go. Leave my land.* The soldiers turned a corner and Amadullah poured the Coke into the muddy soil and threw away the can.

Just past noon, a Toyota pickup with heavily tinted windows parked at the edge of the muddy lot. A man stepped out. He had light brown skin and wore a gray *shalwar kameez* and sandals. He looked like a northerner, though he didn't have the almond-shaped eyes of many Tajiks. 'Good day,' he said.

His Pashtun wasn't as good as the other American's. And he stood too tall, like the soldiers on the patrol. Not like the other American. John Wells, the CIA man had called him. That one carried himself with his pride hidden away and so he had fooled Amadullah.

'Good day.'

'I understand you have something for me.'

'Not here.' Amadullah nodded at the convoy parked a few hundred meters away.

'I know a place three or four kilos away. Protected. Safe.'

Amadullah nodded. The man went back to his Toyota. For the second time, Amadullah was opening himself to capture. But then, if the Americans had wanted to take him, they could have already.

A kilometer down, the American turned off Highway 1 and onto a dirt road bordered on both sides by mud walls covered with grapevines. Amadullah and Jaji followed. After ten minutes, they reached an abandoned cluster of farmhouses, a minivillage that had seen heavy fighting. Bomb craters pocked the earth. Bullet holes scarred the walls. The American parked in the shadow of a two-story farmhouse. Amadullah pulled alongside. The American stepped out and nodded for Amadullah to follow. Amadullah didn't. He reached under the passenger seat for the pistol hidden there.

The American walked over to his window. 'Where is it?'

'What's your name?'

'Shadow,' the man said.

Enough American arrogance. 'Your true name.'

The man's eyes shifted to the Makarov in the passenger seat. 'Frank.'

Amadullah still thought he was lying, but *Frank* would have to do. He led Frank to the pickup, shoved aside the sacks of bricks. Jaji found a pry bar and popped open the Dragunov's crate to reveal a hard-sided plastic case.

Inside, a sniper's tool kit: the rifle, four ten-round magazines, an eight-power scope, a cleaning rod in three pieces, a cleaning kit, and pouches to hold it all. Plus a bayonet and a knife for close-in work. Unlike some of his nephews, Amadullah wasn't a fanatic about weapons. As far as he was concerned, AKs worked fine. Still, the Dragunov was impressive. The center of its stock was cut out to save weight, and it had a long, low profile, with a skinny muzzle. It looked light and lethal.

Frank popped open the Dragunov's bolt, pulled a tiny penlight from his pocket, and shone it down the barrel. The grooves etched inside nearly glowed.

'Chrome,' Frank said. 'Very cool.' He closed the bolt, snapped on the scope, hefted the rifle to his shoulder, cocked his head, put his eye to the sight. 'Nice and easy. Not a beast like the .50.' Frank was more relaxed now that he had the Dragunov in his hands, Amadullah saw. The Taliban had men like this, too, men who loved weapons. Usually they didn't care much for people.

'Have you fired one before?'

'Once or twice. So you're Amadullah Thuwani.'

'You know my name.'

'Of course. There's a bounty on your head. Fifty thousand dollars.' Frank put down the Dragunov, snapped off the scope, as if to say, *Don't worry. I won't try to collect.*

'Only fifty thousand.'

'If you want a higher price, you need to do more than nail a patrol or two.'

'Now that your friend Stan has given me the missiles, perhaps I will.'

'The missiles?'

So you don't know, Amadullah thought. He shouldn't have spoken. Stan had kept the secret from his own side. Now Amadullah wondered whether he could turn the mistake to his advantage by telling Frank more. He might have found a cheap way to stir up trouble. Yes. 'I give you a Dragunov, he gives me SA-24s. A good trade, I think.'

'SA-24s. Russian SAMs.'

Amadullah nodded.

'What's your target?'

Amadullah decided he'd said enough. He couldn't be sure what Frank would do if he found out that the other American wanted to kill the head of the CIA. 'I shouldn't tell you this, but do you know the man called Omar al-Douzani?'

'The leader of the Douzani tribe.'

'He lives in Pakistan. South Waziristan. And travels in convoys, armored trucks. Sometimes with Pakistani military escorts. Your friend Stan told me that with these missiles I could destroy him from five kilometers away. Ten. And then our business can expand.'

'Stan gave you the missiles to use against Douzani?'

Sometimes the Americans needed everything said straight out. 'Yes.'

'And where does the heroin come in?'

'The powder opened the connection, gave us trust in each other. When Douzani is gone, his family will break. He has no sons anymore, only cousins and nephews.'

'They'll all fight to control his tribe.'

'Yes. When that happens, some will come to me for help. I'll choose which one to support, or maybe I'll sit back and let them fight. Either way, I'll feast on them. By the time the Douzanis are done with their war, you'll need a truck for all the powder I can sell you.'

As Amadullah spoke, he found himself believing his own story, the surest sign that Frank would believe him, too. It wasn't even a lie, just a version of the truth that Allah hadn't yet called into being. Frank stepped back and folded his arms. The Americans couldn't hide their emotions. Amadullah could almost see what Frank was thinking: *Stan should have told me. He trusts this Pashtun, this* Talib, *more than me.* Good. Let Stan and Frank try to untangle their own lies. While they wrestled, Amadullah would decide what to do with the missiles.

Amadullah leaned his bulky body over, picked up the Dragunov. 'You still haven't told me why you need it.'

'I may have to clean up a mess.' Frank smiled, and Amadullah saw the anger in him, the real and true cruelty.

'This makes a good broom.'

Francesca watched the Afghans drive off and stowed the crate in the secret compartment welded to the bottom of his pickup. At Highway 1 he turned left, southeast toward Kandahar. *Calibrate and recalibrate*, snipers learned. *Check and double-check before you pull that trigger. You have every advantage until you shoot, so take your time.* Now Francesca laid his hands on the wheel and tried to calibrate what Amadullah had told him.

On the surface, everything made sense. Stan wanted to use Amadullah to assassinate other Talib leaders, ones the CIA couldn't find. The drug trafficking had been a way to reach Amadullah and convince him that he could trust Stan. But the more he considered the story, the less Francesca believed it.

If Stan had planned to turn Amadullah all along, why go to such great lengths to hide the trafficking from his own bosses and everyone else at Kabul station? Why not just get someone senior at Langley to sign a finding for the project and use the Ground Branch, the agency's paramilitary arm, to handle the pickups?

The SA-24s also bothered Francesca. The Russians knew they couldn't build helicopters that could match American designs, so they'd spent a lot of time developing surface-to-air missiles as a cheap countermeasure. The SA-24 was their top-of-the-line rocket, as good as or better than anything the United States had. By all accounts, it could make mincemeat of Chinooks. Probably Black Hawks and Apaches, too. In all his years fighting in Iraq and Afghanistan, Francesca had never seen one. Yet Stan had somehow delivered two to Amadullah. Using them to attack a ground convoy, even one with armored vehicles, seemed a major waste. An RPG or basic antitank missile would be much more effective at much lower cost.

Of course, Stan might have other reasons for going to the trouble of delivering the SA-24s. He might have imagined that the SA-24s would impress Amadullah.

Or . . . Amadullah could be lying. The missiles – assuming they existed at all – could be meant for another target. One that flew on helicopters or jets that were vulnerable only to the most sophisticated missiles. An American target.

Francesca wondered whether to call Stan, confront him, demand an answer. Then he thought of the Dragunov in the secret compartment. Let Stan and Amadullah play whatever game they wanted. Francesca had his own game. He was already thinking about how he might use the Dragunov on Coleman Young or John Wells. Maybe when he was done, he'd give Stan a taste of the rifle, too. Make him a hero the easy way, with one trigger pull. He could see the headlines: *High-Level CIA Officer Shot to Death in Kabul . . . Taliban Claim Responsibility.*

No, Francesca would keep his mouth shut, wait for the right moment to find out what Stan was doing. Check and double-check. Calibrate and recalibrate. At that moment, Francesca understood more than ever why he loved being a Shadow. The trigger pull was the only true moment in the whole damn war. Everything else was a lie.

TWENTY-TWO

Langley

As soon as he hung up with Exley, Shafer started the process of putting together a Facebook profile for 'Mindy Calhoun.' Mindy lived in Tempe, Arizona. She was twenty and a business major at Maricopa Community College. Her interests included the Green Bay Packers, Shia LaBoeuf, Kim Kardashian, and 'Hot men in uniform! American only!'

Mindy's profile had a half dozen photos, each naughtier than the next, though none pornographic enough to attract the attention of Facebook's censuring software. The photos came from Corbis, though with a little help from the Directorate of Science and Technology, Shafer had tweaked them. Anyone who tried to find the originals through the image-recognition engines on the Internet would come up empty.

Mindy had a heart-shaped tattoo on her wrist and a blue mermaid for a tramp stamp. She looked ready for a few years as a Bud poster girl followed by a long career at Hooters. Within minutes of her creation, she had more than a hundred Facebook friends, mostly bots like her who lived in the CIA's servers. That number was enough to make her credible to the soldiers whom Shafer wanted to friend. He picked guys from the South whose profiles showed no connections with Arizona. None of the facts on Mindy's page were checkable except for her enrollment at Maricopa. Anyone who called the college would have found out that she didn't exist. But as Shafer had expected, soldiers weren't interested in running background checks. Forty-two accepted Mindy's friend request within twelve hours. Several sent back messages that would have made Shafer blush if he were the blushing type. A couple guys were dumb enough to send pictures, too. Shafer wondered whether he'd been this horny when he was eighteen. Probably. And he hadn't even been coping with the extra surge of testosterone that came with fighting a war.

After a day, Mindy had enough real soldiers as friends to make her profile believable even to someone who might have reason to be cautious, someone like Tyler Weston. So Shafer reached out to Weston. Yr super-cute, he wrote. *And coming home soon . . . That's awesome!* A few hours later, Weston friended her: *Me and my boys love college girls. Got more pics?*

And so Shafer had the chance to examine Weston's roster of 332 friends, including Rodriguez – though not Roman. He worked through them, trying to find the Special Forces officer whom Young had described to Wells. He came up with three candidates on his first pass. But upon closer inspection, none of the three looked right. The first had rotated home a month earlier. The second operated mainly in the mountain provinces east of Kabul, not in southern Afghanistan. The third, a Ranger lieutenant named Allan Rose, operated out of Kandahar, but he had an airtight alibi. He'd been on a mission in Kandahar province on the night Young had seen the suspect at FOB Jackson.

Shafer expanded his search, friending Rodriguez and Roman. But he came up short there, too. Then inspiration struck. He turned to Jake Weston, Tyler's older brother. *Your bro's hot but yr even hotter . . . I luv bad boys . . .*

Ninety minutes later, Mindy and Jake were friends, at least by Facebook's definition. And on Jake's page, Shafer found D. Lorenzo, who had only two photos in his publicly available profile. The first showed him from the side, wearing a white T-shirt and a floppy hat. The hat hid Lorenzo's face, but not the oversize ace of spades tattoo on his equally oversize bicep. The ace was a favorite of Delta ops. Under 'location,' Lorenzo had posted *Kandahar*. Under 'works at': *I could tell you . . . but I'd have to kill you. Seriously*. The second photo showed a single round, long and copper-tipped. A .50 caliber bullet. A sniper's bullet.

Shafer searched public and military records and couldn't find Lorenzo. He wondered whether the name was an alias. Then he remembered that soldiers who wanted to protect their privacy while still giving friends a way to find them often used middle names instead of last on Facebook. Bingo. Within ten minutes, Shafer had him. Daniel Lorenzo Francesca. He'd joined the Army fourteen years before and grown up a half mile from Tyler and Jake Weston. Before Afghanistan, he'd been based at Fort Bragg, the home of the Deltas. Now his personnel file listed his status as *deployed/unavailable*, the Army's usual euphemism for a soldier on Special Operations duty.

Shafer called Wells, who was back at Kandahar. Technically, General Nuton had banned Wells from every base he controlled, including KAF. But the airfield was so big that as long as Wells stayed away from Nuton's headquarters, the general couldn't know he was there.

'I have good news, John.'

'David Miller.'

'Better. I found the middleman. Name's Daniel Lorenzo

Francesca. He was a sniper in Iraq, Special Ops, and he joined Delta about five years ago.'

'Sniper.'

'He might have killed more guys than you.'

'Unlikely.'

'Jealous, John? He's finishing his second tour in Afghanistan. Looks like he's based at KAF.'

'You have a photo?'

'I'm working on it.' For obvious reasons, the Special Forces kept the names and faces of their operatives secret. The Deltas were doubly cautious. 'I'll get one from the North Carolina DMV. I'd rather not tip him yet.'

'He may already know. I'm looking for him.'

'Fair point.' The mole had probably warned Francesca after Wells showed up in Kabul. 'Even if he knows we're looking, let's not let him know he's been found. Anyway, his file's strange.'

'Define strange.'

'As in, he seems to have gotten special language training. A few years ago, he went to the Defense Language Institute in Monterey for six months to learn Pashtun.'

'So?'

'So that's unusual. JSOC usually views these guys as too valuable to pull them from the field that way. Plus I can't figure out which Delta unit he's part of. After Monterey, his assignment is listed as Delta/D71, no company or squad.'

'D71.'

'Correct.'

'You're sure he's our guy? You're putting a lot on this Facebook connection.'

'*Sure* is too strong. But he's the best candidate.'

'Get me the photo and I'll see what Coleman says.'

'I'll do better than that. I'll get you six guys and you can run a lineup.'

'Good. And let's say Coleman recognizes this guy. What then? I go talk to him? Ask him about his heroin trafficking? Because I have a feeling that's not going to do it. And I don't think CID or the Deltas are going to want to hear about it either.'

'I have a plan.'

'Do tell.'

'Three steps. The first at Kandahar, the second here, and the third at FOB Jackson.' Shafer explained.

'I don't like it,' Wells said when he was finished. 'It feels like tying a goat to a tree and waiting for the lion to show up.'

'Except the goat's got a gun.'

'So's the lion.'

'You have another way, I'm listening. But the hour's getting short, John. Duto leaves in less than a week. Anyway, it's Young's call, not yours, right?'

'All right. I'll ask him. Meantime you'll send me what I need?'

'I'll FedEx it tonight to the KBR office at KAF. Project manager there named Alan Sussman owes me a favor.' The breadth of Shafer's connections always surprised Wells. But then Shafer had been in the game a very long time.

'Sussman.'

'Yeah. He'll hold it for you, and that way it doesn't have your name on it, just in case somebody's looking for you. Meantime I'm going to see if I can trace Francesca up the chain, figure out who in Kabul he might know.'

'Facebook again.'

'I wish. But based on everything we've seen, our mole's more careful than that. And speaking of careful. Watch out for this guy, okay?'

'Don't worry about me, Ellis.' Wells sounded almost personally offended at the suggestion that this Delta operative might pose a challenge to him.

'I'm just saying –'

'I know what you're saying. I've never liked snipers. Takes a special kind of nasty.'

TWENTY-THREE

Forward Operating Base Jackson

Besides its brigade aid station, FOB Jackson had a combat stress clinic where a psychiatrist and a social worker talked to soldiers. Guys mostly came voluntarily, though sometimes commanders ordered them in. As Colonel Brown had told Wells, troubles at home were the biggest source of strain. Nearly every base had a Morale, Welfare, and Recreation center offering free Internet access. Many guys e-mailed their wives and families every day. But the constant contact didn't always help. Deployment didn't change relationships. Soldiers who'd had strong marriages in the United States had strong marriages in Afghanistan. For others, being in touch was more curse than blessing. Guys fought with their wives about child care, or freaked out after seeing pictures on Facebook of their girlfriends hanging out with other men. Military shrinks called the problems MWR syndrome.

The stress clinic at FOB Jackson was a simple one-story plywood building topped with sandbags and protected by a twelve-foot blast wall. Soldiers who didn't want to be seen going in the main entrance could sneak through a gap in the rear wall that opened to a motor pool parking lot. Wells took that route, jogging up three wooden steps to an unlocked door.

Inside, he found himself in the clinic's break room, which held a coffeemaker and a shelf of paperback books and pamphlets about alcoholism, drug abuse, and family violence. An old-fashioned office clock ticked slowly, and vaguely depressing motivational posters covered the walls: 'Fear Is Nothing to Fear,' 'Six Ways to De-stress Yourself.'

'Hello?'

But no one answered. The clinic had officially closed for lunch at noon, a half hour before. Wells walked to the first door on the left, stepped inside. The room was windowless, six by six. Young sat on a plastic chair, leafing through a pamphlet with a light blue cover: 'Signs Your Drinking May Be Getting the Better of You.'

'Coleman.'

'Mr Wells, sir.'

'Call me John. Please.'

'I'm more comfortable using your last name.'

Wells had gotten that answer from enlisted men before. 'Your choice. Sorry I'm late.'

'No problem, sir. Catching up on my reading.'

'Worried about your drinking?'

'No, sir. I don't drink. Been thinking what I ought to do when my contract's up and I'm wondering about social work. Dealing with Oak Cliff kids like me. I'd have to get my BA first.'

'You're not going to re-up.'

Young shrugged as if the question didn't merit an answer.

'You been okay the last few days? No problems with Weston or Rodriguez?'

Another shrug.

'For what it's worth I'm guessing you'd make a good social worker, Coleman.'

'How's that?'

'You listen more than you talk. Probably the key to success.'

'In social work.'

'And life in general.'

'Yes, sir.'

Wells laid six pieces of paper on the desk, each with a headshot from the North Carolina Department of Motor Vehicles. Six men stared up, their lips curled into forced smiles. *I've wasted a half day renewing my license already. Get me out of here.* 'Recognize anybody?'

'It's one of these men, sir?'

'That's for you to answer. Take your time. Even if you're sure right away.'

Young examined the shots one by one. Methodical and cautious. Wells looked away. He didn't want to tip Young. Finally, Young nodded and picked up Francesca's picture. 'This guy.'

'Definitely?'

'Yes. First I wasn't sure, but them big elephant ears gave it away.' For the first time since Wells had met him, Young smiled. 'He thinks he's some bad, too. I can see it even in this.' Young tapped the DMV photograph. 'Staring at the camera like he's got better places to be. Tell me I'm wrong.'

'You're not. His name's Daniel Lorenzo Francesca. He's buddies with Tyler Weston's older brother, guy named Jake. He's a warrant officer based at KAF. A bug-eater.' Regular soldiers called Special Forces operators *bug-eaters*, because their training supposedly included ways to survive on a diet of worms.

'A Delta?'

'Yes and no.'

'What's that mean?'

'He's part of a separate unit inside Delta. Called D71. Ever heard of it?'

Young shook his head. 'What's that about?'

'He's gotten special language training, that's about all I can tell you. Speaks Pashtun. One more thing I have to tell you. He was a sniper in Iraq before he joined Delta.'

Young wasn't smiling anymore. 'So he's a sniper. Tier One. Speaks the language. And he's got some mysterious job that even the CIA can't figure.'

'That's about right.'

'Sir. Question. What part of this is supposed to make me feel good?'

'I guess the fact that we found him.'

'So now what? You grab him?'

'Did you ever see him carrying drugs? Or even Weston or Rodriguez?'

'You know the answer's no.'

'Hear him talking about the deal? Or what happened to Ricky Fowler? Or anything illegal at all.'

'The closest I got to this guy was maybe a hundred feet. I never heard anything. Maybe if I had ears like him.' Young shook his head. 'Don't tell me you can't do this. You're not some MP, sir. You're CIA.'

'Even the CIA can't grab a Delta operator for no reason.'

'You believe me? About the drugs and what happened to Fowler and everything?'

'If I didn't, I wouldn't be here.'

'Mr Wells, sir. You run the guy down and sneak back here and bring me these pictures and I say it's true, it's really him. Then you say you can't do anything about it. What is that?'

'I didn't say I can't do anything about it. There's a way. But it puts you on the line. Because this guy will go after you for sure when we pull his chain. From the minute I go back to Kandahar, you have to figure that you're at risk every time you go outside the wire. Maybe inside, too.'

'Tell me.'

Wells explained. When he was finished, Young picked up Francesca's headshot, stared at it as if it might confess. 'Boxed me, didn't you? Know I can't say no after that speech I made. Why it pays to keep your mouth shut.'

'You can always say no.'

Young ripped the headshot, straight down the middle, tearing Francesca's face in two. 'Let's get him.'

Back at Kandahar, Wells picked up the FedEx package that Shafer had sent and then left the KBR compound, walking south along the busy two-lane road to the base's main gate. Trucks churned by as he dialed a number he'd burned into his brain the year before.

Two rings, then: 'Brett Gaffan.'

'You answer that way, it makes you sound like a telemarketer. "This is Brett Gaffan, have I got a deal for you."'

'What have I done to deserve this honor, John?'

Gaffan was a former Delta operator who had recently worked with Wells on a mission that had started messy and ended messier. He had saved Wells's life on a hill in the Bekaa Valley. Despite that fact, or maybe because of it, they'd hardly spoken since the end of the mission. Just a couple vague promises to get together. Civilians didn't understand this side of the military. Men risked their lives for one another and then walked away with hardly a backward glance once the fighting was done. Combat was combat and life was life. The two didn't always have much in common.

'Long time no speak,' Gaffan said.

'Sorry about that.'

'Sure you are. So come on, out with it.'

'Out with what?'

'You're calling me from a blocked number, not your own phone. And it sounds like you're at a truck stop somewhere. Lots of diesel engines. And it's like seven a.m. here. You must be out of the country, probably on a base, probably Middle East.'

'Afghanistan.'

'I know you want something, so let's avoid the awkwardness and get to it.'

'Am I that obvious?'

'As a matter of fact.'

Wells could hardly deny his ulterior motives. 'You still keep close to your old buddies?'

'Some. Why?'

'Anybody in Kandahar you really trust?'

Gaffan hesitated. 'One guy, sure. A master sergeant, Russell Stout. We haven't talked in a month or so, but I'm pretty sure he's still there. Good guy. By the book. No-nonsense.'

Meaning that he wouldn't necessarily be buying whatever Wells was selling. 'Noted. Can I talk to him, use your name? I'm looking for an op who I think is based here.'

'Want to tell me why?'

'It's complicated.'

'Isn't it always? At least give me his name. I might even know him.'

'Daniel Francesca. Sniper.'

'Nope.'

'He got into Delta about when you left. He looks like a bad guy. I just want help getting a look at him.'

'Really. That's all you want.'

Wells imagined Gaffan holding the phone away from his ear, deciding whether to toss it across the room. *Oops. We got disconnected. And then my phone stopped working. Sorry I couldn't help.*

Wells stayed quiet and eventually Gaffan coughed into the phone, an almost embarrassed cough. An I-can't-believe-I'm-letting-you-use-me-yet-again cough. They both knew he would say yes, defer to Wells's judgment. Gaffan was a very good operator, but he wasn't a leader.

'I'll ask him. But if he's not comfortable—'

'I get it.'

'I assume you'd rather meet him off base.'

'On KAF should be fine. We'll find somewhere out of sight. This place is, like, five square miles.'

'You have a funny way of treating your friends, John.'

'Better than my enemies.'

'True that. When you get back, you owe me a beer, and this time I'm collecting.'

'Done.'

Four hours later, Wells sat on the steps of an abandoned trailer at the southwestern edge of the airfield. With the surge done, Kandahar was already shrinking. This part of the base was mostly empty. The dirt fields around Wells were littered with trailers, pipes, barbed wire, earthmoving equipment, and a hundred other bits of slowly rusting steel. The United States military had brought this equipment at unfathomable expense a year or two before. Much of it had never been used. Now it was turning into salvage.

Wells saw headlights approaching and stood and waved. A Jeep pulled up, and he stepped in. The driver was wiry and lean and deeply tanned. He was in his early thirties, but his close-cropped gray hair made him look older. Wells pulled the door shut and they rolled slowly west, toward the wire.

'Sergeant Stout?'

'Call me Russ. You know this is the first time I've ever seen this part of KAF?'

'Not much reason to go over here.'

'I guess not. So what's up?'

No-nonsense, Gaffan had said. Wells decided not to dance around the question. 'You know a warrant officer named Daniel Francesca?'

'Sure. Danny. Odd guy. In 71.'

'You don't mind my asking, what is 71?'

Stout turned right, north along the perimeter road. He looked at Wells: *Why do you want to know?*

'I have reason to believe Francesca's dirty.'

Stout shook his head. *Not enough.*

'That he and a senior CIA officer are working with a Talib commander to export heroin. Funding the insurgency and passing operational information to the commander.'

'You can't be serious.'

'I came a long way to make this up.'

They rode for a while in silence. 'What kind of evidence you got?'

'It's circumstantial, but it's solid. A couple weeks ago, he was seen on another base with a soldier and officer who we think are the pickup team. We've checked and he had no reason to be there.'

'That's not enough.'

'I agree. I'm not planning to do anything. Just asking questions.'

'We created 71 maybe four years ago. *D* for Detachment. Detachment 71, two-man teams that can operate outside the wire on their own. There're only three here, three at Bagram, maybe one down in Helmand.'

'So they can pass as local.'

'That's the idea. Local enough that they can get down Highway 1 and through the villages without getting stopped or jacked anyway. Danny and his spotter, guy named Alders, they're good.'

'I didn't know you guys ever went out under NOC in teams that small.'

'Not before this. It's kind of a pilot project, and there're only a few guys who can do it anyway. You have to have the language down.'

Something about what Stout had said bugged Wells. He wasn't sure why. He moved on.

'What about Francesca? You said he's odd.'

'You know snipers. How can that not get to you? Plus he's on his third tour. He and Alders call themselves the Shadow Patrol. It's sort of a joke, but sort of not, you understand. And he has this weird high-pitched giggle that comes out sometimes, not necessarily when anybody's made a joke. Like he's a hyena or something.' Stout demonstrated.

'I can see why you wouldn't want him babysitting.'

'Definitely not.'

'These 71 teams live in your barracks?'

'Yeah. You know where we are?'

Wells shook his head.

'This high-sec compound close to the main airfield terminal. Called Bengal. On the maps it's just listed as extra officers' housing, but if you walk by you'll see fifteen-foot walls, barbed wire, lots of aerials. We even have a helipad inside, although we can't use it except if we declare CMS.'

'CMS?'

'Critical Mission Status, like we think we can catch Mullah Omar but we have to go immediately. Otherwise the Air Force controllers hate any air traffic south of the runway. For regular missions we go from the helo ramps on the north side like everybody else. Anyway, the 71 teams almost never go out by helicopter. They have local vehicles and they wear local clothes outside the wire. True black ops. When they're at Bengal, they hang out a little bit, eat with us and work out sometimes, but mostly they stick to themselves and practice speaking Pashtun.'

'And you have different missions anyway.'

'Right. You know what we do. Go out in traditional teams, mostly on modified Black Hawks that can refuel in the air. On my first tour, seven years ago, we rode in GMVs.' The GMVs were the Special Forces equivalent of Humvees, modified with smoke-spouting canisters and .50 caliber rifles on top. To save weight, they had lighter armor, sometimes no armor at all.

'Dune buggies.'

'Maximum speed and firepower. Those were fun. Too bad we can't use 'em now, but a big IED will just vaporize them. So mainly we go airborne, these night raids. But the 71s, they just take their pickup trucks, drive off base, and disappear. Sometimes they support us, sit on an exfil route for a house or villa we're targeting, pick off stragglers once we get them moving. But mostly they just go their own way, do whatever it is they've been tasked for, come back a few days later needing a shower and a hot meal.'

Stout turned right and headed east along the northern edge of the base. To the north, a blimp hung eerily in the night sky. Its cameras watched the mountain where insurgents tried to set up rockets to fire at KAF. Wells wondered what the Afghans – most of whom had never seen a plane that wasn't a threat to bomb them – made of the blimps.

'I'm guessing they don't keep their vehicles inside your compound.'

'Heck, no. They mostly enter and leave at night. We've got a side entrance that dumps guys into the back of a DFAC. In case somebody's keeping an eye on the front gate. You know, going outside the wire the way they do, no armor and soft-skinned vehicles, they'd be dead in an hour if they got made.'

Stout had just given Wells the break that he needed. 'They use local weapons?'

'From what I can see, generally no. They like the .50 for the range. Their pickups have a hidden compartment welded underneath the bed for their rifles, their uniforms, whatever else they're using.'

'They carry American uniforms?' Wells didn't understand, and then he did. 'If they get to the point where someone is checking that closely, their covers won't hold anyway.'

'Correct. They're not trying to live in a village for months or anything. Not looking to infiltrate AQ like you did back in the day. Just get scalps and go.'

Francesca was in an ideal position to move the drugs, Wells saw. He could move freely on both sides of the wire. Wells wondered why he didn't pick the stuff up himself instead of depending on Weston and Rodriguez. But snipers preferred to keep their distance from the enemy. Francesca might figure he and his spotter wouldn't be safe in a face-to-face meet.

Stout reached the eastern edge of the airfield, made another right turn and bumped south, toward the center of the base.

'One last question and then I have a favor. I know you don't know him that well, but does Francesca strike you as the kind of guy who could do this?'

Stout was silent for so long that Wells thought he didn't plan to answer. Then he laughed, a short, sharp bark. 'I'm not sure what kind of guys any of us are anymore. What's your favor?'

'I need to see where Francesca parks his pickup.'

'You said you weren't planning to do anything.'

'I'm not. Not unless he gives me reason.'

Stout went quiet again. Then he pulled the pickup to the side of the road. A Humvee behind honked and flashed its brights and he waved it by. 'You want me to hang one of my own out. Detachment 71, it makes no difference, the guy's Delta. On no evidence, no photos, no SIGINT, nothing. Gaffan asked me to talk to you and I've known him a long time, so here I am. But I got to tell you that inside the community, a lot of guys don't like you. The whole Muslim thing, it's just weird.'

Wells felt his temper rise. 'Ask me what you want, but don't question my faith.'

'Guess what I'm asking you is, which one, John? Which faith? Islam or America? The way you quit the agency, went to work for the Saudis.'

The ones who don't know me, is this how they see me? Even now? Wells had thought he put these questions to rest on his very first mission after coming home, when he'd stopped the Times Square bombing. And maybe he had for a while. But the way Duto used him in the Midnight House mission, and then the way he'd quit and gone solo afterward, had obviously started the whispers again. Wells felt a lowing in his stomach. Even among these men, he was an outsider.

Wells could have explained everything. But Stout hadn't earned the right to ask. 'Gaffan's friends with both of us. He'll tell you who I am. I've been straight with you, every word. If I'm right about Francesca, he's gonna go after the sergeant who made him. I promised that guy I'd protect him and I'm gonna keep my word. As for Francesca, I'm telling you I won't lay a finger on him unless I'm sure. My word's not enough, then we're done talking. I'll find another way.'

Stout exhaled, long and deep, like a truck releasing its air brakes. Wells didn't say another word. Neither did Stout. Didn't tip his hand. Just put the Jeep in gear and rolled south, toward the heart of the airfield.

PART THREE

TWENTY-FOUR

Langley

Colonel Gary Cunningham commanded the unit officially known as 1st Special Forces Operational Detachment – Delta. He was only a full bird, but plenty of generals would have given their stars to have his job. His conversation with Shafer went three minutes, two minutes longer than Shafer expected.

'Colonel.'

'Mr Shafer.'

'Thanks for taking the time to talk.'

'Always happy to improve agency-military cooperation.' Cunningham spoke with the light lilt of south Virginia. He'd been born in Roanoke.

'Glad to hear. I know you're busy, so let me get to it. I have a request for you.'

'Request away.'

'I'd like your files on a warrant officer named Daniel Lorenzo Francesca.'

'How do you know he's one of ours?'

'Please, Colonel. You're not denying it, are you?' Shafer made a finger pistol and pulled the trigger, pow-pow. In truth, he enjoyed making these kinds of messes.

'I'm neither admitting nor denying. I'm asking you how you know.'

'His jacket indicates he's a Delta op.' The jacket was the section of Francesca's personnel file that would be archived and made publicly available after his retirement. It included the basic facts of his service: deployments, dates of promotion, awards. Shafer was asking for the full file, including disciplinary record, aptitude tests, and notes from commanders. The permanent record, in the words of a 1950s high school principal.

'I'm not going to give you access to my personnel files. And for the record, I am still neither confirming nor denying that this man is one of mine.'

'You have a funny definition of agency-military cooperation, Colonel.'

Silence. Shafer pushed on.

'I understand he's in a pilot project, two-man sniper teams. Official name is Detachment 71.'

'We're going in circles here, Mr Shafer. I just told you I will not confirm or deny anything about Mr Francesca. Might as well ask me to pull my pants down and cough for you. As for that project' – and Cunningham's voice turned into a sneer – 'maybe you should talk to your boss about it.'

In his anger, Cunningham had answered a question that Shafer hadn't thought to ask. 'Fair enough, Colonel. I'll do that.'

'And now you need to tell me why you're asking about my officer.'

'All I can say is that I'm conducting an investigation and his name came up. I'd like his record. Since you've declined, I'd ask you at least to do me the courtesy of not informing him that we've spoken.' A request that ensured Cunningham's next call would go directly to Kandahar.

'What kind of investigation?'

'The criminal kind.'

'With due respect, Mr Shafer, you are on very thin ice. If you have evidence that one of my men has broken the law, you'd best tell me about it so I can open an Article 32 if necessary. I wouldn't want you to interfere with the military justice system. That's a crime. And if you don't have hard evidence, if this is a fishing expedition, I will make you pay. You come clean on this now and maybe I won't call OSD' – the Office of the Secretary of Defense – 'and turn it into a real tornado.'

'Anyone who knows me will tell you I love tornadoes, sir.'

'Do you now.'

'And wicked witches and cowardly lions, too.'

'Well, then, Dorothy, why don't you—' Cunningham ended the conversation with an anatomically impossible suggestion and slammed down the phone.

'Pleasure talking to you, too, Colonel.'

The easy part was done. Now Shafer faced a trickier conversation. He took the internal stairs to the seventh floor. He was huffing when he arrived at Duto's windowless anteroom. He sat heavily among the whispering praetorian guard, wishing he had a magazine. Something transgressive, a Hustler, maybe. Or, even better, Mother Jones. No one spoke to him, but after a half hour a secretary nodded him in.

Shafer found Duto with the phone to his ear. He wore a lightweight blue suit that was cut to emphasize his chest, and a shirt so white that it nearly glowed. Again Shafer marveled at how far Duto had come. Maybe Wells was right. Maybe Duto was thinking White House. Though he had no ideology, as far as Shafer could tell. Like Nixon, Duto wanted power strictly for its own sake. To reward friends and punish enemies.

Shafer sat in the leather chairs nearest Duto's desk. A briefing book sat on the polished wood and Shafer reached for it. Duto slapped at his hand.

'I'm as excited as you are, Chairman.' Duto wheeled his index finger, the universal sign for *get on with it*. 'Yes. Seeing the place in person is the only way to understand it. And we'll make sure you meet lots of Afghans.' A long pause. 'Goes without saying that your safety is our paramount concern . . . Of course . . . Of course . . . Great.'

He hung up.

'Senator Travers. He wants to see the real Afghanistan. And also he wants a zero-risk trip.'

'A safari of sorts.'

'And equally authentic. We leave in three days, Ellis. Hour's getting short. You and the boy wonder close?'

'We've found the soldier in charge of running the trafficking.'

'And I care because?'

'Because he's the one guy who knows the mole's real name. He's a Delta named Daniel Francesca.' Shafer watched Duto for signs of recognition, didn't see it. 'And also because Colonel Cunningham, the Delta commander, is going to call you screaming from Fort Bragg in about fifteen minutes. Probably the E-Ring, too.'

'You been making friends again, Ellis.'

'Ever heard of Detachment 71?'

Duto smiled. For real. An uncommon sight. Duto pretended to smile a lot, but usually his eyes didn't follow his lips.

'You're kidding me. Francesca's in 71?'

Shafer nodded.

'Where's he based?'

'Kandahar. Tell me about 71, Vinny.'

'I suspect you already know, but 71 started four years ago. Technically it's still a pilot project. The Pentagon wanted true black ops capability, so JSOC created two-man sniper teams that can operate outside the wire for medium-term missions, anywhere from forty-eight hours to two weeks. They received extra language training, six months of immersion at Monterey. They wear local clothes, drive local vehicles, carry local IDs. No uniforms, no official or unofficial connection to us. Complete deniability.'

'Nonofficial cover is our job.'

'They aren't intelligence officers. They handle military missions where standard infiltration by helicopter or convoy is impossible. Sit on top of ratlines. Or let's say we have intel that a Talib commander may visit a village in the next seven days, but nothing more specific. A 71 team could set up outside the village and wait for him.'

'So what's it a pilot for? Infiltrating Iran? Pakistan? You can't have liked this, Vinny. Giving the military even more power.'

'I expressed my concerns, that's true. Explained that this kind of covert action capability had to be managed closely.'

'I'll bet. Lo and behold, you send me and John out to find a mole. Lo and behold, we stumble onto a program you hate. Fool me once.'

'I know where you're going but you're wrong.' Two years before, Duto had asked Wells and Shafer to investigate the murders of a team of CIA operatives. He hadn't told them he hoped their investigation would help him rid himself of a rival.

Shafer walked around Duto's desk and stood by the triple-glassed, bulletproofed, sound-dampened window that offered unobstructed views to the Potomac. Langley had once been on the very edge of the federal sprawl. But the government had grown and grown. Bits of the military-intelligence complex were all around them. The turf wars and lies had grown, too.

Shafer looked over his shoulder. 'You love a marked deck, don't you, Vinny? Won't play without one.'

Duto lifted his hands, like a man with nothing to hide. Like a politician. 'Truth, Ellis. I had no idea what you and John would find. Or that this guy was involved. Dumping 71 would be nice, sure, but the whole program is maybe fifteen guys in all. And for now it's only running in Afghanistan. This is about the mole, as far as I'm concerned.'

'Funny thing is, you might be telling the truth. But you lie for sheer sport, Vinny. Even when I want to believe you, I have a tough time.'

'Can we step back here? Start by telling me why you think Francesca is the right guy. Last we spoke, Wells found something at Daood Maktani's house in Dubai. Then he went to that base to give a speech. Did you find Maktani? Did he give you Francesca?'

'No. Maktani, David Miller, whatever you want to call him, he's gone. Nothing from him in weeks. I have a bad feeling about it. I see dead people. Most likely Amadullah took care of him.'

Duto didn't even pretend to care about Daood Maktani's fate. 'Okay, so he didn't give you Francesca. Where'd it come from, then?'

'So Wells gave the speech at FOB Jackson.'

'I know that part.'

'Right. Afterward, a sergeant down there went to Wells, told him guys in his platoon were involved in big-time trafficking. Also that he'd seen an SF operative meeting them and he was sure the op was picking up the drugs.'

'You didn't tell me this.'

'I'm telling you now.'

'This soldier narced on his buddies? That seems like a long shot.'

'Yes and no. Wells and I worked the speech so that anybody who knew about the dealing would sense we were reaching out. We figured somebody had to know. We just needed him to be pissed off to raise his hand. Talking to Wells, it's not like calling CID. Anyway, that's what we figured, and it worked.'

'That's why it was so important that Wells stay in RC South?'

'Correct. So then I tracked down Francesca, connected him to the Stryker soldiers. And earlier today Wells went back to FOB Jackson and got a positive identification from the soldier.'

'But you've got no hard evidence.'

'No. Circumstantial only. But why would a Delta hang out with a couple random Strykers?'

Duto nodded. 'And you see Francesca as your best bet to find the mole. Not Amadullah?'

'Amadullah's gone. His phones are dark. When we ran satellites over the compound, we found the women are there but most of the men are gone.'

'So the mole is rolling up his network. Wells came over, got him nervous. Now he's shutting down.'

'Looks that way. Plus I'm not sure that Thuwani knows who the mole is. The mole's always used Daood as a cutout. Which leaves Francesca.' Shafer hesitated. 'But something else is bothering me. I still can't figure what this is *about*. What the mole wants.'

'Motive is overrated.'

More proof that power was the only principle Duto understood. Because he had no ideology, he assumed no one else did either. 'Motive is everything.'

'It's simple. Our guy saw a chance to make some money doing business with the Taliban. He's greedy.'

Shafer rattled his head back and forth. 'You know Kabul station better than that. Tribal leaders don't take checks.' The

CIA sent cases of hundreds and twenties to Afghanistan every month, money that got handed out to friendly locals in return for receipts that were smudged thumbprints. Audits were impossible. A corrupt case officer could simply invent sources and pocket the cash he was supposedly paying out.

'There are other ways to steal, sure.'

'Then why go to this much trouble? It's like he wanted to build a relationship with the Thuwanis and used the drugs as a way in. But I don't know why.'

'Francesca can tell us.'

'Let's hope. I'm looking to connect him with Kabul station, but so far I've come up dry. I suspect whoever's working with him is a childhood friend, or high school. Something not in the records.'

'And you don't have the evidence to challenge Francesca directly.'

'No. And like you said, we're getting short on time. We have to yank his chain, make him come out and play.'

'So you called down to Fort Bragg, baited the colonel.'

'Correct.'

'I assume John's ready on the other end.'

'John's always ready.'

TWENTY-FIVE

Kandahar Air field

Posters of kittens and puppies covered the walls of the trailer that Francesca and Alders shared. Francesca had bought the first one six months before at an online store that offered free delivery to all military post offices. Two tiny cats tugging on a bright yellow thread of yarn. Across the top, sky blue letters proclaimed, 'Playtime.' He hung it over his bunk when Alders was at the gym.

'Seriously,' Alders said when he got back.

'Seriously.'

'Playtime.'

'Playtime.'

Alders didn't say anything else. So Francesca bought more. He avoided anything ironic, like the poster that proclaimed in heavy black type, 'Kitten thinks of nothing but murder all day.' Just cats and dogs running through meadows, splashing in pools. One for every kill. His reward to himself for a job well-done. If anyone had asked, Francesca would have insisted the posters were a joke, and they were. But they were something else, too, a way to remember that the world did have happiness even if he could no longer feel it.

Now he lay on his cot, hands clasped behind his head, looking at his favorite poster, a tiny Chihuahua with absurdly big ears. Her head was tilted as if she'd just heard her name and couldn't decide whether to answer. Francesca called her Holly. Sometimes he imagined that when he got home he'd go to a shelter and get a real Holly. But he knew what would happen if he did. He'd play with her, buy her treats. But one night she'd pee on the floor, or he'd get tired of her yapping. He'd tell her to stop and she wouldn't. Then he'd pick her up and snap her neck and toss her in the trash. Killing humans didn't bother him. Why would killing dogs? He supposed he could live with a perfectly trained husky or shepherd, an animal that answered to him and him alone and never barked except in warning and never disobeyed or begged for food. But a dog like that would basically be a robot. He didn't want a robot dog. So he was left with the posters.

He and Alders were due to ride out at two a.m., deep into the Arghandab River Valley, which stretched northeast from Kandahar City into Zabul province. For most of its length, the valley ran roughly parallel to Highway 1, which was about twenty miles to the south. The apparent proximity was deceptive. A rugged ridge of hills and low mountains split the valley from the highway, with only a handful of dirt tracks offering passage. In reality, the central Arghandab was as deeply isolated as anywhere in Afghanistan.

Over the last couple months, a Talib cell had planted five huge IEDs in the valley. Three had been found and disarmed. Two hadn't. The most recent was the biggest yet, four hundred and twenty pounds of explosive from surplus Russian artillery shells. It had blasted through a Gator armored truck and killed everyone inside, four soldiers and a reporter and photographer from the *Times* of London. Strips from the truck's armor were found fifty yards down the road. The reporter seemed to have been sitting directly over the bomb. He couldn't be found at all.

The Talib cell planting the IEDs was clever. The valley was a soft target, because it had two American combat outposts but no major bases. The closest was FOB Jackson, which was on Highway 1 and focused on that road. No big bases meant no blimps and less helicopter and drone surveillance, which made it possible for the cell to dig bigger holes and plant bigger bombs.

Even so, the Army's EOD squads, its bomb experts, hadn't understood at first how such big bombs had been planted in the middle of the valley's main road. Then an informant in Qalat, the capital of Zabul, told a military intelligence officer that the cell was posting spotters on the road miles from the bomb sites. That way they had advance warning of American patrols. And to reduce the odds that a drone might spot them, they created diversions while they planted the bombs. They sent men out to take potshots at American patrols or rocket a combat outpost. Anything to draw attention from the road.

The informant also explained that the leader of the cell wanted to press his luck. He believed that the Americans wouldn't expect another attack so soon. He hoped to plant another bomb within the next seventy-two hours east of Toray, a part of the road that hadn't been hit yet.

Under normal circumstances, stopping a single IED-planting cell would be considered a relatively low-value mission and left to local units. But a bomb big enough to blow out a Gator got attention at the regional command level, especially when a reporter was involved. And aerial surveillance had revealed an ideal sniper hole near the road, an abandoned grape hut that had a clear line of sight to the target area the informant had mentioned. So Detachment 71 had been asked to send a squad.

When he heard about the operation, Francesca volunteered. Weston had told him about the speech that Wells gave to the Strykers at FOB Jackson. Francesca didn't think it was a coincidence. Wells was closing in. Francesca wanted to have the option of taking Young out. Being close to FOB Jackson would give it to him.

The digital clock on Francesca's bedside table beeped. Nine o'clock. Time to get ready. He reached for his pistol, which hung over his bed next to Holly's poster. He pulled the pistol's clip and examined the rounds for dust or scratches, then wiped them down with a chamois cloth. He was about to do the same with his spare clip when a knock interrupted him.

'Francesca? Major wants to see you.'

Major Steven Penn commanded the Delta squads at Kandahar. He was a black man, tall and solid and more than happy to be first through the door. His office was all business, not a single family picture, no hint where he'd grown up or had gone to school.

'Sir.' Francesca gave his crispest salute.

'Mr Francesca.' Warrant officers were addressed as 'Mister,' because in the military hierarchy they ranked between commissioned officers and enlisted men. 'Sit, please.' Penn nodded at the wooden bench beside his desk. 'You ever heard of someone named Ellis Shafer?'

Not the question Francesca expected. Or the name. 'No, sir.'

'Are you certain?'

'Yes, sir.'

'Seems he's heard of you. Do you have any idea why the CIA might want to investigate you, Daniel? Any idea at all?'

John Wells. 'No, sir.'

'This' – Penn hesitated – 'man Ellis Shafer works for the CIA. He had the insolence to ask Colonel Cunningham for your file.'

'Sir. May I ask if he said why?'

'He did not. But it's no secret that our friends at Langley are not a hundred percent on board with what we're doing.'

For a crazy half second, Francesca wondered whether Stan had planned this twist all along, to set *him* up, take down Detachment 71. No. He couldn't see how that would work, much less how the missiles fit in. No, Young had snitched to Wells and Wells had chased him down. Francesca wasn't sure how. Didn't matter. What mattered was that Wells and this Shafer were onto him.

But the Delta commanders didn't know why. They figured that the CIA was making a play against Detachment 71. So Francesca had caught a break. Penn and Cunningham didn't know whether he was dirty. And they didn't want to know. Knowing would make protecting the project harder, and protecting the project was their priority. They were giving him a heads-up, a chance to fix whatever was wrong.

And fix it he would.

'Anything at all you want to tell me, Daniel?'

'No, sir.'

'You still want to go up into the Arghandab? Because I can assign another team.'

'Yes, sir. One hundred percent.'

'Glad to hear it. Dismissed.'

Francesca saluted and stalked back to his trailer and grabbed one of his untraceable spare phones. He left the Delta compound and punched in a Kabul number. Stan picked up on the second ring. 'Twenty minutes,' he said.

Francesca didn't want to go back to the compound and leave again. To pass the time, he walked over to the Boardwalk, the airfield's equivalent of a town square, a block of shops and restaurants. At the Boardwalk, guys who never got outside the wire could eat Nathan's hot dogs and KFC and buy leather jackets covered with maps of Afghanistan. Of all the things that Francesca hated – and these days his hatred seemed almost infinite – he hated the Boardwalk and the falsity of the pretend soldiers on it most of all. The Air Force ought to drop a nuke on the place.

Stan called back right on time. 'What's going on?'

'Your friends are asking about me. Called my commander. Said my name came up in an investigation.'

'They say what they had?'

'Not as far as I know.'

'They mention me?'

'No. I need to find the freelancer.' How they'd agreed to refer to Wells. *No names on these phones, ever*, Stan had said.

'I suspect he's close to you, but I don't know. Let me handle this. Sit tight.'

'You said that before. This is out of hand. I'm taking care of it.'

'Give me a chance to find out what they know.'

'I'll think about it,' Francesca said, knowing he wouldn't. He hung up. Stan rang again a few seconds later, but Francesca didn't answer. He had another call to make, this one to FOB Jackson.

When he got back to the trailer, Alders was cleaning his weapons. 'Heard Penn was looking for you. Anything I need to know about?'

'Later. In the truck.'

They cleaned their weapons and went for a final briefing for the Arghandab mission with the captain who ran 71. If all went as planned, they would reach the grape hut – a tall mud building where Afghan farmers dried grapes into raisins – an hour before sunrise. There they would hide themselves and the truck. The insurgents didn't have drones or satellites, so vehicles were invisible once they were parked inside.

Drones had made repeated runs in the last forty-eight hours to be sure the grape hut was empty. But the Talibs wouldn't risk planting an IED if they believed that a drone was nearby, so all surveillance would be pulled once Francesca and Alders got to the hut. In fact, much of the valley would be closed to both helicopters and drones for the next five days, both to encourage the bomb makers to get to work and to reduce the chance of friendly fire.

As the briefing dragged on, Francesca's attention slid to the other operation he was planning. It would be easier. A turkey shoot, really. First Young. Then, with any luck, Wells, who was likely to come running once he heard that Young had been killed.

So he was risking his life to protect one group of American soldiers while killing another. The irony was perfect. The *world* was perfect. Francesca bit the inside of his lip to keep from laughing.

Just before two a.m., Francesca and Alders drove out through Gate 1, on the base's southern side. Each man wore a brown *shalwar kameez* and had a short-stock AK tucked behind his seat. As usual, the Barrett was hidden in the compartment under the Toyota, along with their uniforms and night-vision scopes and any other gear that might identify them as American. Tonight the Dragunov was down there, too. Alders carried a

GPS that had been specially programmed with the Afghan road network. But the GPS had been hidden inside the casing for a cheap Nokia, a common brand in the Afghan countryside.

They were wearing what Special Operations guys called ballistic underwear, basically heavy-duty fire-resistant boxer briefs. The underwear was useful for snipers, who did a lot of crawling on stony ground. The military was considering giving it to every frontline soldier. Any IED big enough to take off arms and legs could blow off more sensitive areas, too. A little bit of extra protection was good for morale. Of course, any Afghan would know that the briefs weren't local. But if a Talib got close enough to see his underwear, Francesca figured he'd be dead already. Or wishing he were.

Francesca followed a convoy of supply trucks toward Kandahar City. At Highway 1, the trucks swung west toward the city. Francesca turned right. Suddenly they were alone. Past midnight, the Afghan roads were deserted aside from military convoys. The Talibs had learned the effectiveness of American night-vision equipment and rarely tried ambushes after dark. Ordinary Afghans didn't own cars and had little reason to risk nighttime travel. They locked themselves in their compounds and waited for the sun to set them free.

As the lights of Kandahar faded to specks in his mirrors, Francesca swung left off Highway 1, north on a narrow track that rose up a gentle hillside. After a few minutes, the Toyota crested a ridge and the Arghandab River Valley stretched out below. In the moonlight, it looked almost beautiful. During the day, the grape fields were brown and drab. Now they were black oceans marked by whispery, bare-branched almond trees. Farther north, the pomegranate groves near the river rose thick and lush. Insurgents launched ambushes from the groves, moving under them in fortified tunnels. But at this hour they were as peaceful as the Garden of Eden. Far past the river, the mountains of central Afghanistan soared, their snowcapped peaks glowing white.

'This land is your land, this land is my land,' Francesca burst out. 'From California to the New York – sing it with me now—'

Alders punched him. Hard.

'Not nice. You know, Alders. You're the only one left I can take.'

'Promise you'll tell me when you decide I'm as bad as everybody else.'

'Yeah?'

'Give me a chance to get out of range of that Barrett.'

Francesca's giggle echoed off through the cab of the truck. Even he could hear how crazy he sounded.

'What was Penn talking to you about?' Alders said.

Francesca told him.

'CIA? So we have something to take care of.'

'Thought I'd have to convince you.'

'All this time together, you still don't know me. You think I didn't guess where this might go?'

'Good, because I already talked to Weston.' Francesca walked Alders through his plan.

'This going to be today?'

'Think so. He'll tell me soon as he's sure.'

'You ready on the Dragunov?'

'A rifle's a rifle.' Though Francesca wasn't entirely sure. He'd been able to practice on it only once. The Dragunov fired a high-powered AK 7.62-millimeter round, a smaller bullet than the .50 cal. As a result, the Russian rifle was shorter, lighter, and easier to carry than his own. But it couldn't match the Barrett's range. The differences were typical of American and Russian engineering. American weapons designers put a premium on technical excellence while barely considering the practical problems soldiers might face in the field. The Russians built less capable systems that were easier to carry and use. Ultimately, though, Francesca figured that if he could get within five hundred meters, he'd be fine. The Talibs sure killed enough guys with Dragunovs.

At the base of the valley, Francesca turned right. They drove northeast on the narrow road connecting the villages along the Arghandab River. An IED would obliterate the Toyota, but Francesca wasn't worried. The insurgents saved their bombs for American vehicles, not random farmers who happened to be foolish enough to be out after dark.

For ninety minutes, neither man spoke. The silence in the truck merged with the silence outside. A valley full of phantoms. The road had no signs, no gas stations, no restaurants to mark their path. For a while, Francesca wouldn't have believed they were moving at all if not for their progress on the GPS. But finally it beeped. Alders squinted at the tiny screen. 'Almost here. Maybe another hundred meters.'

Sure enough, a few seconds later Francesca saw a dirt track hemmed by four-foot-high walls on either side. He turned right. Fifty meters in, he stopped, cut the pickup's lights. Without a word Alders slipped out and knelt beside the pickup. Thirty seconds later, he slid back into the cab and handed Francesca a night-vision scope. Francesca slid the cylinder over his right eye, leaving his left uncovered.

Through the eyepiece, the world looked green and black and oddly two-dimensional, like a 1950s television. In a world without electricity, night optics offered huge advantages. Soldiers could lock on insurgents who had no chance of finding them. But because the equipment blunted depth perception, most soldiers no longer wore full goggles. They favored scopes that covered one eye while leaving the other exposed. With practice, their brains learned to process the weirdly divergent information coming from each eye and create a complete picture.

Francesca eased off the brake, rolled deeper into the silhouette world ahead. The grape hut was directly ahead, a long, narrow building, maybe fifteen feet high. It had narrow slits for windows, like a medieval fortress. Another hut had once stood nearby, but an explosion had destroyed it years before, nearly leveling it. The first hut had partly survived. Its southern wall had been shattered and was crumbling into the mud. But its north side, which faced the valley road, was intact.

Francesca nosed the pickup through a cut in the wall near the hut. The Toyota's tires sank into the dirt, but he downshifted and clicked on the four-wheel drive. On the southern side of the hut he found a jagged hole, maybe ten feet wide. 'Home sweet home,' he said.

He edged the pickup through the hole into the hut. He cut the engine. Inside the hut, the blackness was absolute. Without his eyepiece, Francesca would have been blind. With it, he saw that the hut held dozens of simple wooden racks. Farmers used them to dry grapes into raisins. The grapes had long since disappeared, leaving the racks, and a faint sweet odor, as the only evidence of the hut's initial purpose.

Francesca's feet crunched over metal. He reached down, found brass casings and an 82-millimeter mortar tube. Francesca sniffed the tip of the tube. He didn't smell gunpowder. The mortar hadn't been used in years. He tossed it aside.

The back of the Toyota appeared to be filled with junk: old bicycles, foam bedrolls, rusted steel rods and sheets, and a couple of blankets. None of the stuff would have attracted notice at a checkpoint. Francesca and Alders pulled it all out. They slid two of the rods into holes the size of quarters that had been drilled into the Toyota's front bumper. They laid one end of a steel sheet over the rods. The rods and sheet had been machined to fit together as easily as LEGO blocks, with an equally satisfying click. The far end of the sheet lay atop the Toyota's cab. The sheet was seven feet wide, six feet long, just big enough for Francesca and Alders to lie side by side with the Barrett between them, its muzzle poking out of one of the hut's narrow slits. A firing platform.

Once the platform was set, Francesca and Alders stretched the brown blankets over it and the truck. The Toyota was brown and covered with dirt and mud anyway. Inside the grape hut and under the blankets, it would be basically invisible, even during the day. Francesca climbed onto the platform. Alders reached down for the Barrett and lifted it to him, grunting at the weight of the rifle. Francesca pulled up the Barrett and snapped its legs into place. Alders handed him another camouflage net and he draped it over the Barrett's muzzle to hide the steel.

Then Francesca settled back and slipped off his eyepiece. He put his eye to the Barrett's infrared scope, which had far sharper resolution than his own. He found himself looking at an empty green world, the stillest of nights. No grapes had been grown in the fields around here for at least a year. Even the mice seemed to have disappeared.

He was six feet off the ground, with an open view of the road to the north, no farmhouses or high walls for a mile east or west. The position was close to perfect, concealed and with a huge field of fire. These Talib bomb-planting cells usually had no more than four guys. If they set up the way he expected, Francesca could kill them all in under a minute.

Sniper fire was confusing and terrifying, even for experienced infantry. Typical firefights happened at close range, distances no more than a football field. As a result, when an ambush began, soldiers instinctively assumed the enemy was close by. They needed several seconds to realize that they were under sniper attack. When they realized they didn't have any way to counterattack, they typically dove and froze, trying to present as small a target as possible. But during a sniper attack, going to the ground was suicide. Francesca could put a round in a stationary target from a mile away. Unless perfect cover was available, the best solution was to scatter and regroup. Run. But by the time the Talibs figured that out, they'd be dead.

Alders handed him a bottle of water and Francesca took a long slug.

'How's it look?'

'Real good. Whyn't you sack out? I'll take first watch.'

'You sure?'

'Yeah. I'll call it in, let them know we're here.' Their sat phones worked everywhere in Afghanistan – everywhere in the world, in fact – and they were supposed to report when they arrived and every eight to twelve hours afterward. Francesca tried to stick to the schedule, mainly because the Delta commanders got nervous otherwise. When they got nervous, they were apt to do stupid things, like put up a rescue bird. He reached for the sat, made the call.

He'd just hung up when his other phone vibrated. Afghan cellies. Amazing. He didn't even know where the tower was. Probably somewhere on the ridge behind them. The caller identification showed a local phone. Had to be Weston.

'You in position?' Yep. Weston.

'We're where we need to be.' Francesca didn't appreciate this kid's attitude. He'd considered taking Weston and Rodriguez out along with Young. In fact, he was still considering it.

'Okay, I still haven't heard whether it will be today or tomorrow. Should know soon.'

'Call me when you do.' Francesca hung up. Put his eye to the rifle's infrared scope. Listened to Alders snore gently on the ground below. And smiled as he watched the empty night.

TWENTY-SIX

The transmitter was two inches long, no wider around than a dime. Half the size of the eraserless pencils that miniature golfers used to count putts. Shafer had told Wells that the geeks called it an intermittent locator. As long as whatever it was attached to was moving, it reported its position every forty-five minutes to the military's Iridium satellite network. Each transmission lasted only five milliseconds. Otherwise the bug stayed silent, offering no electronic evidence of its existence.

If the transmitter stopped moving for more than forty-five minutes, it offered one final update on its location. Then it shut down. It broadcast so infrequently that it was basically undetectable. Plus it transmitted on a nonlinear cycle. Even Shafer couldn't explain what that meant. But he promised Wells it would enable the bug to beat every electronic countermeasure in existence.

Shafer had sent Wells three transmitters in three different colors. One gray, one brown, one black. They had no on/off switches or lights. They looked like plastic junk. He'd also included a handheld GPS that would track the transmitter. And a note. *Be nice to them. You'd be surprised what they cost.* Wells never remembered Shafer worrying about budgets before. Either the transmitters were seriously expensive or the man was getting strange about money in his old age.

Despite his anger, Stout had shown Wells where Francesca kept his pickup, a muddy parking lot near Kandahar's giant PX. Aside from a razor-wire fence, the lot looked ordinary, full of pickups, SUVs, and Humvees. A small sign beside the front gate said 'Reserved/TF86 Vehicles.'

'TF86 doesn't exist,' Stout said. 'This lot is SF only. Everybody keeps trucks in here. The Canadians and Brits, too. It's unlocked during the day, but there are always a couple of guards. They work for Sandton. That's a private contractor that JSOC uses a lot. They look like they're just hanging out, fiddling with a truck, but they'll challenge you at the gate. At night, it's locked down and alarmed. You need a key and a code to get in. And if you look at the gate, you'll see the surveillance cams.'

Wells looked. Two cameras, both watching the gate. He liked the setup. Hidden in plain sight. Though it didn't help him any.

Stout pointed to a beat-up Toyota pickup near the back of the lot, one of the rattier vehicles. 'That's Francesca's. You can't see it from here, but underneath there's a compartment where they hide their rifles and unis.'

'That's definitely theirs? They never swap with the other squads?'

'No. So that's it. All I can tell you.'

'Thank you.'

'You're not welcome. And don't ask me to get you inside the lot. In fact, don't ask me about anything else, or *for* anything else.'

They didn't speak again until Stout dropped Wells back at the KBR trailer where he was holed up. Wells sat on his bunk and closed his eyes. He owed Shafer a call and he ought to be figuring his next move. But he was stuck on what Stout had said to him as they were driving. *Which faith? Islam or America?* He seemed to be failing both. His mind turned to the man in the hills outside Muslim Bagh. They'd prayed together. Then Wells had killed him. How could God view his words as anything but a mockery?

Islam had helped Wells survive all those years in the North-West Frontier. But now he no longer could explain what he believed, or why. Was he clinging to his faith strictly to separate himself from the other Americans who were fighting this war? To prove to the men he killed that religion played no part in his quarrel with them? They certainly didn't agree.

Eventually Wells tired of asking himself questions without answers. He knelt and lowered his head to the floor and recited the first surah over and over. The prayer itself was a tonic. The Arabic soothed his lips, even if he no longer trusted himself to understand what it meant.

In the morning he put on a regulation Army uniform complete with a colonel's eagle on the chest. In the trailer's mirror, he found he didn't look like a colonel. Even in the Special Forces, colonels didn't have beards like his. He pulled off the insignia. He slipped on his Red Sox cap and his Ray-Bans. A smile twitched his lips as he remembered the morning Anne had given him the sunglasses.

He drove back to the lot Stout had shown him. Sure enough, two guys tinkered under the hood of a Ford Expedition near the front gate. One flagged Wells down. 'Morning.'

Wells stopped, lowered his window. 'Morning.'

'Haven't seen you before. You certain you found the right lot?' The guy sounded South African to Wells. Lots of security contractors were.

'Pretty much. Guys at Bengal sent me here to park. Problem?'

The guy looked at Wells, his beard and shades and killer's hands. 'No problem. Welcome to KAF.'

Wells parked three spots down from Francesca's Toyota, positioning the Land Rover between the pickup and the guards. He looked around, didn't see anyone else in the lot. He stepped over to the Toyota. Its bed was filled with metal rods and sheets that Wells guessed could be assembled into a firing platform. He pulled out the transmitters. The brown one more or less matched the Toyota's paint. He peeled off the backing on two of its six sides, exposing an epoxy superglue. He pressed it in the corner of the bed behind the passenger seat. Once it stuck on, it was practically invisible. He would have put it on the undercarriage, but it needed a direct line of sight to the atmosphere.

He slid back into the Land Rover and headed out. He didn't want Francesca wondering why an unfamiliar vehicle was parked near the Toyota. As he passed the Expedition, he lowered his window. 'Change of plans,' he said. 'See you soon.'

'Happy hunting,' the guard said.

Wells saluted him casually, one pro to another.

He called Shafer. 'Good to go.'

'I'll call Cunningham tomorrow morning my time. Maybe ten a.m.'

'Seven-thirty p.m. here.'

'Look at you, doing the math. So you can expect that he'll be on the phone to KAF pretty much the second he hangs up.'

'No chance he'll cooperate?'

'I call him, back-channel him, tell him one of his guys may be a criminal target and I want his file. And I won't say why, won't show him any of the evidence. Plus I act like an asshole

336

on top of it. He's more likely to send a hit squad up here than help me.'

'All these years I thought being an asshole was your personality. Now it turns out it's part of your cover.'

'Cute. Like talking to my wife. Anyway, figure Cunningham sounds the alarm to the Delta commander at Kandahar, I believe it's a major named Penn. That guy tells Francesca. Who gets off base soon as he can come up with some legit operation that gets him pointed toward FOB Jackson.'

'You're sure the Deltas won't lock him down while they check this out on their own?'

'If I gave Cunningham something concrete, maybe. Not this way. They start kicking over rocks, they don't know what they might find. Best not to look.'

'Speaking of things that hide under rocks, what about Duto? He know where we stand?'

'Not yet. I'll talk to him after I set the hook with Cunningham. Don't jump down my throat for asking, but do you have anyone backing you up over there? Gaffan's buddy?'

'Look, if that bug you gave me works—'

'It works—'

'Then I'll know where Francesca and Alders are hiding. And they won't know I know. If that's not a big enough edge, I'd better find a new line of work.'

'Modern dance instructor.'

Wells hung up, called Anne.

'John?'

'Hello, babe.'

'You're wearing the Ray-Bans, aren't you?'

'How'd you know?'

'You'd only call me things like *babe* when you're wearing them. Rocker John.'

'I've been called lots of things over the years, but I assure you Rocker John isn't one.'

'Tell me you're almost done over there.'

'I am. Honestly.'

'You gonna get the bad guy?'

'I always do.' Almost.

'Then we'll live happily ever after. You and me and Tonka makes three. He told me how much he missed you this morning. Said you're not a good owner, but you're his favorite anyway.'

'Tell him I miss him, too. And you, Anne. Can't wait to see you.'

'I love you, John. Whatever it is you're doing, be careful.'

'I love you, too.' A word Wells had rarely used with Anne. A word that felt right today.

He spent the afternoon getting his gear together. Then he had nothing to do but wait. He went back to his trailer and slept. No point in wasting energy he would need soon enough. He woke after sunset to a call from Shafer, who explained what had happened with Cunningham and Duto.

'So Duto knew about 71 all along,' Wells said.

'He swears he had no idea that the trail would go that way.'

'You believe him?'

'It doesn't matter. Train's way down the tracks.'

Shafer was right. They couldn't stop chasing Francesca now. As usual, Duto had played them.

'One of these years, I'm going to pay him back.'

'*Inshallah*, my friend. Knock 'em dead.'

'I'll do my best.'

It was nearly eleven p.m. when his local phone rang. Young.

'Coleman.'

'Out of nowhere, Weston told us to be ready for an op in the next twenty-four hours. Motorcycle registration in the Arghandab.' Insurgents favored motorcycles, so the military was trying to track them with tamper-proof registration stickers. Never mind that the insurgents had an endless supply of cheap bikes. Registration offered a measurable benchmark for commanders to meet. The military loved measurable benchmarks.

'Where exactly?'

'He says we don't have final orders yet. But the most likely spots are a couple roads that run from Highway 1 and up into the valley. Pretty near the base. Eighty to a hundred miles northeast of KAF. You know where I'm talking about?'

'More or less.'

'More or less does not promote confidence, sir.'

'When you know more, you call me. I promise I'll be there.'

'That's more like it.'

So Weston was getting his platoon off FOB Jackson. Which meant Francesca would be leaving KAF soon enough. Wells's GPS was plugged into the feed from the transmitter on the pickup. Wells waited for it to ping.

And waited. The hours dragged. Midnight passed. One a.m. Maybe Francesca wouldn't leave base until tomorrow. Or maybe Young was wrong. Maybe Francesca wasn't part of this scheme after all. Two a.m. Wells tried to sleep, couldn't.

At 2:30, the GPS beeped. A single blue dot indicated that Francesca's pickup was ten miles outside of the airfield. He'd taken the bait. Wells knew where he was heading. North and east, deep into the Arghandab River Valley. Toward 1st Squad, 3rd Platoon, Bravo Company, 1st Battalion, 7th Stryker Brigade. Toward Coleman Young.

Part of Wells wanted to chase them immediately, but moving

at this hour would be a mistake. Francesca and Alders couldn't do anything until Young was off FOB Jackson. Best to let them get set in their sniper hole, then go after them.

Wells set his alarm for 5:30, before dawn. He closed his eyes and dreamed of a wave that started in the Hindu Kush and swept down and down, through the poppy fields, the empty Registan Desert, over the mountains in Pakistan, all the way to the sea.

Soon as he woke Wells checked the GPS. Something was wrong. Three transmissions – covering a ninety-minute period – showed motion northeast in chunks of thirty miles or so. The third transmission came in around four o'clock. But after that, the locator went silent. At least two more transmissions should have followed by now. If the pickup had stopped, the transmitter should have reported that, too. Wells called Shafer. 'What's going on?'

'Probably they've stopped somewhere where the transmitter doesn't have line-of-sight to the atmosphere. It'll keep pinging every forty-five minutes until the signal goes through and it gets an answer.'

Wells thought of the metal firing platform he'd seen in the back of the pickup. If Francesca had set that up and it reached over the transmitter, it would block the signal. 'If there's metal in the way—'

'Metal's not good. But it will keep trying.'

'Meantime I'm just supposed to guess where they holed up.'

'I'll put some calls out, see if I can get a handle on what their official mission is.'

'You think the Deltas are going to tell you that after the way you left it with Cunningham?'

'You do your job, John. Let me do mine.'

Shafer hung up. Wells rose and showered. He pulled on a

shalwar kameez and covered it with a brown windbreaker for the ride and packed a nylon bag with his kit. Everything he was carrying would pass for local, even the GPS and his binoculars. For weapons he had a knife strapped to his leg and three Russian RGO-78 grenades and his old Makarov and silencer. No AK. Even a short-stock would be impossible to hide. Anyway, a long-range gun battle with Francesca would be suicide. An AK had an effective range of maybe a hundred yards. Francesca could be lethal from ten times that distance. Wells would need to ambush him close in.

His new motorcycle was parked outside his trailer. He'd bought it the day before. It didn't look like much, a Chinese-made Honda knockoff with an air-cooled 250cc engine and wire wheels. The word *Hando* was painted in white on its gas tank. No one would ever confuse it with a Ducati. Its speedometer went to two hundred kilometers an hour, but Wells figured the wheels would come off long before then. But Wells had looked it over closely before buying it. It was mechanically sound, and the tires and shocks were solid.

In any case, anonymity mattered more than performance. Anonymity translated into surprise, and Wells had learned over the years that tactical surprise beat firepower. Bar brawls or gunfights, the guy who hit first won. Maybe not always, but close enough. In Hollywood, fights went on and on and on. In the real world, they didn't take long. Once a punch or kick or bullet knocked you down, going back on the attack was nearly impossible. You kept getting hit until the other guy stopped. Sometimes he didn't stop until you were dead.

Francesca seemed to have learned the same lessons. His dirty pickup was what Wells would have used if he'd needed to carry a sniper rifle. And like Wells, Francesca and Alders operated without uniforms, or backup to bail them out. A casual observer might not see much difference between Wells and Francesca.

But somewhere Francesca had lost himself, forgotten his purpose. Forgotten that anyone could pull a trigger, take a life. The act itself was simple. The *why* was what separated soldiers from serial killers. Wells hadn't forgotten the why. So he hoped. He put his bag on the back of the bike, slipped the key into the ignition.

The morning traffic on Highway 1 was picking up as Wells headed east, shielding his eyes from the sun. The flatlands of southern Afghanistan turned cool in the mornings at this time of year. Wells shivered under his windbreaker as he followed Francesca's trail north off Highway 1 and into the Arghandab Valley.

Even by Afghan standards, the valley was a backwater. A half dozen children swirled around a woman in an electric-blue burqa. A donkey dragged a cart inch by inch, whining with each step, as a gaunt man with skin the color and texture of leather clapped a switch across his haunches. Two Afghan soldiers leaned against a pickup truck, cigarettes in hand. One had painted the stock of his AK pink and covered the muzzle with rhinestones. *Don't ask, don't tell*. Afghans on both sides of the insurgency had a strange fondness for tricking out their rifles. The soldiers eyed Wells as he passed, but didn't bother to stop him.

Wells reached the last point the transmitter had signaled just over two hours after leaving Kandahar. He pulled over and looked for any sign that Francesca and Alders had stopped nearby. Open fields lay north of the road, toward the river. To the south, a narrow cart track passed through a handful of farm compounds. Wells didn't think the Toyota would fit on the track.

Anyway, he could see a stream of smoke coming from one compound, and kids playing on the roof of another. Wells couldn't imagine how Francesca and Alders would have hidden themselves in an occupied house. They had to be squatting someplace abandoned.

Wells rolled on. The landscape stayed the same for the next few miles. Compounds and the occasional grape hut sat south of the road. North, toward the river, the pomegranate groves thickened. Still, this part of the Arghandab was much less fertile than the land nearer Kandahar, the trees less dense.

The road passed through a village. To the south, several shops occupied a plaza, the Afghan version of a strip mall. At the far end was a garage big enough to hide the pickup. Wells stopped outside the plaza's first store, walked in. Three men hunched over sewing machines, working long strips of white cotton. Posters taped to the concrete walls showed their offerings. The men barely acknowledged Wells. In these tiny villages, outsiders were suspect, especially if they weren't Pashtun.

'Good morning.'

'Morning,' the man nearest Wells mumbled. One of his eyes was a deep, ugly red, the skin around it swollen and tender. Severe conjunctivitis. In the United States, a doctor would cure that infection with a few cents of medicine. Here, the man might go blind.

Wells leaned over his machine. 'I see you do excellent work.' The man grunted and fed cloth through as the machine clucked. Time to get to the point. 'I'm looking for two men who might have stopped here early this morning. Before sunrise.'

The man raised his head to stare with his weeping eye at Wells. The machines halted one by one until the shop was silent. 'No one's stopped here.'

'They were driving a Toyota, a pickup.' Wells reached into

343

his pocket for a wad of afghanis. 'Are you sure you haven't seen them?'

'No one's stopped here. And who are you?'

Wells backed out. As he got back on the bike, the sewing resumed. He didn't understand why the tailors had been so unfriendly. He put the bike in gear, rolled by the garage. A side door was open and he could see inside. Empty. They hadn't stopped here. Wells pulled back onto the road.

Past the village, more dirt tracks ran south, though most petered out before the ridgeline. Just three roads in this part of the valley ran over the ridge and toward Highway 1. If what Young had said was right, the Strykers would be on one of those roads sometime today. But Wells needed more. He hoped Shafer was making progress on unearthing their official mission. To find them without the transmitter's help, he had to pin down what they were doing. And he had to lock them down soon, so he could track them as they moved on Young. Only then would Wells have the proof he needed to take them out. Right now he had only circumstantial evidence. He had to catch them in the act.

Worst-case, if Wells couldn't find them, he could try to cover Young directly as the Stryker platoon registered motorcycles. But Francesca would be expecting him. Finding and tracking Francesca as he moved on Young would give Wells his only real chance of beating Francesca's firepower advantage.

As he started to ride again, his phone buzzed.

'Told you, let me do my job,' Shafer said. 'Point one. That road you're on has turned into an IED alley. Four soldiers and two British journos got creamed last week. That got noticed all the way up to RCS HQ.'

No wonder the locals were giving the fish eye to outsiders,

Wells thought. They couldn't stop the Taliban from planting bombs, but they were worried that more casualties would provoke a big American counterattack, the kind that flattened villages. 'What's point two?'

'Point two. Yesterday the drones at KAF, in fact all air support, was ordered away from a sector of the valley sixty kilometers long and thirty wide. Lockdown for five days. Reason given is Special Operations mission, otherwise unspecified. How much would you like to bet your friends are setting up, waiting for Red Team to plant another IED? Makes for great cover.'

'It's even better than that. The mission gives them an excuse to be out here. The no-fly zone means that when they kill Young, the Strykers can't hit back. They go back to their original nest, take out the IED cell, come home to Kandahar. Mission accomplished. They just need to put a few miles between where they're supposed to be, the official post, and the Young kill.'

'Sounds right.'

'So I should be looking for a nest near the road, within a mile or so. Not on the ridgeline. An abandoned farmhouse, something like that. With room to hide the pickup.' Wells was thinking out loud now.

'I hear more, I'll let you know.'

Wells hung up. Now he could focus on houses within a few hundred yards of the road, with an open field of fire. Plus the firing position had to be big enough to hide the Toyota. Only a few buildings could meet all those conditions.

Still, he had a lot of ground to cover. Francesca and Alders would have reached the nest between four a.m., the time of the locator's final transmission, and 4:45, when it should have reported again. Even if they had needed ten minutes to hide the pickup and put the firing platform together, they could have driven for thirty-five minutes, enough time to get as much as twenty miles east of the final location the transmitter had recorded.

Wells headed east, watching both sides of the road. For a few minutes, the valley became more densely populated. Compounds and villages tumbled together, the Arghandab's version of suburban sprawl, unlikely ground for a sniper's hole. Then the land opened up again. And Wells came on a good spot for a nest, a damaged grape hut with an unobstructed view of the road. The hut's narrow windows made for good firing ports, and a dirt track led directly past it. Wells couldn't risk taking the track. But he knew that in Francesca's position he would have chosen the hut, or a place just like it.

Wells rode until the hut disappeared. He'd take his chances in one-on-one combat with anyone. But snipers were different. He felt as if he'd appeared at dawn for a duel and found himself holding a slingshot instead of a pistol. A half mile was a long way. Ten New York City blocks. Nine football fields. From a half mile, Wells couldn't even see his enemy's face without binoculars, good ones. Yet an experienced sniper like Francesca had a good chance of putting a bullet in a target's chest from the same distance.

Wells pulled the bike over at a primitive gas station, the first he'd seen in fifty miles. Again he called Shafer. 'I need a visual, a satellite pass.' Wells gave the coordinates. 'It's a grape hut, a big one. ASAP.'

'Really. You don't want to wait a few days.'

'I'm not in the mood.'

'This guy's got you a little bit spooked, doesn't he?'

Wells didn't answer.

'All right. You know it's past midnight here, but I'll make it happen as fast as I can. Could be anywhere from fifteen minutes to six hours, depending on what we have overhead. I'll call you when I know.'

Wells propped the motorcycle on its kickstand, reached into his bag for a bottle of water. He drank deeply. A couple kids stared until he waved them on. In these villages, any stranger was conspicuous. He couldn't stay in one place too long, but he didn't want to ride farther from the grape hut. Thirty minutes later, Shafer called.

'You must be living right. NRO had a Keyhole passing Kabul. The overnight targeting officer is an easily impressed sort. He ran a quick series.'

'And?'

'I can't see them firsthand because he won't send them to my Gmail account. NRO's funny that way. And the shots aren't great because they couldn't get the KH directly over, they had to angle, and the roof is mostly covered. But he swears he can see a pickup truck inside.'

'What about people?'

'He said he didn't see anyone, but that I shouldn't read much into that because the imagery is so dirty. No need to thank me, John—'

One of the kids was wandering close again, giving Wells an excuse to hang up. *What next?* Finding Francesca was only half the battle. Young hadn't called yet. So Wells didn't know where the Strykers were running their motorcycle registration. Until Wells knew exactly, he couldn't position himself to intercept Francesca. Why wasn't Young calling?

His first instinct was to leave the valley floor, head south into the hills, find a promontory where he could overwatch the grape hut. But the Arghandab's geography was trickier than it first seemed. The hills were a smaller version of the Bitterroot Range in Montana, where Wells had grown up. They rose as much as twenty-five hundred feet above the valley floor. Gullies and draws cut deep into their sides. Once he got into them, moving east to west across them would be very difficult. Maybe impossible. The GPS could tell him where he was, but not where he needed to go. He needed a good map for that, and he didn't have one. He would also have to ditch the motorcycle, which was his only major tactical advantage. Worse, he wouldn't have cell service once he left the valley floor, so Young would have no way of reaching him. No.

He had two other alternatives. He could sit where he was, wait for Young to call. Or he could take the high-risk option, set up on one of the three north–south tracks that went over the ridge. But if he chose wrong, he would be stuck ten or more miles away from the ambush, with no easy way to get to the right spot. He couldn't justify taking a one-in-three gamble that could leave him badly out of position. Playing linebacker growing up, he'd never liked the guys who went for the big pick instead of batting the ball away. When they were right, they got the glory, but when they were wrong, they gave up a touchdown and the whole team paid.

Then he realized. He took off his windbreaker and stuffed it in his bag. At the gas station, he filled up and bought two big stacks of wood. He bundled them on the backseat of the bike to hide his bag. He left his pistol and grenades inside the bag. He couldn't risk Francesca spotting them through the scope.

He mounted up and headed west. Toward the grape hut.

At the dirt track nearest the hut, he swung left, south, bouncing over the ruts. He tried not to think about the fact that Francesca was surely tracking him from inside the hut. This close, the .50 caliber would blow through him and leave an exit wound the size of a softball. At least he wouldn't have to worry about bleeding out. He'd die instantly.

But he had to trust that Francesca wouldn't shoot a random farmer on a motorcycle. Francesca had no reason to believe that Wells could have tracked him here. And Wells could pass as local better than anyone.

Halfway to the hut, Wells still couldn't see the pickup. He wondered whether Shafer or the NRO had made a mistake. Finally, maybe a hundred yards from the hut, he saw a blocky shape inside the narrow windows. The hut was a great position. Even this close, Wells wouldn't have seen the truck if he hadn't been looking. At a hundred feet, he saw the first hint of a sniper nest, camouflage netting around one of the slits. He still couldn't see the muzzle of the rifle.

Just past the hut, Wells pulled over. He was safer here, on the south side, with the hut between him and the rifle. The .50 caliber was big and heavy and hard to maneuver. He put the motorcycle in neutral and dropped the kickstand, but left the engine running. He pushed aside the bundles of sticks so he could reach the bag and the pistol inside.

'Hello,' he yelled in Pashtun. 'Uncle?'

No answer. Walking into the hut would be a mistake. If they were sure he'd seen the Toyota and the firing platform, they'd shoot him. But they wouldn't do that unless they had to. They would think he lived nearby, and they wouldn't want to get the locals upset. Instead, one of them should come out, challenge Wells, tell him to get lost.

But no one did.

Wells switched off the engine. Waited. Nothing. No whispered voices in English or Pashtun. No movement inside the hut. No scrape of metal on clay as Francesca repositioned the Barrett. Wells unzipped the bag, grabbed his pistol. He stepped over the cut in the wall and into the compound. The hut's mud walls were pebbled and uneven. Sprigs of weeds were growing in some of its slatted windows as nature began to reclaim its soil. Wells saw fresh tire tracks in the dirt. No doubt the Toyota had come this way. He looked close, saw two more sets of tracks atop the tire treads. They were narrower. Bicycle tires.

'Hello?' he yelled again. Then ran for the hut. No sense waiting now. If they were inside, they were laying a trap for him. If they weren't, he needed to find out.

They weren't.

The pickup was there, the firing platform, and the rifle. But Francesca and Alders were gone. Wells bent low, looked for bicycle tracks. He found them near the pickup's back gate.

Wells pulled out his cell. The reception was fine. But something had gone wrong. Young hadn't called. Now Francesca and Alders were on their way to ambush him. If he couldn't find them, stop them, he would have himself to blame for Young's death.

Not this time. Not after what had happened in Mecca.

Wells sprinted out of the hut, back to the motorcycle. He turned back. To the valley road. He had one chance. Three roads led to Highway 1. He had to figure out which one Francesca and Alders had taken. He couldn't guess. If he guessed wrong, he would lose an hour or more. He had to be sure. *How?*

TWENTY-SEVEN

Francesca strained up the hill, cranking the pedals under his leather sandals, staring down at the dust beneath his front wheel. He raised his head, saw Alders pulling away around the next bend.

'Slow down,' Francesca yelled. In English. A tactical breach. He didn't care. The road was rutted and steep, barely wide enough for two bikes side by side. A small car could scrape through, but it would need a new paint job afterward. In an hour of riding, Francesca had seen only two motorcycles, both coming north, toward him.

At least the air was cool up here. The folds of the hillside hid the sun. Still, Francesca would never again question the manhood of the riders in the Tour de France. He found Alders waiting at the top of a sharp left turn. 'Not too bad from here,' Alders said. Francesca pulled over, waited for his breath. Alders gave him thirty seconds, then rode off. Francesca followed, cursing. But Alders was right. After one final turn, the road flattened out and opened into a narrow saddle. Scattered pine trees and mulberry bushes broke the rocky soil. To east and west, the slopes climbed steeply. It was the best natural pass across the ridge for ten miles in either direction, which was why the road ran through it. Though *road* was a highly generous term.

Francesca looked back the way they'd come, across the Arghandab Valley. The pomegranate groves that bordered the river were maybe ten miles north and fifteen hundred feet lower. Closer in, smoke rose from a grape field. The nearest fire department was at KAF, so the fire would be burning awhile.

Alders pulled out a plastic-coated terrain map. They'd left their GPS back at the hut so they couldn't be tracked. But Francesca didn't need the map. He felt comfortable with the terrain up here. He could see where to set up.

The far side of the ridge, the southern side, sloped gently toward Highway 1, where FOB Jackson was located. The road they were riding turned slightly left as it emerged from the saddle, running south-southeast. About five hundred meters ahead, the road bisected a small village. Maybe forty compounds. Weston had told Francesca that the platoon would set up there, stickering motorcycles and checking out some of the houses. A presence and registration patrol.

The day was clear, the wind low. Assuming Weston did his job and got Young into the open, Francesca expected the shot would be easy. After the kill, he and Alders would head back the way they'd come. The platoon would have little chance to chase them. The Strykers could get only as far as the saddle. On the northern side, the road was too narrow and steep for the big trucks to navigate. On the bikes, Francesca and Alders could easily outrace anyone foolish enough to chase them on foot. The no-fly zone meant that they didn't have to worry about drones or helicopters. And Francesca planned to ditch the Dragunov. Taking it back to the grape hut and then KAF could only cause trouble. So even if some overzealous Apache pilot violated the no-fly zone and came over the ridge, he'd see nothing but a couple of Afghan farmers on bicycles, miles away from the kill zone. Once they were back at the hut, they would hang out and wait for the Talib IED-planting cell to show.

Weston had called just after sunrise. Francesca hadn't slept at all, but he felt great, thanks to two greenies. Breakfast of champions. He felt the vibrations of every mote of dust in the grape hut. He was in tune with the world. He was *alive*.

'Got the okay from my CO. We're gonna roll this morning. Little bit sooner than I thought. You cool with that?'

'We're always cool, Lieutenant. Where we talked about before?'

'Yes. The village is called Mohammed Kalay. We'll be there at ten-thirty. Eleven at the latest.'

'Roger that. Eleven. And your boy will follow orders long enough to give me a chance to engage?'

'He hasn't said no to a mission yet. I don't see him starting now.'

'And you haven't heard anything from the other one?' Meaning Wells.

'The one who came and talked? No.'

'You do, you let me know.'

'Will do. When you're in position, will you signal?'

Yeah, I'll signal. Coleman Young getting his throat ripped out. That's the signal.

Francesca hung up. Alders was still snoring. Francesca squeezed him on the shoulder. Not hard. Guys who spent their lives in nests like this didn't like being woken too suddenly. Alders sat up, wiped a hand over his mouth.

'Was I lucky enough to get blown to hell while I slept or am I still stuck in this tar pit?'

'Sad to say you're still alive.'

'Why did you wake me? I had a good one going.'

'Your favorite nurse again?'

Months before, Alders had told Francesca that he had a nurse fantasy, not the usual candy striper but a chubby, big-breasted East Indian who gave him a rough massage with a barely happy ending.

'I should never have told you that.'

'True. Ready to rock and roll?'

'Our Talib friends?'

'Our other friends.'

'We just got here.'

'I know, but this way's better. Get it done quick, come back, chill.'

Francesca hadn't told Alders that he was still thinking about taking out Weston and Rodriguez with Young. He figured he'd see how the trap set up. A game-time decision.

They rode off a few minutes later in their brown *shalwar kameez*. They had three hours plus before the Strykers arrived. The grape hut was about thirteen or fourteen miles from the saddle. Francesca figured they would have plenty of time. Then they hit the hills. For the last couple miles, he'd wondered whether walking might be faster. The ride had taken so long that they burned through most of their cushion. By Francesca's watch, they had about forty-five minutes to pick their spot, get settled. Less time than he would have liked.

Francesca pulled the bike off the road, left it behind a rock, grabbed the canvas bag that held the Dragunov's hard-sided case. He walked east, keeping back from the ridgeline. The saddle turned steeper, blending into the hill above. Loose rocks cut at Francesca's sandals. He wanted to gain maybe forty or fifty feet of elevation, make the shot easy to take, hard to trace.

Alders ranged ahead and closer to the ridgeline. About a

hundred yards east of the road, he waved Francesca over. Above, a dry streambed crosscut the hillside, running southwest. It fell over the ridgeline thirty yards away from where they stood. A tangle of mulberry bushes marked the spot. Francesca and Alders could set up in the streambed between the bushes, which offered great cover. Aside from the last few feet, they wouldn't even have to crawl or crab-walk to the position. They could walk without fear of being seen from the fields below.

'You see.'

'Long as it has the right angle.' If a boulder or the folds of the ridge blocked Francesca's line of sight to the village, the position was useless, no matter how good the cover. He cut over to the streambed. It was dry, six feet wide, a couple feet deep. This part of the Arghandab Valley didn't get much rain. The runoff that fed the river fell in the mountains to the north. Just shy of the ridgeline, Francesca unzipped the bag and pulled out his binoculars and a thin brown blanket. He unrolled the blanket. He wanted to keep his gown clean. On the ride home, even the most oblivious Afghan police officer might notice a man in a dirt-covered *shalwar kameez*. He squirmed forward on the blanket, ignoring the stones poking at him. At the edge, he propped himself on his elbows, raised his binoculars.

Perfect.

The contours of the hill made him nearly invisible to the villagers below, but no rocks or outcroppings blocked his view. The mud houses and compounds started a quarter mile away. Inside them, villagers did what Francesca had decided Afghans did best: not much. In one compound, three men sat against a wall, drinking tea from a battered brass kettle. Outside another, a bony farmer dragged a rake slowly through the earth, as an equally bony cow grazed nearby. Two empty burqas floated high in the air, ghosts on a clothesline.

In the center of the village was an empty dirt field, a town square of sorts. The Strykers were sure to park there. None of the walls between him and the square were high enough to matter. The fluttering burqas were a lucky break, too. Their movement would make gauging the breeze easy. Francesca hardly even needed Alders.

'Look good?'

'That it does.'

Alders crawled up beside him, holding the rifle and his bag of gear. Francesca edged left and traded the binoculars for the Dragunov. 'Too easy,' Alders said.

'There's no such thing.' Francesca slid the Dragunov's scope over the rifle's barrel, which was designed with a metal rail that made attaching the scope a cinch. He flipped a latch to lock it in place. Next he reached for a magazine. He'd brought four, all loaded with ten rounds of 203-grain steel-jacketed 7.62-millimeter ammunition. The bullets could smash Level IV armor plates that stopped regular AK rounds.

At five hundred meters, even a perfectly aimed shot from the Dragunov could go wide of its target by six inches. Instead of a head shot, Francesca planned to aim for Young's chest and fire a three-shot burst. Unlike most sniper rifles, the Dragunov was semiautomatic. Each squeeze of the trigger fired another round. At worst, the first burst would shatter Young's vest and knock him down. With ten rounds, Francesca would have plenty of chances for a kill shot.

Francesca locked onto the farmer bent over his rake. *I could kill you and you'd never know where your death came from. Not where or why.* The excitement went beyond words. Death and life were his to give. He dropped the safety and put a finger to the trigger, his mouth open and every breath a rapture. After a long moment, he flicked up the safety, pulled back. *I've let you live. Forget Allah. Pray to me tonight, old man.* He draped brown netting over the Dragunov's muzzle and rested his head on his arms and waited for the Strykers to come. Waited for prey.

TWENTY-EIGHT

Wells stopped at the intersection of the valley road and the easternmost of the three tracks that led over the hills. He jumped off and squatted low, looking for bicycle tracks in the dirt. If Francesca and Alders had come this way this morning, their narrow tires should still be visible. But the treads Wells saw were far too wide to belong to bicycles. He pulled out his binoculars and followed the track into the hills. No bicycles, no men walking.

Fifty yards down, three boys played soccer, kicking a ragged ball with the studied indolence of teenagers everywhere. Wells stepped toward them. 'Have you been here all morning?' The boys looked at one another. The ball never stopped moving.

'Have the Americans taken your tongues? Answer me.'

The tallest boy grinned at Wells, a confident smile that somehow reminded Wells of his own son. 'Yes.'

'Have you seen men riding bicycles this way?'

'One man. My uncle Hamid. He lives down there.' The boy nodded to a low-walled compound about a mile down the road.

Wells hurried back to his motorcycle. He could eliminate this track. Two left. The second intersection was barely ten miles west, but Wells wasn't sure how long he would need to reach it. Forty miles an hour on the Arghandab road equaled a hundred and twenty on an American highway. Any faster and he would pop a tire.

Wells swung the bike around, headed west. In the last two hours, he'd gotten to know this strip of road: the one-room store that seemed to sell nothing but potatoes and apples, the skinny German shepherd chained to a tree who barked madly when Wells passed. The grape hut that Francesca and Alders were using as a bed-and-breakfast.

Finally, the second ridgeline road. Wells pulled over, looked for bicycle tires.

There. Two thin tracks, not quite side by side. Wells pulled his binoculars, looked up at the hills. Nothing. And no kids to ask.

The road passed a handful of compounds on its way to the ridgeline. The bikes could have belonged to local farmers. Even so, Wells decided to go with his gut, chase the tracks. He turned south. The road was so rutted and rocky that he couldn't get out of second gear. Francesca and Alders must have had an even tougher time. The slowest chase in history. A 250cc Honda knockoff after two bicycles. Wells smiled, but only for a moment. He didn't understand why Young hadn't called him, warned him. He might be too late already. Francesca might be taking aim at this moment—

No. He pushed the thought away. He rolled the throttle and the motorcycle zipped ahead, bouncing beneath him, past grapevines and almond trees. After about fifteen minutes on the track, he passed the last farmhouse and came upon a patch of dried mud that stretched all the way across the track. If he saw the bike tires here, he'd know that Francesca and Alders were ahead. If not, he'd wasted even more time.

Wells bent his head to the mud with the desperate hope of a poker player peeking at his last down card, needing an ace. And saw . . . fresh tracks. He rode on, more confident now, as the road rose in earnest into the hills. Wells wended his way between ruts deep enough to snap his ankle. Wells saw now why the Arghandab Valley was so isolated. Farmers couldn't use these tracks to ship their produce to Highway 1 and the rest of Zabul. Even a well-built four-wheel-drive SUV would have a tough time with this hill.

Wells took a curve too fast and the front wheel chopped into a rut. The bike tilted precariously left and the back end kicked out. Wells pulled his left foot off the peg and stepped sideways onto the muddy track. His toes jammed into a rock, sending a jolt up his leg. The bike stalled. As he struggled to keep it from going down, his right leg touched the superheated exhaust pipe. He tried to pull away, but the bike moved with him, the pipe searing his gown into his calf. Finally, Wells regained his balance and jerked the bike up. He stood in the track, grunting in pain. A bright red burn the size of a silver dollar rose from his right calf. His left foot throbbed angrily. He wasn't exactly mortally wounded, but the odds that he'd win a foot chase with Francesca had just plunged.

Wells gritted his teeth and put the motorcycle in gear and rolled on. First gear. No faster. He'd be useless if he broke a leg. Anyway, Francesca and Alders couldn't be that far ahead. On bikes, they'd be lucky to make five miles an hour.

Minute by minute, turn by turn, he rose up the hill.

Ten minutes later, he reached the saddle. And saw their bikes, sprawled carelessly a few feet from the road. Eureka. Wells stopped, looked left and right. The bikes lay to the left, east, so Francesca and Alders had probably gone that way. But he didn't see them, or any obvious position.

He could leave the road, ride up the hill. But they'd hear the engine coming their way long before he found them. He couldn't ride and shoot at the same time. They'd take him out easily. He could ditch the bike and go up the ridge on foot. But if they were close, and they probably were, they would hear the motorcycle cut out. And wonder why it had stopped instead of passing over the saddle. Or . . . if the Strykers hadn't arrived yet . . . if he had even a few minutes . . .

Wells rode to the southern edge of the saddle and put the bike in neutral and looked out. The village lay a few hundred yards below. No Strykers, but Wells saw a convoy of blocky vehicles maybe five miles away. They'd be at the village in ten minutes, fifteen at most.

He eased back into gear, rode over the ridge and down the hill. As he left the safety of the ridgeline, he was intensely conscious that Francesca had to be above, watching through his scope. He kept his eyes forward. No reason to look anywhere but the village ahead. No reason to be nervous. He was just a farmer out for a ride.

Then he closed on the village, or it closed on him. The compounds splayed out around the road. He came to a muddy open square and what must have been the only shop in town. Four teenagers stood beside its open doorway. Just what Wells had hoped to see. He pulled up beside them, parking beside a wall that hid him from the ridgeline.

'Nice motorcycle,' the biggest of the four said.

'What's your name?'

'Razi.'

'You know how to ride, Razi?'

Razi squared his shoulders. 'Of course.'

'Then you can have it.'

'What?'

'The bike. You can have it. I'll give it to you.'

'You're not funny. You're stupid.'

Wells raised a hand. 'Allah cut out my tongue if I'm lying. Let me tell you what I need.'

When Wells had explained, Razi shook his head.

'Why do you want this?'

Wells nearly told the kid not to ask, then decided the truth would work better. 'There are men hiding in those hills. I want to get to them and this is the best way.'

'Then what?'

Wells heard the rumble of the Strykers' diesel engines in the distance. They couldn't be more than five or six minutes away. 'Yes or no, Razi? Yes or no?'

The kid looked at the others. He didn't want to seem scared in front of them, Wells thought. Peer pressure worked every time.

'Yes.'

Wells stepped off the bike. He pulled off his bag and the branches that had covered it and tossed the branches on the ground. Razi took his place at the handlebars. Wells slid in behind him and put the bag between them and rested his hands on Razi's shoulders. Without a word Razi put the bike in gear and turned them around and took them back up the hill. Wells was glad to find that the kid rode smoothly.

As they emerged from the square into the sun, Wells peeked at the eastern slope of the saddle. He saw a big boulder that might have been Francesca's nest, and a couple of thick shrubs. But he couldn't look too closely and risk tipping off Francesca. Instead he tucked his head into Razi's shoulder and visualized what he would do when the bike reached the ridgeline.

TWENTY-NINE

Francesca watched the Strykers come up the road through the open fields. They dwarfed the crummy mud houses and everything else they passed. They were a ways off, but they would reach the village soon enough. They were moving twenty-plus miles an hour, faster than Francesca had expected, especially since the lead Stryker had to push its mine roller up the hill.

Still, they were running a few minutes late. On a routine mission like this, somebody always fell behind schedule. Not that the schedule mattered. The village was tiny. The platoon wouldn't run across many motorcycles. The guys would hang out for a couple hours, knock on some doors, get back to FOB Jackson in plenty of time for dinner. Another mission complete. Another day closer to home.

Then Francesca heard the whine of a motorcycle engine. It was close by, coming up the hill behind them, the same road they'd ridden up. The bike sounded small, a couple hundred cubic centimeters. The engine was revving high, like the rider was in first gear. It made the last turn, reached the saddle, stopped. Alders started to get up, but Francesca put a hand on him to keep him down. A few seconds later, the bike moved on, to the edge of the ridgeline. It idled even more briefly, like the rider was looking over the ridge down at the village. Then it moved south.

'What was that?' Alders said.

Francesca raised a finger to his lips and scooted forward as the bike came into view. It looked to be a Honda knockoff with a 250cc engine, just like the two they'd passed on the way up. A bunch of branches hung off the back, like the bike had a wooden Afro. The motorcyclist was a big guy with a big beard and a brown *shalwar kameez*.

'Why'd he stop on the saddle?' Alders said.

'Probably saw the bikes, tried to figure it out.'

'And then on the ridge?'

'Maybe he saw the Strykers.' Then Francesca realized. 'Could be he's part of that IED cell.'

'I still hate the timing.'

Francesca didn't like it either, but the guy looked local. Anyway, if Francesca took him out, they'd lose any chance at Young. 'I'm gonna let him roll.'

The guy reached the square in the middle of the village, disappeared behind a mud wall. Francesca could still hear the bike idling. He looked down the road. The Strykers were closing, under three miles out now, steaming up the hill.

'I don't like it,' Alders said.

Francesca ignored him. The biker was no threat. And if he looked like he was becoming one, Francesca could take him out in seconds. He wasn't wearing armor. Francesca would have seen it under his gown.

A minute later, if that, the bike emerged from the square. Now it was coming back north. Now the guy who'd been riding was on the back. A teenage kid was up front. The branches were gone. The passenger was holding some kind of bag.

'Told you,' Francesca said. 'Dude's ACF' – anti-coalition

forces – 'all the way. Getting out of Dodge before the cavalry gets here. Bet you a hundred bucks I catch him planting an IED back at the hut and I take him then.' Francesca liked that idea. *Watch him now, kill him later.*

'He stops on the saddle, we're gonna have a problem.'

'He's not stopping.'

The bike came up the road, its little engine humming *chugga chugga choo*. Francesca let it come, didn't even scope it. He was staying focused on the Stryker convoy, less than two miles away now. He wanted to hit Young quick, soon as he had a clear shot. Weston and Rodriguez, too. Snip those loose ends. If Alders got pissed, so be it. The man couldn't exactly file a complaint with CID. But Francesca figured Alders wouldn't be upset, not after what he'd said in the truck. Alders had turned out to be stone-cold after all.

The bike disappeared from sight as it approached the ridge. Then it was on the saddle. It slowed, might even have idled for a second. Then it revved and disappeared down the back side toward the Arghandab, its engine fading.

'Told you,' Francesca said. 'No problem. Show's about to start.'

THIRTY

When the bike got to within fifty yards of the ridgeline, Wells tapped Razi's arm. The kid downshifted. Wells stood, put his hands on Razi's shoulders. Razi nodded to Wells's unspoken command and tapped the rear brake lightly as they hit the saddle. Wells kicked his right leg over the seat and jumped.

He landed cleanly. Even so, he felt like someone had put a spike through his left foot. He grabbed the pistol and two grenades. He stuffed the grenades in his gown pockets, ducked behind a tree close by the road. Behind him, the motorcycle's engine revved as it rolled away down the hill. Wells had offered Razi the bike in trade for the one-minute ride from the village to the saddle. The deal was more than fair, aside from the chance of sudden death by sniper. Though Wells had kept that risk to himself. Anyway, Francesca had stayed quiet and the bike was Razi's now. He'd earned it. Wells hoped he had fun with it.

Wells didn't think Francesca or Alders would leave their nest to investigate a passing motorcycle, especially since they could hear it disappearing. But he stayed behind the tree for fifteen long seconds before standing and stalking east, up the hill, pistol loose at his side. He scanned for the nest, the glint of metal, the shadow cast by an arm or leg. Nothing. He heard the Strykers now, their big engines rumbling. They must have reached the village.

Then he saw the streambed and the mulberry bushes.

The Strykers were so big that only two could park in the central plaza. The third and fourth stopped at the edge of the village, a hundred meters away. Francesca focused on the two in the center of town.

'You ready for this?' he said to Alders. 'Blue on blue?'

'It is what it is.'

The Dragunov's scope was marked with chevrons and graphs that formed a primitive but effective range-finding system. Francesca marked distance to target at 525 meters. The black burqas were limp on their clothesline. The breeze had stopped.

The lead Stryker's ramp inched down. One by one, men stepped out. Francesca watched through the scope. *Americans*. With American uniforms and helmets and M-16s and M-4s. No. Not Americans or Talibs. Not friendlies or enemies. Targets.

Weston was fifth man out of the Stryker. Soon as his feet touched dirt, he started directing traffic. He sent two men to the eastern edge of the square, spread the rest around the Stryker. They were loose and relaxed, Francesca saw. No one expected trouble. For just a moment, Weston looked up the ridgeline, like he was trying to spot the nest. But his eyes slid by Francesca and kept right on going.

Francesca moved to the second Stryker. The ramp had dropped. Two men out already. A third emerging. Rodriguez. So Young was in there, too. Young was in Rodriguez's squad. He'd be out in a matter of seconds.

Even better, here came Weston, walking over to Rodriguez. 'Three for the price of one,' Francesca said.

'It is what it is,' Alders said again.

Francesca wondered whether Alders thought he had some profound wisdom there. Because he didn't. But Francesca didn't argue. They'd come to the silent moment before the lightning. Francesca steadied his hands, slowed his heart. He thumbed down the safety, put his eye to the scope, slipped his index finger through the trigger guard.

And he waited.

Young walked down the ramp, took a half step onto the muddy ground. Francesca's finger tightened on the trigger—

Young turned and walked back into the Stryker like he'd forgotten something. Rodriguez stepped toward the ramp. He seemed to be yelling. Probably asking Young what the heck he was doing, telling him to get his butt out of the truck.

Then Francesca felt as much as heard a presence behind them. A scuffling on the dirt, leaves crackling. He couldn't explain exactly how he knew. But he *knew*.

'Check the six,' he whispered to Alders.

'What?'

'Now.'

Alders didn't argue. He reached for his AK, pushed himself to his knees, turned—

And then everything happened at once.

Wells climbed to the streambed and angled down. Following the draw would give him the best chance of spotting the nest without being seen. Forty meters from the bushes, the streambed dipped between two refrigerator-size rocks. Wells walked between them. Another step and he could see almost to the ridgeline. A brown blanket. And two pairs of sandaled feet side by side. His first glimpse of Francesca and Alders, not face-to-face but face-to-foot.

Wells took another step, raised his pistol. And suddenly the man on the right sat up and turned. Alders. Holding an AK. His mouth popped open as he saw Wells.

Wells pulled the trigger, a quick one-handed shot. He didn't have time to aim. The bullet caught Alders high in the chest, close to the shoulder, and pushed him down. Wells fired again, missing. A geyser of dirt exploded up from the streambed. Alders grunted in pain and kicked himself backward toward the ridgeline, cutting off Wells's angle.

Wells stepped forward, but Alders put up a couple wild shots so Wells couldn't charge. Wells shifted his aim to Francesca as Francesca pulled in his legs. Wells fired twice and missed both times. Only one for four now. Alders returned with the AK. This time the shots were close, and Wells threw himself down to the streambed. At this range, even a half-aimed burst could connect.

'Drop it!' Wells yelled.

Alders answered with another three-shot burst. Wells raised the Makarov, fired two shots blindly. Six gone now from the pistol's ten-shot clip. But he needed to keep Alders and Francesca down. Wells had them pinned and facing the wrong way. They wouldn't want to go over the ridgeline and expose themselves to the soldiers in the village unless they had to. But if Francesca could get himself and his rifle turned around, he'd have a serious firepower edge.

'Last chance!'

No answer. Wells raised himself to his knees, shifted the Makarov to his left hand. With his right, he reached into his gown for a grenade.

Alders was hit bad, Francesca saw. The right side of his gown was already inked with blood. His big front teeth were chomping at his lower lip as he tried to keep quiet. Francesca had no idea how Wells had tracked them here. The answer hardly mattered, not now.

Down in the village, the Strykers had taken cover. If Weston had any sense, he would delay as long as he could, give Francesca a chance to work this mess out for himself. But eventually he would have to send a couple squads up here to search the ridgeline. Francesca needed to be gone by then. He would have a tough time explaining why he was up here carrying a Russian sniper rifle.

He had to take out Wells and get back into the Arghandab. Let Weston and Rodriguez run his corpse over with a Stryker until it was unrecognizable. Meanwhile Francesca would get back to the grape hut and call in a medevac for Alders, tell some story about how he'd gotten pegged while he was out taking a piss. It wasn't a great plan. It left Young alive. But Young had no evidence and wouldn't be big on talking anyway, not after he saw his buddy Wells get creamed.

'You win,' Francesca said. He squeezed Alders's hand. 'We surrender.' Wells was too close for Francesca to tell Alders what he planned. Even a whisper would carry. He'd just have to hope Alders got it. Alders winked. Good enough. Alders turned and pushed himself up with his good hand. Francesca grabbed the Dragunov and got ready to launch himself over the ridgeline. He would spin and stand and fire through the mulberry bushes. He wouldn't have much of an angle and he'd be shooting uphill. But he had a sniper rifle against a pistol and that should be enough.

Alders stood up unsteadily from the streambed, every breath a struggle. His right arm dangled uselessly. He wasn't holding the AK. Francesca was still hidden. Wells was on his knees, holding the grenade low and close against his body so Alders couldn't see it. As grenades went, the RGO-78 wasn't great, a modern version of an old Russian design. It weighed about a pound and looked like an oversize green egg with a ridge in the middle. If Wells could drop it within five meters of Francesca, it would be lethal.

'Francesca!' Wells yelled. *'Now!'*

'He's coming,' Alders said. 'I promise—'

Alders was talking too much, covering, and then Wells heard Francesca scrambling at the edge of the streambed. Wells put the grenade to his teeth and pulled the pin and released the handle and tossed it up, aiming for the ridgeline. The grenade arced high, end over end, desperate and beautiful as a field goal try with no time left. Wells knew as soon as he threw it that he'd left it short.

'Grenade,' Alders yelled. 'Grenade!'

Alders dove. Wells went down, too. These RGOs kicked fragments thirty meters.

Boom. The explosion echoed off the hills, louder than a single grenade had any right to be. Alders cursed and Francesca screamed and Wells crawled down the streambed on hands and knees, the stones scraping the burn on his leg. Alders came to his knees and raised his trembling left hand. Shrapnel had cut open his arms, and the front of his gown was black with blood. His mouth was a hole in his beard. He would be dead in an hour unless one of the Stryker medics down the hill could stanch the bleeding.

'Yield,' Alders said. In English. Reminding Wells that he was an American. An American soldier. In his eyes, Wells saw the truth of the surrender. No trick this time. Suddenly the Makarov weighed a thousand pounds. Wells had never killed an American.

'Tell me the truth. Why you were here.'

'You know why.'

'Say it and I'll let you live.'

'Coleman Young. Please.'

Alders had given up any claim to mercy with the false surrender. He'd given up any claim when he'd come here to murder Young. Wells raised the pistol.

'You said—'

I lied, Wells thought. He squeezed the trigger. Twice. In the chest. Alders slid against the side of the streambed and his dead eyes accused Wells.

In the silence, Wells could hear Francesca's ragged breathing.

'Alders,' Francesca said from just beneath the ridgeline. Wells couldn't see him or the Dragunov.

'Francesca. Tell me who you're working for.'

'You gonna let me live, too?' Francesca giggled. 'That what you'll do for me?'

'I'll do you a bigger favor. Kill you now. No trial, you don't spend fifty years in Leavenworth. Go out like a man. Your parents, your buddies, they never know you're a traitor.'

Wells reached into his gown for his second grenade. Would Francesca move left or right along the ridgeline to protect himself from more grenades? Or would he stay close to the streambed for the most direct shot with his rifle? Yes. He'd stay close, try to end this now. Wells grabbed his second grenade from the gown. His last grenade. His extra Makarov magazines were back in his bag, too. He was down to two rounds.

'Fair enough,' Francesca said.

Wells pulled the pin on the grenade. If he left it short, the ridgeline would protect Francesca. If he put too much on it, it would slide down the hill. Wells didn't throw it. He rolled it down the dry streambed, hard. Then he jumped out of the stream-bed and dove down behind a rock and waited for the explosion.

It came too soon. The grenade had blown before falling off the ridgeline. Even as the echo died, Francesca yelled, 'Missed.' Wells raised his head and saw Francesca standing up, spinning, holding a rifle chest-high, where he could get an angle and fire up the streambed. Francesca snapped off three quick shots before he realized Wells had moved. But Wells had no angle either, and with only two rounds left, he couldn't afford to miss. He waited, expecting Francesca to hide under the ridgeline again.

Instead, Francesca stepped forward. He went to one knee in the streambed next to Alders's body. He swung the Dragunov slowly left to right, covering the trees and rocks on both sides of the streambed. From where he waited, he couldn't see Wells. But Wells still had no angle on him, and they were only about twenty-five meters from each other, and Wells would have to give up his cover to move.

'Americans dressed like Afghans killing each other with Russian guns,' Francesca said. 'How about that?' Wells had the crazy thought that Francesca sounded like Keith Jackson calling college football. 'I know you've only got a couple rounds left in that peashooter, Johnny. Make 'em count.'

Wells reached out, felt the edge of a rock with his fingertips. He reached for it, couldn't get to it. He inched down, quietly. Let Francesca talk. The Dragunov swung side to side, never stopping. Francesca was waiting for any move, any sound.

'I *heard* Alders surrender. How do you shoot a man, he's got his hands in the air, he's begging for his life? Tell me that.'

Wells got his hand around the rock, found it was the size of a baseball. Just right.

'Tell you what, Johnny. I'll tell you who I'm working with. And when you meet him in hell, you tell him the Shadow sent you there. And be sure to ask him about the missiles, will you?'

Moving only his arm, Wells flipped the rock high into the air. He didn't care where it landed as long as it reached the other side of the stream, the downhill side. It bounced off a tree and landed on the scree with a crack, and Francesca swung the Dragunov around toward it—

Wells came to his knees and lifted the Makarov and squeezed the trigger twice, knowing these were his last two rounds, knowing that if he missed Francesca would finish him—

He caught Francesca once in the chest and once in the belly. The shots spun Francesca sideways and he fell against the side of the stream beside Alders. He tried to bring the Dragunov back around on Wells, but couldn't. The muzzle dragged uselessly on the ground. Wells stood, jumped down, walked to Francesca, knelt beside him. The shots had caught him high and low. Ugly wounds, probably mortal. Francesca put a hand on his stomach and looked dumbly at the blood trickling through it.

'Who you working for?'

'You think you're any different than me, John? That what you think?'

Yeah, somewhere on the way, you stopped caring who you killed. Wells heard American voices in the distance. When they got here, they'd see the Dragunov and the AK and three guys dressed like locals. They'd open up long before Wells could explain he was American, much less the truth of what had happened. Weston would understand, of course, but Weston was no friend. Wells had to get off this ridge now. Ride Francesca's bike back down the hill and go from there.

'Finish it off,' Francesca said. 'Don't be a bitch.'

'Last time. What's his name? You call him Stan, I know that, but what's his name?'

'Wrong question, John. The right question is why? And the answer is, Why *not*? Why *not*, why *not*, why *not*.' A breath between each repetition, as if the two words held Francesca's whole being.

Wells reached down for his knife. Then stopped himself. He wouldn't give Francesca the pleasure.

'Do it.'

'Not without the name.'

Wells stood, stepped away. Francesca went silent. Then spoke one last time.

'Lautner.'

Wells turned back.

'Pete Lautner is Stan. Now *do* it.'

They locked eyes. Francesca nodded and Wells knew he'd spoken true. Wells pulled his knife and knelt in the dirt and lifted the blade high.

The voices on the hill were louder now. Wells wanted to offer some final words. But none came. He couldn't wait. Francesca closed his eyes. And Wells grabbed his hair and pulled back his head and plunged down the knife.

EPILOGUE

DOD IDENTIFIES ARMY CASUALTIES
The Department of Defense announced today the death of
two soldiers who were supporting Operation Enduring
Freedom.

Chief Warrant Officer William F. Alders, 34, of
Linwood, W. Va., and Chief Warrant Officer Daniel L.
Francesca, 33, of Orlando, Fl., died in Zabul province,
Afghanistan, of wounds suffered when their unit was
attacked with small arms fire. They were assigned to
the US Army Special Operations Command, Fort Bragg,
NC.

The release was standard, though a careful reader might notice
that it used the passive voice to describe the incident: '*their unit
was attacked*,' not '*insurgents attacked their unit*.' The families
of Francesca and Alders were told only that they died in hand-
to-hand combat after their position was overrun, a story that was
true as far as it went.

Of course, the Deltas who helicoptered from Kandahar to
retrieve the bodies knew that Francesca and Alders had been
killed close to fifteen miles from their assigned position and
weren't carrying their Barrett. But the Deltas didn't have to be

told to keep their mouths shut. The less said the better. Some questions were best left unasked.

Wells crashed in a KBR trailer at Kandahar the night after he killed Francesca and Alders. The next morning he shaved his beard, the thick black clumps piling in the sink, nearly clogging the drain. He put on his cleanest shirt and borrowed a Hyundai from the KBR lot. When he gave his name to the gate guards at the Delta compound, he half expected that they'd put him on the ground and cuff him. The frontline guys might not have figured out exactly what had happened. But the major who commanded the unit knew of Shafer's call to Cunningham. He had to suspect Wells was responsible for killing his guys.

Instead, the guards waved him in and asked him almost politely to wait in his car. A few minutes later, a black man about Wells's age strode toward the gates. He had a square jaw and shoulders that hardly fit under his uniform. He slid into the front passenger seat and nodded to Wells.

'Steven Penn. I run this unit.'

'Major.'

'Let's take a drive.'

Wells rolled through the gate and into the endless airfield traffic.

'You came here to tell me what happened?'

'As much as I can.'

'I want you to feel you can be straight with me.'

'I always get nervous when somebody says that.'

'I'll put it this way, then. I'm not taping this. Why do you think we're talking in your car and not my office?'

Wells decided Penn deserved the truth. 'Francesca had a Dragunov. I don't know where he got it, but it was practically new. They were set up on that ridge targeting a Stryker platoon. I found them, came up on them, killed them.'

'You killed them? Just like that.'

'Just like that.'

'Then you called your boss Shafer and told him to tell me where to find the bodies.'

'I didn't want them to rot and I knew the Strykers would leave them.'

Penn squeezed his hands together. 'Why would my men do that? Engage American soldiers?' Whatever anger or regret Penn felt, his voice was perfectly controlled, barely a whisper. Wells explained what Francesca and the Strykers had been doing. Penn listened in silence until Wells finished.

'You're sure?'

'It's why they were up there. One of the Stryker soldiers was talking to me. They were planning to take him out.'

'Any more of my men involved?'

'I don't think so. It looks like a CIA officer was running them, running the ring.'

'Which is why you're in on this. Why Shafer called Cunningham. Setting the hook.'

'Yes.'

'Why didn't you just tell us?'

'All we had was one enlisted man's word and a couple pieces of circumstantial evidence.'

'And you didn't think we'd want to hear about it anyway.'

'That's right.' Though now that he'd met Penn, Wells thought he and Shafer had made a mistake. The Delta officer seemed like a problem solver, not a blame dodger. If Wells had come directly to him, they could have found a less dangerous way to smoke out Francesca and Alders.

'Was this about taking down Detachment 71? Some Langley power grab?'

'I don't play those games.' Though Vinny Duto does. 'This

was, is, about a problem in the CIA. A mole working with the Talibs. The director asked me to find him and the investigation ran this way. To drug smuggling and then to your guys. Honestly, I didn't expect that.'

'And have you found the mole?'

Wells nodded.

'Care to share?'

'I expect you'll find out soon enough, but I'd rather not.'

They drove in silence toward the cluttered junkyards in the southwest corner of the base. The wind had turned southerly, bringing with it the stench of human waste. The tons of feces that Kandahar's inhabitants generated every day had to go somewhere. Before being pumped into the fields outside the base, it was chemically treated at an artificial lagoon on the airfield's west side.

'Had to take us this way,' Penn said.

'It always this bad?'

'During the summer, guys wake up thinking they've crapped themselves.'

'A big thinker might wonder if that smell isn't a metaphor for the war, the waste we're leaving behind.'

'He might. I just leave the windows up and breathe through my mouth.'

'A wise man.' Wells turned back toward the center of the base.

'Thank you.'

'For turning?'

'For what you did.'

The words were so unexpected that for a moment Wells wondered if he'd misheard.

'If my guys were doing what you said . . . and you're right, why else would they be up there . . . then they were cancers.

And I failed as a leader. Failed them and myself. It was happening right in front of me. I didn't see it. I let them get out of control.'

'You're not a mind reader. And wars do strange things to the men who fight them.' At the end, when he'd closed his eyes and offered his neck to the knife, Francesca had smiled. He'd been relieved. Wells would swear to it. *War is endless grief.* 'What will you tell your men, Major?'

'As little as I can.' Penn paused. 'And are you planning to deal with the Strykers, too?'

'Yes.'

Penn seemed to want to ask Wells how, but he didn't. Neither man spoke again until Wells stopped outside the Delta compound. Penn extended a hand. 'Wish we could have met under different circumstances.'

'Me, too, Major. Maybe one day stateside we'll have the chance.'

Penn opened his door, hesitated. 'Do you think we can win over here?'

I don't even know what that word means anymore. 'I think you, me, everybody else, we'll all do our jobs until somebody has a better idea.'

At that, Penn saluted and left.

'I tried to call you, tell you where they'd be,' Young told him a few hours later. 'But they shut down the coms that morning.' He explained that when a soldier was killed in action, the Army cut cell service as well as the sat phones at the Morale and Welfare rooms. The Pentagon didn't want wives or parents hearing about casualties through the military grapevine before they were officially notified. A soldier in the brigade had stepped on an IED on the morning that Francesca and Alders had gone to the ridge, and so the phones had been cut.

'I have to ask, Coleman, how come you rode up there anyway, knowing I might not be there?'

'May as well lie on my back and spread my legs if I'm gonna stay home. That what you would do, Mr Wells?'

'Death before dishonor.'

'I figured it would work out and it did. Saw Mickey Mouse up there with his throat cut. Still the lieutenant and the sergeant and Roman, though.'

'I'll handle them.'

'Like that?'

'Not like that.'

'What then?'

'Roman's the weakest of the three of them, I have that right?'

'Stupidest for sure. Spends most of his time on his PSP and he's not even good at that.'

Stupid didn't necessarily mean weak. Still, Wells figured Roman was his best bet. That night, as Roman walked back to his bunk from the showers, Wells stepped out from between two trailers, tapped him on the shoulder.

'Walk with me, Kevin.'

Roman's eyes darted like tadpoles in a muddy pond. 'Sir?'

'Walk with me. Now.' Roman's shoulders slumped and he fell in beside Wells, who led him to the same maintenance lot where Rodriguez and Young had faced off. The maintenance guys were gone for the night. Wells walked Roman to a narrow aisle between a Stryker and a blast wall.

'You know who I am, Kevin?'

'The guy who talked to us last week. John Wells.'

'That's right. Know why I'm here?'

'No, sir.'

Wells hit Roman, low and hard in the solar plexus, pivoting into it, getting all of his two hundred and ten pounds behind the punch. Roman's stomach was a little bit soft and Wells connected solidly, more solidly than he'd intended. If he'd been holding a knife, he would have buried it to the hilt. As it was, he felt the contact up his arm and into his shoulder. Roman doubled over on his fist like a folding chair. Wells pulled his arm back and Roman put his hands on his knees and gasped.

Wells gave him a few seconds and then put his right hand under Roman's shoulder and tugged him up and stepped close. Roman was still struggling for breath. His eyes jumped wildly before settling on Wells. 'Tonight. You're going to call CID, tell them about you and Rodriguez and Weston.'

'I don't—'

'Don't tell me you don't. And don't tell me you can't.'

'They'll kill me. I swear they will.'

Wells put a hand under Roman's chin and squeezed his throat. 'Tyler and Nick won't kill you. But I will. Here or back in the States. Like I killed Francesca. I'll do you just like that.'

Francesca's name did the trick. Wells had figured as much. Francesca was a Delta. A sniper. The baddest of the bad. And Wells had nearly taken his head off his neck. Roman pushed out his lips, though actual speech seemed beyond him.

'You don't have to tell them what Tyler did to Ricky Fowler' – Wells figured the murder would come out quickly once the Army opened the investigation – 'but you need to tell them about the drugs. CID's got that twenty-four-hour hotline. You call it tonight, tell them you want to come in tomorrow to Kandahar. Tell them you had an attack of conscience. You know what that is, Roman?'

Roman shook his head.

'Didn't think so. Now you tell me what you're going to do.'

'I'll call them tonight.'

Wells stepped back and hit Roman again in the stomach. Not

as hard this time. Wells didn't want to kill him. Even so, Roman doubled over and coughed, quick faint breaths, an old dog panting after a game of fetch. Wells flexed his knees to get low and hit him once more, a rising right that connected with the tip of Roman's jaw, bone on bone. Wells grunted with the impact. A sweet pain filled his hand. Roman's eyes rolled back. His head snapped up. Then gravity took over and he crashed to the hard-packed dirt. Wells watched for a couple seconds to be sure Roman was still breathing, hadn't swallowed his tongue. Then Wells walked away, shaking out his hand. Truly he hadn't felt so good in months.

As soon as Wells passed Peter Lautner's name to Shafer, a team of techs at Langley began checking every e-mail in their servers, every phone call, every trip, every expense report. They hoped to find evidence of a connection between Lautner and Francesca or Alders, or even better between Lautner and Amadullah. At first, they came up empty. In the two-plus years since his wife's death, Lautner had been very careful, unusually careful, to keep his official CIA account free of anything personal.

But within twenty-four hours, even before Wells went to FOB Jackson, the techs scored a hit. Stored on the agency's computers at Langley was an e-mail four years before to Lautner from Daniel.L.Francesca@us.army.mil. A few days later, Lautner had written Francesca back. He'd sent the e-mail not to Francesca's military account but to another address, DLORFHK@gmail.com. It didn't take much imagination to realize the account probably belonged to Francesca. With the NSA's help, the CIA cracked the Gmail address and found three suspicious messages. Two were nothing more than short strings of numbers, possibly phone numbers, though they didn't match any numbers in the NSA's worldwide database. The third was yet another Gmail account, with the password attached. Shafer checked it, found it empty. Probably Francesca and Lautner had used it to send messages to each other. One man wrote a message, saved it as a draft e-mail. Once the other read it, he deleted the draft. That way, the message was never permanently stored anywhere, and never left a trail for the NSA to trace.

Shafer and Wells believed that Lautner and Francesca had met face-to-face or used burner phones for all their important conversations. In truth, Francesca's last words were the only real proof that Wells had of Lautner's involvement. Wells thought he understood now why Gabe Yergin, the station's operations officer, had acted so oddly during that first interview at the Ariana Hotel. Yergin had suspected Lautner, but he'd had no real evidence. So he'd done everything possible to raise Wells's hackles without openly voicing his suspicions.

Lautner himself had added to the confusion. Because he'd been so overtly hostile, Wells had imagined he couldn't have anything to hide. In fact, Lautner had outplayed Wells. He'd guessed how Wells would read his anger and then used that knowledge to his advantage. He was very tricky and very good and he had left only the faintest footprints on this operation. As far as Wells could see, Francesca, Daood Maktani, and maybe Amadullah Thuwani were the only three men who could connect him directly to the trafficking. The first two were dead, and now that he'd left his compound in Balochistan, Thuwani was impossible to find. Anyway, he would have less than no interest in helping the CIA.

And so, two days after he shot Francesca, Wells found himself standing on the roof of the German embassy, waiting for Shafer to call. He'd flown to Kabul from FOB Jackson the night before and decided that the Germans would probably be better hosts than his friends at the Ariana. Duto and the agency's congressional paymasters were scheduled to fly to Kabul in hours. Wells still didn't know how Duto planned to deal with Lautner, or whether he'd be involved.

His sat phone trilled. '*Guten morgen*.'

'And guten morgen to you, John. Though it's one a.m. here, so maybe *guten night-en* would be more accurate. We okay to talk?'

'Believe so. I'm on the roof. Looking at beautiful Kabul. Snowcapped mountains to the west, helicopters to the north, Taliban all around.'

'Sounds romantic.'

'What am I doing here, Ellis?'

'I've never seen Duto this way. Like he's paralyzed, doesn't want to believe it's Lautner. He wants to talk to you, go over it again.'

'Sure.'

'Sit tight for fifteen minutes.'

An hour later, the phone rang again. No preamble.

'We don't have enough. No prosecutor would charge him. A few weird e-mails and hearsay from a dead sniper? And what exactly will you say on the cross, when the defense asks how you happened to hear Francesca's last words?'

'You sound tired, Vinny.'

'Tell me you're sure about this. How can you know Francesca was telling the truth?'

Because men don't lie to their executioners. 'I know.'

'If we could find the money. Lautner must have it somewhere.'

'Forget the money. This was never about money.'

'What would you do?'

'You know what I'd do.'

'Just answer me.'

'Francesca's dead. Lautner knows it's over. He's not stupid.

He knows. Show him that you know, too. Order him home. Now. The next flight out. Make the call yourself, so he can't dodge it. But don't give him a reason. Don't even let him pack. Push him, make him react.'

'And what do I tell my congressmen when they ask what happened to the station's deputy chief?'

'Have you heard anything John just said?' This from Shafer. Wells heard the exasperation in his voice. 'He's telling you there's a real chance Pete Lautner's going to make himself a one-man welcoming committee and strap on a bomb when you get there. Do I have to spell it out for you? Blow himself up. Like Marburg did to his wife and his brother. *That's* what this is about. Not money. Revenge. *Get him out of there.*'

Duto grunted, low and pained. Then he spoke two words, so quietly Wells hardly heard him. 'All right.'

Wells stayed on the roof for a while and then went for a walk. The gate guards tried to convince him to stay inside but he shook them off. The Afghans looked curiously at him. Now that he'd shaved his beard, he had a harder time passing. But he had a pistol on his hip and the sun was high in the sky and Western soldiers were all over downtown Kabul and nobody said a word. He felt like a tourist who'd gotten lost.

He had nearly looped back to the embassy when his phone rang. Shafer.

Lautner had locked the door to his office and put his 9-millimetre in his mouth and vented his brains on the wall. No note. But in his lap, a copy of the official after-action report on Marburg.

There wasn't anything to say, so Wells didn't say anything.

'Duto's postponing his trip,' Shafer said eventually. 'You can head out whenever.'

'I assume I'll be getting a medal for my honorable service. Maybe a small private ceremony at the White House.'

'It's best for everyone this way. You know.'

Wells hung up. Lautner, dead. Wells felt no surprise, but when he tried to walk, his legs weighed a thousand pounds. Afghanistan was just lines on a map, as fictional and fleeting as any human creation. Land couldn't be cursed. The idea belonged to a different century. Yet at this moment, the taint felt as real and sharp as the mountains around him.

Twenty miles south, Amadullah Thuwani gobbled down the last remnants of his lunch, roast lamb and rice. He hadn't heard anything from the Americans since he'd handed over the Dragunov. He wondered whether the CIA man had forgotten him. No matter. He still had his twin treasures, the surface-to-air missiles the man had given him.

And one day he'd use them.

By the time he reached North Conway, Wells was exhausted through his bones. Two days of flights and layovers. He'd traveled commercial the whole way. For the moment, he couldn't bear the steel embrace of the American military. So he'd flown through Dubai and Frankfurt and Dulles, gleaming airports all, filled with purposeful men and women and the baubles of the twenty-first century. Duto had tried to make him stop at Langley for a debrief, and Shafer had offered to put him up. Wells had ignored them both and caught the first flight to Boston and found a cab at Logan willing to take him to New Hampshire, a dented Crown Vic. 'Cost you five hundred dollars and I'm gonna need that up-front,' the driver said, aggressively, like he was waiting for an argument, but Wells just nodded and reached for his wallet. As they rolled northwest on 93, Wells stared out the window at the office parks and bent roads and gray New England hills and wondered again whether a land could be cursed. Or a people.

Outside Manchester, the snow began, a sudden squall, big soft flakes that poured from the lead-white sky and melted instantly on the highway.

'Has there been much?' Wells said, his first words since Logan.

'First real storm all year.'

Wells decided the storm was good luck and then decided that exhaustion had made him fanciful. Soon enough he'd be seeing omens in jet contrails. He closed his eyes. When he opened them again, the driver was rolling up outside the old farmhouse Wells shared with Anne and Tonka. The snow was still falling hard, sticking now, coating the earth, hiding its scars. Gray smoke rose from the chimney into the gray sky.

'Here you are,' the driver said.

Wells left him behind, walked into the yard. Tonka looked out from the living-room window and started to wag his long bushy tail with absurd speed. All the welcome any man could want. The door was unlocked. Wells pushed it open.

'I'm home.' The word low and solid in his throat. The only word he needed. 'Home.'

ACKNOWLEDGMENTS

Thanks to Neil, Ivan, Leslie, Tom, Marilyn, Matthew, and everyone else at Putnam who makes John Wells come to life. Thanks to Heather, who battles tirelessly for the best deal, and Dev, who watches the watchers. Thanks to my family for all your support and thoughtful comments. And, of course, thanks to Jackie, wife, friend, and partner.

I also want to extend a special thanks to Lt. Paszterko, Capt. Field, and the rest of the 'Hard Rocks' for putting me up, and putting up with me, in Kandahar last year. Seeing the United States military in action is a privilege and honor. Stay safe.

As always, thanks to anyone who got this far, and please do write me at alexberensonauthor@gmail.com with comments and suggestions. I promise to do my best to write back. (And if you're not sick of me yet, you can follow me on Facebook and Twitter.)